Michael Carson was b
the Second World V
schools, he then became a novice in a religious
order, but decided the religious life was not for
him. University followed, then he took up a career
as a teacher of English as a foreign language and
has worked in the Middle East, Brunei and Africa.
He is the author of the Benson trilogy (*Sucking
Sherbet Lemons*, *Stripping Penguins Bare* and
Yanking Up the Yo-Yo), *Friends and Infidels*,
Coming Up Roses, and a collection of short stories,
Serving Suggestions. He now lives in Wales.

Demolishing Babel

Michael Carson

BLACK SWAN

DEMOLISHING BABEL
A BLACK SWAN BOOK : 0 552 99568 1

Originally published in Great Britain by Doubleday
a division of Transworld Publishers Ltd

PRINTING HISTORY
Doubleday edition published 1994
Black Swan edition published 1995

This book is set in 10½pt Linotype Melior by
Phoenix Typesetting, Ilkley, West Yorkshire.

Black Swan Books are published by Transworld Publishers Ltd,
61–63 Uxbridge Road, Ealing, London W5 5SA,
in Australia by Transworld Publishers (Australia) Pty. Ltd,
15–25 Helles Avenue, Moorebank, NSW 2170,
and in New Zealand by Transworld Publishers (N.Z.) Ltd,
3 William Pickering Drive, Albany, Auckland.

Reproduced, printed and bound in Great Britain by
Cox & Wyman Ltd, Reading, Berks.

For the Unknown E.F.L. Teacher
and
For Angela Burt – The Teacher's Teacher

rule 3. *Rule the roast (roost).* The OED gives no countenance to *roost*, & does not even recognize that the phrase ever takes that form; but most unliterary persons say *roost* & not *roast*; I have just enquired of three such, & been informed that they never heard of *rule the roast*, & that the reference is to a cock keeping his hens in order. Against this tempting piece of popular etymology the OED offers us nothing more succulent than 'None of the early examples throw any light on the precise origin of the expression'. In seven out of the eight pre-18th-c. examples quoted the spelling is not *roast* but *rost* or *roste*; but the OED philologists would doubtless tell us that *rost(e)* could represent Old-French *rost* (roast), & could not represent Old-English *hróst* (roost). Writers should take warning, at any rate, that *rule the roast* is the orthodox spelling, & that when they have written it the compositor must be watched.

Fowler's Modern English Usage,
(1926 Edition)

Book One

Elementary

The vapour trails of jets furrowed blue sky. On this hot Sunday afternoon the three Sues, in Sue's car, followed a removals van from the Demolish Babel Oxford Street school to Heathcliff College on the edge of Hampstead.

The van contained office equipment and files with the names and details of the teachers and students who were attending this year's summer school. The three Sues watched these items being loaded into the large room next to the main door of Heathcliff College.

The men, as they lifted and carried, placing everything where they were told, asked for tea.

'Sorry,' said Sue. 'The kettle doesn't come until tomorrow. It's Agnes's.'

'She's the office supervisor,' added Sue.

'There's a drinks machine in the corridor, but it was a bugger last year,' concluded Sue.

The men finished their work. Sue signed the chitty and they left.

'They weren't much use,' observed Sue.

'The fat one seemed quite cuddly,' said Sue.

'Let's ring Agnes and tell her it's done,' said Sue.

Sue rang Agnes Fogherty, who had excused herself from helping the three secretaries with the move because she needed to take her cocker spaniel to her mother's house in Southend. Sue got the answering machine.

'We've got everything into the office,' said Sue in a put-on, put-out, puffed voice. 'We're as ready as we'll ever be, Agnes.' She put the receiver down.

'I can't believe it's come round again,' said Sue.

'It isn't that time, is it? Christ, Sue, when you have one we all feel the fall-out.'

'No, not that,' said Sue. 'The summer school. It only seems like last week since we were packing up.'

'That's time for you,' said Sue, straightening out a paper-clip.

'Goes like the clappers,' said Sue.

'What's that paper-clip ever done to you?' asked Sue.

'It's my nerves,' said Sue.

'What have *you* got to be nervous about? You should be

over the moon. You'll be able to spoon with your precious Keith,' said Sue.

'*Spoon* – is that what you call it?' said Sue sarcastically.

Sue ignored her. 'He *is* teaching on this year's school, isn't he?' asked Sue.

'Definitely. I have the teachers' list in front of me as I speak. *Keith and Lynn Weaver.* You ought to be ashamed, Sue.'

'I am,' said Sue, 'but I can't help myself.'

'You're a slave to your passions, Sue, that's your trouble,' said Sue.

'And what about you? You're not so pure, and don't you think you are!' said Sue vehemently.

'All the old crowd of teachers are coming,' said Sue, perusing the teachers' list.

'"The cream of English teachers flown back to Blighty for the Demolish Babel English Language Summer School,"' said Sue, putting on Sir Dennis Harlow's voice.

'It's hard to credit, isn't it? Don't they have homes to go to?' asked Sue.

'Who?' asked Sue.

'The teachers, that's who,' replied Sue.

'Sir Dennis likes continuity. He's always saying it.'

Sue looked at Sue knowingly.

'Well, continuity is one thing, but it's not true what they say . . . ,' said Sue.

'What's not true?'

'Well,' said Sue portentously. 'They say that rolling stones gather no moss, but it's a great big lie – at least, as far as the teachers are concerned. They're covered in it, if you want my opinion. Talk about travel broadening the mind! That's not true, either.'

'I've always wondered about that,' said Sue.

'What?' asked Sue.

'Travel broadens the mind. I mean, when you think about it, what you broaden in one direction gets stretched in another. It stands to reason. You know, like a sponge or chewing gum,' said Sue.

12

Sue thought about that. 'Perhaps you're right, but it isn't necessarily so. Maybe there's an increase in the critical mass.'

'Hark at Magnus Magnusson!' said Sue.

'Well, I like all the teachers. The summer school's fine just the way it is. It's nice that some things stay the same. That's what I think.'

'Don't be too sure,' said Sue.

'How do you mean?' asked Sue, straightening out another paper-clip.

'What I mean is that there are signs and portents,' said Sue.

'Come again?' asked Sue.

'Jordan Bostock's report. He wants changes made. And Jordan Bostock may look like an ordinary teacher, 'cept he's better turned out, but he's got shares. He wants Eric Trotter off the school, and that's just for starters,' said Sue.

'Oh, no! Eric's lovely!' said Sue.

'How old d'you reckon he is?' asked Sue.

'Jordan Bostock? Forty-fiveish, I'd say.'

'No, not Jordan Bostock. Eric Trotter.'

'He's kicking eighty.'

'It gives you hope in a way,' said Sue.

'Arthur Arthur's coming back, too. Egypt's loss is our gain,' said Sue, studying the teachers' list.

'I don't like to think about it,' said Sue.

'Lots of scholarship students this year,' said Sue.

'Dennis can't say no,' said Sue.

'He's not the only one,' said Sue.

Sue pulled a face, then threw the ruined paper-clip into the basket. 'I fancy a drink,' she said.

'Why not?' agreed Sue.

'Yes, why not?' added Sue.

The three Sues locked the office, leaving the stationery and equipment alone in the centre of the silence that suddenly returned to the deserted rooms and corridors of Heathcliff College: a silence which, once broken by Agnes turning the key in the lock the following morning, would not return until the summer school was over.

13

*　　*　　*

The following day, a little before one, Arthur Arthur was sweating up the west side of the Finchley Road towards Heathcliff College. A heavy piece of soft luggage hampered his progress, resisting his thick right leg with each step. He felt as if he were wading up a river whose fast current at each moment threatened to rip his legs from under him, send him back the way he had come, out of control.

'I help?' asked Arthur's companion, a tall thick-set Egyptian whom Arthur had befriended in the queue at Cairo airport.

'No, Eisa lovey. You've got enough of your own to carry,' Arthur replied.

Eisa, perhaps not understanding, took hold of one of the straps of the heavy bag. Arthur started to protest but, feeling the relief, the sudden untrammelling of his leg, how reaching their destination suddenly seemed possible, let it happen. He used his free hand to pull his sweat-glued Hawaiian shirt away from his bulging stomach. He bothered the cloth down at the back so that its tails covered his wide hips.

They soldiered a further two hundred yards up the hill.

'Here's a good place to cross,' Arthur told Eisa as they reached a pelican crossing where some people were waiting for the lights to change. 'It's not far now.'

'Yes, my teacher,' Eisa replied. He put down his heavy suitcase and rubbed chafed hands. Sticky sickles of blackness punctuated his palms. The long flight from Cairo had deposited grime all over him, though everything had appeared to be clean enough. Still – God be thanked – he had arrived safely. He looked up at the blue sky, then over at Arthur, who had also put down his bag and was wiping the sweat from his face.

Eisa was grateful to have made a friend on the plane. And not just a friend but a teacher on the summer school. As soon as he arrived, he would wash, pray and then write to Leila to tell her that all her fears were without foundation. Even Leila, a pessimist by nurture, would

14

have to concede that things could not be better. He was already in England. Now it only remained to master the language of the English and all would be well.

'Bloody hot, isn't it?' Arthur remarked. 'It's going to piss down, though. I can feel it. All those clouds we passed through over the Channel are heading straight for us. It'll bucket down shortly.'

'Yes, my teacher,' repeated Eisa, though he had not understood.

There, he's said it again, thought Arthur Arthur. Who the hell teaches them these things? He can hardly speak a word but manages *my teacher*. It isn't as if it's appropriate. It might have been at one time. It might have served. But not now. Not now.

A woman in front of them turned her head, giving Eisa an up-and-down look. Then she returned to talking to her friend next to her. 'We'd had it six months. Got it at Jones Brothers in the winding-up sale they had. It had a lovely rocking action. Grand for Dad. Then the springs went. Just like that,' she said.

'There goes the light,' said her companion.

Eisa, remembering the look, wondered if the women were talking about him.

'Not in any hurry to stop, are they?' said the woman. She looked to left and right. 'It was a Parker-Knoll, too.' And she gave her companion a look of bruised trust before walking out into the road.

Arthur Arthur stepped forward to grab her but stumbled over his large bag. He saw a flash of blue, a space where the woman had been.

A car trying to race the red light had struck her a glancing blow. The woman was thrown forward. Arthur could hear the wind leaving her. She spun. She spun like a top along the road. A bollard stopped her, reversed the spin, took her legs from under her, leaving her at last in the gutter.

The car brakes screamed. It stopped on the empty road ahead. There was a long silence. Then Arthur heard what sounded like a puppy being stepped on. The lights of the car flashed twice. *He's locking the bloody thing!* he thought. *He's bloody locking the bloody thing!*

People ran to help the woman.

The driver tried to join the group around the victim. They smelled alcohol and a rat on his breath and would not accept him. They told him to wait for the police.

Eisa took off his jacket to pillow the woman's head but he could not make the group around her understand. Arthur Arthur called police and ambulance from a box nearby. The emergency services said they already knew. He and Eisa stood around. Then, reasoning that there were plenty of people to bear witness, Arthur Arthur took Eisa's arm, told him to try to forget about it and stole him away – up the *via dolorosa* of the Finchley Road.

As a woman died four hundred yards to the south, Nathan, the thirteen-year-old son of Rachel Pales, was admiring himself in the glass door of Heathcliff College. He gave the door both profiles, jived a few times, hoisted up his baggy jeans and winked at his reflection. Then he ran off to bang the Coke machine outside the Union shop.

In front of the machine Nathan closed his eyes tight to recite his magic mantra of gibberish or some foreign tongue. He repeated the formula three times and punched the machine hard. He waited, then tried again. He looked around, fearing a third attempt. But there was no-one about. The Union shop was closed for the lunch-hour. He risked another blow.

The third punch hurt his hand, and he comforted it in the warm place under his arm. The hand felt his bones and reminded him how too-thin he was. His old PT teacher, who couldn't do PT himself but just leaned his bottom against the stage apron, had said that he needed dynamic tension and, remembering, he tensed himself. The impregnable Coke machine hummed a snigger back at him. Nathan turned away and mooched unhappily into the garden between the library and the quadrangle.

The first student to arrive at the Demolish Babel Summer

School saw Nathan's back. 'Excuse me,' Muchtar said.

Nathan turned, expecting retribution for his assault on the Coke machine. He prepared an angry excuse about malfunction and swallowed pocket-money, then lost his anxiety when he saw the brown man next to a large piece of luggage. 'Yeah?' he asked, hitching up his jeans.

'My name is Muchtar. I am looking for the reception of the summer school. Can you tell me where it is?'

'Easy. I'll take you,' said Nathan.

'You are a very kind young man,' said Muchtar.

Nathan shuffled for a second but did not say anything. They walked towards Reception.

'I think you are too young to be a student on the summer school,' said Muchtar.

'My mum works here,' said Nathan. 'She's the head teacher. She writes books, too.'

'Oh, that is interesting,' Muchtar replied. 'What kind of books does she write?'

'Textbooks.'

'What is her name? Perhaps I have heard of her. You see, I am a teacher in my country.'

'Rachel Pales.'

'Ah, yes. She is very famous. We have many of her books. And your father, what does he do?'

Nathan did not reply at once. They had reached the entrance to Heathcliff College. 'I don't have a father. He was killed in a car-crash. He was from Kenya.'

'I am sorry,' said Muchtar.

Nathan shrugged. 'Don't worry about it. It was a long time ago.'

He showed Muchtar through the door that had been his mirror. As it swung shut he saw, along with his reflection, parked cars and the red church in Kidderpore Avenue wandering across the pane. Muchtar waved his thanks from the other side.

Chance had brought Nathan back to the place where his mother had told him to wait for her. But she should have been there an hour before. If she was much later, he would miss karate practice and his chance to show off

17

the new trainers while they were still in mint condition.

Lonely again, Nathan sat down for a moment. Then he remembered his refuge. He ran off across the quadrangle, down, three at a time, the steep steps by the launderette. He stood at the foot of the tree, wondering for a moment how he had ever climbed it, waiting for the sight of it to rekindle memory of the route upwards. But the ten feet of trunk between ground and lowest branch offered no foot-holds. Then the knack came back and he was prising himself up, using his back wedged against the brick wall of the library as a brace.

In a minute he was figuring out the toe-holds into the heights of the tree, aware that he was walking into the sky; the busy patterns of summer leaves making him invisible from the earth. He did not know why, but his sudden vertical walk through a green jungle was exciting him. He touched himself, supporting his body by one thin arm, but stopped when he saw that his hand was black from the London muck sticking to the bark.

It could not be much farther now. He had left treasure in a hole in the trunk, waiting for someone long after he had died to come, discover it and wonder. He looked down, feeling again the security of the place, how his weeping in the hidy-hole high above London had remained a secret between himself and the leaves.

Arthur had gone back to Egypt and forgotten him. Nathan's letters from London had failed to elicit a response. Even the Christmas stocking full of the things that Arthur loved to eat, but could not afford to buy in Egypt, had produced no response. Yet Arthur had seen his tears as the bus took him away to the airport; Nathan still feeling the pressure of Arthur's handshake, knowing that with each second rotating wheels and engines would remove his friend farther and farther away.

That day a year before, bursting with the need for ritual, keeping Rachel, his mother, waiting, wondering, worrying her car-keys, he had disappeared up the oak tree and left Arthur's gift in the hole, propitiating gods, invented or remembered, with his mantras.

18

Above the last safe branch he found the hole. A year of grimy weather had stiffened the knotted handkerchief, as if it were saturated with snot. Inside were Egyptian coins that Arthur had given to him. They had grown dull in their hiding-place. He looked at his poor booty, thinking there should have been something else. He smoothed out the handkerchief, remembering the tears he had wept and dried with it, tears he had thought would never stop. He had proved then that he was incapable of making a stiff upper lip or, rather, that a stiff upper lip does nothing to hold back tears. Another lie. Perhaps a stiff lip could dam English tear-ducts. But not his. He was not English. The looks he got every day told him that he was not English. Nathan Pales was something else, something not yet quite clear but something to do with the tales of dark beautiful kings that Arthur had told him – with all the students he saw and studied at the summer school – and he had wanted Arthur to stay in touch to teach him more.

He held the coins in the palm of his hand. Then he made a fist around them, and was about to throw them into the rustling green of the air when the pain from the blow he had given the machine came back to the fist and sparked an idea. He put the coins into his pocket.

He descended the tree, swung from the lowest branch and dropped to the grass. He ran across the lawn to the Coke machine and pushed the coins into it. Reciting his mantra, Nathan pressed the button for Coke. With a rumble the machine laid a frozen can. Then, to his delight, a salvo of silver coins exploded through the guts of the machine and into the change-tray.

Nathan Pales walked with a spring in his step back towards Reception. He found himself a place in the sun and sat down, leaning against the rough brick of Heathcliff College. The Coke can farted satisfactorily as he flicked it open like an ad. He sat there, warmed and cooled, looking as if he was waiting for his mother, but really waiting to see what this year's summer school would reveal.

*　　*　　*

19

'Where were you?' Nathan's mother, Rachel, asked him. 'I've been here several times in the last hour and not a sign of you.'

'Same here,' he said.

Rachel rattled her car-keys. 'Are you coming or aren't you?'

'It's too late now. I've missed karate.'

'Well, I've got to get back to the Oxford Street school. Do you want to come for the ride? I'd like the company.'

'When are you coming back?'

Rachel looked at her watch. 'Say five?'

'I'll stay here,' he said.

She looked at him, thinking. 'OK,' she said. Then she turned on her heel and walked away, hoping Nathan knew how aggrieved she felt.

Nathan knew and cared and tried not to care. He finished his Coke, crushed the can, set it down beside him and closed his eyes. Under the warm sun he fell asleep as the world began to arrive for the Demolish Babel Summer School.

Teresa was having less good fortune with the drinks machine outside Reception. It had already swallowed a large number of odd-shaped alien coins without result when Teresa decided it wouldn't hurt to insert her nylon comb into the slot to prod the machine either to excrete them or to release coffee into the waiting plastic cup. She prised the comb backwards and forwards, uttering Catalan curses between her small white teeth.

A tired-looking woman wearing a pink eye-patch passed her and said hello. Teresa thought too late to ask assistance, but the woman had disappeared. Her foot-falls echoed like church as she took herself down each loose board of the wooden stairs to the dining-room. Then suddenly, as if rubbed into existence by a miracle-hungry foreigner, a small brown man was standing next to her. Teresa seized her chance.

'Please,' she said.

'Yes? My name is Muchtar. How may I be of assistance?'

Teresa let go of the comb to show Muchtar her predicament.

'Dear lady,' said Muchtar, frowning at the comb, 'what have you done?'

'I want coffee. Much. I put coin where is comb now. Coin come down dri . . . dri . . . dri . . . in here.' Teresa pointed to the reject-coin slot. 'I do again. Dri . . . dri . . . again in here. And so et cetera. Coin in machine. No coffee. I want coffee. So . . .' And Teresa's dark eyes flashed. 'I do this . . . what is call?'

'You kicked the machine with some force,' said Muchtar helpfully.

'That is! I kick him and again and again. Nothing.'

Muchtar nodded. 'Then?'

Teresa gestured to the comb. The sight of it rekindled her anger, and she kicked the machine once more, waited a decent interval for some sign of acquiescence, then made an insulting gesture to it.

'I think we should try to remove the comb. First things first, you know.'

Muchtar rotated his shoulder-blades a couple of times to show he meant business, grasped the comb and pulled. Nothing happened. He tried again, with the same result.

'See?' said Teresa.

Muchtar saw. 'I think we must beg assistance,' he said.

'But I want coffee and I want comb!' gasped Teresa.

Muchtar frowned and twinkled at Teresa, like a man who knows what he likes but doesn't like that he likes it. 'You are very wilful,' he said. 'There is coffee downstairs. One of the teachers told me.' There was some pride in Muchtar's voice, as if by being vouchsafed such information by a teacher he had realized an ambition of many years' standing. He put his right arm around Teresa's left upper arm, making to lead her down the stairs towards the dining-hall.

Teresa did not seem particularly keen to go with Muchtar. She pulled away. 'No. I try again.' She stood squarely in front of the machine, wriggled as if in front

21

of a mirror to make the hem of her petticoat disappear, and seized the comb. She pulled. The comb did not budge, and Teresa started banging the worn white surface of the machine – where many before had banged – with the flat of her hand.

'You are practising but you make no progress,' said Muchtar teacherishly.

'What's going on here?' asked Agnes Fogherty, Demolish Babel's office supervisor, appearing suddenly in the space where only a second before had been the firmly closed door of Reception.

'This machine . . . ,' said Teresa.

'The lady has been experiencing difficulties with the coffee machine,' Muchtar explained.

Agnes Fogherty pointed a finger at Muchtar. 'Don't tell me,' she said. 'Mr Muchtar, isn't it? Malaysia. I've done you, haven't I?'

'Yes, but . . . ,' began Muchtar.

But Agnes had turned to Teresa, Muchtar from Malaysia having been done. 'This machine was working this morning,' she said. 'I obtained an excellent oxtail soup at eleven-thirty.' Then she caught sight of the protruding comb. She approached it. 'What is this?' she asked, pointing an accusatory finger at the comb.

'I don't know the English,' said Teresa, her Latin spirit deserting her – as it had deserted many another – when confronted by Agnes Fogherty.

Agnes regarded Teresa.

'It's this lady's comb,' said Muchtar, trying to be helpful.

Agnes, sensing that he would understand better, turned to Muchtar. She raised herself to her full height, causing Muchtar to diminish, as if the ground beneath him had dropped a foot without warning. Then she gave Teresa her sternest sideways glance to make sure she had noted the transformation; that opposition was of no avail. She had, after all, been around teachers long enough to glean from them that one had to start out tough. It was no good being soft and then trying to retrieve the situation. She started out tough. 'In all my years as office supervisor at Demolish Babel, I have never seen the like,' she began. 'We're off to a fine start, aren't we? In a few hours a large number of students of English from all parts of the globe will be arriving. "Ah, good!" they will say as they pull their heavy suitcases through the door after their exhausting journeys from God knows what area of darkness. "Ah, good! A coffee machine. Let's revive ourselves after our long journey, with a cup of freshly brewed coffee." But what will they see as they approach the machine? They will see a *pink* comb in the place where by rights there should be a clear passage for the insertion of a coin of the realm. They'll say such things as "England isn't what it was", "In Tokyo the coffee machines work". They will not know that an early arrival at the school – doubtless unacquainted with such mechanically sophisticated machines – had taken it into her head to use her *pink* comb as a tool of destruction.'

Teresa was looking from Agnes Fogherty to Muchtar, her expression delicately balanced between incomprehension and pleading.

'First impressions. You and I – we both have to worry about first impressions. They last far longer than a cup of coffee, young lady. Never in all my years have I . . . ,' concluded Agnes inaccurately. In her twenty years as secretary at the Demolish Babel English Language School she had seen, she felt, all but a scant inch of everything.

'I have told the lady,' said Muchtar, smiling towards Teresa, 'that there is coffee in the dining-room.'

Agnes consulted her watch. 'Well, there shouldn't be. It's almost two.'

'But maybe . . .'

'And, anyway, that does nothing to solve the problem in hand. What is your name?'

'Teresa Carreras.'

'You haven't reported to Reception. On your briefing notes you are instructed to report to Reception the moment you arrive.'

23

Teresa looked down abjectly at her third-best-but-favourite trainers, bought in Valencia just before the Olympics. Why, she had met Manuel while wearing them! They had been rough with Mediterranean sand! Wet with sweat from walking in La Mancha! How could she be standing in them now in this place of rough brick and echoing shouts? She dropped a tear. It hit the B of Benetton on her left trainer.

Muchtar saw the tear, and his gaze accused Agnes Fogherty.

Agnes had also seen the tear. She addressed Muchtar. 'They'll try anything to worm their way out of a problem,' she tried. 'In a few hours I'm going to have lots like that. Not to mention the staff. I can expect no consideration, I suppose.'

Another tear fell. This one landed on the blond wood of the floor, next to a coffee stain the exact shape of New Guinea. Miss Fogherty saw it, looked up into Mr Muchtar's beseeching eyes and said, 'Well, I suppose we'd better get you registered, young lady.'

She was about to take Teresa round the arm to lead her into Reception when a large piece of soft black luggage pushed open the swing-door leading out to Kidderpore Avenue and was then kicked into the building by a desert boot that had seen better days. It was followed by a large white English Language teacher well known to Agnes Fogherty.

'Agnes! Another summer school! We have been spared to fight another summer!'

'Arthur Arthur, it's you,' said Agnes Fogherty.

'Yes, it's me, lovey. Another year of sowing seed in the fecund wastes of upper Egypt is behind me! I have returned.'

'This way, dear,' said Agnes Fogherty to the still-grieving Teresa. She deftly performed one of her characteristic about-turns. 'I suppose it isn't the end of the world. I'll call Dominic in Maintenance about the machine.'

'Am I the first?' asked Arthur Arthur.

'No. Lynn Weaver came this morning.'

24

'Good-o! Is Keith with her?'

Agnes Fogherty twisted her face, making her neck tendons stand out. 'No.'

'No?'

'She'll explain, Arthur. While you're at it, ask her about her eye-patch. I didn't dare. I was worried about what might pour out. You know what she's like.'

'Ask her about her *what*?'

'Doesn't matter.'

'Where is she?'

'God knows.' Miss Fogherty caught sight of Eisa. 'Who's this?'

'This is Eisa. I got talking to him on the plane. Eisa lovey, this is Agnes. Anything you need, Agnes is the one.'

Agnes gave Arthur Arthur a look. 'I'm *Miss* Fogherty to the students, Arthur – unless they're buying the drinks.' She gave up all attempts to minister to Teresa, passing her back to Muchtar, who placed both his hands on her shoulders in a fatherly fashion. Agnes Fogherty looked at the large man beaming behind Arthur Arthur. 'Is he enrolled on the summer school?' she asked Arthur Arthur.

'Yes. You'd better be extra nice to Eisa, Agnes. He's had a bit of a shock.'

Agnes did not enquire further. 'Well, you'd better all register.'

'What is this, Mr Arthur?' Eisa asked, pointing at the pink comb.

'It's a comb, Eisa. A comb,' said Arthur Arthur.

'A comb,' repeated Eisa.

'And what colour is it?'

'It red.'

'Almost, but not quite. Think of a colour very close to red.'

Eisa had a go. His big face puckered up. He stroked his chin.

'It's pink. Pink,' said Arthur Arthur after a decent interval. 'Lots of lovely things are pink. Like me, for instance. Pink.'

'Bink,' said Eisa.

'That's right. Your *p*'s need attention, Eisa lovey. Oodles of language lab for you. It's a pink comb.'

'It's a bink comb.'

'Whose is it, by the way?' Arthur Arthur asked Agnes. But Agnes Fogherty was glaring at the keyboard of her computer and did not reply.

'It's Teresa's,' said Muchtar.

'It's Teresa's,' repeated Eisa.

'Very good, Eisa,' said Arthur Arthur. 'You're a fast learner.' He appraised Eisa. 'You're as bright as a button.'

'You very good teacher,' said Eisa.

'Maybe I am, Eisa lovey, but a key's only as good as the lock. And your lock is absolutely fabulous.'

'What is "lovey"?' asked Eisa.

'Same same "Habeebi",' said Arthur Arthur. And he slipped Eisa a wink before heading for Reception. 'Are the three Sues here?' he asked, looking round the empty room for Agnes's assistants.

'Everyone's been asking me that. Rachel wanted to know, too. They're seeing to the books, I hope. Something of a crisis. They'll be here later on,' said Agnes. 'There you are, dear.' She presented Teresa, now recovered, though still resentfully subdued, with the key to her room. 'You're 405 Churchill Hall. That's through the door out there. Up three flights and—'

But Muchtar interrupted. 'I can show the young lady to her room. It is next to mine,' he said.

Agnes eyed Muchtar suspiciously. 'Well, it shouldn't be. There must have been a cock-up. The three Sues, shouldn't wonder. Anyway, dear, the keys can be a little on the temperamental side. Slovenly university students occupy the rooms when the summer school is not in session. You may find that after inserting the key in the lock you will need to pull the handle of the door sharply as you turn it. Alternatively, you might have to insert the key, lift the handle while pushing it away from you. You get the idea?' She smiled outwardly, pushed the key into Teresa's hand while her head turned away to view the messy pile of papers on her desk. 'Anyway, it's a bit like life – a matter of trial and error.'

Muchtar nodded, taking responsibility. He made to lead the wounded Teresa from Reception.

'Ask "Whose is this?", Eisa lovey,' commanded Arthur Arthur.

'Whose this?' Eisa asked, holding the pink comb aloft.

'Is my!' exclaimed Teresa. She seized it from Eisa's huge hand and beamed a huge smile at her benefactor.

'Where are you coming from er . . . lovey?' Eisa asked his new friend.

'From Spain.'

'Cordoba! Sevilla! Al Hamra!' said Eisa.

'You are in Spain?'

Eisa looked mystified. 'No, Ingiltra. England.'

Teresa and Eisa smiled at one another, like Robinson Crusoe and Man Friday confused on their island of melting ice. Arthur Arthur had gone to bag himself the best of all available rooms. He could be heard pleading with Agnes Fogherty for a double for old times' sake. Agnes, famous for her lack of sentiment, told Arthur Arthur he was no longer part of a couple. 'Agnes lovey! Look at me!' replied Arthur Arthur.

'Yes, you have put on a bit of weight since last year. Lots of walks on the Heath for you, Arthur! Just don't tell Dennis about your double.'

'Thanks, Agnes. Tell you the truth, Eisa and I've had a bad fright. A woman was run over in the Finchley Road just now. Right in front of us.'

Agnes shook her head, tutted and searched in her pile for Arthur's key.

Just then, Nathan, yawning, opened the door and gave the coffee machine a cute kick as he passed. It gurgled and a stream of hot black coffee poured into the cup. Nathan stopped, wondering. But only for a second. A trio of foreigners was suddenly approaching him, all smiles. He smiled back and shuffled about.

'It is the helpful young man!' beamed Muchtar.

'Ah, *felicidad*!' cried Teresa. She squirmed out of

27

Muchtar's clutches and seized the cup. Then she sat down on the step next to the telephone kiosk, toasted Nathan, Eisa and Muchtar, and a relieved Agnes Fogherty, who would not now have to get in touch with the dreadful Dominic of Maintenance.

'Hello, Nathan!' called Arthur Arthur, coming out of Reception. 'You've grown! How's your mum?'

'She's OK, I suppose,' Nathan replied coldly.

A few minutes later Nathan was tip-toeing back up the stairs, away from the dining-room. He had gone there fresh from his triumph to watch the television – for the room doubled as the TV room – but, seeing Lynn Weaver sitting alone there, thought better of it, even though he felt curious about her eye-patch.

Nathan knew Lynn well, was always being told by his mother to call Lynn *auntie*, had photographs on the shelf at home of Lynn hugging him when he was younger. But he did not want to meet her now. When he was safely out of sight of the dining-room he breathed a sigh of relief and ran off towards the garden.

But Lynn Weaver was too deep in one of her interior monologues to notice Nathan. 'I'm not just a piece of carry-on luggage, Keith,' she was telling a plate of tough lemon meringue pie.

She had told each course of her dinner similar things. The celery soup had been informed that she was fed up with landing in one more arrivals-hall; the steak and kidney pudding that this was no longer a life she wished to lead; the salad that other couples had homes. 'Do you know what a home is, Keith? A home is a place to which people return to put their feet up. Normal people come home. Normal people do not taxi from the airport past street after street of homes to . . . to . . . this.'

'This' was the empty dining-hall of Heathcliff College, a room she knew well from previous summer schools, but a room which, no matter how many free lunches it

28

offered her, could not inspire affection. 'This' was also her seedy double study-cum-bedroom in Churchill Hall, its walls faced with rough brick that grazed her arm each morning when late for class, its only decoration a white notice-board covered with student graffiti, with fire and sexual precautions.

'This is it,' Lynn told herself as she walked over to the coffee machine to the right of the buffet table and pressed its button, remembering to pull the cup away when only half-full, let the weakening water drain away, then repeat the procedure to obtain a cup of coffee whose strength suited her. Funny how the details of life at the summer school came back. It had been the same with the door-keys. In a trice she was lifting, pulling back, pushing, as if she had never been away.

Lynn sat down again, pushed her unloved pudding out of eyeshot, and sipped the strong coffee. 'Yes, this is it all right.' She thought of her rebirth on the floor of the Ali Kapu Convention Centre at the Shah Abbas Hotel in Isfahan. 'It's up to you, Lynn. Look around. Behold The First Day Of The Rest Of Your Life,' Nigel Khayaam had said. 'This is it.' Nigel Khayaam had thought that the expression contained all the wisdom of the ages. He had not said it as Lynn had said it since. She looked at herself in the concave surface of her pudding spoon, stopped short. *What's happening at the Shah Abbas Hotel now? What became of Joan and her Baha'i opium-addict husband? What was his name? Gone. Where are all my students now? Were they killed in the war with Iraq? And what about all those girls who told anti-mullah jokes, sneered at the idea of covering up their faces, doted on Tom Jones? Where are they?*

She and Keith had been forced out of Iran by the revolution. At the airport they were strip-searched by fanatics; Lynn's small collection of gold puzzle-rings lifted out of her bag, looked at, unravelled and not returned by a woman who had reminded Lynn of a nun relieving a child of her dinner-money. Had the woman, she wondered, managed to put the puzzle-rings back together again? She hoped not.

29

'Is this seat available?' asked Muchtar.

Lynn smiled, looking round the dining-room with its twelve tables, each capable of seating ten people, and all empty.

'Please,' she said to the man.

'Thank you,' said Muchtar. He sat down neatly, like a diplomat about to sign a peace treaty under the gaze of the world's media. 'We have met before. Don't you remember? I asked you about meals,' he said, smiling broadly.

'How silly of me. I'm tired out, I'm afraid. Are you a student?' she asked, thinking of all the other times she had asked that opener in this room. It was Lynn's seventh summer school. Or was it the eighth? Faces from the past scrolled through her brain like a class attendance-list, some as they appeared in the mug-shots on the common-room wall as part of a getting-to-know-you exercise, others bedecked in their last-night pantomime costumes. It's funny what you remember, she thought. It is not at all funny what you forget.

'Yes and no. I am an English teacher in my country. I am here on the teachers' course.'

Lynn nodded. 'You'll be with Rachel Pales. Rachel always does the teachers' course. Where are you from?' Faces of foreigners scrolled again. Brown leaves in misplaced address-books.

'Malaysia. Do you know Malaysia?'

If it's on a map, I know it, Sunshine. 'Yes,' she said, 'my husband and I worked there once.' More than once. She stabbed at the first posting. 'Kota Tinggi.'

Muchtar beamed. 'I am not Malay, of course. Not by race.'

'You're Tamil, aren't you?'

The man's beam widened, and for a moment the brightness of his expression made Lynn forget Keith and his quest, and her exile. She had made him feel at home. 'Yes, I'm from KL. That's—'

'Kuala Lumpur. Which part?'

'You know KL? I'm from near the station. My dad has

30

a shop,' said Muchtar, trying to look at Lynn's good eye and ignore the eye-patch.

'It's a beautiful station. They were fixing it up last time we were through there. It always reminds me of the Brighton Pavilion. All those domes and minarets.'

'But now I and my family live in East Malaysia. Sarawak.'

'Where in Sarawak?' Lynn asked, thinking of an eighteen-month stint in Kuching ten years before, a time both she and Keith had been content – until the Malaysian government had done away with their posts.

'A small town near Miri.'

'I know Miri,' said Lynn. 'We went to the Niah caves to see the bats and the swiftlets.'

'The caves are wonderful.'

'Yes. A bit slippery, though. All those droppings,' she said. As she, Keith and . . . who else? . . . had been waiting for dusk at the mouth of the cave, a collector of swiftlet nests fell from his climbing-pole to the floor of the cave. She and whoever was with her had cradled him, covering him with their anoraks, while Keith ran off with the other collectors to get help. She could re-call his terrified eyes and her inability to say anything that would comfort him. She had followed the man's gaze, watching the clouds of bats passing over the dark ceiling of the cave, then dispersing into the dusk, flying away in their millions to cloud the sheer lapis curtain of the sky, the living cloud forming fluid countries, islands and continents, as the swiftlets concentrated to take over the cave for the night, exchanging homes with the bats quite peaceably. What had happened to the nest-collector? They had asked the man at the guest-house. He had not held out much hope. All for soup, too. 'Er . . . are you alone?'

'Oh, yes. I have left my wife and children in KL with my dad. I am missing them. What about you?'

'My husband won't be arriving until tomorrow. He's gone for a job-interview.'

'Where?'

'Italy. Rome.'

'I think you British are very lucky. The world is your oyster,' said Muchtar wistfully.

She stifled a yawn, but not well enough.

'Perhaps you require more coffee. May I obtain you another?'

'That's kind. Thank you. Black. I'm jet-lagged.' She studied her palm as she lifted it to her face to bite her bitten nails: the flesh flushed from dragging too much carry-on baggage; her finger cut by her wedding-ring.

Muchtar got up, his brown hand holding his tie against himself. Lynn wondered what kind of husband he was. Beneath the charm he was probably quite stern.

But what if Keith gets Rome? Dismantling their possessions from the university bungalow in Kano and shipping them off to Rome! It would be better to give them away to the deserving poor. That would at least stop the beasts at Customs from grabbing them.

Lynn thought of the empty cartons that had greeted them in her father's garage in Leominster after their first posting abroad. Probably they'd been shipped all the way from Port Sudan in that condition. She could still see the Dinka blankets, the wooden pillow-stalk, the masks. The rest she had forgotten, though sometimes she would search about for a cassette, a stapler, a skirt. If anything was lost, she would think of those rifled cartons in her dad's garage. Where were their contents now? Why didn't we learn then?

She looked at her watch, adding hours, wondering if the bats were coming out of the caves in Sarawak as she sat in the empty echoing dining-room. No, it was too late.

'Do you live in England?' Muchtar asked her, placing her coffee carefully on the table.

Lynn could not help laughing. 'No, we're just visitors. I mean, we don't have a home here. My husband and me, we teach abroad.'

He frowned. ' "My husband and *I*", isn't it?'

Here we go, she thought. She decided not to be drawn into it.

'Yes, you're right. Silly of me,' she said. 'It's just something I say.'

'Where have you just come from?'

'Nigeria. Kano.'

'You must be very tired.'

She was looking down at the milk entering the whirlpool of the weak coffee. She didn't take milk in coffee. She looked up at the man and nodded.

'I don't know your name. My name is Muchtar.'

'Lynn Weaver.'

He held out his hand. 'How do you do?' he said.

'How do you do?' Lynn replied, shaking Muchtar's hand weakly.

'Just as I thought!' he exclaimed.

'Yes?'

'Yes. That's the right answer.'

'To what?'

'To "How do you do?". At home I was teaching from a new textbook which said "I'm fine" is fine, but that's not right. "I'm fine" is the answer to "How are you?", isn't it? "How do you do?" you answer 'How do you do?" That's correct, isn't it?'

Lynn had been here before, too. She had visited all the little stations along the line leading to that Shangri-la known as Language Proficiency. The trouble was that each station had sidings and loops and places for uncoupling and time for discussions on the merits of the window-boxes. 'Well, it depends,' she said.

Muchtar's face fell. She knew why it had fallen. He wanted a rule, a bit of certainty in his life, a prescription that would make him better. But Lynn, born to prescription, had been weaned on Descriptive Grammars. 'It's hard to give a hard-and-fast rule,' she said. 'You see, if enough educated English-speakers say something often enough, it . . . it sort of . . . er . . . becomes correct, even though it might have started out as an error. Many English-speakers would reply to "How do you do?" with "Fine, thanks".

33

You really can't be too dogmatic about grammar. But you know that yourself as a teacher.'

'No, I don't know that,' said Muchtar vehemently. 'I don't know that at all. In my classes we have rules, and the rules are to be obeyed.'

Lynn looked at Muchtar. She was glad she wasn't Rachel Pales, who took the teachers' course at the summer school. 'That depends . . . ,' she said again.

'In the old days there was right and wrong, and the British knew the difference,' said Muchtar.

'Times have changed,' she tried, seeing her room in Churchill Hall, investing it suddenly with unexpected qualities of enchantment. She could imagine herself snuggling down in the bed and swooning asleep, the muted roar of traffic in the Finchley Road lulling her with the knowledge that she was somehow privileged to be able to sleep while the city carried on its tiresome routine.

'If you'll excuse me, Muchtar,' she said, 'I think I'll go to my room. I haven't slept since the day before yesterday.'

Lynn collected her dirty dishes – adding Mr Muchtar's coffee-cup to the pile – and took them to the kitchen. The summer school lasted for three weeks, and she knew from experience that it was not a good idea to alienate the kitchen staff.

'Don't I know you?' she asked the young man by the washing-up machine.

'Don't think so,' he said.

'Weren't you here last year?'

'No, this is my first time.'

'My mistake,' she said. 'I must be confusing you with somewhere . . . with someone else.'

Molly O'Connor arrived in mid-afternoon, staggering into Reception just at the moment when Agnes Fogherty, the first wave of crisis behind her, was in the act of sitting herself down to partake of a Sweet Afton and a few pages of her newspaper.

34

Molly knocked her Molly knock, then peered round the door. 'It's only me, Agnes,' she said diffidently.

'Molly!' said Miss Fogherty. 'You know there's no-one I'd rather see. Have you had a good year?'

'Good-*ish*,' replied Molly, setting down her small suitcase neatly. She took off her plastic rainhood, pulled the ends so that it folded into a limp plastic ruler in a trice, while a magnetic field of water drops cascaded around. 'Sorry,' she told Agnes Fogherty and the bedewed folding chairs. 'Still, I shouldn't complain.'

'It's raining, is it? That's good. We need it. I expect He laid it on just for you. You've changed your hair. It looks nice.'

Molly felt her hair, almost guiltily. 'Does it? It's shorter. I took the scissors to it. I had trouble with the back. Did it by feel. A mirror's no help at all. I'm not sure about it.'

'No. You never are, Molly,' said Agnes with certainty.

Molly smiled at the old joke between them. 'Anyway, I know how busy you are. I'll just take my key and get out from under your feet.'

'You must be tired,' said Agnes, looking closely at Molly's face for signs of change. As both women were in their late forties, Agnes tended to use Molly's progress as a mirror for her own. 'Still, you're looking as fresh as a daisy.'

'I'm tired-*ish*,' Molly replied. 'We had to change planes in Dubai. It's such a palaver. I asked them if I could stay on board, but they wouldn't hear of it. And before I forget . . .' Molly O'Connor took the rattan duffel bag from her shoulder, placed it on the floor and rummaged in it. 'I shouldn't encourage you in your vices, Agnes,' she said, taking out a yellow carton of Sweet Aftons.

'Molly, you shouldn't be spending your money on me.'

'Sure, they give them away in Dubai!' replied Molly. 'Did I tell you that Father Keogh has given up? He's wearing nicotine patches now. He won't be parted from them. The fundamentalists up-river keep him supplied.'

Agnes Fogherty took a drag on her cigarette. 'We'll have

35

a good natter when the invasion's over,' she said. 'I've got you your favourite room. The one over the entrance with the view of the church across Kidderpore.'

'That's great,' said Molly. Agnes gave Molly her key, and she signed for it.

'You haven't got a tan yet, have you?'

'I stay out of the sun,' said Molly, turning the door-key in her hand, anxious to take her first look at the church. 'It's too much for me.' She picked up her suitcase. 'Am I the first?'

'No. Arthur and Lynn beat you.'

'How are they?'

'Lynn's a bit subdued. Apparently Keith's on the move again. He hasn't arrived yet. An interview in Rome.'

'Rome!' said Molly, impressed.

'Yes, Rome would suit you, wouldn't it, Molly?'

Molly nodded. Then she looked at her duffel bag and wondered if it would. What about the children and Tankiti and the Falls of Sense? It would be no life if she couldn't go to the Falls of Sense!

'I'd have thought Rome would suit Lynn better than where she is,' Agnes said. 'She thinks differently. Bent my ear about staying put as soon as she saw me. Talking about ears, she's done something to her eye.'

'Oh dear, she hasn't! What?'

'I didn't ask,' replied Agnes. 'I didn't want to open the floodgates, if you know what I mean.'

Molly did know, and nodded. 'The poor thing's tired of moving about. She and Keith have two whole pages of my address-book all to themselves! I can understand why she gets fed up.'

'So can I. It's not the travel, more the travelling-companion that would get me down, if you get my drift,' said Agnes.

But, if Molly did, she didn't let on.

'Arthur's just the same,' Agnes continued. 'He seems to have bounced back.'

'I heard about Harry.'

'I gave Arthur a double room. It took some juggling.'

36

'That's nice,' said Molly, elsewhere. 'I wasn't able to bring Tankiti.'

'Who's Tankiti?' asked Agnes.

'Shame on you, Agnes! Don't tell me you've forgotten the blue-eyed boy of St Cedric's!'

Agnes had forgotten, but made a snapping gesture – Ah, *that* Tankiti – with her free hand.

'Dennis offered him a scholarship. He even sent me Tankiti's plane ticket.'

Agnes rummaged for her scholarship list. 'What's his surname?'

'St Cedric.'

Agnes wondered about that but decided not to ask. 'So he's St Cedric, Tankiti, is he? No . . . yes, he's here under "C". The three Sues have left out the "Saint". Couldn't believe it, I expect.' She crossed Tankiti St Cedric off her list. 'So why isn't he here?'

'It's a long story, Agnes. I'll tell you when me head's stopped spinning. I better hadn't take up any more of your time.' She waved to a mystified Agnes Fogherty and left Reception.

Molly was trying to reconstruct the knack needed to open the main door of Churchill Hall when she heard a sound she knew. Castors attached to hard luggage rolling along an uneven pavement and, over this sound, the birdsong of Japanese in high and low register. As she struggled with the key she could already see the approaching students in her mind's eye: the American style of their clothes, their impeccable shining hair, the hand-before-mouth of the girls when they laughed. The *Demolish Babel Summer School This Way* sign, placed on the pavement, fell over with a crash. All the sounds were coming back. Molly put down her suitcase, turned the key and opened the door of Churchill.

'Please . . .'

Only twenty clattery wooden steps rose between her and her room opposite the church. How often at the mission she had sweated and dreamed of cool London and her little room above the entrance, the deciduous trees in full leaf, the temperateness . . .

'Please . . . madam . . .'

Molly O'Connor let the door shut and turned. The knack would come back.

A dozen Japanese students, each leading a large suitcase with wheels on one corner, stood gazing at her. The suitcases had changed since last year. The colours bolder, one two-toned – the exact coffee-and-cream of her dead dad's Triumph Herald – the carrying-arms bent slightly to give better traction. How clever, she thought. It's obvious but you'd never think of it till you see it!

'Welcome!' Molly said expansively.

The students bowed and Molly bowed back and the girls laughed behind their hands while the boys held on tight to gravity. 'First things first,' said Molly. 'You need your room-keys. Reception is this way.'

She pointed the students towards Reception, reassuring the boy with the wispy moustache, who seemed to be the leader, that she would guard their luggage. She heard their chirping as they filed into Reception to face Agnes Fogherty; smiled as she caught snatches of Agnes slowing down words and increasing volume – her way of translating instructions into Japanese or, indeed, any other language. 'You're all in Stocks! Same key for both doors. To get there, you go outside. Turn right. Along the corridor. Out the door. You'll see the sign for Stocks. Up the stairs . . .'

'Everything all right?' Molly asked them.

The leader looked confused. He shook his head, frowning at his key.

'Come with me,' she said. They followed her, chirping. She thought of St Francis and the birds. She helped them lift their cases up the stairs. *What have you got in here, the crown jewels?* She showed them the knack needed for opening their doors. Then, when the tatty bedrooms revealed themselves, she felt herself redden at the offence they must cause what she imagined to be Japanese sensibilities.

When they were settled, she conducted the boy with the

moustache down to the dining-hall, where Nathan and the kitchen staff were sitting around watching television. The television sounds, amplified by the brick and the sound-box ceiling, stripped the thin layers of forgetfulness from the strong impressions of previous years. The clattering and tinkling from the kitchen, together with a radio tuned to a pop station; the hubbub of conversation at the tables. Volume turned up and up to a pinnacle of life. She thought of the rainforest cacophony around St Cedric's.

'You can watch television while you eat. It'll help your English,' Molly told the Japanese. She watched the lead Japanese as he nodded thoughtfully. How beautiful he was, she thought. How well turned out. A credit to some mother worrying, a confusing world away. Then she saw the shrunken head of the Japanese soldier sitting in the Kass longhouse next to a statue of St Martin de Porres and a Sony tape-recorder with a cloth over it. She had tried to get Tankiti to rid himself of the head, to give it a decent burial somewhere in the forest, but he wouldn't. His father had taken the head, he said. His spirit would be angered if it were removed. I'll convince him that what I did was the right thing. It belonged in the forest. I'll win him round. If he could have come here and seen these lovely people, he'd have agreed. I'll tell him that. Yes, I will! I'll have him confessing his pagan stubbornness to Father Keogh; I'll . . .

Bidding farewell to the Japanese, Molly made for her room. She had opened the door, taken in the sight of the church across the road, heard the sigh the automatic door-closer made, before she realized that she didn't have her suitcase.

She approached St Anthony before returning downstairs knocking at the door of Reception. 'Agnes . . .'

Agnes Fogherty did not look up. 'It's over there, Molly. I found it sitting outside the door of Churchill, in full view of Kidderpore Avenue. Anyone could have walked off with it.'

'Stupid of me.'

'You got involved, didn't you?' said Agnes accusingly.

'They seemed a bit lost.'

'Yes, well, they've got to get used to being a bit lost. It's part of the human condition, being a bit lost. And you know what Dennis says, don't you?'

Molly looked lost.

'"Never show when you can tell." It's one of his Ten Language Teaching Commandments.'

'Yes, of course.'

Molly took the suitcase and fled back to her room. The bed had been placed under the window. That was different from last year when it had been against the wall, under the grubby notice-board. She took the old armchair and pulled it into the middle of the carpet, facing the window. She unlaced her black shoes and took them off. Wedged into the crenellations of the soles were flecks of red earth from the St Cedric mission in Mulu, Borneo. The earth had survived the ride down-river, the drive to the airport, the long flight. She smiled to herself, sat down in the armchair, put her feet up on the bed.

The rain clouds had passed away, and the afternoon sun shone again on the red Victorian church. She had seen it so often while away, conjuring it up in the middle of her work, doubting that it could exist on the same planet as Mulu. But now, despite the evidence of the red earth, all the dictates of common sense, she was having the same trouble believing in Borneo.

Still, that always happened. That was one of the strange things about travel. To counteract her doubt, she conjured up the names and faces of all her children there. She heard the door between the corridor and the stairs creak, go silent for a second, then shut with a little bang. Exactly like last year. A pity no-one had thought to fix it, but this aural Braille was comforting somehow. She returned to reciting the names of her children, worlds away in Borneo. Then, before she knew it, deep sleep had sent her soul zooming home in the winking of an eye.

*   *   *

Despite her best efforts, Lynn Weaver could not sleep. She lay on the single bed farthest from the window, which looked out over the concrete quadrangle and some noble trees to the Finchley Road. Once or twice she drifted deliciously down below the surface of consciousness, but a bad-tempered horn, or a car taking the Finchley Road in second gear, jolted her back, wide awake, to common day.

The traffic seemed worse than last year. But each year everything was judged to have deteriorated since previous years. It was one of the comforting things about returning to England for the staff of the summer school. No matter how tough their lot abroad, returning to England always invested life elsewhere with the rosy unreality of a post-card of paradise landing on a grubby Monday-morning doormat.

Lynn lay on the bed for half an hour, counting the horn-blasts. Eighteen. Then she thought of Keith, jet-lagged in front of an interview board in Rome.

A prolonged horn-blast might have distracted her. She was suddenly making a new life for herself in Rome. But, as soon as she was conscious of nosing round that obvious trap, she forced her mind back to her garden in Kano. She and Keith were going to teach the summer school, pop in on their parents and then return to Kano. That is how it was going to be. She was not going to Rome. Friday was watering the garden every day, waiting for his Levi jeans and his cassette-recorder with tape-to-tape recording, along with a long list of cassettes. Friday was going to set up as a tycoon in the market selling the copies he hatched from the machine. She was going to help Friday with that, and he was going to help her create the best garden between Jos and Marrakesh. Rome was out, and she would tell Keith that when he showed up.

She got up, wondering whether she should push the beds together. She decided not to, brushed her teeth at the washbasin, ran the red face-flannel under the cold tap, held it to her face and breathed through it. A cup of tea might help, she told herself.

41

In the deserted kitchen she filled the kettle. She remembered the kettle from last year, remembered that it did not switch itself off; that the chain restricted its movements. She was able only with difficulty and a clanking of chains to pull it to a position under the cold tap. Sitting down on one of the armless uneasy-chairs she looked around the kitchen. The ironing-board had made it through another year, as had the iron – also chained. It was odd the way things appeared to stay just as they had been. She had hardly given Churchill Hall a thought during the year away. How many girls had been made pregnant since last year? Had there been any suicides? Burglaries? Prowlers?

'Lynn!'

She looked up, only then noticing that the room was full of steam. Making his way through it, his arms open wide to embrace her, was Arthur. 'Arthur!' She dodged his embrace, running instead to turn off the kettle. Then she ran to him and let herself be hugged. 'That's nice. That's really nice,' she said.

'Any time, lovey. Any time. What's the matter with your eye?'

She touched the patch. 'It started as a scratch from the cat but it turned nasty. Did you get my Christmas card?'

'Yes,' he said, hangdog. 'I'm sorry I didn't get in touch. I only managed to get as far as H in the address-book.'

'Don't worry about it. I thought that was probably how it was. I half-expected to get one of Harry's little gems, though. How is Harry?'

Arthur had turned away from her, looking in the cupboard for tea-bags. 'Ginger-nuts and digestive bickies! Dennis never lets us down in the food department, does he? You heard about his knighthood, did you?'

'Yes. I was very pleased. Never thought he'd get anything like that. He doesn't seem the type.'

'Will a mug do?' he asked.

' 'Course.'

'I wonder how they dressed him up for his trip to the Palace? He couldn't have gone in one of those batik shirts, could he?'

'I expect Porn-Chai would've taken care of that. She's good at it.'

'Jordan Bostock's going to be miffed, I should think.'

'You know, I don't think I've thought about Jordan Bostock since last year,' said Lynn. 'Do you think he'll be coming back this year after what happened?'

'He'll be here,' replied Arthur. 'He's got a hide like a rhinoceros. And he's got a stake in Demolish Babel. A stake through its heart. He'll be here all right. Has to check his investment.'

'Pity. I'll never forgive him,' said Lynn.

'No. Me neither. Fucking Judas,' replied Arthur. He placed the mugs of tea on the table and struggled to open the packet of digestive biscuits, pulling at the packing with his fingers.

'Let me,' said Lynn.

'I haven't got any nails.'

'Me neither, but I can usually manage it.' The plastic wrapping tore for her easily. 'How's Harry?' she asked again.

Arthur looked at her. 'Harry's dead,' he said. 'He died in February.'

'But . . . I thought . . .'

He nodded, smiled with his lips in the way he had, winked with a cold unsmiling eye, and patted her hand. 'We all thought he'd last longer. He thought so himself.'

Suddenly, not wanting to, wanting to, tears were leaking out, and not only for Harry. 'I can't believe it,' she said. 'I mean . . .'

Arthur looked at her, thinking how easily Lynn wept. He could see her bidding farewell to him and Harry the previous summer, her face a puffy mess after a morning of partings. Harry had said something to him as he waved which had made him laugh. What? He was forgetting things about Harry. Day after day memories leaked away.

'I know what you mean,' he said. 'I buried him with my own hands and I can hardly believe it sometimes. Here . . .' He gestured to the brick walls of the kitchen. 'When I landed in this afternoon and met Agnes again I

43

kept looking about me, expecting Harry to come out from behind a blackboard with a "Durrrurrr! The Wicked Witch of the South has come North! Miraculo! Miraculo!" No such luck, of course, but a side of me thought he might have died as far as Egypt was concerned, but been spared for the summer school. He was two different people. One for here. One for there. Does that sound daft?'

Lynn touched her eye-patch. 'It just won't be the same without Harry,' she said. Then she thought how useless she was in such a situation. She'd been lucky up to now in that department. Charmed lives in her immediate vicinity. Still, as in so many other departments, it looked like the charms were beginning to lose their gilt. 'Are you managing OK?'

'Oh, yes. The school's been busy. We – I – can't come near to satisfying the demand. Not much money in it. Never was. It's been the devil's own job scraping together the fare. I took a few groups of tourists from the steamers for days out on donkeys.'

'Do you still get payment in kind?'

'Oh, yes. A chicken one day. A few sweet-corn. Lots of good spuds recently, from a chap I got through First Certificate.'

'God, I'd love to see you in action.'

'You should visit.' Arthur stopped. Then he said, 'The whole village turned out for Harry's funeral.'

'That was kind.'

'Payment in kind, remember?'

'Er . . .' Lynn couldn't go on. '. . . No, it doesn't matter.'

'Come on, Lynn, out with it. I don't mind talking about it, you know. I rather like it, in fact. And if that sounds odd . . . well, when have I ever seemed anything else?'

'He didn't suffer too much, did he?' she asked guiltily, feeling that he would think her mawkish.

'No, lovey. Egypt took care of that. He took the tablets the doctor gave him in London. We went back home rattling. Whenever I looked at him he was popping pills. Then he got an intestinal bug. He couldn't shake it off.

44

The flesh fell off him. He took to his bed and he was gone a week later.'

'So you had a few good months after the summer school?'

'Yes. Very good. When he got sick I made arrangements to take him to Luxor and then by train to Cairo. One of Harry's students from his University of Cairo days owns a clinic. But when it came to it Harry refused point-blank to go. I was pissed off with him at the time but, looking back, I think he made the right decision. People would drop in all the time. I'd have to shoo out crowds every night.' He drained his tea. 'If it had to happen the way it happened, it couldn't have been better.'

'And you're all right, are you?'

Arthur turned away. 'Great. How's Keith?'

'He's fine. He isn't here yet. He's having a job-interview in Rome.'

'Still got itchy feet, have you?' he asked standing to fix himself another cup, offering to make her one. She shook her head. He must have forgotten their talk last year.

'He has. I want to stay put. If he gets this job, I don't know what I'll do. I've read him the Riot Act. Enough is enough.'

'But Rome'll be better than Kano, won't it?'

By way of reply, Lynn gave Arthur a look and pulled her straight black hair back behind her ears.

'You ought to wear it up,' he said.

'Too much of a bother,' she said.

'Then, cut it short. It'd suit you short. How many countries is it now?' Arthur asked.

'Thirteen in seventeen years, and we were in Saudi and Malaysia twice.'

'You should write a book.'

Lynn didn't seem to be listening. 'I've tried it short. It doesn't help.'

'Harry often used to say, when I got my knickers in a twist about pensions, savings and property – the lack of – "But think of the alternative. Comprehensive! Or, worse, the Demolish Babel Oxford Street school!" And that was always enough to calm me down straight off.'

'But you stayed put in Egypt. You're part of the community. You kept your wanderlust in check. Not like Keith.'

'The wander maybe.' Arthur looked at his spoon, turning it between his fingers. 'I'm not so sure about the lust. I suppose Egypt suited us. We struck lucky. Who knows, maybe Roma will be it.'

'We're not going to Rome, Arthur. Correction: *I'm* not going to Rome.'

'But . . .'

A man with grey hair down to his shoulders, wearing a red and blue batik shirt, blue jeans and Birkenstocks, appeared at the door. 'Rome! I should think not indeed! You've got the Demolish Babel Summer School to do!' he said.

'Dennis, how are you?' said Lynn.

Dennis Harlow hugged Lynn and then repeated the embrace with Arthur. 'In a bit of a pickle, as usual. You haven't seen the three Sues, have you? I've been waiting for them at HQ all day. No sign of them. I don't suppose you could give me a hand with some books, could you?'

'Why not?' said Arthur.

'Congratulations, by the way,' said Lynn.

Dennis looked mystified.

'Your knighthood.'

'Oh, that! Thanks. It came like a bolt out of the blue. Still, I like to think that it was more a slap on the back for everyone who has laboured to spread the English language far and wide. Now, we'd better shift those books. I'm double-parked. What's the matter with your eye?'

Lynn's hand lifted, reminded. She opened her mouth to reply but only managed to see Dennis Harlow's back through her good eye as he strode from the kitchen.

Arthur, noticing Lynn readying herself to be hurt, opened the door at the top of the stairs and blew a kiss to make her better. They trundled down the loose wooden steps. 'He doesn't change, does he?' he remarked.

46

'No, not really. Thank God, I say. He takes us on every year.'

'A scholar and a gentleman!' said Arthur.

The door at the top of the stairs closed slowly, then banged. But the sound did not disturb Molly O'Connor, who was dreaming of a prayerful visit with Tankiti to the grave of the Japanese shrunken head on the banks of the Kass river, three hundred yards downstream from the Falls of Sense.

Jordan Bostock arrived at Heathcliff College walking in the wake of a group of eight Italians. He had wanted to overtake them as they shambled up the Finchley Road from the Underground station, shouting in Italian above the roar of the traffic. Now he was glad that he had not. For he saw Lynn and Arthur standing behind the open hatch of Dennis Harlow's Volvo Estate, being presented with piles of books reaching from hip to chin.

He pushed himself into the midst of the group as they went into the tunnel below Molly O'Connor's room. Then, knowing the geography, taking advantage of the students' momentary befuddlement, he slipped through the door into Reception, thinking dark thoughts about Dennis. He had obviously hired Lynn and Keith, Arthur and Harry yet again, despite the report he had written at the end of last year's school. Under the heading *Establishing Goals* Jordan Bostock had intimated that some new blood was needed, new blood who would revitalize the summer school, reorientate it towards the businesslike future with conservative methodologies. But Dennis as usual had just let things slide.

In Reception, Agnes Fogherty did not notice Jordan at first. She had her hands full with new arrivals. He saw that it was the usual muddle. Keys not working, arguments with minicab drivers over fares, with students over fees unpaid. He thought again of his previous year's report, of the carefully argued prose under the heading *Processing*. If

47

Dennis had acted on his recommendations, all this would be proceeding like clockwork.

'Try this one. It can't do any harm,' said Agnes Fogherty to an African who had made two trips to his room, only to find that neither offered key fitted.

'Pardon?' asked the African.

'TRY THIS ONE! IT CAN'T DO ANY HARM!' repeated Agnes, louder. Her version of African-French. The African took the key and retreated, muttering.

'Elle veut que tu essaies cette clé,' whispered Jordan Bostok helpfully.

The African beamed. 'Vous parlez français?' he asked.

'Je possède cette langue comme la mienne,' Jordan Bostock replied.

Agnes stood up and addressed the Italians streaming into Reception. 'Leave your luggage outside, please! Form an orderly line.'

The Italians looked at one another.

'LEAVE YOUR LUGGAGE OUTSIDE, PLEASE! FORM AN ORDERLY LINE!' she repeated.

'Vuole che lasciate fuori i vostri bagagli e che vi mettiate in coda,' Jordan Bostock told them. They smiled and complied.

Agnes caught sight of him. 'Ah, it's you, Mr Bostock! Thank God! Can you help me out? I've been saving your room for you. The same as last year. Private bath, just the way you like it. I'll hand over the keys if you'll do a spot of . . . er . . .' – she sought around for a phrase that would appeal to Jordan Bostock – 'crisis management for me. The three Sues should be here but the stupid inconsiderate girls have let me down.'

Another recommendation unacted upon, thought Jordan Bostock. Dennis should have given the three Sues the push. Not to mention Agnes Fogherty. But Dennis was hopelessly sentimental. Jobs for the drones. Dennis had not even been able to take a trip to Thailand without marrying his bar-girl, setting up her hill-tribe family in a souvenir shop in Phuket. Dennis was hopeless. His good idea thirty years ago – doubtless sired by the unacceptable

48

sort of LSD – had made him the shambling captain of the SS *Demolish Babel*, a loose leaky vessel which, buoyed up by the surging demand for English, resolutely refused to sink.

'What can I do?' he asked.

'Well, there's a student who's been flourishing a plug in front of me for the last half-hour, saying "No good". Now, where is he? I haven't been able to get an ounce of sense out of him.'

Jordan Bostock caught sight of a large man sitting on a director's chair in the corner, his knees describing nervous arcs. In his hands he held a plug and chain like a flower. Jordan pointed to the student: 'Him?'

'Yes. Ask him what the problem is.'

'ما هى المشكلة ؟' asked Jordan Bostock.

'أنا أَسف جداً' said Eisa.

'السيدة تقول انت عندك مشكلة' said Jordan.

'الحوض صغيره جدا . ايضا انا مشتاف للعوده الى وطنى، السدادة بتاعت' Eisa replied.

'He says his plug is too small.'

'Is that all?' asked Agnes. 'I suppose every plug in Egypt is an exact fit, is it? Tell him to put a hankie round it.'

'No, Agnes. I won't tell him that. What's Maintenance doing? It's their job to make sure everything fits.'

'In a perfect world . . . ,' said Agnes, looking around her desk for something to take her mind off Jordan Bostock.

But then the Italians were bearing down on her. 'Name?' she asked.

'والمياة لن تتسرب إلى المجارى من الحوض' said Eisa to Jordan.

'الله يقويك و انا ايضا' Jordan replied.

'He says the water won't go down the drain.'

'Room two one six. You go outside . . . So why is he worried about a plug . . . ? Turn left. Straight through. Up the stairs. You can't miss it. Now you. Name? NAME?'

'But that's not the point, is it? Where's Dominic?' asked Jordan.

'Two two one, Dora Russell. If you're quick, you can catch up with the other chap. Go on. Hurry! He's trying to fix the desk-light for a Japanese girl in Stocks. Apparently it caught fire. Next! NEXT!'

'انا مازلت حزين،' said Eisa.

'انا اسف، سأحاول حل المشكلة' Jordan replied. Then he turned to Agnes. 'He says it is very inefficient.'

'Spell your name. Your name. Spell! A, B, C. Well, tell him my sister went to Cairo and got stuck in a lift,' said Agnes. 'What now?'

The African was back standing in front of her, holding his key.

She grabbed it from him, rummaged in a pile and gave him another one. The African stood there.

'Qu'est-ce qu'il y a, encore?' asked Jordan Bostock.

'La clef rentrait. Il y avait déjà quelqu'un dans la pièce. Elle etait très en colère quand elle me vît,' said the African.

'He says there's somebody in the room. The key worked, but it's the wrong room.'

'He'll just have to wait until the rush subsides.' She addressed the African. 'Have a seat.'

The African followed her gesture and went and stood in the corner next to Eisa, who got up, offering him his chair. They both stood. Eisa showed the African his plug, and the African showed Eisa his key. They talked for a while, aiming resentful looks in Agnes Fogherty's direction.

Dominic, the maintenance-man, came in, holding a partly immolated desk-lamp. 'Look what the Jap girl did to it,' he said, pained. 'Not only that, she's buggered up the whole circuit right along the corridor. Talk about bull in a china shop.' He turned, glaring at a Japanese girl wearing a T-shirt which said *This and that and tell your mother* in Gothic script. She had brought both her hands up, covering her mouth. Tears stood in her eyes. Eisa appeared from nowhere and put an arm around her shoulder, murmuring words of consolation in Arabic into her ear. Agnes, pretending not to, watched them and marvelled for a moment at human diversity. Then she stopped.

'She very sad, madam,' Eisa said.

'Yes, I can see that. Dominic, get this gentleman a plunger for his plumbing. You' – addressing the Japanese girl – 'come here, dear. COME HERE DEAR! Good. Now, don't be upset. Worse things happen at sea.' Pearl Harbor, she thought. 'What's your name? WHAT'S YOUR NAME?'

'Satoko.'

'Satoko. What a pretty name! Now, there's nothing to worry about, Satoko.' She looked at Dominic. Why didn't someone make him wash? She pursed her lips, then smiled. 'This nice gentleman will get you a new lamp from the stores.'

'A bleeding rice-cooker into the bleeding light socket, I ask you,' said Dominic. 'Buggered the whole system. Don't they have fuses in Japan, then? We could make a fortune exporting good British three-pin plugs.'

'Dominic. Plunger. Dominic. New lamp. Dominic. Out,' commanded Jordan Bostock.

'It's you, is it?' said Dominic to Jordan Bostock, making for the door. 'I dread this time of year.'

'Well, if you did your job for the rest of the year you wouldn't need to dread *this* time of year, would you?'

'The students. There's no keeping up with them. I spend the whole bleeding year unblocking U-bends. Bugger me. I mean, I'm as broad-minded as the next man. You need to be round students, don't you? If it's not U-bends, it's the bleeding hose-pipe ban. Do you know how long it takes to water the tubs?'

Jordan and Agnes looked at Dominic unsympathetically.

Dominic disappeared, muttering.

'He's applied for a job in Saudi Arabia,' said Agnes Fogherty. 'Quality assurance with British Aerospace.'

'He doesn't stand a chance. In Saudi things *work*,' said Jordan.

51

'He says he's got an interview,' continued Agnes doggedly.

'I don't believe it.'

'He's convinced he's going. He's already passed his AIDS test with flying colours. He reckons nothing can stop him.' Agnes twinkled. 'You might run into him there, Mr Bostock.'

'I doubt we would move in the same circles,' said Jordan.

Agnes Fogherty turned away, pulling a face at her computer screen.

There was a momentary lull. Jordan Bostock found himself listening to the silence. But he listened too long.

'Avez-vous trouvé une solution à mes problèmes?' said the African.

'Excusez-moi. Un minute, s'il te plaît. Er . . . Agnes, can you give this chap a room?'

'Name?'

'Sebastian Palumbo,' said the African.

'Ah, yes. Mr Palumbo. From Senegal. You're one of our scholarship boys.' She handed the scholarship boy a key. 'Go out the door—'

'Agnes, if you give me my key, I'll take Mr Palumbo to his room.'

'Ah, yes, Mr Bostock. Here you are.' She handed him the keys to his de luxe room with some ceremony. 'So nice to see you again,' she added, dredging up sincerity from an area of experience she did not have, though she often had to draw upon it. After all, Agnes had been the one who had typed up Jordan Bostock's report after the previous year's summer school.

Jordan thanked her crisply and was about to leave when the three Sues exploded into Reception.

Actually, only two of Demolish Babel's typists were called Sue. The third was called Karen. Karen had been called Sue so often that she had finally given up, not being that fond of the name Karen anyway, and answered to the name of Sue.

The three Sues regarded the summer school as a well-earned break from normal routine in the head office of Demolish Babel in Oxford Street. They had, in fact, been at Heathcliff College all day. After an early-morning wine-run to the Majestic Wine Warehouse in Sue's clapped-out Morris they had staggered back to Sue's room where they had decided to sample a bottle of Bulgarian Merlot. And one had led to another.

'Mr Bostock!' shouted Sue, and the two remaining Sues followed her across the room to kiss the flinching Jordan Bostock hotly.

'Have you had a good year in Sodding Arabia?' asked Sue.

'Can't complain,' said Jordan.

'You heard about Dennis's gong, did you? He's been a sod to work for since,' said Sue.

'A sodding sod,' added Sue.

'You're drunk,' said Agnes.

'Not drunk, Agnes,' said Sue. 'A little tipsy.'

'Merry,' added Sue.

'Yes, *merry*'s the word,' concluded Sue.

'It's been hell here,' said Agnes. 'I'm going to put my feet up tomorrow and let you three handle the rest of it.'

'Sorry. We're still recovering from moving everything in yesterday,' said Sue.

'While you were skiving, Agnes,' said Sue.

Agnes glanced at Jordan Bostock, but said nothing.

'We're weak-willed, that's our trouble,' said Sue.

'And easily led, into the bargain,' said Sue.

'I think I'll go to my room,' said Jordan Bostock. 'I'm rather tired after my journey.'

The three Sues regarded Jordan, tipsily mimicking sympathy.

Dennis poked his head round the door. 'Where have you lot been? Hello, Jordan,' he said.

'Congratulations, Sir Dennis,' said Jordan Bostock.

'Your turn will come, I should think,' replied Dennis. 'In the mean time, the Radio Rentals man's come with the tellies and videos. We could do with a hand.' He addressed Agnes Fogherty. 'Where do they live, Agnes?'

'Same rooms as last year, Dennis. I've got the keys here.' She smiled sweetly, and Dennis walked over to the desk and took them from her. 'Don't forget to lock up after. You know how they walk.'

'You're telling me. I say, Jordan, you couldn't help us shift them, could you? Come on, Sues.'

'I wouldn't take the Sues if I were you. They're a bit the worse for wear,' said Agnes.

'They're not, are they?' He turned to them. 'You're not, are you? Already? Did you arrange for the photocopiers?'

Sue looked shocked. She turned to her friends. 'I didn't. Did you?'

'We didn't,' said the two Sues.

'Phone the people, would you, Agnes? I don't know why I keep you three on. There are plenty of other Sues who'd give their eye-teeth for your jobs,' said Dennis.

The three Sues looked at one another knowingly. Sue exploded with giggles, then shut her mouth hard.

'Give us a hand, would you, Jordan?' asked Dennis, holding the door of Reception open.

'I've promised to show this student to his room,' said Jordan Bostock, gesturing to Sebastian Palumbo, who was leafing through an old copy of *English Teaching Extracts*.

'Well, he can help, too. He looks like a good strong lad,' said Dennis. He appraised Sebastian, 'Goodness, he's tall! Got Tutsi blood somewhere, shouldn't wonder.'

Jordan Bostock translated, and Sebastian followed Jordan Bostock from the room, thinking that helping out must be something the recipient of a Demolish Babel scholarship was honour-bound to do.

They left Reception to Agnes Fogherty and the three Sues. Sue started doing her Jordan Bostock impersonations, while the other two Sues discussed the merits of Sebastian Palumbo. Agnes Fogherty said that of all

54

the students so far checked in a couple of the Italians had been the choicest. Sue asked which of the teachers had arrived, hoping that she might catch sight of Keith Weaver, her favourite, at dinner. Then Sue said it was time to break out another bottle. They should try the Bull's Blood this time. A steal at £1.99. Agnes Fogherty counselled restraint but, when the bottle arrived with four glasses, joined in. Then, just as they were trying to find the key to close Reception and go down to dinner, Rachel Pales, the teachers' teacher, arrived, looking for Nathan, and they all tried to assume a patina of seriousness and sobriety.

Dennis and his helpers had placed yard-high piles of textbooks all round one side of Rachel Pales's bedroom. She stopped worrying about finding Nathan for a moment when she saw her name emblazoned on the shiny covers of her bestselling *English for Your World*, volumes 1 to 5. Teachers' Books, Students' Books, Workbooks, Tapes, Tapescripts, Videos.

What a lot I got! Rachel said to herself, as she often did.

But her books consoled her only for a second. On the way up to her room she had seen Jordan Bostock helping Dennis unload video-recorders. Damn his eyes, she thought. I can't face the evil little jerk. I can't. He's poisonous and he poisons the summer school.

She tried to dismiss him from her mind, but he wouldn't go. Jordan Bostock had power; owned a large minority interest in Demolish Babel and had the ear of several of the other major shareholders. So far, Dennis – with Rachel's support – had tried to resist the onslaught for change, for turning Demolish Babel from an English Language school for every foreign Everyman into a money-making machine serving moneyed interests on the make.

Over the years Dennis and Rachel had lost many a

battle in the war against Bostock's Boys. The Oxford Street school now played host to armament procurers in search of the latest jargon; would send teachers abroad to train people in all the new-fangled vices that the late twentieth century had managed to sire – vices carried around the world from mouth to mouth through the medium of English. But the summer school remained intact. It was meant to break even and only that. All profit was ploughed back into scholarships. Its students were drawn from every continent, all walks of life.

But Jordan Bostock wanted to change all that; to reorientate Demolish Babel totally; to sack its staff, who returned year in year out like moulting migrating geese to its easy-going nest; to double the fees, and starch and press the English on offer so that it fitted only the world's doers and movers.

God rot him, thought Rachel Pales. Then, catching sight of Nathan's karate kit in the corner of the room, she searched about for her car-keys.

Arthur Arthur, on the run from Lynn, opened Rachel's door without knocking. She appraised him, noting the extra weight he had put on. Arthur smiled, but Rachel asked him stonily, 'Why didn't you reply to any of my letters, Arthur?'

His smile disappeared. 'Harry . . . ,' he said.

But Rachel was not satisfied. 'Precisely. Harry. I'd have thought I had a right to be kept informed. He was once my husband, after all. I know it all happened a long time ago and it's a small thing as big things go but—'

'I'm sorry, Rachel. Thanks for your letters. I appreciated them.'

'Harry died in February and I learned about it from that OUP rep. Do you think that's fair?'

Arthur stroked the cover of *English for Your World*, volume 1. 'I asked him to tell you, Rachel. I've just not been able to rouse myself to write. Everyone got the same treatment. It wasn't just you.'

'But I'm not *everyone*, as you well know.' Rachel approached Arthur, looking at him steadily. He took a moment to look for changes in her face. God, she was wearing well. Who would ever believe that Harry had left her for him? The whole world, except the three concerned, would have shaken their heads and pronounced Harry certifiable. 'The grown-up thing to have done would have been to inform me. When are you going to grow up?'

She waited for him to reply, but he just looked back at her steadily, the ghost of his old smile nudging up his fleshy cheeks.

'I was in two minds about whether to invite you here at all. If it hadn't been for Dennis insisting, I might have got someone else.'

He didn't believe her, but it hurt him just the same that she could even contemplate a summer school without him.

'I'm sorry,' he said.

'Granted,' Rachel replied briskly.

'Can I go now, please, Teacher?' he asked.

'Certainly not. You've got to give Teacher a big hug first.'

'Hello, Rachel Pales,' Arthur said.

'Hello, Arthur Arthur.'

Rachel looked at her watch. He watched her switch back to type, their hug in a trice consigned to the remote past. 'I should go and find Nathan. God knows what he's up to. I don't think you'll be in his good books this year. You didn't write to him at all! Not once. He spent days on your Christmas stocking. I told him I didn't know what he saw in you.'

'No. I saw him at Reception a while back. He's grown.'

'Yes, I wish he'd stop it. He's a real Jekyll and Hyde these days.'

'Hormones,' said Arthur. 'How old is he now?'

'Thirteen.'

'God, is he?' Time, he thought.

'He's embarked on the dark ages, Arthur. Sometimes he's quite beyond me. I wish he'd been a girl. You know where you are with girls.'

'Do you?' Arthur asked. He smiled. 'Talking of girls, Lynn's here.'

'Well, *most* girls. How is she?'

'Keith's not with her. He's in Rome. An interview.'

'They're not moving again, are they? God, I don't know how they do it. Lynn's letters were full of how much she's enjoying Kano. She's adopted a local stray apparently. How can she possibly be contemplating another move?'

'She isn't. It's Keith.'

Rachel nodded knowingly. 'When's he coming?'

Before Arthur could reply Nathan appeared at the door. 'Mum,' he moaned, ignoring Arthur.

'Hello again, Nathan,' Arthur said.

'Hi,' Nathan replied *en route* to picking up his karate kit.

'I'd better get you back home,' Rachel said.

'Don't I get a kiss?' Arthur asked Nathan.

'No,' Nathan replied.

'You should have been nicer to Arthur,' Rachel told Nathan as she locked the door of her room.

He did not reply, merely walked away from her down the corridor. She watched him go, unsurprised, thinking of Lynn and Arthur; of untidy lives that managed to get themselves folded and shipped back to London each year for the summer school.

They made her feel neat and tidy in comparison. Her ten years abroad – five two-year contracts with the British Council, each planned to provide new experiences, the mastery of new languages – had led her logically into textbook writing and the responsible job she now held at Demolish Babel. She had lost Harry to Arthur in Oman, but that had been more a relief than a loss. Two years married to Harry had taught her – as it had taught Harry – that she was not made for marriage. She had settled back with a contented sigh to single life, almost grateful to Arthur for taking Harry off her hands.

But a drunken goodbye-party at her next posting,

Mombasa, had led to a one-night stand with a Kenyan teacher and caused Nathan to appear, uninvited.

Now, as she ferried Nathan around between football and friends, steel-band practice and maths crammer, while juggling her many responsibilities at Demolish Babel, she felt that in the small world of several London postal districts her life was on its way to becoming as chaotic as the other teachers'.

Rachel wondered about Arthur. She had wanted to ask him questions, to know how Harry had become infected. As far as she knew, Harry had been monogamous. She had broached the matter with Harry at the previous year's summer school, and Harry had said he thought an injection at a village clinic was to blame. Well, that was possible. But, even if it were true, where did that leave Arthur?

I'll get Molly O'Connor to tackle him, she thought.

She closed and locked the door. Then she took out her organizer and made a note: 'See Molly.' She put the thick book back into her bag. She walked along the corridor, tired out, dreading the activity of the next three weeks.

The glass door at the top of the stairs closed behind her with a little bang.

'Tankiti, don't!' shouted Molly O'Connor, the noise startling her out of sleep. She sat up in bed, looked at her travel alarm-clock – a gift from her Auntie Mary, the sight of which always sparked a prayer for her soul. Time for dinner, she said to herself, the nightmare already forgotten.

The following morning at ten, all the teachers of the summer school, except Keith Weaver, were squeezing into the kitchen on the top corridor of Churchill for the first staff meeting.

'Right,' said Dennis Harlow, sitting with Rachel Pales behind the kitchen table, fingering samples of books and materials arranged neatly on its surface. 'Right,' he repeated, as Arthur Arthur caught sight of Molly O'Connor, sitting cross-legged on the floor out of the way, and greeted her with a long 'Oooh, Molly!', got down on his hands and knees – like St Vincent de Paul to a Parisian down-and-out, she thought – preparatory to embracing her.

'I heard about Harry.'

'Say a prayer,' he said. 'I may as well sit down here beside you. It's easier than getting up.'

'Right,' repeated Dennis indulgently. 'Welcome to the Demolish Babel Summer School. I think nearly everyone knows everyone else.'

Rachel whispered to Dennis. 'Ah, yes. We have two teachers who are with us for the first time: our lab teacher . . .' He could not remember the teacher's name. 'Would you care to introduce yourself, dear?'

A young dark-haired woman disengaged herself from the crush on the line of easy-chairs. 'I'm Florence Partridge,' she said and made to sit down again.

'You can do better than that, Florence. Tell us about yourself.'

Florence stood up straight again. 'Er . . . I'm twenty-seven.'

'A mere child!'

'Thank you, Arthur,' said Dennis. 'Yes, dear?'

'And I've been head of Audio-Visual and Media Resources at the Quick School of Languages in Madrid for the past three years,' continued Florence.

'Ah, the opposition! How is Mr Quick?'

'We never see him,' said Florence.

'Yes, that's what we hear on the grapevine – the grapevine that Mr Quick partakes of rather liberally,' said Dennis. He looked round, laughing at his own joke. Molly smiled at him, seeing that no-one else was bothering.

Rachel noticed Florence reddening. She smiled her sorry-about-that smile at Florence. It was an expression she had become fluent in since working for Dennis.

'Right. Thank you, Florence.'

Florence Partridge returned, relieved, to the crush on the seat, apologizing to Jordan Bostock for trapping his jacket.

'And we also have an exotic young man who is teaching the summer school for the first time. An American! Take a bow, Aaron!'

A tall dark man, wearing a grey skull-cap attached to the back of his curly head of black hair with two hair-clips, stepped forward and bowed.

'I thought it high time,' said Dennis, 'that we had a native American-speaker on the team. After all, Britain is merely a small offshore island. The variety of English that is – I die pronouncing it – becoming the norm around the world is American English. A great many of our students in past years have asked why there isn't any input from across the Pond.' He addressed Aaron directly. 'I hope you don't mind being the token Yank, Aaron.'

'Not at all,' said Aaron. 'I feel privileged to be taken on board.'

' "Taken on board," ' beamed Dennis. 'You see what a mint, producing all manner of valuable linguistic coinage, Aaron's going to be. Tell us about yourself, Aaron.'

'Sure. My name is Aaron Lippmann and I'm from Brooklyn. I got my Master's in Applied Linguistics at the University of Buffalo. I've taught in Kenya on the Peace Corps and currently I'm working with Russian immigrants in Tel Aviv.'

'Right, I think that's it as far as introductions go. I'll hand you over to my assistant, Rachel Pales, whom I think you all know. She'll conduct the rest of the meeting. I'd better go down and see that the three Sues are doing their bit. I'll see you at dinner. We've got a surprise guest.'

And Dennis excused his way to the kitchen door, and disappeared.

The staff relaxed. Rachel saw it happening, was happy that it was happening. She shuffled her papers, smiling as Arthur asked Molly about her year; as Lynn explained Keith's lateness; as Aaron, his voice booming confidently above the more subdued English buzz, was asking old Dr

61

Eric Trotter, another hardy perennial of the school, where he was from.

'New Zealand,' Dr Trotter replied. 'But that was many moons ago, laddie. Almost fifty years.'

'What's the difference between yoghurt and New Zealand?' Aaron asked Dr Trotter.

Rachel tapped her coffee-mug with her pen.

The hubbub subsided, except for Molly O'Connor. 'So I said to him, "Tankiti, it's just not right to have a Japanese head in your longhouse. Why won't you let Father Keogh give the poor soldier a decent burial?" Now, as a rule, Tankiti's quite open to suggestions but—'

Rachel tapped her coffee-mug again.

'Sorry,' said Molly O'Connor.

'Ladies and—'

Eric Trotter was laughing reedily. 'Yoghurt's a living culture! That's a good 'un. I'll try to remember to tell Moira that one,' he said.

'Ladies and gentlemen,' repeated Rachel, 'I'll keep the meeting short. Most of you know the ropes by now. This afternoon you'll all be needed for the interviews to assess the students' level. We'll use the results of this to help us assign students to the appropriate classes. Now, we have already drawn up a tentative list, based on the written tests we sent to all applicants by post. But what we've found in previous years is that some of the students get help from family members, teachers, etc. So an oral helps to clinch matters.' She handed out a stapled sheaf of papers to all the teachers and explained the pitfalls of trying to sort students out into classes.

Jordan Bostock raised his hand. Rachel had known he would. 'I think it would be sensible to sit the whole student body down to a battery of objective tests. Spend the whole first day of the course on it, if necessary.'

'But which objective test, Jordan? Our students have come by their English in so many different ways, by so many different methods.'

'I've brought the whole battery of tests that we use at the

King Saud Academy. They're highly reliable. A standard deviation second to none.'

'Keep it clean, Jordan lovey,' said Arthur. Molly shushed him.

'What did he say?' Dr Trotter asked Aaron.

'A standard deviation second to none,' said Aaron.

'I never got the hang of standard deviations. I just couldn't get my bonce around them,' Eric Trotter said.

'Have your tests changed since last year?' asked Rachel coldly.

'No, we haven't felt the need to change them,' Jordan replied coldly.

'Still structuralist? Then, I think not, Jordan. As I recall, your material only tested grammatical accuracy. Our criterion is always communicative competence.'

'But grammatical accuracy is what we're trying to achieve! You can't have communicative competence without it,' said Jordan.

'Here we go again!' said Arthur Arthur.

Rachel addressed Arthur. 'No, we're not going to argue again. I am not saying that Jordan is wrong, just that he doesn't see the whole picture.' She turned back to Jordan. 'I think this is worth repeating for the benefit of Florence and Aaron. We're trying to achieve *communicative competence*, Jordan. The odd grammatical mistake – so called – may not interfere with communication. I know our methods here are messy, but eclecticism is messy. It's like democracy. That's messy, too.'

'Students like a prescriptive course. Rules help. They're hooks for them to hang their linguistic coats on,' said Jordan. It was clear even to Aaron and Florence that this was an old argument in the Demolish Babel Summer School meetings. 'It's just not helpful to the learner to present them with a descriptive map of the language. It's about time we consigned descriptive grammars – and all the trendy textbooks based on them – to the dustbin.'

There was silence. Everyone knew that Rachel – apart from her textbooks – was the author of one of the most popular descriptive grammar books available.

Arthur Arthur tried to lighten the mood. 'Captain Sensible wages war on Wonder Woman! Look, loveys, we go through this nonsense every year. Prescriptive and Descriptive. Now, I'm not against a bit of discipline . . .'

There was laughter from those who thought they knew.

'What did he say?' asked Eric Trotter of Aaron.

'He's not against a bit of discipline.'

'There's not enough of it,' said Dr Trotter.

Arthur Arthur continued, 'But I'm also in favour of large helpings of Romance!'

'Hear! Hear!' shouted Lynn.

Jordan Bostock, not for the first time, felt everyone was getting at him. 'B.F. Skinner's work – refined for language teaching by Lado and Fries – has never been bettered,' he said. 'Now, you know Chomsky has repeatedly asserted that his linguistic theories have absolutely no relevance for—'

'I think we'd better get on to trips,' said Rachel. 'Who'll do Brighton this year?'

Jordan Bostock looked at his hands.

'I will,' said Arthur.

'Right. Arthur. Who'll go with Arthur?'

There was a sudden silence.

'Thank you very much,' said Arthur.

'I'll go with you,' said Rachel. 'Stratford?'

Eric Trotter volunteered and said that Moira, his wife, would accompany him. 'What are we going to see?'

'*Edward the Second*, I think,' said Rachel.

'Never seen it. Heard it on the World Service once,' said Dr Trotter. 'Missed the ending, though. All sorts of hisses and crackles.'

'Maybe you didn't miss the ending,' said Aaron.

Lynn and Molly O'Connor volunteered for Oxford. Jordan, who hated trips, was pressed into accompanying Aaron to Hampton Court.

'And Florence can go to Greenwich and the Thames Barrier with Keith.' Rachel made some notes. 'The Welcome Dinner is at seven. May I just remind you to circulate?

A teacher at each table. Please don't congregate into a little teachers' coven. I know I can rely on you. And any problems, I'll be around all day. So, until the interviews this afternoon, you're free.'

Arthur got up and made for the chained kettle. He held it out. The chain clanked. 'Poor disciplined thing! Here's some cool water for you!' And he held the mouth of the kettle, stretching on the end of its chain, under the cold tap.

'What did he say?' Eric Trotter asked Aaron.

'I missed it,' said Aaron.

'Me too,' said Eric Trotter. 'It happens all the time. Come and meet my missis.'

'I'd be glad to.' And Dr Trotter took Aaron's arm, standing up stiffly with the aid of the arm and his ebony walking-cane. They walked slowly out of the kitchen and turned left along the corridor.

Jordan Bostock, waiting until they were safely ahead, followed after by himself.

'I don't know why he bothers doing the summer schools,' said Arthur when Jordan had gone. 'He could buy and sell the lot of us.'

'They earn a lot in Saudi Arabia, I'm told,' said Molly.

'And he's been there twenty years, getting them ready to wage war in a twentieth-century manner. Have you ever talked to him about stocks and shares? There's nothing he hasn't got a finger in.'

Lynn said, 'I quite enjoyed Saudi Arabia. Both times. But maybe I only think I did. Keith couldn't stand it, though.'

'When's he due in, Lynn?' Molly asked.

Lynn looked at Rachel. 'Oh, any time now. Any time,' she said.

The dining-hall had been transformed for the Welcome Dinner. Bunches of balloons, nudged about by the ceiling fans, hung from the strip-lighting; uniformed waiters and waitresses, brought in especially for the affair from Holloway Cottage Catering, placed rolls on plates; the tables, for the first and last time in the course of the summer school, were covered in cloths; bottles of Bulgarian wine in two colours stood next to large jugs of weak lemon barley water.

Arthur Arthur took his seat at a so-far empty table farthest from the high table, where Sir Dennis and Lady Porn-Chai were to sit, along with their guests. He poured himself a glass of red and sat, siren-like.

Muchtar made a bee-line for Lynn at her table halfway up the dining-hall. He had been shopping. He pointed to his cardigan.

'Cashmere. Pure cashmere. Do you know what they cost in KL?'

'Sorry?' Lynn asked, worried about Keith missing his dinner.

'In KL they cost three times what I paid.'

'I expect Mr Muhattir has lots,' said Lynn.

'He is a fine man, our president,' said Muchtar.

'He is, thump!' replied Lynn dogmatically. She was already a little drunk from a session at the bar with Arthur. 'He's ravaged the rainforests of Sarawak and Sabah, and' – she pointed pointedly to Muchtar's bargain sweater – 'I should think he has a closet stuffed full of cashmere sweaters.'

Muchtar, not being a Malay yet having been partly financed at the Demolish Babel Summer School by a bursary from Mr Muhattir's Ministry of Education, muttered that his leader was a very good man.

'Just watch him when things get tough,' asserted Lynn. 'When all the assets of Malaysia are exhausted and there's nothing left except making peat from coconut husks. He'll be in his Proton Saga and off to spend his ill-gotten gains in a minute.'

'He is working for his people,' said Muchtar.

'Pull the other one,' she said. 'What about the Chinese? What about *you*, for crying out loud? You're not a Malay. If you're a *Bumiputra*, I'm Dewi Sukarno.

You're discriminated against in your own country! I'm amazed you don't know that. Still, you're here to broaden your mind.'

'You are wrong, madam. As with "How do you do?"'

She looked at him. What did that mean? 'Call me Lynn,' she said.

Muchtar said nothing. Lynn, embarrassed by the brown man looking at his plate, glanced around, hoping to see Keith striding into the room to carry her away on his white charger to another table for another chance.

The hall was filling up. The three Sues had been sent to gather together the slow students.

'Anywhere! Sit anywhere!' said Sue to Ito, the Japanese student who had asked Molly O'Connor for aid. Ito made to sit on the still-empty top table.

'Not there,' said Sue.

'But . . . ,' said Ito.

'Yes, I know Sue said anywhere. Anywhere but there.' Ito got up. He seemed about to head towards Lynn and Mr Muchtar, but thought better of it when he saw Lynn smiling at him more siren-like than perhaps he considered seemly. He sat instead at a table by himself. There, another Sue approached him and said, 'Sit *with* somebody, Ito. It's no good being by yourself, is it? You'll never improve your English that way, will you?'

Ito stood up and, seeing a group of Japanese making for a table by the window, joined them. Soon they had sat down, completely filling the table.

Sue approached. 'No national groups!' she said, imitating what Sue had said about a table filled with Turks. 'It's against the rules.' She pointed to alternate students. 'I want you, you, you, you and you to go and find yourselves another table.'

The Japanese looked at one another. Sue took Satoko by the arm and led her off, sitting her down between Mr Palumbo from Senegal and Mr Ezekiel from Niger, thereby interrupting an animated conversation in French on the state of Sierra Leone. Then Sue returned for another Japanese to throw to the lions of the international community. She chose Ito, who was beginning to think being moved about was part of some inscrutable English ritual. He tried to explain to Sue that he had eaten half his bread roll, but Sue was in no mood to take time from her busy schedule to wait for the slow-cooker of Ito's hesitant English to boil. She placed him in the centre of a table with Italians at both ends and some subdued Eastern Europeans in the centre.

Ito sat becalmed, all at sea, worrying about the half-eaten bread roll back on his ex-plate on the table near the window. He glanced across in time to see Jordan Bostock take his seat there, while Sue manhandled a group of protesting Spaniards into the places vacated by the other Japanese. He saw Kaori, a girl he admired, gazing towards him wistfully. He held his head up high.

'You look sad, said Jordan Bostock to Mitsuko.

'I am from Japan,' replied Mitsuko quietly, automatically answering the question she was usually asked first.

'What is your name?'

'Mitsuko.'

'Welcome to England, Mitsuko,' said Jordan Bostock.

Teresa was talking animatedly in Spanish to her companion next door but one to her, ignoring Mitsuko, who was next to her.

'Los Juegos Olímpicos fueron estupendos. Unos amigos de mi padre tenían una reserva en bloque. i Hemos visto todo!'

'Yes, I agree,' said Jordan Bostock. 'The Olympics were wonderful. A really good show. But I think you should talk about them in English. That's what you're here for. It's the rule.'

'What is rule?' asked Teresa.

Jordan translated.

'I no like rule. I wan' to speak in my language.'

Jordan told Teresa in Spanish not to be so selfish and inconsiderate. Didn't she realize that she was excluding Mitsuko from the conversation?

Teresa started to sulk. She looked at her plate.

Mitsuko, of course, had not the least idea what had been said, but she understood the implications. Overcome with embarrassment, she, too, looked at her plate.

'Where are you from in Japan?' Jordan tried.

Teresa's next-door-but-one companion leaned forward and said, '¿Quién se cree que es?' to Teresa, drowning out Mitsuko's reply.

'This is too much,' said Jordan. 'I really must insist that you use English.'

Assumption pursed her lips. 'This is vacation,' she said.

'I'm sorry, Mitsuko,' Jordan said.

Mitsuko stood up. 'Excuse,' she said and ran off out of the dining-hall.

'Now, see what you've done! I hope you're satisfied,' said Jordan to the Spaniards.

They shrugged.

'This seat taken?' Aaron Lippmann asked Jordan.

'Well, actually—'

Aaron sat down. 'I didn't catch your name,' he said.

'Jordan Bostock.'

'Jordan. Hey, you Jewish?' asked Aaron.

'No. I work in Saudi Arabia.'

'You ain't Jewish.' He turned to Teresa and put out his hand. 'The name's Aaron.'

Teresa smiled sweetly. 'Teresa Carreras. I am coming from Spain,' she said, then looked over at Jordan and scowled. She reached into her bag and produced a packet of Marlboro, opened it and offered cigarettes to Aaron and Assumption.

'I don't,' said Aaron. 'Used to but I kind of decided I liked breathing better.'

Teresa shrugged as Assumption took a cigarette. She did not offer one to Jordan.

'I'm sure you shouldn't be smoking,' began Jordan. Sue came over.

'I'm sorry. You'll have to wait until after the pudding before you can light up. Hope you don't mind.'

Teresa pulled on her Marlboro and exhaled a plume of

smoke just to the right of Jordan's ear. 'Franco es muerto,' she said.

'Hey, what's your surname, Teresa?' asked Aaron.

'Carreras.'

Aaron turned to Assumption. 'And yours? What's your surname?'

Assumption looked befuddled. Teresa translated. 'Rodriguez,' she replied.

'Thought so,' said Aaron. 'Crypto-Jewish. Any Spanish name ending in ez. Hey, you aren't Jewish, are you?'

Assumption shook her head, not having understood the question.

'No, but I bet you used to be. When Ferdinand and Isabella came to the throne you converted. I was at a conference at the Taos Methodist College in New Mexico. Thousands of Crypto-Jews made it to the New World, closely followed by the Inquisition. They went over into New Mexico to escape those bastards. There are still a lot there. A guy at the conference wept when he discovered he was Jewish. He said he'd always known he was different but it wasn't until the conference that he realized why. Hey, Loyola, the founder of the Jesuits, he was Crypto-Jewish.'

Jordan, irritated by the conversation and the cigarette smoke, said nothing. He watched Eric and Moira Trotter tottering into the dining-hall and, finding the nearest tables full, making their way to Arthur's table, where sat a group of Gulf Arab students.

Lynn, seeing the Trotters, wanting to be with them but trapped by a silent Muchtar, could only watch their slow progress up the long room.

'Room for two little ones?' asked Eric Trotter.

''Course, loveys. Take a seat,' said Arthur. 'I was just filling in my friends here about how a good Muslim can get pissed without breaking the rules. A Spanish gadget called a *porron* does the job.'

'He very bad man,' said one of the Arabs, taking a swig of lemon barley water.

70

Eric Trotter moved up next to Arthur and reached for the bottle of Bulgarian red.

Moira Trotter seized it from him. 'Eric, no!' she said.

Eric looked mournful. 'Trouble-and-strife,' he said, addressing the three Arabs. 'You've got it right.'

'What is "trouble-and-strife"?' asked Omar.

Eric Trotter pointed to Moira Trotter as she lowered herself down between Omar and Nasser Muhammad. 'She is. "Trouble-and-strife". . . wife. It's cockney slang. If you're in my class, I can teach you lots.' He put his left hand up and pointed a finger behind it towards Arthur Arthur. 'Ginger beer . . . ,' he began.

'Thank you very much,' said Arthur.

Eric Trotter made another swing for the wine. Moira Trotter slapped his hand.

' "Trouble-and-strife," ' said Omar to Moira Trotter.

'There's no fool like an old fool,' Moira told Hussein, across the table from her.

Eric accepted a glass of lemon barley from Omar. 'Thank you, young man. It seems that yet again I am going to have to get sozzled on atmosphere.'

He commenced so to do. 'Have any of you men been to Ghana?' he asked.

'Spare us, Eric,' said Moira.

Eric ignored her. 'Have any of you men been to Ghana?' he repeated.

'Ghana? What is Ghana?' asked Nasser Muhammad.

'Ah, I see. You don't know where Ghana is, don't you?' He reached into the pocket of his dinner-jacket and took out an old Parker fountain-pen. Then he took a paper napkin, unfolded it and drew a map of sub-Saharan Africa on it with a shaking hand.

'You old fool,' said Moira.

Eric took no notice of his wife. He completed the map, dotting in borders, blotting in Lake Chad. He held up his map. 'Nigeria, Niger, Chad, Sierra Leone, Dahomey, the Central African Republic – rum place that, don't go. And this is . . .' He looked at Arthur,

71

who was beginning to look bored, having heard it all before. Then he pointed to Omar: 'You,' he said.

'Ghana,' said Omar.

'Good lad. Ten on ten. This is Ghana. Me and the "trouble and strife" worked in Ghana before, during and after independence. A real bobby-dazzler of a country it was then. A good time was had by all. I was prof of English at the University of Accra. Well, along comes Nkrumah. It was fine at first. We put his picture on the wall next to the lion head and went on as per normal. Then Nkrumah said that he was replacing all the expats with folk who were nearer to his own physical and political complexion. Not only that, but money could not be transferred out of the country. Well, that left me and the "trouble and strife" up Shit Creek good and proper. We had a big stash of cedis salted away.'

'I never wanted to leave,' said Moira. 'If I'd had my way, we'd still be there.'

'That's all very well, Moira, but with no exchange of dosh we—'

'Forget it, Eric,' said Moira without hope. She shook her head across the table, first to Arthur – but Arthur had glazed over – and then to Hussein. 'He just won't let it alone. He's like a dog with a bone when it comes to his cedis. I hear him rabbiting on in his sleep. "Cedis this and cedis that . . ." Silly twerp!'

'Anyway, we left Ghana with only what we stood up in. This is after ten years' work, mind!' continued Eric, oblivious to criticism. 'So, to cut a long story low, what I want to say is that my cedis have been accruing interest ever since. All we need is the spare dosh and we can go back to Ghana and have a bloody good binge.' He appraised the Arabs, whom he supposed to be affluent. 'Now, what I'm suggesting is that if you scrape together the ready for the tickets we could be off to Ghana straight after summer school. Me and the trouble-and-strife have three spare weeks before they need us in Ulan Bator.'

The Arabs, not having understood much of what Eric Trotter had said, nodded.

Moira addressed Arthur. 'You're fed up with his bloody cedis, aren't you? I can see that. Imagine how I feel. I keep telling him to donate it to charity, but he won't hear of it. I should have married Harry Cartwright. He had a till. Mum always used to say, "Moira, whatever else you do make sure you marry a man with a till." I wish I had now.'

Eric Trotter made to sneak his hand around the wine-bottle, thinking his wife was distracted. She slapped his hand without moving her gaze from Arthur.

'That hurt, Moira,' Eric told her. He addressed the three Arabs. 'I bet you lot wouldn't put up with that sort of treatment.'

'Your wife is correct,' said Omar piously. 'Alcohol is very bad.'

'Oh, yes! Oh, yes!' said Arthur knowingly. He had seen Omar, Nasser Muhammad and Hussein, pouring raucously out of a taxi the previous night.

'It's my pancreas,' said Eric. 'I'm a martyr to my pancreas.'

'And don't you forget it,' said Moira severely.

Eric turned to his wife. 'I'm not allowed to forget it, am I, Moira? It's got so bad that every time I look at you I think, "I've got a dicky pancreas".'

'Thank you very much,' said Moira. She turned away from her husband, caught sight of Molly O'Connor and waved.

Molly O'Connor, sitting near the high table, did not notice Moira Trotter. She was looking round anxiously, hoping to catch sight of Agnes Fogherty, for whom she was saving a seat.

But the rainbow-hued chaos, the amplified babel of conversation, the United Nations of folk into which her jet had dropped her, made Molly forget Agnes for a moment. Next to her sat Eisa. He had already eaten his roll. What would he eat with his starter? She looked at him.

73

Such a nice face. Not good-looking in the least, too fleshy and round for that, but kindly. She took her own bread roll and, in a quick movement, transferred it on to Eisa's plate.

Agnes Fogherty arrived at last. 'God, I'm sorry, Molly. The nobs shouldn't be long now. I just hope Dennis can keep his dinner down. He's been hitting the gin.'

'Who's the celebrity?'

'I've never heard of him,' said Agnes.

'What's his name?'

'Peter Salt.'

'*The* Peter Salt! That really is exciting,' said Molly.

'If you say so. Who is he?'

'He's the most influential professor of linguistics in Britain!' said Molly.

'Is *that* all?'

'Yes. He's provided English Language teaching with linguistic insight after linguistic insight.'

'How's that?' asked Agnes, for something to say. She was watching Sir Dennis guiding in his guests, positioning them on the top table. Harry English, a major shareholder in Demolish Babel, whom Agnes distrusted because he had vociferously supported Jordan Bostock's report; Lady Porn-Chai, Dennis's Thai wife – what was that on her head? A tiara! A bloody tiara! Typical. A representative from Sir Dennis's publishers and, of course, Peter Salt, whom Sue had told her had felt her up on the stairs.

'Yes, that's him,' said Molly. 'I didn't have a notion what a language function was until I read his book, *Communication Is All*. It opened my eyes. Until then I had been mired in structuralism, Agnes.'

'What's structuralism?' Then, seeing Molly's face, she said to herself, *No, cancel that!*

Molly was shocked. 'I'm amazed you don't know. Why, you were with Dennis when he started. His first book was pure structuralism. Teachers used to spend most of their classroom time putting students through hoops. Agnes, it was so boring! It was supposed to make correct language automatic! Of course, now we know that it doesn't work like that. I'd go into a drilling coma sometimes, it was so boring.'

'A drilling coma?'

'Yes, you'd take a sentence and change it, just supplying a different word. Like this: "I like Mary. *You.* You like Mary. *John and Mary.* You like John and Mary. *Know.* You know John and Mary. *He.* He knows John and Mary . . ." And I'd just go on and on and forget where I was. I'd be thinking of what I was going to have for tea and what was on the World Service. I tell you, Agnes, it was shocking. Students would sometimes come up to the front and give me a good shake.'

'Who are John and Mary?' asked Agnes.

Molly pointed a finger at Agnes. 'You've hit the nail on the head, Agnes! Who *are* John and Mary? They were just words. There was no context. Terrible when you think about it.' She looked up at Peter Salt at the top table. 'But he saved us from all that.'

'So you don't do that any more.'

'None but the most benighted teacher does. I can think of one who is unreformed – but it would be uncharitable to name names. He isn't a million miles from where we sit,' she confided, thinking of Jordan Bostock.

A waitress placed a prawn cocktail in front of Molly. 'I haven't had one of these since . . . since . . . last year. Lord, I do enjoy the food on the summer school, Agnes.'

'Those salads tire me out,' said Agnes.

'Of course,' said the man from Tongue to Tongue Publishing, 'I'd say we were ready for a switch in methodology. We've just about saturated the eclecticism market.'

'Say again?' asked Professor Salt.

The man from Tongue to Tongue Publishing said again.

'Yes, I hear what you're saying,' said Professor Salt. 'I've been dialoguing my creative side and, things being what they are, I wonder if it isn't time to adopt a more prescriptive approach. I read an American paper in *Language* the other week. A Professor Sphencler was advocating a return to what he termed *the catachrestical grammar*. It's a good phrase for a concept whose time might well be coming round again.'

'Like hell,' said the publishing man.

Peter Salt regarded him.

'I mean, hell's back, if you get me. You know, hell? A vicar was talking about it on Morning Service.'

'Yes, but I don't quite see . . .'

'All I'm saying is that discipline's back. Head down in the classroom, learning by heart, hell – they're all back.' He nudged Professor Salt. 'And woe unto that man who is found wanting and stuck with a load of dithery eclectic codswallop!'

'So you like the idea?'

'Yes, yes,' replied the publishing man, already seeing his presses in Macau disgorging a completely new crop of grammars and textbooks for assembly in Hong Kong and worldwide distribution to a hungry English-language-learning world always in search of the Rosetta Stone.

'For too long, it seems to me,' continued Professor Salt, also hearing the roar of the presses, mistaking the sound for insight, 'we've been pushing English through its functions; asserting that foreigners can take the language like a hugely comprehensive phrasebook. I wonder if we've gone too far in that direction. After all, the world wants rules again. It's tired of being lost. It's tired of change that leads down the drain.'

'Right you are. My own thoughts entirely. It's time to reverse the eclectic movement. It's become a nightmare.'

'I have a few ideas churning around,' said Professor Salt, who had started the eclecticism ball rolling in the first place. 'Mind you, it's just a gleam in my eye at the moment.'

'We'd better act sharpish, mind,' said the man from Tongue to Tongue Publishing. 'You know what they say, don't you?'

'What?' Peter Salt was thinking fast.

'If the salt loses its savour . . .'

'Not a chance, mate. Not a chance!' said Peter Salt. 'I'll call you in the morning.'

'Ladies and gentlemen, welcome to the Demolish Babel English Language Summer School,' said Sir Dennis Harlow. 'My name is Dennis, and I just want to say what a pleasure it is for all of us to have you here. English is, of course, the new world language. It is the *sine qua non* for success. Lest I sound chauvinistic in this matter, let me assure you all that I in no way wish to denigrate your own native languages. Jolly good, I am sure, they all are. It is just a matter of happenstance that English has come out top of the heap. English has given the English people a valuable asset in these difficult days. Building the most economical and dependable car we may have passed on to other hands; clothing the world; administering the world – but we do have our language to sell and we do it, I really must say, rather well. This year I was given a knighthood. I am now Sir Dennis Harlow. But was this accolade for me alone? No; rather, it was for all the practitioners, some of the best of whom are sitting among us today.' Sir Dennis gestured expansively. 'Will all the teachers stand up and take a bow?'

The staff of the summer school stood up, and Sir Dennis named each in turn. Then Professor Salt was introduced. He stood up and spoke about the need for radical changes in teaching methods which would lead over green fields, back to that Shangri-la called Square One. *Square One!* he thought, while most of the students in front of him worried because they could not understand a word about what was in store for them. But Professor Salt was not thinking of his immediate audience. He was having one of his linguistic insights: desks worldwide groaning with brand-new materials, ground out by himself. *The series will be called Square One! Student Texts, Teachers' Books, Workbooks, Cassettes, Videos, Tapescripts, Laserdiscs, IBM-compatible computer software. Square One!*

Professor Salt caught Jordan Bostock's eye and winked discreetly.

Book Two

Lower Intermediate

Until the waitress brought round the cheeseboard – like a uniformed Salome showing off the head of John the Baptist – the meal had amused Satoko. It had, after all, contained lots of fine ingredients for filling a succulent letter home. As she prodded a roast potato around her plate, she already saw herself back in her room, writing to her best friend Suzuki, telling her about the chewy prawns in a milky sweet red sauce. Such tiny prawns, prawns that should never have been picked from the ocean – mere babies abused.

And how would she describe the meat? The pith and sinew of the toothbrush sticks of the Omana tree? A hot futami mat? No, language was not adequate. She had taken a forkful and chewed it many times but had finally had to give up and put the cud discreetly into her napkin. Yet all around her people were loading bits and pieces into arrangements on forks, together with the dark brown things she only dared to poke, hoping they would do the decent thing and crawl away out of her sight. Yes, it had made her want to laugh and shiver all at the same time. A bit like watching *Gremlins* on her video.

And the next paragraph of the meal. What had the man with yellow on his chin called it? Pudding? This upholstered in a sweet and sticky sauce. Yes, that was funny, too. It had all been funny until the cheese.

When the cheese arrived the aroma fuming from it reminded Satoko of a distillation of all the smells in the sweaty crowded arrivals-hall at Heathrow, mingled with the blocked-up toilet on the charter flight from Osaka. The cheese did not amuse Satoko at all. She got up, smiled an expression of acute embarrassment to her companions, then ran from the room.

Sue, having a quiet fag by the telephone, had spotted her and asked if anything was wrong. Satoko could only shake her head and flee up the stairs through Sue's acrid smoke.

Once in her room, Satoko felt better. But only for the seventeen syllables of time it takes to recite a haiku. When she saw her homely rice-cooker sitting on the bed, she felt

81

bad again. For she had a vision of that same rice-cooker at home on the oilcloth-covered table in the three-mat kitchen of her family's flat in Osaka. Her mother bustling past it, her reflection made dumpy then pencil-thin by the distorting polished steel of the appliance. Satoko seized hold of the rice-cooker and held it to her, thinking of her mother, who had loaned it to her for her trip, along with a large bag of grade 1 Japanese rice, a thick book of dried seaweed and the plea that she make herself rice in the cooker each day while surrounded by barbarian corn. She had tried to obey her mother's instructions to the letter but that had brought a flash of angry foreign power and the surly intervention of Dominic. The rice and cold-water stains still littered her bedspread, like a wedding that has ended in tears.

Satoko, cradling the rice-cooker to her front, reached over the bed for the book of seaweed. She opened it, popped open the airtight pack, inhaled the aroma of home and thought how the air in the packet was Japanese air. There it went! Lost, dispersing into the seedy room full of the stench of old smoke and petrol and student trainers. She could scent its diaspora. Lying down on the bed, she peeled off a sheet of the wine-red seaweed, held it up to the light and saw the magical shapes of childhood through it. Goblins and samurai warriors and geisha girls and Shinto priests and landscapes from fans swirling in the wild whorls of the dry seaweed. She folded it, and pushed it into her mouth like a gag. Then, as her saliva melted its taste, making her miss the rice she usually placed inside it, she thought of her family curled on aired futons, the fans nodding around the room, whirring away mosquitoes and Osaka humidity. She began to weep then, pulling the familiar broken rice-cooker to her by its flex, holding on to it tightly, as a refugee holds on to her last poor possessions.

> *I remember*
> *My little caged bird singing*
> *long*
> *To be on my way . . . ,* she thought.

Then somebody was knocking at the door. It was a

gentle knock, so different from the one that Dominic had ejaculated earlier in the day. A polite knock it was, as delicate as Shinto bells beseeching becomingly on behalf of the Ancestors. The bad-smelling maintenance-man's knock had been an invasion, a staccato canon, warning that a bad-tempered barbarian – a second Commodore Matthew Perry – was demanding admission to an area of private dreams. This knock, on the other hand, was reassuring while assured. Japanese.

In Japanese, Satoko asked who was there.

'It's me. Mitsuko. Please may I come in?'

Satoko had met Mitsuko at the airport in Osaka, had exchanged a few words with her in the Immigration line at Heathrow. 'Come in,' she said.

Mitsuko entered the room, and the two girls at once began commiserating with one another about their situation. Satoko talked of the evil-smelling food that looked like tofu but smelled of everything distasteful. Mitsuko sympathized, stroked the violated rice-cooker. She told Satoko that she felt sad, too. She recited her own haiku about home, and both girls wept sentiment for a moment.

Then Mitsuko cheered up. 'I have news,' she said.

'Yes?'

'Yes. Very close to here is the home of Grid Reference. I have found it on my map.' She showed Satoko a pop person's map of London which she had cut out of a Japanese music magazine. 'We are here,' she said. 'And Grid is there.'

'Yes, he is very near,' said Satoko. 'But do you think he will see us?'

'I am sure he will,' said Mitsuko. 'Sandra Sayorama of *Top Pop* saw him. He gave her tea.'

'Let's go!' said Satoko.

'Yes, but we must dress up for him!' said Mitsuko. 'Do you have suitable attire?'

'I think so, though I had to pack it while Mama's back was turned. Do you?'

Mitsuko snapped her fingers, tossed her hair and chewed as though she had a cud of gum in her mouth. Satoko, placing the rice-cooker on the bedside table, darted over to her hard suitcase and produced a black leather cincture of a skirt. 'And make-up? Have you suitable make-up?' asked Mitsuko.

Satoko gave Mitsuko a look of disdain, the look that Michael Jackson shot at her from her Video Walkman, which made her feel strange. 'Of course! I have the complete palette of Nigomishi New Wave Paint for Sensitive Skin.'

'Do you?' asked Mitsuko admiringly. 'I only have a few items from Sunrise in the West range. It is very inferior to yours, I think. But my father is very strict about cosmetics.'

Both girls thought of their fathers, and bowed inwardly. Then they forgot their fathers and remembered their quest. They arranged to meet in half an hour to make their pilgrimage to the pop star's mansion next to Hampstead Heath.

Molly O'Connor was drawing the curtains of her room when she saw the elderly woman sitting alone on the bench in front of the church. She completed the action, trying to remember where she had seen her before. She sat down at her desk, reached for her class list and ran through the names.

'That's Astrid from Brazil,' she said to herself.

She tried to dismiss the sight of Astrid on the bench from her mind. There was the important first lesson to prepare, after all. But as she inspected her textbook and teachers' book she found herself unable to concentrate. There had been something sad about Astrid at the interview. Of course, it might have been nerves. Still . . .

Molly got up with a sigh.

'Is there room for a little one?' she asked Astrid.

Astrid nodded without a smile, and Molly sat down uneasily next to her.

'You seem sad,' Molly said.

'You are correct,' Astrid replied.

'But why are you sad? Tell me.'

Astrid lifted her face mournfully to the street-lamp, which was turning from pretty red to filthy yellow-orange in the navy-blue dusk. 'I should not come,' she said.

'You mean, "I should not *have* come", don't you?' Molly replied, ever the teacher.

Astrid shrugged, shook her head. 'I don't feel belonging.'

'Well, you won't if you don't join in! You Brazilians are great at joining in. And don't you dare contradict! I saw *Black Orpheus.* Oh, I know what you Brazilians get up to at the drop of a hat! You see Lent in with a good shake! No greasy old pancakes for you!'

Astrid shrugged. The night was clammy. Molly looked across the road at the lighted window of her room, wondering if she wanted to be inside. No, I don't, she thought. I'm here for the students. 'Go on, join in!'

'Nobody wants an old woman,' said Astrid.

'That's rubbish!' said Molly, wondering if it was. 'You're as old as you feel. Didn't you see Mr Molina from Spain? He's at least eighty, I'd say. And he's having a grand old time. He was surrounded by laughing youngsters at dinner. It doesn't matter how old you are. It's your attitude that's important.'

Astrid shrugged again. 'I should not have come back here,' she said.

'You're right. Well done! You're a fast learner. But that's no way to talk. You're here now. Now, look, I'll tell you something. You're going to be in my class. I'll make sure you have a good time' – Molly's heart sank when she saw the mournful way Astrid received that news – 'even if it kills me.'

Molly noticed Satoko and Mitsuko sneak out of the entrance, turning left along Kidderpore Avenue. Where did they think they were going at this time of night? Shouldn't she warn them? And what had they done to themselves? Gone were the American clothes, the fresh complexions. Black make-up double-underlined leather jackets and skirts. They even wore black leather caps. She thought of the Japanese head from Tankiti's longhouse. *I was right to take it. Never been righter.*

'Look at them, Astrid!' said Molly. 'Where do you think they're going at this hour? They ought to be joining in, too.' Astrid, however, did not seem to have noticed the two Japanese.

'Everything has broken,' she said. Then she caught sight of Satoko and Mitsuko, followed them, frowning, until they disappeared round the corner. 'We have like these in São Paolo.' Then she looked up at the sky and forgot them. 'There is a hole there. It creeps up my continent. It sucks out all the goodness. The sun is now an enemy.'

'The ozone layer, you mean? Yes, it is shocking,' said Molly. 'We'll be talking about ecology in class.'

'Talk! Talk! There is always talk. There is no action. My balcony garden is covered in dust. Every leaf has thick dust,' said Astrid.

'Oh, yes. Cities can be very dusty,' said Molly. 'I blew me nose this afternoon and—'

'My apartment is on the bottom floor. I must have bars or the children will come in my garden and destroy. I am in prison. It was not always the same.'

Molly's heart went out to Astrid. 'Do you live by yourself?'

'Now alone. Alone. Alone always,' she said, like a Mahler song.

'Things get a bit out of hand when you live alone. I live in Borneo, by the way. I'm a lay missionary. Of course, there are lots of people around, but I suppose you're always alone-*ish* inside and everything. It's best not to think about it too much.'

'They have destroyed the rainforest there,' said Astrid.

'Well, I wouldn't say they have destroyed it. They're biffing away, though. They're having a really good old go.'

'Those whom pull down are the only who push up through the compost.'

'I've never thought of it that way. Look, why don't we go for a walk? That was a really rich dinner. Mind you, it

86

was a treat for me. I loved the pudding. In Borneo they perform miracles with sago but we don't get much sponge cake. Now, the fundamentalists up-river, they have some lovely puddings. All flown in, of course. Have you ever had pecan pie? It's heaven. The fundamentalists give it me whenever I see them. I think when they see me they think *pecan pie*. Still, if they think they can buy me off with pecan pie they've got another think coming . . .'

Astrid did not seem to be listening. She stood up. 'Where will we walk?' she asked.

'There are some lovely houses in the neighbourhood. You'll like the gardens,' tried Molly. They walked along Kidderpore in the direction of central London. 'Do you have children?'

Astrid gulped as if she were about to sneeze. Molly had a 'Bless you' on the tip of her tongue, but the expected sneeze turned into a sob; the sob into a flood.

'Do you want to talk about it?'

Astrid reached into her bag and took out a large handkerchief that shone in the dark. She opened it, and the folds were like black lines inked across the cloth. She blew on it. Molly put her arm around Astrid's shoulder – an action which accelerated the tears.

'Will you be my friend?' Astrid asked.

'Of course I will,' said Molly. 'What do you think I'm here for?' And she looked up through the hole in the ozone layer, thanking everyone up there for a task.

'I see Molly's found her first wounded bird,' said Agnes Fogherty, standing next to Lynn in the queue for the bar.

'Has she? I think I should be the first on her list,' Lynn replied. 'Make that a pint,' she told the student barmaid.

Agnes took no notice. 'I knew that Brazilian woman was going to be trouble as soon as she asked me why the hot and cold taps were separate.'

'How do you mean?'

Agnes aimed an index finger at Lynn. 'You're a mind-reader, Lynn. That's exactly what I said to the old buzzard. She went on and on about mixer taps. Mixer taps in the bathroom, I ask you! Typical kraut. They'll be agitating for bidets next.'

'I thought you said she was Brazilian,' Lynn said.

'And I'm the Queen of the May. She may have a Brazilian passport, but I know a kraut when I see one. And I think I've seen this kraut before. I've been racking my brains.'

Lynn looked round, searching the vicinity, her good eye open wide for Germans. 'Now, you mustn't stereotype,' she said. 'You know what Dennis says about stereotypes, don't you?'

'Yes,' said Agnes with a sigh.

Lynn, seeing the coast clear, turned back to Agnes. 'I've got a German in my class. I'm dreading it. I'm really scared. Nervy, you know. My grammar isn't what it was.'

But Agnes wasn't listening. 'I must look through the files. I'm almost certain she's been here before. It was the mixer taps that rang a bell. I sometimes forget a complaint but never a complainer.'

'There's no sign of Keith yet. You haven't any messages, have you?' asked Lynn, off humming her own leitmotif.

Agnes shook her head. 'Can I get you a drink?'

'No. I'm getting them in for Arthur and Eric Trotter. I'll get you one.'

'Half a Guinness,' said Agnes.

Lynn completed the order. 'It's just not like him not to keep in touch,' she said. She wondered about that. 'At least, not when he's got something important on.'

Agnes watched the Guinness settle. 'Well, I listened to the news just now and there've been no plane crashes. He'll turn up.' Bad pennies always do, she thought.

Lynn was busy giving Agnes a withering look when a glass smashed in the corner of the common room. Sue screamed.

'Will you look at the three Sues? They just get worse,' said Agnes.

'The state of this room. I feel quite sorry for Dominic.

I just don't know why people don't keep the newspapers neatly,' said Lynn.

'Don't feel sorry for Dominic. He deserves everything he gets,' said Agnes. She flicked the ash from her Sweet Afton on to the carpet Dominic would have to hoover at dawn. She took two of the drinks and walked over to the huddle of teachers.

'Welcome, Agnes!' said Arthur. 'The pint's mine. The gin's for young Eric Trotter.'

'Where's Moira?' asked Agnes of Eric Trotter.

'Gone to bye-bye,' said Eric Trotter. 'No staying power.'

'That's not fair,' said Lynn, who often saw Dr and Mrs Trotter as Keith and herself farther down the endless expatriate road. 'Anyway, I know for a fact you shouldn't be drinking.'

'Call this drinking? This isn't drinking,' said Eric Trotter, trying to conjure up blurred neon bar-signs in the blurred past. 'Did I tell you about the stomach-pump doctor of Mombasa? He set up shop right in the middle of the red-light district. Every bar had his number next to the telephone. He reckoned he'd have enough to retire in five years.'

'And did he?'

'Well, that was thirty years ago. But he wasn't there when I last visited. Could have done with him, too. I don't know what they put in the gin. Did I ever tell you about the time me and Moira got invited to a shindig with the Karamoja?'

'Yes,' said Arthur.

'They made a mean beer with cow's blood and maize.'

'I always get nervous before a new class,' said Lynn. 'Each time feels like the first time.'

'One of them wanted to marry Moira.'

'They'll love you, lovey,' said Arthur. He belched.

'Charming!' said Agnes.

'She was hitting fifty. I told her to jump at it.'

'Sorry, Agnes. It's the rich food. I'm not used to it. What did you think of Old Salt, by the way?'

'I do not understand', said Lynn, 'why him and Dennis

couldn't simplify their English for the speech. I looked around and I knew that most of the students were mystified.'

'Best left not understood,' said Arthur.

'They're out of touch,' said Eric Trotter. 'Only interested in the next lot of textbooks. Thought it was a bit rum what Salt was saying, though. Looks like we're going to be back to square one again. When I started in this lark we were teaching grammar rules the whole time. It's a long way round to find yourself back where you started. I don't call that progress.'

'There's no such thing as progress,' said Arthur. 'Human life is a treadmill under a spotlight. The reason we don't get off is that we're scared of the darkness all round.'

'That doesn't sound like you. Who said that?' asked Lynn.

'Lotsa people, lovey,' replied Arthur. 'Everyone who's reached the age of reason, shouldn't wonder.'

Lynn noticed Muchtar coming in. She hunched forward. When she looked up Muchtar had sat down by himself with a paper. Yes, she thought, Molly's going to have her work cut out.

'There's the usual queue at the phone,' said Agnes.

'I could teach them how to use their phone cards,' said Lynn, preparing her lesson out loud.

'Well, I've been telling those rich Arabs about my cedis,' Eric Trotter said. 'I bet they've got the ready. If a gang of us could get out to Ghana, we'd have an incredible binge. A binge of binges!'

'He's still trying to spend his cedis, I see,' said Lynn to Agnes.

'Every year it's the same,' said Agnes. 'I thought that he'd managed to get that Dutch bloke from last year – the one with the shiny suit – to go in with him. It looked as if he'd finally cracked it. I'm sure I remember him leaving in the Dutchman's BMW.'

'It can't have come to anything,' said Lynn. She turned to Eric Trotter. 'What happened last year? I thought it was all sewn up.'

90

'The chap got cold clogs,' said Eric Trotter. 'Said he was drunk when he offered to sponsor us.'

'But didn't you leave with him?'

'Sure. But he only took us to the airport. I reckon he felt guilty about his cold feet. Still, I'd already decided that it would be a hiding to nothing to binge my cedis with him. He was a bit of a dullard. Remember how pathetic he was in the panto?'

'He could hold his booze,' said Arthur, who could, too.

'Maybe so, laddie. But I think those Arabs are a better bet.'

'Between you and me, I don't think they understood anything of what you were saying,' said Arthur.

'Well, we'll just have to say it again. Repetition. That's the ticket. Never fails. They could write us a cheque without thinking, I reckon. Did you see the Rolex on the one opposite me?'

'I don't know why he doesn't just forget about his damned cedis,' said Agnes.

'It gives him an interest,' Lynn said. 'At least he can get at his cedis. Still, treasure on earth and all that. If it isn't moths, it's mullahs. We got back to travelling light after Iran.' She listened. 'Er . . . wasn't that a telephone?'

'Reception's shut,' said Agnes automatically.

'But, Agnes, it might be Keith!'

'I'm never going to be able to get there before it stops,' said Agnes, making not the smallest attempt to stand up.

'Telephone's ringing,' said Rachel Pales, on her way home, her head full of domestic logistics.

'Go on, Agnes. Please!'

Agnes handed Lynn the key to Reception, and Lynn rushed out of the common room, hearing the telephone jangling. She willed it to continue; forgot the steep step outside the door of the common room – void where ground should be – and gave herself a fright, a fright that echoed down eight – or was it nine? – previous summer schools. One more thing I never learn, she thought.

A minute later she was back with the group in the

common room. She returned the key to Agnes who, from the look on Lynn's face, could see that the call hadn't been from Keith.

'It was some Italian mother wanting to talk to her beloved son,' said Lynn.

'What did you do?'

'I told her to call at a respectable time. I said everyone had gone to bed.'

'That's not like you. I've known you to look for a student high and low. You're second only to Molly in that.'

Was she? she thought. 'Am I? I don't think I am.' Still, it might be nice to be like Molly. Did Friday in Kano count? Would Friday lift her up? 'Another Guinness?'

'Not for me,' said Agnes. 'Anyway, it should be my round.'

'You entered late. It's Eric Trotter's.'

'Who's taking my name in vain?' Eric asked.

'I don't know what we'll do with Keith's class in the morning,' said Agnes, thinking out loud.

'Maybe it won't come to that,' said Lynn. 'Talking about classes, I'd better go and do some preparation.'

'I'd have thought you could teach anything with one arm stuck in the door.'

'No. Used to. These days I really have to get everything sorted out in my mind. The old memory . . . ,' said Lynn.

'I'm rather worried about Lynn,' said Agnes.

'She's not worth worrying about, that one. Daft name, Lynn. Never liked it.'

Dr Trotter chirped up. 'Whose round is it?

'Yours, but I'm going. Buy Agnes a half of Guinness.'

'Right-o. See you in the morning.'

Lynn smiled and left the common room, thinking how good it felt to be with them all again. As she passed the entrance she saw Molly coming through it with her charge.

' 'Night, Molly.'

' 'Night, Lynn. We still haven't had our chat. See you tomorrow,' called back Molly.

Astrid looked at Lynn's back as if she were a rival. 'I have kept you from your friend.'

'Nonsense! I'm here for you. I can talk to Lynn any time. Now, off you go and get a good night's sleep.'

Astrid nodded. 'The sandman is coming,' she said sadly.

'Yes, and he's going to sprinkle sand in your eyes to make you drop off. Do you feel better?'

'No,' said Astrid. 'I shall never.'

'Don't forget to say your prayers!' Molly said.

Astrid gave Molly a sad little wave and climbed the stairs like Marie-Antoinette to the gallows. Molly watched Astrid's ascent with an uneasy combination of concern and relief.

'Excuse me,' said Muchtar.

'Oh, hello?'

'I am Muchtar. From Miri. We have much in common, don't we?'

'You're not from Borneo, are you?' said Molly. 'Small world! Will you have a drink?'

Muchtar consented to an orange juice. Molly paid, figuring that she could have bought a litre of juice from the unhappy Iranians in the shop across the Finchley Road for the price it was costing her at the bar. 'Let's sit down somewhere we can hear ourselves think. Will you look at that ashtray? It's amazing there hasn't been a fire with all those crisp-bags. Now, tell me, Mr Muchtar, what do you do in Miri?'

'I am a teacher.'

Molly stepped back a pace. Her smile, Muchtar felt, transformed her face, used every line to paint a picture of surprised joy. He felt himself lifting. 'You're not! So am I! I work at St Cedric's in Mulu. Have you been to Mulu?'

'Yes. I have gone walking with my students in the jungle. We climbed the pinnacles.'

'I know the pinnacles. I've never been up them. No head for drops. But Father Keogh takes a group from St Cedric's there from time to time. I tell you what I *have* done! I climbed Mount Kinabalu last year. I went with the top class and we did it with no trouble at all. After, we went to Kota Kinabalu and they had a little plaque made for me. It said "Good Luck Teacher" in lovely letters. Isn't that nice, Mr Muchtar?'

Muchtar grinned. 'I, too, have climbed Mount Kinabalu.'

'Was it clear from the top? We could see all the way to Sarawak in one direction. When the sun came up after that devil of a climb I thought I was in heaven! And aren't the guides wonderful? They seemed to know instinctively just when you needed help and when you didn't. Whenever I slipped, a guide would be there saying sorry, as if he felt he had to apologize for the bad manners of the mountain.'

Muchtar nodded. He had been smarting from Lynn's straight talk at dinner and from what a German girl called Ursula had said. She had cornered him earlier in the day with a searching interrogation on the immorality of orangutan sanctuaries. Muchtar had been feeling very much on the defensive.

'Now, tell me, Mr Muchtar, what do you teach in Miri?'

'English and History.'

'So you're with Rachel. You'll have a good time with Rachel. She gives good value. She'll work you, mind. I often think I should take her course one year instead of teaching. It might recharge the old batteries.'

'St Cedric's is a Catholic mission, isn't it?' Muchtar asked.

'Yes, it is. Are you Catholic?'

'No. Muslim. I'm sorry about your problems at St Cedric's,' he added.

'Yes. Well . . .' She stopped, thinking about them, Then she pushed them away, almost physically. 'Still, we just have to hope and pray that things work out for the best.'

'We need the wood for our development.'

'I know,' said Molly. 'It's just the Kass are such lovely people and they don't want much.'

Muchtar wanted to say that he thought the Kass needed to be civilized; that they ought to be brought down from the forest and resettled in the villages by the river, there to grow coffee, pepper and vegetables. But instead he nodded and shrugged a what-can-you-do?

'Now, tell me about your family, Mr Muchtar.'

94

Muchtar took a deep breath and then exhaled over Molly
a litany of sons and daughters, maladies and mathema-
tical achievements, Ordinary Level examinations obtained
in extraordinary number. They sat amidst the hubbub and
the detritus of ashtrays and newspapers, inhabitants of
an exotic island who, loaded by history and circumstance with weapons to wound one another, chose to
lay them aside for the night.

The majority of the classrooms at the Demolish Babel
Summer School were located in a long terrace of
Edwardian houses which stood, like upright elderly
gentlemen, stubbornly determined not to be intimidated
by the common roar of the Finchley Road.

Each year it took no time at all for teachers and students
alike to hate the Finchley Road with a passion: its noise
and its smoke, the purgatorial slog up it from the Tube
station, the amble down which turned into a trot no matter
how leisurely one intended to make the trip.

To cross the Finchley Road meant pressing a button to
stop the whole flow of traffic and, for some of the more
self-conscious students, a long few seconds exposed to the
invisible glare of the natives proceeding into and out of
London at law-lacerating speeds, sitting morosely – and
some thought resentfully – at full-stop for foreigners.

The road was never far from their thoughts. In class,
despite the double-glazing, the Finchley Road roar lost
word-endings, hid explanations and doubled blackboard
writing. The classrooms became stifling, but to open the
windows brought all communication to a standstill.

The following morning Lynn took her central-intermediate
class into room 10 of 317 Finchley Road. On the way up
to it, she pointed out in her teacher's voice the wood of
the banisters and floor, the mirrors set into the panelling
of one wall, the plaster scrolling around the ceilings. It
was nice to imagine, she told a French woman whose

95

name she could not remember, a large middle-class Edwardian family inhabiting the place. The clip-clop of horses outside. The gas-lamps. The stability of it. She lingered on the stairs repeating new words, happy with the informality, dreading the door closing on her classroom with her on the inside with something to prove, new students watching her, all expecting an entertaining and instructive show exactly tailored to their needs.

The class she arranged in a semi-circle around the teacher's desk, placing a name-card in front of each student. As she did this she thought of Keith. During the night she had imagined him dead on a marble slab, a label tied to his big toe. In his absence, Dennis Harlow had reluctantly agreed to take Keith's lower-advanced class.

'Right, then,' Lynn said, as she often did. 'Right, then. My name is . . .' She wrote her name on the board. 'L . . . Y . . . N . . . N. That's my first name. W . . . E . . . A . . . V . . . E . . . R. That's my surname.'

The German woman put her hand up. That was ominous. *I mustn't stereotype! I mustn't! I've taught lots of lovely Germans in my time. They were no trouble at all!*

'Ursula,' said Lynn, reading from the card.

'Which is correct, "first name" or "Christian name"?'

'Both. But "Christian" is perhaps not appropriate if one is not a Christian.'

'Which is more widely used?'

Lynn thought confession the better part of valour. '"Christian name", I think.'

Ursula nodded and started writing in her notebook.

'Of course, "surname" can also be called "last name".'

'And frequency of use?' asked Ursula.

Lynn smiled at Ursula, thinking fast. I'm going to have to watch you, she thought. I wonder if I can get you pushed up a class. 'Both are readily understood. It's six of one and half a dozen of the other.'

The African put up his hand.

'Sebastian?'

Sebastian Palumbo, who had finally had his room-key

problem sorted out, said, 'I do not understand what do you say.'

'You don't understand what I said. Right.' *What did I say?* 'Er . . . yes.' She explained the idiomatic meaning, wrote 'dozen' on the board, practised the expression by asking the class about pairs of items retrieved from her bag. 'Which is better? This book or that one?'

'It's six of one and half a dozen of the other,' they replied.

Ursula put her hand up.

'Ursula?' smiled Lynn.

'Think of this,' said Ursula. 'I go to a shop. I want a six-pack of beers and six eggs. They are before me. I point. I say: "Six of one and half a dozen of the other." This is correct. Yes?'

'Well, I suppose so,' said Lynn, digging the thumbnail of her right hand into the finger of chalk.

'But they are not the same. There is a difference from beer to eggs.' Ursula looked round, smiling at her joke.

'Yes,' said Lynn. 'There is a difference *between* beer and eggs.' She increased her speed, hoping she would cause Ursula to get lost but not be able to bring herself to admit it. 'However, the former is idiomatic and the latter is literal. Try to keep the phrase for using in situations like the one we practised just before. Right, then,' she said, turning away from Ursula to take in the rest of the class. She saw out of the corner of her eye Ursula's hand going up. She chose to ignore it. 'Right, then, we are strangers to one another. I want you to do two things.' And she instructed the class to write down ten *probing* questions they would use to learn about their classmates. She taught *probing* by having the students imagine she was a dentist. She probed one of the Turk's teeth with her pencil. Lourdes winced. Outside a line of cars heading for London was at a standstill. The driver of a gold Rolls-Royce was looking up at her with what Lynn took to be a smirk on his face. *You bastard!* she thought. *Come the Revolution!* She wrote *probe* and *probing* on the board. She glanced

97

out of the window, but the grand car had gone. She went around the class, seeing how the students were managing with their questions.

Ito, the Japanese, seemed to be doing well. Ten perfectly formed, if dully polite, questions. The Turks were having trouble with their modal auxiliaries. She'd have to sort that out at some point. Ursula had written ten perfect probing questions and was leaning back in her chair, pulling at her great mane of golden hair, readying herself to be bored.

'Go on, give us a few more,' Lynn told Ursula.

Ursula looked at Lynn, then set to work.

Having checked all the questions, she divided the class into pairs, telling them to find out about their partner. They were to make notes and be ready to present a thumbnail-sketch – she explained the term – to the class. It was a *getting to know you* exercise, she said.

Then, as each student talked about his partner, Lynn noted down their mistakes. She was pleased to see that Ursula was having some trouble with the Present Perfect Simple. The Present Perfect Simple was one of Lynn's favourite tenses. She knew, she felt, all its quirks and exceptions. It took second place in her armoury only to the Remote Past.

As she was coaxing tiny whispers of English from Ito she heard a great thud on the ceiling.

'My goodness, what is this?' exclaimed Mahmoud, the oldest of the Turks.

'It's Arthur's class, I expect,' said Lynn.

'What is he doing?' asked Sebastian Palumbo.

'Who knows?' Lynn said. That was true. Nobody did know. Arthur Arthur was extremely secretive about his classes. He wedged a chair against the door to prevent intrusions.

'Lourdes, tell us about Ito.'

'Ito is from Japan. He is twenty-three and he is a student. He is not married. His favourite food is rice,' said Lourdes.

'Yes?' asked Lynn. 'Is that it?'

'I think he does not understand many questions,' said Lourdes.

'That isn't true, is it, Ito?'

Ito looked at his desk.

'Very well. Ito, tell us about Lourdes.'

Ito stared hard at his notebook for a long time. His eyes narrowed to slits. He frowned a frown beyond his years. 'Lourdes is French. Her surname or last name is . . .' He held his notebook out for Lourdes to read. Lourdes helped him. 'Her surname or last name is Moreau. Her first name or Christian name is Lourdes. She is a student. She wants to engineer. She has two brothers and one sister. Her father is very kind and so is her mother, too. This is the end of my probe.'

'Er . . . ,' said Lynn.

Another bang from upstairs, followed by gales of laughter. What a contrast to my dull class, she thought. She'd have to quicken up a bit. 'I think what we'll do, class, is talk to another person about the person you heard talking to us about the first person they were talking to.'

They looked at her. 'Like this,' she said. She seized Ito as her visual aid. Ito flinched at the sudden touch. When she had finished with him she dropped him back into his seat, made a papal gesture of inclusion. 'Right, then, you do the same,' she said.

After a decent interval she called a halt to the activity and had students ask her probing questions about her own life. She listed the countries in which she had taught; feeling, in spite of everything, a thrill of pride at how her career covered the blackboard. It justified her somehow; showed callow Ursula that she had kept a wide sample of the world's population happy in class. Then she distributed the textbooks and got down to the lesson of the day, only then recalling that she had meant to tell the students to seek out a student of the Open University – whose students were attending their own summer school nearby – to interview.

Never mind, I'll do it at the end of the class, she

thought. But when the time came her head was full of Keith, and she forgot.

At 11.30, after coffee, the student body were rounded up by the three Sues and taken to the physics lab for the first in a series of talks, laid on for the Demolish Babel Summer School. All were encouraged to partake, even those whose shallow English would be out of its depth in the deep structures of most of the talks.

'Come on, let's be having you!' Sue told the group surrounding Arthur.

They looked to Arthur for clarification. Arthur was unable to say anything, as his mouth was full of Mars Bar, so he nodded and they trailed after Sue, who was looking hawkishly to right and left to make sure no prey was escaping. She caught sight of Satoko and Mitsuko making for the stairs. 'And where do you two think you're going?'

Satoko glanced at Mitsuko mournfully. Having failed to meet up with Grid Reference the previous evening, having stood out in the road for three hours in the hope that he would return from whatever glittering gathering he was attending, they had determined to cut the talk and meet a rap group called Two Short Planks for coffee. Sulkily they turned and let themselves be corralled up Kidderpore Avenue towards the physics lab.

On the way Sue prised a grieving Astrid off her bench outside the church; then, just when she thought she'd got everyone, she caught sight of Sebastian Palumbo reaching up to draw closed one of the curtains of his room. Sue noted the room. She'd be back for Sebastian.

'No sign of him?' Rachel asked Lynn.

They were standing at the back of the lecture theatre, readying themselves to close the double-doors from the outside and then bolt back to Rachel's room for a leisurely coffee.

'None,' said Lynn.

'There are some seats at the back,' Lynn told a group of students from Arthur's class, standing dispiritedly in the aisle, finding no room to join the others. 'Go on. The chap's waiting to start! There just isn't any room next to your chum. Mix! It's good for you.'

The group moped their way to the back row where they made Astrid, sitting alone, like a damned gargoyle, move up.

Jordan Bostock, chatting with the speaker, stood up to introduce the lecture.

'Time to go,' whispered Rachel. She and Lynn started to close the heavy doors, feeling merrily guilty to be on the outside, hearing Jordan say: 'No country in the world has more daily newspapers than the United Kingdom. To help you understand which newspapers are which we have . . .'

They made for the stairs.

'He's a bore, that one. The talks get better later in the week,' said Rachel.

'So why have him?' Lynn asked.

'Ask Dennis. I think he feels sorry for him.'

'Yes, but . . .'

They were passing Churchill Hall, and Sebastian Palumbo was pulling shut the remaining curtain of his room. Rachel noticed. 'There's one who hasn't gone. Shall we go and have it out with him?'

'That's Sebastian. He's one of mine,' said Lynn, looking up at the blank blue window, thinking of Friday watering her garden in Kano. 'Leave him to it. He's probably still jet-lagged. He seemed very tired in class.'

Agnes Fogherty came out of Reception. Lynn thought she had news for her, but all Agnes said was 'You haven't seen Sue, have you? I've rounded up two of them but the other Sue's escaped.'

'No,' said Rachel, not sure which Sue Agnes was referring to.

'I gave her specific instructions that after she'd got everyone safely installed at the talk she was to come

101

straight back here. Of course, I should know better than that by now. I keep hoping they'll improve. I got Dennis to give them a good talking to. He's not as tolerant of the Sues as he was. And not before time, if you want this worker bee's opinion.' Then Agnes saw Lynn's question bubbling up. 'No. But rest assured if and when I do I'll drop everything to come and tell you.' Lynn nodded. Agnes and Rachel exchanged glances.

'Lynn and I are going to have a little chat in my room,' Rachel said, 'in case you need me.'

Agnes nodded knowingly.

On the way upstairs, Lynn asked Rachel, 'You don't know something I don't, do you?'

'No, I don't think so. But I . . .' Rachel stopped. She wanted to say what was on her mind with a cup of tea in her hand.

Five minutes later, after an encounter in the kitchen with Moira Trotter, dressed in her candlewick house-coat, Rachel led Lynn to her room.

'I don't know how she fills her time. She never seems to go out,' said Lynn.

'She's very partial to Ellis Peters. Anyway, she probably enjoys just mooching. How old would you say she is?'

'Seventy?'

'At least that, I'd say. Excuse the state of the room.'

Lynn noted how different the room was from hers. Still, Rachel had a home to go to. Rachel had no need to make her room mimic a home. Lynn, used to her homes going up and coming down like pop-up constructions in children's books, had tacked up pictures of her garden in Kano, the old market, close-ups of a beaming Friday; had spread a patterned Isfahan cloth over the Formica table. The previous day she had pushed the beds together in anticipation of Keith's arrival. If things had worked out, she would have arranged herself around the back of his question-mark body, told him what was going to happen, how the best was going to be made of their present situation.

Rachel cleared a width of her bed and dumped the books on the floor. Lynn picked one up. 'I'd kill for these in Kano,' she said.

'Short of books, are you?'

'They're on order. They've been on order since we arrived. I don't know what happens to them. Nicked, I should think. In the market I'm always coming across sacks of maize which say, "A gift to the people of Somalia from the people of Iowa" – that sort of thing. I expect the same thing happens to our books.'

Rachel looked at Lynn hard. 'You've no idea what's happened to Keith?' she asked.

'No. None. I'm expecting him. He'll get a rocket when he turns up, I can tell you.'

'What I wanted to say is,' continued Rachel, 'I think it's time we told the authorities. The police, the Italian embassy, that sort of thing.'

'I thought that was what you were going to say. You think there might be something really wrong, don't you?'

'Don't *you*?'

Lynn did not reply at first. She fiddled with her eye-patch. 'He might not have the number of the school.'

'But he can find these things out!' said Rachel. Then she added, as if speaking to Nathan, 'Don't fiddle with your eye-patch. You'll only make it worse.'

Lynn dropped her hand at once. 'He's never missed the start of something before.' She laughed mirthlessly to herself. 'It's the finish that he always misses.'

Rachel looked hard at Lynn. Yes, she thought. I know things that you don't. Poor idiot. I know, for instance, that Keith was playing around with Sue on the last school; that he pursued a German girl called Heidi until the girl complained to Agnes Fogherty. I know he's basically out for himself. How could Lynn not know? Everyone else knew. 'It beats me why you let him go off to Rome alone like that. Why didn't you go with him?'

'Because,' replied Lynn, 'I had made it clear that I did not want him to go.'

103

'But he went all the same.'

'Yes. But I haven't finished with him yet.'

'He's always won up to now. What makes you think that this time will be any different?'

'Because I've never dug my heels in so firmly before. I just told him straight: "You can go for the interview in Rome if you want to but don't think I'm going with you. And don't think I'm going to follow you to Rome if you get the bloody job. I'm staying put."'

'What was his reaction to that?' Rachel asked. Couldn't she *see*?

'He didn't really react. He just went on with booking the tickets.'

'Did you travel as far as Rome together?'

'No, I took the direct flight on Nigerian Airlines. Keith left later in the day. His flight went all around the houses. Cairo, Tripoli, Rome.'

'Did you see his ticket?'

'No. Why should I?' Then she began to see what Rachel was getting at. 'But he definitely went there. I saw the letter from the school. He was very impressed by the letterhead. What are you getting at, Rachel?'

'I'm not getting at anything, Lynn. I just need to be sure. If we ask the airlines and the embassy to make enquiries, we need to know that he actually went to Rome.'

Lynn nodded, as if she understood what it was all about. 'Dennis is behind this, isn't he? I know how he hates filling in. He's scared stiff of students.'

'That's true in a way,' Rachel replied. 'And he does want me to ring around for another teacher if Keith doesn't show up soon. That's partly why I want your permission to tell the authorities.'

'So what do you think?' asked Lynn.

'I don't know. Did you part amicably?'

'Not really. I was in a mood. I always get in a mood at Kano airport. I was dead nervous because I thought Customs would try to take my presents off me – I've

104

bought you some Tuareg salad-servers, by the way. They tried to, said they were national treasures, but I made a scene.'

'So what do you think?'

'Rachel, what do you mean what do I think? Haven't I already told you that I haven't the least idea what to think?'

'All right, Lynn. Can I ask Agnes to contact the police?'

'Can't we wait until tonight?'

'I think we've waited long enough already.'

Lynn looked at her hands. 'Shall I go to Agnes?' she asked.

'Don't worry. I'll do it.'

'I just don't want to leave Kano, Rachel! I've got friends there. I've got promises to keep.'

And miles to go before you sleep. 'Yes, but this hasn't got anything to do with that, has it?' Rachel asked.

'Hasn't it? I don't know what to think.'

Lynn stopped, looked over at Rachel. Does she want me to tell her something wise? Rachel thought. Well, hard cheese, love.

Lynn shrugged off the question, waiting for Rachel to reassure her. She sighed at her silence. Then she said, 'I don't think he's going to come back, Rachel. I think he's gone for good.'

'Come on, Lynn! It's early days.'

'But you know what worries me most about that? What worries me is that I won't be able to go back to Kano without Keith. He's the one with the real job. I'm just tagging along for the ride.'

Rachel, though not given to concealing her true feelings, said, 'I'm sure it won't come to that. He'll turn up. Don't worry.' Then, after a moment's uncomfortable hesitation, she hugged Lynn clumsily.

Ezekiel, the headmaster of a primary school in Zinder,

Niger, was feeling uncomfortable in the lunch-queue. He had so far only managed to make friends with Sebastian Palumbo from Senegal. And Sebastian's English was not very good. He kept speaking to Ezekiel in French. Also, Ezekiel had not been placed in the class he wanted. He was an English teacher, after all. He did not belong in Aaron's class. The trouble was that no-one seemed prepared to listen to him when he broached the topic of moving to Rachel Pales's teachers' class where, he felt, he might learn something of use.

Also, the other students on the summer school seemed to shy away from him. Ezekiel was not sure why. True, he was older than many of the students, but even the two middle-aged Chinese he had tried to engage in conversation the previous evening had quickly made an excuse and left him to himself.

Ezekiel decided he must be positive, not be discouraged, put into practice what he taught his pupils at home. He smiled amiably up at a towering Scandinavian blonde standing next to him in the queue. She looked back at him, her face as blank as Lapland, then looked away towards the food-cabinets.

He turned round towards the back of the queue, more in hope than in expectation of seeing a friendly face. There, standing out a head above the other students, was Sebastian Palumbo. Ezekiel surrendered his place and went to join Sebastian.

'I did not see you at the talk,' said Ezekiel.

'I did not go,' replied Sebastian, watching the students emerging from the kitchen with their trays. 'What is that?' he asked Ezekiel.

'It says it is Macaroni Cheese. And Lemon Cheese Pudding,' Ezekiel replied.

'It is all very yellow,' said Sebastian. He felt hungry after his morning with Sue but was not sure he was hungry for the yellow things on plates.

'It is food,' said Ezekiel happily. 'If you don't want the hot food, you can have cold food from the buffet!'

'I want meat and rice.'

106

Ezekiel thought it strange that Sebastian should be so unadventurous. 'Here every meal is a great feast. I shall be fat when I go home to my family.'

'This food is difficult to digest for me,' said Sebastian.

Ezekiel said nothing. He was thinking of his family, wishing they were with him in the queue for this great lunch. Then he was back to the outskirts of Zinder, to the school where he was headmaster, to the small prefab adjoining it, where now his wife would be cooking one or two items in a pot.

Everything Ezekiel saw he wanted to share with his family. The trees outside his window, the room itself, the electricity that did not keep failing, the bounty everywhere.

He looked around the crowded dining-room. Were all the students' thoughts, like his, beaming homeward? Did others feel as he did? The man from Albania had told him that he had never seen such food as was on display at the summer school. Ezekiel had nodded. Perhaps there were some who were not amazed, who did not miss their homes, for whom travel was a frequent occurrence, such feasts of no significance. For Ezekiel that realization doubled his own amazement.

Both Ezekiel and Sebastian were at the summer school on scholarships. Ezekiel had been recommended to Dennis Harlow through a missionary who had once studied with Dennis. Ezekiel had never been out of Niger before, had only ever visited the capital, Niamey, on three memorable occasions. He had never dared dream of such a thing happening.

'What was it about?' asked Sebastian.

'Excuse me?'

'The talk. What was it about?'

'I did not understand everything. A man was talking about the newspapers. Different types of people take different newspapers. Only stupid people buy the little ones. Top people buy the big ones.'

Muchtar was standing behind Ezekiel and Sebastian in the queue: 'English! Speak English!' he told them.

107

Sebastian nodded and smiled at Muchtar. 'Forget,' he said.

'"I forgot,"' corrected Muchtar.

'Thank you. "I forgot." I am with my brother. He speak French with me and I . . .' Sebastian stopped.

'Yes?' asked Muchtar.

'Er . . . and I speak French with he . . . him.'

'Very good,' said Muchtar. 'Did you enjoy the talk?'

Ezekiel made a noncommittal French gesture with his head. 'Most. The man's accent was difficult,' he said.

'But do you see what is happening? It is fascinating! The English used to control the world and now they cannot control themselves! Nudes! I ask you! So much disagreement! The man who looks at *The Times* dislikes he who looks at the *Mirror*,' beamed Muchtar.

Ezekiel thought he had not quite understood, that what he thought he had understood was a misunderstanding. He nodded and smiled. 'Ah . . . ,' he said.

Encouraged, Muchtar confided further insights. 'Our teacher − I am on the teachers' course − she does not *know* anything. All the time she "thinks that maybe this is a good idea" or "sometimes we say this" or "on the other hand I have heard people say that". She cannot say, "This is right" or "Do it this way". It is very pathetic.'

Ezekiel nodded and moved up the queue. He was now in sight of the sweating kitchen staff ladling great gummy spoonfuls of macaroni cheese on to plates.

Ezekiel said, 'I, too, am a teacher. I want to be on the teachers' course.'

'The class is full,' said Muchtar.

Ezekiel nodded and said, 'Ah . . .'

Sebastian saw Sue turning from the buffet table with a plate of greens. She winked at him. Sebastian turned away.

'Which one did you have?' Sue asked.

'Him over there,' said Sue.

'Which one? The little one talking to Mr Muchtar?'

'What do you take me for? Not him. The other one.'

'The tall one?' asked Sue.

'Yes, him,' replied Sue.

'Agnes reckons he's trouble,' said Sue.

'She would,' said Sue.

'What was it like?' asked Sue.

'Just the job,' said Sue.

Sue looked at Sue as she cracked a carrot stick with her big teeth. 'I'm keeping myself nice for Keith,' said Sue.

' 'Course you are,' said Sue. 'You ought to be ashamed. Least mine isn't married.'

'Bet he is. They all are,' said Sue. 'I hope you took precautions.'

'I'm on the Pill,' Sue whispered back.

'Not those precautions. The other precautions.'

'What other precautions?' Sue asked.

'May I sit with you?' asked Molly O'Connor, holding a plate piled high with macaroni cheese.

' 'Course,' said Sue.

'You should really be circulating,' said Sue, anxious to know what other precautions she should have taken.

'Spare me. I've had a morning of it,' said Molly.

'That's not like you,' said Sue.

'No, but my class really put me through it.'

'Tell me about it,' said Sue.

'No, don't,' said Sue.

Molly looked at her plate. 'I've forgotten my salad.' She stood up and went to the buffet table to compile a salad for herself.

'What precautions?' Sue asked.

'Well, there's a lot of it in Africa,' said Sue.

'A lot of what?' Sue asked.

'Christ, you're thick,' said Sue with satisfaction.

'Well, all I can say is that he had a lot of it,' said Sue, knowing how to rile Sue.

'You'll be sorry,' said Sue. 'And when you're sorry don't forget who told you you'd be sorry.'

'You're just jealous,' said Sue.

'And what sort of morning did you two have?' asked Molly.

'Same as usual,' said Sue.

'I missed mass,' said Molly. 'Slept right through the alarm. Must be jet-lag. You think you're over it but you're not.'

The Sues nodded.

'Where's the other Sue?' asked Molly.

'She's off with Dennis,' said Sue.

'I could do with seeing him about my class. They're a lovely lot, but . . . Oh, I don't know.'

'It takes time to settle in,' said Sue.

'Maybe that's it. But have you seen the way Arthur's class are sticking to him like glue? It always happens. Mine just rushed off. He always makes me feel jealous.' Molly took a forkful of the macaroni cheese. 'Mmm, this is good. We don't get much cheese in Mulu. Is that all you're having, Sue?'

Sue smiled. 'Yes, I made a pig of myself at elevenses.'

'You can say that again,' said Sue.

'Well, it doesn't show on you. I wish I had your figure.'

'A good figure doesn't buy happiness,' said Sue.

'No, I suppose not.' Molly forked a radish in. 'This is my first radish since last year.'

'How's everything at St Cedric's?' asked Sue.

'Well, did I tell you about the trouble we were having with the American fundamentalists?'

'No, I don't think so,' said Sue. 'I remember you telling us about the loggers.'

'Well, the loggers are still at it. They won't stop until the whole place as far as the mountains is fit for nothing. No, they're still a cross. But the latest problem is these American fundamentalists. They've got more money than sense. They fly everywhere. They've got a spanking new mission up-river from us, and all their food is flown in from the States, by all accounts. You wouldn't believe what flows past St Cedric's. And it has to come from the Yanks' place. There's no-one else up there. Coca-Cola tins, polythene bags. I wouldn't mind but they've started getting at our people. The kids keep turning up with T-shirts on that say "Honk if you love Jesus". I ask

110

you! They give the kids chewing gum. Still, it's what they're doing to the tribes in the interior that worries me.'

Molly stopped, split again, momentarily far away from the dining-room, across the globe in the mountainous area between Sarawak and Kalimantan.

'What have they done?' asked Sue.

'They've got two Piper Comanches,' said Molly. 'And they've been flying them into the mountains and making contact with the mountain tribes.'

'How do they land them?' asked Sue, who had a practical turn of mind.

'Search me, but they do,' said Molly. 'But do you know what they've been doing? They've been making the tribes up there totally dependent on them. They give out sweets and soft drinks and condensed milk in tubes to anyone who comes for a service. Then they bring in gadgets, outboard motors, fridges. Once the tribes are dependent on them they threaten to leave them without. So the tribes all become fundamentalists.'

'But isn't that what you do?' said Sue. Then, seeing Molly's hurt expression, she added: 'I mean, haven't you changed the people's way of life, too? I'm sure you did it for the best. You stopped them shrinking heads, didn't you? That has to be a good thing, doesn't it?'

'We're not like those fundamentalists,' said Molly.

'No, I'm sure you're not,' said Sue. 'What's on this afternoon?'

'Arthur's taking a group to Highgate Ponds for a swim.'

'Who's taking the girls?'

'I am,' said Molly, ripping her mind away from fundamentalists. 'No-one else wanted to. It'll be too cold for me. I'll just watch their clothes for them.'

'I'm going to have a nice nap,' said Sue.

'At your age!' said Molly.

'Sue has a punishing schedule,' said Sue knowingly.

'The students are a bit of a handful,' said Molly.

'You can say that again,' said Sue, yawning ostentatiously.

*   *   *

'Come on, loveys, giddee up!' Arthur Arthur shouted at the students ahead of him. 'Don't dawdle!' He turned to Molly. 'Honestly, you wouldn't credit it, would you? Youth has no stamina.'

'They're on their holidays,' said Molly. 'I expect they're enjoying the walk.'

'Well, I'm not doing the Highgate Ponds run again,' said Arthur. 'I'll show them the ropes and leave them to it in future. The afternoons are siesta-time for me.'

'Me, too. I love my afternoon nap. I open a book and read a couple of pages, then drift off. It's really lovely. Sue was just saying at lunch how much she enjoys her naps. Now, that came as a surprise. I—'

'Harry died while I was having a nap,' said Arthur.

'Oh, Arthur! Do you miss him very much?'

'Oh, yes, Molly. All the time.' He shouted at the students: 'Turn right here. Right! Stop when you get to the main road.'

'It's so strange to be here when Harry isn't,' said Molly. 'He came with us to Highgate Ponds last year, didn't he?'

Arthur nodded. 'I didn't want him to come with us, Molly. I tried to persuade him not to.'

'Why? He loved his swimming.'

'I was scared.'

'Scared? That doesn't sound like you! What were you scared of?'

Arthur looked at Molly, and she wondered whether she wanted to hear any more. 'He was so thin, and that sort of thinness tells tales in England in a way that it never did in Egypt. Of course, Harry knew exactly what I was up to when I told him he'd be better having a rest than a swim. He insisted on going.'

'Well, I suppose you were afraid he might have caught a cold.'

Arthur corrected Molly as if he were unscrambling the fractured language of an elementary student. 'Colds were

112

the last thing on my mind, Molly. It was the men at the Ponds I was scared of. They know AIDS when they see it. They've picked it up from the tabloids. I changed into my trunks and when I turned there was Harry standing in his, all seven stone of him, covered in those lesions. The men had stopped playing volleyball, stopped lifting weights, stopped gossiping. They all looked straight at Harry. I wanted the ground to open and swallow us and I hated myself for it. Anyway, we had a shower before going into the water. I stayed behind until the last student had gone and then I followed. The men were talking about Harry and how they thought it a fucking disgrace. There ought to be places for them. I didn't say a word, just walked out on to the jetty. Everyone else was swimming about. I dived in and then looked back. The men had come out to watch us and were talking with the attendant.'

Then Arthur, a different person, shouted: 'Right! Don't wander off! Wait for us!'

'You never told me any of this. What happened after?'

'The attendant came to the diving-board and shouted to Harry, told him to come over.'

'And did he?'

'Yes. Harry seemed totally oblivious. He swam over to the attendant. He said that the others didn't want him to swim in the pond. Harry asked why not. The attendant said it was because he looked sick.'

Arthur raised his voice to the students again. 'Now a busy road. Kerb drill. Look right. Look left. Look right again. If the road is clear, you may cross. With care!' Molly wondered if it was time to ask the question. She thought of Rachel's request for information. But she wanted to know, too. She wanted to know whether her prayers should change from First Conditional to Polite Imperative.

He made the students repeat their kerb drill, only then allowing them to cross. 'Now, we're going along this path. At the end of it there's a famous London pub, the Bull and Bush. Please keep to the path. In the forest are monsters who will eat you up.'

Ursula gave Arthur a benign sneer.

'So what happened?' Molly asked.

'Do you remember Emmanuel, the big Nigerian?'

'Yes. He was a handful, that one.'

Arthur nodded, recalling. 'Yes, he knew the score all right. He was a wise old bird. He'd probably seen quite a bit of it himself.'

'And Emmanuel helped, did he?'

'Yes. Harry was just lying back in the water, watching the attendant. Emmanuel was swimming nearby, asked what was happening and when Harry told him, and I don't know what he told him – I was too far away by then – Emmanuel released a stream of language at the attendant.'

'In English?'

'In Everything, Molly. People walking by the Ponds could hear him. Of course, we didn't understand a word, but we didn't need to.'

'And what did the attendant do?'

'Nothing. Scared stiff probably. He hadn't expected Emmanuel's reaction. He just walked away.'

Molly felt let down, though she wasn't sure why.

Arthur, after a long pause, continued: 'The thing is, Molly, I kept away from it. I swam about pretending I hadn't noticed what was happening. Of course, it was impossible to miss. Nobody was fooled by me, least of all Harry. On the way back to Heathcliff he said, "Thanks for coming to the rescue." Emmanuel and Harry became good friends for the rest of the school. Harry wept when they said goodbye at the end.'

'Does Emmanuel know about Harry's death?'

'Yes. I wrote to him straight away. He wrote back.'

'He was wonderful in the panto. He stole the show. There's no one here this year that can compare.'

'Oh, I don't know about that. You never know until the night. Still, Emmanuel was a one-off. I don't know why I'm telling you this, Molly.'

'Confession's good for the soul.'

'Maybe. But, you know, I don't think Harry ever forgot that incident. I know I didn't. I sometimes think he died

114

while I was having my nap to tell me something.'

'That's nonsense! It's the guilt talking. Guilt is a useless waste of time,' said Molly.

'Anyway, that's why today's trip to the ponds is a sort of pilgrimage. A ritual. I've got to get it right.' Arthur stopped and looked at Molly. 'It's my turn now.'

What did he mean? 'You're all right, though, aren't you?'

'Not really. No.' Then, seeing her fright, he added, 'I mean, I probably am. Not sure. I'm just . . . well, you know.'

She wondered whether she ought to feel relieved. 'I've been wondering, Arthur . . . ,' she said.

'I know you have.'

'It doesn't matter . . .'

'Come on, Molly. Out with it.'

Molly breathed deeply and unleashed bullets she – and many another teacher at the summer school – had been biting for a year or more. 'I've been wondering how Harry could have caught the virus. I mean, did he have an injection with a dirty needle? Was that it?'

Arthur stopped, looking at Molly hard. He wondered whether Molly could be quite that naïve. He looked at her and decided that she could be. 'I'd like to think so, Molly.'

But Molly was not so naïve, had known when she spoke that her opener had been a gentle knock at the door of the subject that so worried her. 'But you're not sure?' she asked.

'Not sure,' he replied. 'To tell you the truth, Molly, I think it was me that infected him.'

'You?'

'Yes. Me.' She had stopped dead in her tracks. He walked on a pace, then stepped back to join her. 'Harry didn't play around. But I did. When he left Rachel for me he said I was the only man for him and he stuck to that agreement. I didn't.'

'Oh, Arthur!' she said.

Arthur took her arm, half-expecting her to push him

away. Instead she gripped his hand under her thin upper arm. They walked on in silence.

At the Bull and Bush, Arthur paused and lectured the students in simple English for a moment or two. He sang them a verse of the song. They trailed up the hill and he lectured them again at Jack Straw's Castle, pointing out the last watering-place for the horses on their way into London and . . . 'So?'

'The first watering-place for the horses on their way out of London,' Ursula said.

'Correct. Good girl. Now we'll cross the zebras. It's the law that traffic has to stop for you once you're standing on the zebra. But don't try the law too hard. It doesn't work like it used to. Not in London.' He stood on the zebra, and a car stopped at once. Molly saluted the driver. They led the snake of students across and on to the Heath.

'It's terrible about Keith,' said Molly. 'Lynn hasn't heard a thing. I heard Dennis saying he was going to get another teacher if he doesn't show up today.'

'That's typical Dennis, isn't it?' replied Arthur. 'He ought to wait a while just to spare Lynn's feelings.'

'He can't face the teaching.'

'Too good for the chalk-face these days.'

'I'm not sure it's that. He's lost his confidence. It's easily done.'

'Yes,' he said. 'Look, Molly, I'm sorry about what I said back there. I shouldn't have. What do you know of such things?'

'I'm not a complete ignoramus, Arthur. We get the *Tablet* posted to St Cedric's. But what I don't understand is why you were . . . er . . . unfaithful to Harry. That's completely beyond me. I can understand Harry leaving Rachel if he wasn't made for marriage, but how could you go off with other people? And how could Harry stand for it?'

'Ah,' Arthur replied. 'You ask hard questions, Molly O'Connor. Harry didn't know he was gay until after he was married. Don't ask me how it happens. It's quite beyond me. It goes to prove that bright people can be thick as a post in certain directions. I've known since I was a

116

youngster. He had acquired the habit of monogamy while I was fumbling about with a succession of one-night stands. It gets into your blood, Molly. I didn't choose promiscuity. It's all there is. Or was. Harry didn't accept it; though, to be fair to me, he knew how I was. We reached a kind of accommodation. It worked. Until AIDS.'

'Have you been tested?' she asked.

The group were coming up the path that revealed the best view over London and, to the east, the skirts of Highgate Hill, with the ponds at its hem. Year after year, he anticipated the students' reaction. He broke free of Molly and gestured over London, like a compère introducing a star turn.

'There you are, loveys! London! And it's all yours!' he said.

'Very beautiful!' said Eisa.

Arthur nodded. He looked out at the view, unmoved.

'No,' he said to Molly as she caught up with him. 'The uncertainty is what keeps me sane. Not knowing, I can think that maybe a needle was to blame. If I knew, I'm not sure I could live with it.'

'Grow up, Arthur,' she said.

He looked at her, wondering if he had heard correctly. Molly looked back at him coldly. 'I'm not just worried about myself,' he said.

'Oh, you're not?' she said.

Arthur fled to Eisa's side. Eisa told him in Arabic how he had dreamed of the accident on the Finchley Road. 'Are you sure the woman didn't die? In my dream she died, Mr Arthur. And – it was a very terrible thing – she blamed me,' he said.

'She didn't die, Eisa,' lied Arthur. 'How many times do I have to tell you. Look, I read it in today's paper. It says she was *comfortable* in the hospital. Now, that's always a good expression to hear. She may have to stay in the hospital for a bit, but she'll be all right.'

'Are you sure?'

Arthur remembered the head wound, the blood in the gutter. He thought of the swaying driver, entered him,

117

pictured his ambivalence. *Just a couple. 'Course I can drive. Middle of the day. Aim the car and soon be home and happy.* Drunk with alcohol or lust. It amounts to the same thing. Me and the shaking drunk-driver are in the same sinking boat.

'By God, I am positive,' replied Eisa's teacher.

Arthur postponed entering the ponds by taking the students to a bench occupied by two men. He went up to them. 'Would you mind moving aside for a minute? I want to show my students what's written on the bench.'

'Anything for education,' said one of the men. Both moved up so that the dedication was revealed. But Arthur was looking at the tell-tale lesions on the face of the man who had spoken. His heart went out to him. He wanted to sit himself down in the space they had made, send everyone away and be with them.

In memory of 'Goldfish', who loved this place. He taught the students 'nickname'.

'He's called Goldfish because he liked to swim in the pond,' said the sick man's companion.

'You ought to be a teacher,' Molly said.

'It's funny you saying that. You're always saying that, aren't you?' said the man, aiming a punch that stopped an inch from the arm of the sick man, turning into a stroke.

'He buddies me to death, this one,' said the sick man.

Arthur looked away towards the entrance to the ponds. 'It's quiet considering it's so hot.'

'That's 'cause it's shut. Pollution. There's a sign on the door.'

'What about the women's pond?' Molly asked.

'I wouldn't be knowing, would I?' said the sick man. He winked at Arthur.

'Sorry,' Arthur told the students. 'Still, you've had a good walk. Maybe we should go and see Karl Marx's grave instead. It's not far.'

The sick man addressed Molly. 'He's a morbid one, your friend. Memorial benches and cemeteries. Take them for a coffee at Kenwood. That'd be better. You could watch

118

the birds in the next pond. They seem to be managing, pollution or not.'

'You're right,' said Molly. 'Thank you for moving up to let us see the bench.'

'You're welcome. Come again.'

They left the men. Arthur looked back and saw that they had moved back together on the bench. He noticed, too, that his heartbeat was no longer ringing in his ears.

'I think this is a very embarrassing exercise for us,' whispered André the Dutchman to Aaron.

Aaron winked at André. 'You don't get off the hook that easily, my friend,' he said.

Aaron strode to the front of the class and addressed his ten advanced English-learners. 'I've just been round the class, and you all seem to feel the exercise is embarrassing. I'm glad about that. Part of the point of it is to embarrass you.'

'But why?' asked Karol the Pole.

'Because', replied Aaron, 'you are past the stage of talking about the easy things. It is time to discuss the hard things. This is a hard thing to discuss. Nobody likes their prejudices exposed.'

The class looked back at Aaron resentfully. It was interesting, he thought, what a United Nations of like minds they could become when threatened. He decided to get the ball rolling himself.

'Samoto from Japan. I'll tell you what pisses me off about the Japanese, shall I? First and foremost' – he pointed to the board, where a number of helpful phrases were written – 'I don't think that you Japanese have beaten your breasts' – again a point – 'about your country's actions during the Second World War. At least the Germans confronted their history. The Japanese, on the other hand, have' – point – 'pushed their history under the carpet' – point – '"Those who forget history are condemned to repeat it"' – write – 'yes, Karol?'

'And what about you English?' Karol asked. He looked over at Samoto for support, but Samoto merely sat Buddha-like, clicking his ballpoint. Karol continued: 'First and foremost, you are hypocrites. This is well known. Also the world's biggest bloody colonial exploiters. Many of the present troubles in the Third World can be put on your feet. You say the Japanese have not confronted their history!' Karol laughed, and Aaron helpfully wrote a phrase to help him. 'Don't make me laugh!' said Karol. 'Your children are ignorant, lacking good manners. People are not kind. You should not criticize nobody.' Aaron wrote, 'People in glass houses shouldn't throw stones.' He wrote feverishly: the board was filling up fast, just as he liked it. He explained what he had written, wrote some more, then turned back to Karol. He explained 'motes' and 'beams'. Karol liked that.

The class behind him was starting to rumble. Ideas, Aaron reckoned, were coming to the boil.

'Thank you, Karol.' He wrote, then repeated: 'I take your point. I stand corrected. Only trouble is, I'm not English. I'm American.'

'I know that. I was giving you the benefit. Double what I said,' said Karol.

Tanya, a middle-aged Russian from Israel, put up her hand. 'You Poles are not so pure,' she said. 'Big beam in your history which you like to push under the carpet now. What did the Poles do to save the Jews from Hitler? I tell you what they did. Nuf-think! Nuf-think!'

Aaron stopped Tanya and explained her mixed metaphor. 'Thank you,' she said. 'And now you want everyone to be good Catholics. You do not have room in your soul for dissent. Always the very extremy path.'

'This is very negative,' said Paula, a beautiful Swiss. 'I do not like all this negative stuff.'

'You think we should' – Aaron scribbled – 'be more positive?'

'Yes, I do. Be much more positive,' said Paula. 'Positive is good.'

'Yes, that's fine, Paula,' said Aaron. 'Very fashionable.

When you stress the positive you' – write – 'white the sepulchre. I like the negative better. It's got the stench of truth. Does anyone have anything negative to say about the Swiss?'

Many hands went up.

Aaron called on André.

'First and foremost, the Swiss stay out of trouble. Nothing interferes with business. They operate a banking system that helps corruption around the world. They exploit the world with their industries. Look at Nestlé.'

'Don't make me laugh!' said Paula. 'What you are saying about Switzerland you can say about Holland. People in glass houses shouldn't throw stones. The Red Cross is nothing, I suppose? Don't make me laugh!'

Yaohan, a large Indonesian lady, interrupted. 'I agree with Paula.' Paula smiled at Yaohan, and Yaohan smiled back. 'I am from Indonesia. We Indonesians suffered many bad things from the Dutch. They did not take care about us at all. They built few schools, just took what they can.'

'Like the British!' said Karol.

'No, you're wrong about the British. The British built schools and hospitals,' said Samanrata, a Sri Lankan scholarship student at Demolish Babel.

'Only to indoctrinate you with the British way of life,' said Aaron negatively.

'What are schools and hospitals without freedom!' added Karol portentously.

'I know why Yaohan likes the Swiss,' said André. 'Because the Swiss banks keep quiet about all the Indonesian crooks who put their billions there. My uncle was an oil-worker in Indonesia and he said that you couldn't help the Indonesians. They are all lazy and stupid.'

'Excuse me if I stress the positive,' said Paula, sweet as a piece of melting Toblerone. 'I was in Bali recently and thought the arts and crafts exquisite.'

'Thank you,' said Yaohan.

'You're welcome,' replied Paula.

'What did the Swiss ever make, except money?' asked André.

'Cuckoo! Cuckoo!' exclaimed Georg from Romania, who had not spoken before.

Aaron, though he was loath to step in when a student discussion was in full flow, could not resist informing Georg that he might be able to make a more eloquent contribution to the proceedings. 'I did not notice you writing down the phrases on the board, Georg! It's always a good idea to write,' he said.

'Right! Right! The English are so self-righteous,' said Georg.

Aaron bit his lip, refusing to rise either to the bait or to the ambiguity.

'I'm not English, I'm—'

'Just double it,' said Karol.

'And add a donkey's tail!' added Paula.

'There is no art in Switzerland. Everything works as clockwork. Everything is rules. I was in Switzerland on my route to here,' continued Georg. 'I was on a train from Zurich airport into the centre. I had a ticket. But there was nowhere to sit. I stood in the corridor, and the railway man comes to me and asks to see my ticket.' He paused while Aaron wrote 'ticket inspector'. 'The ticket inspector says to me, "This is First Class. You must pay three francs." So I say "But there is no seat." So he says, "Sitting or standing three francs more."' Georg nodded, then smacked Switzerland off his hands energetically. He then pointed to the dust at his feet. 'That is Switzerland.'

Paula opened her mouth, then shut it again.

'Don't be shy. Say it!' Aaron said.

'Of course, everything in Romania is wonderful, I suppose!' Paula said. Aaron wrote 'sarcastic' on the blackboard and encouraged Paula to continue in the same vein. Paula did not require prompting. 'All the trains there run on time. Children have rosy cheeks and are well cared for. There is true democracy everywhere. Romanians go around the world stopping wars and alleviating suffering.'

Paula's sarcasm was not lost on Georg. 'We are at least struggling for living!' he said. 'We experience the high of life and the low of life. Not like you Swiss who only know

122

the middle of everything. So safe! So bourgeois! Cuckoo! Cuckoo!'

André said, 'There is no Swiss Rembrandt!'

'Such a pretty, flat little country full of pornography and prostitutes,' said Paula, smiling sweetly at André.

'It's called "tolerance". God made the Earth, but the Dutch made Holland,' countered André.

Aaron saw Samoto's lips move. Hope rose in him. A Japanese speaking in class was an idea too good to be true, but perhaps an idea whose time had come. He calmed the storm. 'Samoto,' he said.

'Those surprising Dutch,' Samoto said.

Everyone was silent, waiting. They waited in vain.

'Is that *it*?' asked Aaron. '*Those surprising Dutch?* Is that all you have to say?'

Samoto, now slapping the back of his left hand with his pen, nodded.

'That's another thing I have against the Japanese,' said Aaron. 'They never speak in class. I once had a class of Japanese back in the States and it was hell. I could have read them the New York telephone book and they'd just have sat there and taken it.'

'At least the Japanese learn foreign languages. Not like the English and Americans,' said Karol.

Aaron turned to Ezekiel, who had contributed nothing. 'Have you any opinions you'd like to share?'

'I want to be in the teachers' class. This one is not suitable for me,' he said amiably.

'But I've already told you, there isn't any room, Ezekiel.'

'But I came to learn better teaching,' replied Ezekiel matter-of-factly.

Aaron thought of saying that he could learn a lot from being in his class. He held it back. 'OK. I'm going to clean the blackboard. Please note down the phrases that are new to you. If you have any problems with anything written there, just ask.'

They did as instructed. Then Aaron divided the class into pairs. Each pair was to tear a strip off his or her partner. He passed through the class.

Paula and Yaohan were together. A bad choice. They were discussing the best hotels to stay at in Singapore.

'Singapore is a place that you could be negative about,' said Aaron.

'I like Singapore,' said Yaohan. 'The shopping is second to nothing.'

'It is very clean and ordered,' added Paula.

'Right. Look, do you know what a role-play is?'

They nodded, having been through enough English Language courses to know full well what a role-play was.

'OK. Will you role-play hating Singapore for me? Practise the phrases I've taught you. I'll be back in a minute and I want to see Singapore on the floor being kicked and spat upon and screaming for mercy.' He passed on.

'*Very* nice,' said Paula.

'The botanical gardens are most entertaining,' said Yaohan.

'And Singapore is *safe*!' said Paula. 'In Switzerland we are having problems with people who take drugs. Zurich, for example, many are taking drugs in the street. In Singapore this would never happen.'

'Yes,' agreed Yaohan. 'In Indonesia I must sometimes beat my breast. The situation in Jakarta does not make me laugh. Many people have a beam in their eyes. It makes me cry.'

'It's no good pushing it under the carpet,' said Paula.

'No,' agreed Yaohan. She read from her notes: 'People in glass houses, etc. I am in the Jakarta Ladies' Circle and we do much good among the beam-eyed poor. We take bandages to the rickshaw-drivers and distribute condoms.'

'Ah, yes. Condoms are essential,' said Paula.

'Ezekiel,' shouted Aaron. 'I won't tell you again! Just drop it, OK? I'm not the person you should speak to. After class you can plead with Rachel, but I doubt you'll get very far.'

'I will beat my breast and show her my beam,' said Ezekiel.

'You do that!' said Aaron, and he went on to listen to Karol and Samoto.

'I eat rice every day,' said Samoto.

'In Poland we eat potatoes. There is rice, but it is very expensive.'

'First and foremost . . . we Japanese . . . enjoy rice,' said Samoto, seeing Aaron listening.

'What do you think of England?' asked Aaron provocatively.

'It is very nice,' said Samoto.

'And Korea? Do you like Korea?'

'I have never visited over there,' said Samoto.

'But I hear that the Japanese are very cruel to their Korean population.'

Samoto was silent.

Aaron addressed Karol. 'It's true, I'm afraid. The Japanese think that everyone who isn't Japanese is a barbarian.'

Karol looked at Samoto. 'That isn't true, is it?' he asked.

Samoto smiled at Karol, then he shook his head, very slightly, very fast, so that his teacher would not see.

Aaron gave up on Samoto. Five minutes later he gave up on the activity. 'OK, class,' he said. 'That's enough free-flow for today. Open your books!'

'About time, too!' remarked Karol.

'He's going to teach us! Good gracious!' said Paula.

'Half an hour go already and still he teach us nuf-think! Nuf-think!' said Tanya.

Aaron saw Samoto making to speak. He went up close.

'"Books give not wisdom where was none before,"' Samoto said.

'Yes?' Aaron asked. 'Yes? That's worth taking on board! Go on!'

But Samoto just smiled.

In full retreat from the International Evening, Lynn passed Teresa in a frilly flamenco gown, pulling on a Special

125

Brew; a group of Japanese, demure in traditional costumes. She continued to flee. A cossack coming out of the lavatory bumped into her.

Forty-eight hours had passed since Rachel had called the police and the British embassy in Rome. Not a word had come back. At tea-time she had been introduced to a young teacher and, though Agnes had done her best to conceal from her why another teacher had turned up at this late stage, it was clear to Lynn that Dennis had taken him on to replace Keith. To cap it all, she seemed to be losing her touch in the classroom. Ursula, fulfilling all the darkest stereotypes of Lynn's nightmares, kept asking grammatical questions that tied her brain in knots. Towards the end of the morning class she had given Ursula a verbal flea in her ear. Then Ursula had cut her dead in the corridor outside Reception. War had evidently been declared.

Once in her room, Lynn drew the curtains tight. She pulled over the easy-chair, fetched the duty-free bottle of Teachers whisky, poured herself a couple of inches into the plastic tooth-mug, sat down in the chair and sipped it.

Yes, it was obvious. Keith had seen her getting comfortable in Kano; going to much more trouble than ever before to make the little university bungalow cosy, to cultivate the garden. It must have seemed to Keith like a sign that she was no longer the footloose girl he had married. She was now the one who moaned that she was tired of the game that involved taking giant strides across the playground globe, was fed up and wanted to play the game that big people played: a bored game with a house and happy families.

Lynn looked at her watch. Eight o'clock. In Kano the sun would have set; Friday have finished giving the garden its evening watering. She toasted Friday with her Teachers. She hoped that the thought of the promised tape-recorder and an assortment of up-to-the-minute pre-recorded tapes would keep Friday diligent. But if Keith didn't return . . .

126

There was a knock on the door.

'Who is it?' Lynn called, automatically making to hide the whisky-bottle under the desk.

'It's only me, Lynn,' said Molly O'Connor.

'Come in.'

Molly tried, but the door was locked. 'Hold on a sec.' Lynn put her tumbler on the side of the basin. She unlocked the door, uncertain about whether she wanted a visit from Molly. 'Come in, Molly love,' she said.

'I saw your light was on through the curtains,' said Molly. 'I was wondering if you were coming to the International Evening.'

'Are you going? Come in.'

'Are you sure? I mean, if you'd rather—'

'Come in, Molly. We haven't had our chin-wag yet.'

Molly looked to right and left along the corridor, worrying about students. 'They seem to be going to a lot of effort,' she said.

'Yes, I saw some of them. Well, come in for a minute anyway.'

Molly did so, holding her Kass duffel bag by its string, letting it enter first, like a dog on a lead. 'There's no news from Keith, is there?'

'None. To tell you the truth, Molly . . .' Lynn reached under the desk and pulled out the bottle of Teachers.

'Sure, I don't blame you a bit. I'd do the same. I've been praying to St Anthony for you.'

'Have a seat, Molly. Will you join me? I've only got a tooth-mug, I'm afraid.'

'Well, I don't usually. Still, why not? It'll be good for my nerves.'

'Say when.' And Lynn poured Molly two inches, the second poured against Molly's frantic protests. 'You'll have me drunk!' she said.

'It'll do you good.' Lynn reached for her own glass. 'This is my second,' she said.

'Cheers!' said Molly.

They sipped the whisky. Then Lynn asked, 'Have you seen Rachel?'

'I saw her running out on my way up. She's got to pick up Nathan from his friend's.'

'I don't know how she does it.'

'Me neither. Nice whisky. Just the job. We don't get much of it at St Cedric's.'

'How is everything there?'

'It's not so good, Lynn. Between the Muslims, the American fundamentalists, the loggers and the tourists, it's becoming very difficult. I sometimes wonder what's going to happen. The Kass are becoming very militant.'

'Have the loggers reached their land yet?'

'No,' replied Molly. 'But they're nibbling round the edges. An acre here and there.'

'But doesn't the Government stop them?' asked Lynn.

'The Government wants to shift the Kass away from their ancestral lands. They don't even acknowledge that the tribe has any title to it. You see, none of the Kass have birth certificates and so they don't officially exist. They can't vote. The Government are just biding their time and then they'll enter the land and start messing things up.'

'No wonder the Kass are becoming militant!'

'They killed four loggers last week.' Molly counted on her fingers. 'Yes, just this time last week. Blowpipe darts. I nearly didn't come. If Father Keogh hadn't ordered me to leave, I'd still be there. I'm worried sick about it. Did I tell you that I was supposed to bring Tankiti with me? Dennis gave him a scholarship.'

'No, you never mentioned it.'

'Lord, didn't I? It really is time for us to have a chin-wag. Anyway, I must have told you about Tankiti. He's been working at the mission longer than me. He was brought in from the forest as a baby by his father. He was in a shocking state apparently. Only Father Keogh was at St Cedric's then. But Tankiti's father had heard that the mission could make him well. He brought the baby in and then left. He never returned for him, and he's been at the mission ever since. You should hear his English. Of course, he's well into his thirties now. He passed all his School Certificate exams through the University of

128

London. He's the closest thing either Father Keogh or I get to family. Anyway, we were all set for our trip over. Tankiti had been really looking forward to it. But on the day after the killing of the loggers he was nowhere to be seen. Just disappeared. I don't know what to think. It might be that he just couldn't face up to the long flight. It might be something else. I ought to be there.'

'You don't think he could have had anything to do with it?' Lynn asked.

'With what?'

'Er . . . the . . . you know . . . what happened to the loggers.'

'Lynn, Tankiti's a Catholic.'

Hitting slap-bang into Molly's blind spot, Lynn nodded as if she had forgotten for a minute.

'Such a treasure,' said Molly, rolling the glass of Teachers between her palms.

Lynn thought of Friday. But I've known Friday less than a year. Molly and Tankiti go back decades. She took a large swig of her whisky and worried about the scratches of the surfaces she and Keith had managed. Nothing could grow in them. Molly's deep furrow had, on the other hand, bloomed. 'I can understand why you must be worried. You and I are in the same boat in a way,' said Lynn.

'Everyone's in the same boat, Lynn,' said Molly. 'But what I've done is place everything in His hands. It's up to Him.'

Ah, yes, *Him*, thought Lynn. Molly's references to the Godhead were the one aspect of Molly that put Lynn off rather. *He* did not have a particularly good record on taking care of individuals and tribes placed in His care. 'Yes . . . well, I expect everything will turn out all right.'

'I don't think so,' said Molly resignedly. 'I have a feeling things are going to get much worse. If you want to know what I think, I think that Kumo exerted a bad influence on Tankiti. Kumo's always been a great one for keeping the old ways alive. Taking off the young men for initiation rites. That sort of thing. It wouldn't surprise me in the least if he got his claws into Tankiti. Unless . . .'

'Yes?'

Molly didn't answer at once. Then she turned on Lynn a have-I-turned-the-gas-off look.

'What?' Lynn asked.

'The fundamentalists!' exclaimed Molly.

'How do you mean?'

'The fundamentalists could have got him. They've been nosing about. They could have got him! Oh, yes!'

'Could they?'

'They'll stop at nothing. They've no morality at all, those fundamentalists. You know, I shouldn't be here. I should be there!' She picked up her duffel bag.

'I'm sure it will all be all right,' said Lynn. 'You mustn't let your mind run away with you.'

'No, I mustn't. I must just leave it to Him.'

'It must be hard for them,' said Lynn. 'They're really stuck between cultures.'

'Oh, don't give me that!' exclaimed Molly. 'You think most people on the planet are not stuck between cultures as you put it? It comes down to moral choices in the end. What do you think is right and wrong?'

'Yes, but the cultural split makes those choices very difficult.'

'Well, Tankiti had the best-possible upbringing. He knows what's right.'

'And what would have been right in this case?'

'To stay at the mission, to come to the summer school with me.'

'Another drink?'

'I mustn't,' said Molly, holding out her glass.

'Why not?'

'That's what Arthur says.'

Lynn thought about that. 'Have you seen much of him so far? I keep getting the feeling he's giving me a wide berth.'

'I'm sure that's not true, Lynn. But, between you and me, I don't think he's happy. I'm very worried about him.'

'He's made a hit with his class again,' Lynn said, feeling the old jealousy.

'That's neither here nor there. He's scared out of his wits.'

'About the virus?'

Molly nodded. 'He hasn't been tested, you know.'

'Well, if I were him I wouldn't get tested, either. Who wants to know they're going to die?'

'We all know we're going to die, Lynn.'

Lynn thought about that. 'I think the odds are that he has it, though.'

'Don't, Lynn!'

'Facts are facts, Molly.'

'Yes, I know, but that's all they are. There's more to life than facts. There's got to be.'

'You're a saint, Molly.'

'Ah, yes. I forgot. That must be it. Come on, let's go to the International Evening. You know it's always good for a laugh. And Arthur will notice if we're not there.'

Lynn stood up and looked at herself in the mirror. She adjusted her eye-patch. 'Do I want to go to the International Evening?'

Molly persisted. 'I promised Astrid that I'd be there.'

'Astrid? Who's Astrid?' asked Lynn.

'You must have seen her. She sits on the bench outside the church looking like a wet weekend.'

Lynn laughed. 'You know, I have seen her. And do you know what I said to Arthur? I said: "Arthur, there's somebody waiting for Molly."'

'And what did Arthur say to that?'

Lynn hesitated, remembering what Arthur had actually said. She thought fast. 'He said he knew exactly what I meant. We pride ourselves on being able to spot them.' Lynn turned from the mirror. 'Yes, why not? Let's go to the International Evening. We're a couple of internationalists, aren't we?'

Arthur stood on the makeshift stage at the far end of the student common room. The student body of Demolish

Babel, many in national costume, ready for their turn, sat crowded in front of him.

'Fingers on lips, loveys!' he commanded. When the students had quietened down, Arthur announced with a rising intonation which reached a climax, then swooped soupily on the last word: 'Welcome to the Demolish Babel International Evening!'

He saw Lynn and Molly arriving late, sitting themselves down in the *cordon sanitaire* around Astrid. 'Now that all the boys and girls are here,' he said pointedly, 'let's get straight down to the business of the evening!'

Much cheering.

'Japan!'

From the back door of the common room, the door leading out on to the quadrangle, the Japanese contingent appeared: the men in lavishly patterned kimonos, the women in obis. They stood in a line across the length of the stage. A piano, being played by Mitsuko, started up. The Japanese sang a song.

'That was good, wasn't it?' said Aaron to Eric Trotter.

'Not half bad, laddie. Still, the Japs only come into their own with the origami demonstration. They always do origami. Grab me a bit if any comes into range, would you? Moira collects it and she's going to miss it if she doesn't turn up soon.'

On cue a long table was produced, loaded down with an elegant meal of rainbow papers. Each student reached for a piece and started folding and cutting intently. Soon blue, pink, red, green and white cranes were taking shape, flying through the Japanese's hands. These were followed by flowers, old men, horses . . . Ito made a teacher wielding a cane which, by pulling a piece of paper from the back, descended on to the back of invisible students. Then they threw their production at the waiting world. Wherever a paper object was thrown a group of eager students stood to grab for it.

Astrid had thought a crane was making straight for her. She knew it was going to land in her lap. But just as the crane had been about to make a perfect landing on her

132

woollen skirt a hand reached out and grabbed it. An Italian boy whooped in triumph and bore off her crane.

'Never mind,' said Molly. 'I'm sure they'll make another for you.'

Astrid was readying herself to be inconsolable. But Satoko, having seen that Astrid had missed the crane intended for her, lobbed another in her direction. But this, too, was grabbed in mid-air by the same predatory Italian.

'Manners!' said Molly, who had half-risen to catch the paper product on Astrid's behalf. The Italian, seeing frowning Molly and distraught Astrid, handed his booty over to Astrid with an elegant gesture, almost as though he had all the time been thinking of Astrid as the natural recipient of his treasure.

'Thank you,' said Astrid.

'That was nice, wasn't it, Astrid?' said Molly.

Astrid did not reply.

Lynn placed her lips next to Molly's left ear and whispered, 'That one's hopeless, Molly.'

Molly nodded. What was Lynn talking about?

A perfect pale-blue paper horse hit Molly on the forehead, then landed unbruised, standing on four paper legs, on her lap.

'You're a little miracle. That's what you are!'

Jordan Bostock worried about what the Gulf Arabs would do. They had come to him seeking inspiration, and Jordan had advised them to go to the embassy. The important thing was, he had said, that the other students learn something about your part of the world. He was sorry he had said that now. The Japanese, while telling everybody nothing about themselves, had shown them everything.

Arthur Arthur had trouble stopping the applause. 'Please, loveys,' he said. 'Please! We're behind schedule. Lots more to do. A world of talent to plunder! Now, put your hands together for the Gulf Arab contingent!'

Much applause but no sign of anybody. Then a television and video were manhandled up on to the stage by Nasser, Muhammad, Omar and Hussein, dressed in

133

shining white thobes and ceremonial cloaks. The equipment was plugged in, the student body invited to watch a film about the renaissance of Arabia with special reference to that country's victory – by the help of Allah – over the hypocritical hoards of Saddam Hussein. Unfortunately, the soundtrack could not be heard by even the most well intentioned at the back. A buzz of chatter soon overtook the volume. This was unrelieved by Omar, who distributed glossy brochures about gas and gas liquid retrieval from under the desert sands, brochures he had brought up in their hundreds by taxi from the office of the Saudi cultural attaché. Jordan shushed the whisperers at the back.

Teresa, nuzzling her Basque boyfriend, brought up from a tapas bar in West Hampstead for the International Evening, replied, 'Shush you! Always you stop people to do things! Fascisti!'

Jordan turned round and paid full attention to the video. It was going on far too long. He had warned the Arabs to keep it short. Now everyone had a glossy brochure and it was being used as a fan in the hot room. Jordan looked around, hoping against hope that this would be the last time the charade would take place. He heard Teresa laugh – and he plotted to steal the last one.

Arthur stood up. 'Yes, I think we get the idea,' he said, and turned off the video. The Arabs looked hurt but recovered when Arthur reminded them of the Sword Dance. They disappeared, reappearing holding gold-tooled silver swords which they waved about in the air while chanting. The back paid attention at first, but the act again went on too long and the world was distracted once more, the sound building up to embarrassing levels.

'That's the trouble with the International Evening,' said Eric Trotter to Moira, who had arrived and was stroking her paper crane. 'They never know when enough is enough.'

'Like you,' she said.

'How do you mean, like me?'

Mrs Trotter pursed her lips and longed for peace and her candlewick dressing-gown to nuzzle her. Candlewick was

Moira Trotter's one extravagance. Renewing her supply of candlewick items was one of the pleasures of returning to London each year. One of the challenges, too. Each year it was becoming harder to find.

'When there's no more candlewick to be had, it'll be time for me to shuffle off,' she told anyone who would listen. And those who listened passed it on until Moira Trotter and candlewick had become intricately interwoven.

Arthur had cleared away the Arabs and their electrical equipment. 'The People's Republic of China!'

Three Chinese men and one woman in a cotton print frock stood at the centre of the stage and sang 'Danny Boy'. Then one of the men stepped forward and made a convincing speech in defence of the Chinese occupation of Tibet, which was received politely, largely because nobody in the audience had understood more than a few words.

'That one tried to sell me a set of books,' said Aaron, pointing to one of the Chinese.

'Me, too,' said Moira Trotter. 'I was in the kitchen and in he came without a by-your-leave. Three volumes in a slipcase.'

'He's probably trying to earn some spends,' said Eric. 'How much did he want for them?'

'Fifty quid.'

'Fifty quid!'

'Tibet!'

The single Tibetan showed everyone how to get into the lotus position, bowed to the tumultuous applause, and left the stage, his hand above his head, as though holding the World Cup.

'Senegal!'

Sue clapped and cheered enthusiastically as Sebastian Palumbo ascended the stage to the rhythm of an African beat. Agnes's suspicions were aroused. Rachel Pales, clutching her car-keys, wanting to put in an appearance before leaving the school for the night to catch Nathan up to no good, thought how

135

like Nathan's father Sebastian was. He moved about the stage in traditional dress, his every economical movement complimenting the music perfectly. Dr Trotter thought of cedis and orgiastic swansongs in his old haunts in Accra; throwing notes and coins to the populace, turning the ramshackle city into Carnival, leaving Moira embalmed elsewhere in her candlewick. Much applause and many encores. But Sebastian knew it was wise to leave your audience wanting more and retired to his seat.

'Niger!'

'I don't know why Arthur Arthur has the two Africans together. More dancing, I suppose,' said Jordan Bostock.

But in this he was mistaken. Ezekiel told a story in simple English about a tricky wild dog who won the heart of a lioness and who never wanted for food. When he had finished he said, addressing Rachel Pales, still standing at the back, 'I am a teacher of English in my country. I want to be better. I want to be on the teachers' course.' He did not elaborate. He did not need to. Every teacher at the summer school – and many a student, too – knew where Ezekiel wanted to be. Where he wasn't.

Rachel, thinking she could after all squeeze in a small one, gave Ezekiel a thumbs-up sign. Ezekiel translated the signal wrongly, and worried.

'Austria!'

Mr Wehrli from Austria gave the audience a yodelling lesson which went down well.

'Italy!' The Northern Italians mimed the final scene of *Turandot*. The Southern Italians showed everyone how to make a Sicilian fish stew, then sang a folk-song.

'The Interval!' shouted Arthur Arthur, and he made for the bar, gaining a head-start on the rest of the audience, the adoring members of his class in hot pursuit.

'I think I'll give the second half a miss,' said Lynn. 'I've got a headache.'

'Do you want me to join you?' Molly asked, wondering what Astrid would say.

'No, don't worry, Molly. I think I'll turn in.'

'Right-o. Don't hit the bottle, will you, Lynn?'

'No, of course not,' lied Lynn. ''Night!' she called over to Astrid.

Astrid nodded sadly.

'You're not going to come out of this if you don't join in, you know!' Molly told Astrid.

'They look so stupid on the stage,' she said.

'Well, you look pretty stupid being a misery on that bench,' retorted Molly. It was out before she could stop it. 'I'm sorry . . .'

'I will go now,' said Astrid, standing up.

'Oh, you're hurt now, aren't you? I shouldn't have said that. Can I come with you?'

'No,' said Astrid, and she walked out of the common room.

The abandoned strains of Middle Eastern jollity reached Astrid as she waited for Molly on the bench outside the church. When the music started her feet tapped the pavement and had continued to do so until, noticing, she had brought them back under control.

Rachel Pales passed in her car and waved. Astrid scowled back.

Then Mitsuko and Satoko emerged, hands hiding smiles, from the front entrance, transformed by their punk uniform, their traditional Japanese clothes left untidily on the floor of their bedrooms.

Astrid saw them and shouted across the road, 'You girls!'

Mitsuko and Sakoto crossed the road to the bench. They bowed. The bow did not go with their attire.

'Where are you going?' asked Astrid. She adjusted her shoes more firmly on the pavement.

The two Japanese viewed the large elderly lady in front of them, a type of elderly lady completely beyond their experience. 'Walk,' said Satoko.

'Dressed in this manner?' asked Astrid.

Neither girl quite understood what Astrid was saying, but both had grandparents Astrid's age who would have acted similarly. They made the short cultural hop and looked at the ground.

'I will come,' said Astrid, thinking that half the world away some disciplined Japanese parents were bowing towards her in spirit, thanking her for protecting their children.

'Please,' said Satoko, pinching Mitsuko to communicate her frustration.

Astrid stood up. 'You go this way, yes?' she asked.

'Yes.' And the two girls fell into line, one on either side of Astrid.

This is most satisfactory, Astrid thought. I am so tired of Molly's talk about street-children. She does not understand the situation at all. Then she said to her companions, 'I enjoy a walk. It is so much better than the boom-boom inside.'

They walked up the road.

'Where are we going?' Astrid asked.

'Walk,' said Satoko.

In Japanese, Satoko said, 'What can we do? We can't take her to Grid Reference's house.'

'Why not? She may bring us luck.'

'But—'

'Are you happy here?' Astrid asked.

'Yes. We are very happy, thank you,' replied Satoko. 'Are you happy?'

'Oh, yes,' said Astrid. 'When I am with good girls I am always happy.'

Satoko wondered about that, translated it into Japanese, returned it to English and, not able to think of anything else to say, said, 'Thank you.'

Astrid stopped on the road. 'I have attended this school before.'

Both girls nodded. Satoko whispered to Mitsuko, 'Maybe we can take the old woman for a short walk and then leave her at Heathcliff College.'

'Maybe,' replied Mitsuko.

'What did you say?' asked Astrid.

'English is difficult,' said Sakoto.

'English is difficult. Like the people,' said Astrid. 'They are worse than before.'

'I gave you a paper bird,' said Satoko.

'Ah, it was you? Yes. Thank you.'

They reached the top of the road, where the West Heath started. The day had ended, and twilight enveloped the Heath with a glow of navy-blue light. They crossed the road.

'Shall we sit here for a while?' asked Astrid, spotting a bench under a tree.

The two girls did not reply. Hope was ebbing away. They let themselves be led to the bench.

'Do you like your teacher?' Astrid asked.

'Some,' said Mitsuko.

'I will sit between,' said Astrid.

Satoko and Mitsuko exchanged glances. They sat down demurely next to Astrid and looked around at the trees.

Satoko saw a man, dressed rather similarly to herself, emerging from some bushes to their right. When he saw them, he turned on his heel and disappeared into the bushes again. Satoko was heartened to see someone in her uniform of preference.

Astrid had seen the man, too. 'In Brazil, too, there are many like that,' she said.

Satoko did not understand what Astrid was saying. She felt that precious time was slipping away and spoke in Japanese to Mitsuko. 'I want to leave this place. I want to go to his house,' she said.

Mitsuko stood up. 'Madam,' she said. 'I feel ill. I want to go.'

'You want to leave me?' asked Astrid, unsurprised.

'I must,' she said. Then Mitsuko gestured to Satoko and both girls stood up and, bowing to Astrid, walked away back to the road.

Astrid watched them go. She had not expected that Japanese girls would be so wilful. The Age, however, was international now. Even the Japanese thought nothing of

139

leaving a helpless old woman on a park-bench with night coming on. Her time had passed.

She saw another man dressed in black leather emerge from the bushes, stand, lighting a cigarette from a lighter. It was becoming dark now. Astrid fancied that he was looking in her direction. He was walking towards her, the cigarette arrogant between his teeth. Then, when he got closer, he stopped suddenly, seeing who was sitting alone on the bench, turned on his heel and walked off.

She thought of the park in São Paolo, the one she took her schnauzer, Popo, to each morning and evening. How was Popo getting on in the kennels? She would not forgive her for leaving her. Only as Christmas approached would Popo relent, take up the offer of Astrid's knee. No, Popo would now be sitting in her cage waiting for the return of her mistress, for a chance to get back into the flat and chew up her slippers, pull the Meissen from the doily-covered tabletops, cause her sorrow, reject her.

She placed her handbag on her knee and pretended it was Popo. She crooned to it, asking for forgiveness. If Popo did not love her, then who would? There was no-one left.

'You all right, love?'

Astrid peered through her tears at the man in black leather. 'João . . . ,' she said.

'It's just that it's dark and I was wondering if you're lost. This isn't the sort of place you expect to see a woman sitting all alone. And it's late! Have you seen the time?'

'I miss my dog,' said Astrid.

The man sat down next to her. She drew away. 'Oh, dearie me. Have you lost it? How long ago?'

Astrid did not answer at once. She was thinking. At last she said, 'A half an hour.'

'What sort of dog is it?'

'A schnauzer.'

'What's his name?'

'She's called Popo.'

The man wondered about that. 'Well, if I was called Popo I'd run a mile, too.' He saw Astrid's doleful expression. He put a leathered arm around her shoulder.

140

'Popo is a good dog. I don't know why she has gone. I have looked for her. Nowhere.' And Astrid, knowing exactly what she was doing, wept a few more of the tears that had become a habit over the last two years.

'Don't worry, love. I've got some friends nearby. We'll look for Popo for you.'

'Please! I cannot manage without my Popo.'

'You live alone, do you?'

'Alone! Always alone!' said Astrid, reprising Mahler.

'I'll be back in a tick,' said the man. He disappeared back into the undergrowth.

There he followed the well-trodden paths. Whenever he came upon another man or a group lounging against trees, he communicated the news of Astrid's loss.

'Poor old duck, she's in a state. I left her weeping on the bench by the road. She shouldn't be out by rights. Keep an eye open, would you? It's a schnauzer. Answers to the name of Popo – though you'd never catch me answering to the name of Popo even if I was ten times as lost as I already am.'

Word spread from mouth to mouth, and soon the night-people of the West Heath – all tensions slackened by a task – were looking everywhere for Popo. Astrid could hear them from her bench. 'Come on, Popo! Come on!' Yes, it was all most satisfactory. She smiled. She smiled inconsolably.

Half an hour later Arthur was passing the bench on his way into the undergrowth. After the International Evening had finished he had darted away, telling his students that he was going to the toilet and would be back in a tick. Instead he went to his room, put on a sweater and set off.

He wondered for a moment what was going on on the bench. Then he recognized Astrid sitting there, surrounded by a group of men. She was still weeping into her handkerchief.

'What's the matter?' Arthur asked.

'The lady's lost her dog. We've been looking but there's no sign of it.'

141

'Mother!' Arthur exclaimed. Astrid looked up at Arthur, alarmed. 'What are you doing here? If I've told you once, I've told you a hundred times . . .'

'She your mother?' asked the man who had first come upon Astrid.

'Yes,' Arthur replied. 'Thank you for helping her out. The truth is that she doesn't have a dog. She has me, though. Don't you, Mother?' He took hold of Astrid's arm. 'You shouldn't be wasting the time of these nice gentlemen, Mother. Come on, let's go home.'

Astrid stood up but said nothing.

'She wanders off a lot,' Arthur told the men. 'I'm sorry.'

'*You're sorry!* I've come all the way from Crouch End!' said the man.

'You know how it is.'

Astrid, still silent, stared malevolently at Arthur.

'Come on, Mother. Time to go home and let these kind men get about their business.' He took hold of Astrid by the shoulders.

She shrugged him off. 'I know you!' she shouted, turning to include all the men around her. 'I know you all!'

'Come on, Mother. That's no way to talk.'

The men were melting back into the darkness of the bushes, looking around furtively, alarmed by Astrid's outburst.

'You'd better take her home sharpish,' said the man from Crouch End. And he added, 'Rather you than me, mate!'

'I'll do that,' said Arthur, grabbing Astrid firmly by the arm and leading her away. 'And thanks again. I won't forget it.'

The man was walking away. He did not turn but waved to Arthur, his hand arcing over his head. He disappeared into the bushes.

They started to walk. Astrid struggled out of Arthur's grip.

'Just behave yourself! You've caused enough trouble for one night!'

She did not reply at once. She turned, looking at Arthur

hard. 'Yes, you used to come here. I remember that. I remember everything.'

Arthur, startled, asked, 'Remember? Remember what?'

'You don't know me, do you? You have forgotten. I think nobody of the teachers remembers.'

'What?'

'João,' Astrid said.

Arthur stopped, thinking. He looked hard at Astrid.

'João,' Astrid repeated.

He continued to stare at her hard, seeing João in his mind's eye. Then the two came together. The young-looking mother doting on her handsome blond son. He fine-tuned the focus of memory and the two images came together. But the second he saw Astrid's resemblance to João – the mother's resemblance to the present incarnation – the image flew out of focus and he was startled by the contrast of then and now. God. Time, he thought.

'João!' Astrid repeated, almost shouting.

'João! Yes! I remember! You know, I didn't recognize you! You're João's mother, aren't you? But you're different. Is it your hair? Didn't you have blond hair? How long is it? Seven years? Eight? How is João? I meant to write but you know how it is.'

But Astrid didn't answer Arthur's questions. 'João is dead,' was all she said.

Book Three

Intermediate

Eric Trotter looked at his pocket-watch. Five minutes to go and the first week's lessons would be behind him. It was odd how each class stretched away interminably at the start and then disappeared in a flash. He wondered why he had never learned the lesson. It might have come in handy.

'Right, class,' he said. 'You've been in England about a week now. I'd like to know what you think. The English are a bit of a mystery to me, to tell you the truth. Any opinions you can give me about them will be gratefully received.'

Paolo from Genoa, he of the long lashes and the antelope eyes so beloved by Agnes Fogherty, made to stand up. Eric Trotter motioned him back to his seat, observing that it was nice to see how well brought up he was. 'People are bad-tempered. They look at me angry,' he said, thinking of his trip to Madame Tussaud's when, on entering the Tube, the waxworks had already seemed to be on display.

Dr Trotter nodded. He turned to the class. 'Do any of you know why?'

'The English do not like people. Only dog,' said Teresa, whose opinion of the English had been hardening from repeated run-ins with Agnes Fogherty, the three Sues and Jordan Bostock. She had also noticed that Agnes had a framed picture of a cocker spaniel on her desk where any normal member of the human race would have mother, father or lover.

'Yes, Teresa, you may have a point. Satoko, what do you think?'

Satoko shrugged. 'They mind their business,' she said, after coaxing.

'Why do you have so many people without homes? Why do people become so drunk?' asked Pablo from Chile.

'That's a hard one,' said Dr Trotter, thinking of the joke about the nun trying to remember Eve's first words to Adam. 'You are, boys and girls, in a country that doesn't know whether it is coming or going. There is very little common ground,' he explained and wrote. 'At least, that's

147

the impression of an old expat.' He turned to Fatos from Albania. 'What do you think?'

Fatos, like many another student at the summer school, was of the opinion that it was preferable to be homeless on the streets of London than in the situation he, his family and friends were in at home. 'You do not know your luck,' he said.

Eric Trotter waited patiently for more from Fatos. But Fatos did not give any more, for to give any more information would mean revealing too much of himself to the group. He had formed friendships with Russians, Ukrainians and Romanians. They ate their meals together largely in silence, but knowing that they shared the same thoughts. They put away huge amounts but were unable to feed the gnawing hunger of their inability to transfer a crumb home. They luxuriated in deep hot baths, slept off too much food under too many blankets – hoping that the memory would warm them when, worlds away, this summer was impossible to credit – and they watched the drinking at night at the bar, unable to buy a round, unless someone better-endowed took pity.

Bored by Fatos's silence, Mr Wehrli, whose Mercedes was parked outside the main entrance to the summer school, asked Eric Trotter, 'Why do you criticize your country? It is disloyal.'

'It isn't my country,' Eric replied. 'If I'm from anywhere, I'm from New Zealand. But Pablo asked a question and I'm giving you an honest answer. You don't have to believe me. Right, any more questions?' Eric looked around.

The class looked around, too, but either there were no more questions or the class were too embarrassed to ask them. Teresa started packing up her books.

'Right,' said Eric, looking at his watch. 'We've got a couple of minutes before the end. Does anybody know what this means?'

He drew a map of West Africa, dotted in borders, printed the names of the countries. Then he wrote *CEDIS*.

Nobody knew.

'Right, I'll tell you, then,' he said.

Arthur was sitting next to Rachel at the front of the Demolish Babel bus bound for Brighton. 'Nathan seems happy,' he said, turning in the bus towards the laughter. 'All the students are looking quite chirpy. They like getting out of London on the trips. There ought to be more of them.'

Rachel wasn't listening.'The microphone won't work,' she said, knocking its business end. She turned towards the driver. 'It didn't work last year, either.'

'Try switching it on,' said the driver, remembering Rachel, too.

'Ah, yes.' The 'yes' boomed through the coach. Ezekiel stopped talking animatedly to an attending Nathan. He looked around, alarmed by the sudden sound.

The Italians who were in Molly O'Connor's class finished the yes by shouting 'Yes, what? Yes please,' as Molly had taught them to the point of cliché.

'This is a slow journey, even on a Saturday, I'm afraid,' said Rachel. 'Notice the seedy suburbs of South London.'

'It isn't bad. It's Catford. I live near here,' remarked the driver.

Rachel ignored him. '"Seedy" means—'

'Ghanaian money!' shouted the Arabs, and some members of Eric Trotter's class.

She covered the microphone. 'Eric hasn't started on his cedis again, has he?'

'Where have you been?' Arthur asked.

Rachel made a face at Arthur before turning back to the microphone. 'But it also means a little bit poor, untidy, run down.'

The driver braked for a zebra. 'In England vehicles have to stop if somebody is standing on a zebra crossing,' said Rachel pointedly.

She'd better not try it, the driver thought, remembering how Rachel had ordered him about on last year's trip to Norwich. Seeing her again had brought it all back. She had

149

managed to be charm itself to her students but had had no time for him.

'Give it a rest, Rachel. I'm sure they'd rather chat among themselves,' said Arthur.

Rachel looked out at the streets of advertising and traffic, seeing useful vocabulary and idioms everywhere, but reluctantly turned off the microphone switch.

'It's nice to see the way Ezekiel and Nathan are hitting it off,' Arthur said, watching a woman picking papers from a dustbin.

'Are they? I wonder why,' Rachel replied.

'They've been as thick as thieves since we started out.'

'Maybe Ezekiel's inherited your mantle,' said Rachel. 'It's a bit worrying really.'

'How do you mean, worrying?'

Rachel wasn't sure what she meant. Worry was her usual reaction to most things concerning her son. 'He's a bit of a mystery to me,' she said.

Arthur thought about that. 'Well, all kids that age are.'

'You're certainly out of favour this year.'

'You've noticed, have you? Did he say anything?'

'No, but he never *says anything*. At least, not about the important things. I'm only his mother, remember.'

Arthur was examining his hands.

'But I do remember those letters he wrote to you, the Christmas stocking he compiled and sent out to Egypt with that teacher,' Rachel said. 'I've never seen him give so much time to anything. I was sure that would rate a reply. He really looked on you as a friend, Arthur.'

Arthur was now clenching his hands into fists. She saw them tremble. He saw her seeing. He hid them between his fleshy thighs. 'How's the shop doing?'

'Quite well. I sometimes think I'm cracked to keep it on. I ought to sell it. Still, it pays for Dot. And Dot's wonderful with Nathan. Of course, it could be much more of a money-earner if I had more time.'

'You ought to change the name,' said Arthur.

'I think it's a good name.'

Rachel, on returning from her time abroad, had bought

herself a seedy three-floor building in the Essex Road, with a shop on the ground floor. This, after refurbishing the accommodation above, she had turned into a health food shop called Inner Cleanliness.

'What are we going to do in Brighton?' asked Arthur, already wanting to go home.

'Oh, I think the usual, don't you? Lunch at the Pavilion and then give them the slip. I could do with a good shop.'

Assumption tapped Rachel on the arm. 'Teresa is sick, madam,' she said.

'How do you mean, sick?'

The variety of sickness soon became apparent. 'Stop the bus!' said Rachel.

'God, it always happens to me!' said the driver, pulling up outside a car showroom. 'People shouldn't be sick on this bus. It's got auto-stabilizers. She must have eaten something.'

'That's probably it,' agreed Rachel tartly, staring at Teresa leaning over a grid, being comforted by Assumption.

'I don't know why they come on trips if they get sick,' the driver observed.

Teresa, deathly pale, returned to the bus and was led down the aisle by an ever solicitous Assumption.

'What is this Brighton?' Eisa asked Lourdes.

'It's a seaside town.'

'Why we go?'

Lourdes shrugged.

'I want see London,' said Eisa. 'All the time, day and night, we are busy. Go here. Sit there. Listen. Speak. Now I have Saturday and we go from London. I want see the Tower of London, the Harrods, the Queen, the Piccadilly Circus.'

'I don't think you use "the" before Harrods.'

'It is belong to an Egypt man,' said Eisa proudly.

'The definite article you definitely don't need,' continued Lourdes, who had spent the whole of the previous morning in Lynn's class on the use of 'the'.

151

'Wife me . . . ,' said Eisa. He was not sure how to proceed. He was not allowed to.

'My wife,' corrected Lourdes.

'You are lady. You have husband.'

'No, I don't,' said Lourdes. 'I live with my parents.'

'Sorry?' said Eisa, but with the wrong intonation.

'I said I live with my parents.'

'Sorry?' repeated Eisa.

'Why sorry? I am not sorry!' said Lourdes.

'Why you no sorry? What old you? What age you?'

'You should say, "How old are you?" Thirty-four,' said Lourdes.

'Wife me thirty-two and have four children. All girl,' said Eisa.

'*Merde!*' said Lourdes, looking out of the window. She addressed the semi-detached houses zooming past. 'My English will become worse around all these errors.'

'You never met your dad?' asked Ezekiel.

'Nope,' replied Nathan. 'I live with Mum.'

'Was your dad English?'

'Nah, he's African. From Kenya. Mum met him when she was working there. He was a one-night stand.'

'I don't understand,' said Ezekiel.

'A one-night stand. A quick one.' Nathan could see that Ezekiel was still at a loss. 'Mum got drunk one night, fancied my dad, had sex and had me nine months later. Don't tell Mum I told you. She told Dot, and Dot told me. She'd go spare if she knew I knew. She thinks I think he got killed in a car-smash. Anyway, I'm a bastard. A real one,' said Nathan proudly.

Ezekiel thought about that. 'Don't you miss not having your dad?'

'Nah,' said Nathan. He looked out of the window. 'Mum makes lots of money. She writes books, you know. And we have a shop, too. She's got plenty of the ready.'

'Do you think you will write books?'

'No. Not me. No way.'

'What do you want to do?'

'Dunno.'

'You have many opportunities here,' said Ezekiel.

Nathan shrugged, then tugged on the zip of his shellsuit, leaving Ezekiel to wonder about the boy's indifference. He looked at his face, the colour of milky coffee. A good-looking boy. But the face changed into the face of his own eldest son, Tanja. He longed for this boy to disappear, to be replaced by Tanja.

He regarded Nathan, who had scrunched down in his seat, gazing intently at the zip of his shellsuit. Ezekiel, accompanied by Sebastian, had gone into central London the previous evening – escaping the Barn Dance by so doing – and priced clothes there. Along Oxford Street the two scholarship recipients had roamed, their mouths dropping open at the extent of goods available, feeling their poverty magnified by every price-tag they read. For, although they received a scholarship, no-one had thought to provide them with spending money. And what was the point in being in so rich a place if one could not prove that one had been there by unpacking bags at home and making the family glad with gifts, brought in by booty?

Nathan was pulling at the zip, bored now by Ezekiel's silence. He seemed to be trying to destroy the object so far beyond Ezekiel's pocket, the object that would have thrilled Tanja.

'Don't do that!' Ezekiel told Nathan.

Nathan moved his eyes to regard Ezekiel. He kept tugging at the zip.

'Don't, you'll destroy it!'

Nathan desisted. 'Man!' he said. 'I'm tired of it.'

Before he could stop himself, Ezekiel said, 'Give it to me, then.'

'Why?'

'Because I have a son who would respect it and care for it.'

'The colours are old. Nobody wears dayglo any more.'

'OK. So give it to me. I never saw such colours before I came to London. My son would cherish it. He would

153

keep it in a plastic bag when not wearing it. In my town he will be the envy of his friends.'

'It's just an old shellsuit,' said Nathan.

'You don't understand, Nathan. In Niger I could never buy my son a thing like that. I saw them in Oxford Street. They cost more than I earn in one month.'

'I don't believe you.'

'Why would I lie about such a thing?'

Nathan considered this, his bottom lip pocketing the upper. He looked into Ezekiel's face, and Ezekiel saw Tanja. 'How old is your son?'

'Thirteen.'

'Same as me,' said Nathan.

'He is like you. Darker, but like you. He is very slim. I think he will be tall. Like his mother.'

'I want to go to Africa,' Nathan said. 'Mum says she'll take me.'

'I think you should.' Should he? he wondered. Should he? Africa would know him at once; steal his shellsuit and his traveller's cheques. Africa would see him as a strange mutation. Still, if he went to Africa he would *learn*.

When the bus arrived in Brighton, Rachel told the students to note where it was parked and not to forget. 'We'll be leaving at five-thirty sharp. Five-thirty. That's half-past five. From here. You've got your maps. The carpark is "B" on the map. I want you all here then. If you're late, I can't guarantee that we'll wait. You'll just have to get the train back to London. Please, if you decide to stay on in Brighton and return by train, tell a friend. Now, is that clear?'

They all nodded.

'So what time must you be back . . . Eisa?'

'Five and half,' said Eisa.

'Five-thirty. Half-past five. That's right. Now, you all have your packed lunches. You can do what you like, but Arthur and I are going to the Pavilion. It's very nice. Historic. It's also a good place to eat lunch. Any of you who want to come with us are welcome. The sea's over there. The shops are that way. It's all on the map.'

Arthur and Rachel stood at the door of the coach doing a head-count.

'How many did you get?' Rachel asked Arthur.

'Thirty-seven.'

'Funny, I got thirty-six. You didn't include the driver, did you?'

'I don't think so.'

The driver was at the back of the bus surveying damage caused by Teresa.

'It's a bloody mess,' he said. 'And somebody's been smoking. This is a non-smoking bus.'

'Sorry,' said Rachel.

'No, you're not,' said the driver.

Rachel gave the driver one of her looks. She and Arthur walked off, trailing about half the students in their wake.

'You shouldn't have acted like that with the driver, Rachel,' said Arthur.

'Why not? He's a wanker.'

'Bad policy.'

'You're a fine one to talk!'

'What does that mean?'

Rachel looked around. 'Where's Nathan?'

'Over there. With Ezekiel. Look, what you said just now . . .'

But Rachel had marched off to corral the Arabs. Eisa shouted like a souk to them in Arabic and was given a withering look by a couple of old women chatting outside a butcher's. He smiled at them to reassure them, but that only seemed to alarm the women more. They retreated, their shopping-baskets a last line of defence.

Ezekiel wanted to go into the Pavilion, to follow the others. But he saw the price posted and decided he could not afford it. 'I will sit down here,' he told Nathan.

'Great,' said Nathan. 'It's boring inside. I was here before. Do you want to eat your lunch now?'

'No. We must wait for the others. Is your mum going in?'

'Doubt it. She wants to talk with Arthur.' He pointed

155

over to Rachel and Arthur sitting on the grass, talking earnestly. 'Arthur's got troubles,' he said.

'I'm sorry.'

'Don't be. My mum used to be married to a man called Harry. This was way before Mum had me. They worked out in Iran or somewhere. Arthur was there, too. Guess what happened! I bet you can't!'

Ezekiel shook his head.

'Harry left Mum for Arthur!'

'I don't understand, Nathan,' said Ezekiel.

Nathan looked hard at Ezekiel, not believing him. Ezekiel stared back steadily at the boy. 'Harry decided he was queer and went off with Arthur.'

'Queer?'

'Gay. Homosexual.'

'Like Oscar Wilde?' Ezekiel asked.

'Like who?'

'It doesn't matter.'

'Anyway, Harry died of AIDS this year, and I heard Mum telling Dot that she thinks Arthur has it, too.'

Ezekiel made to stop his ears. 'Are all English children like you?' he asked.

'I don't get you.'

'What you just said you should not have said. These are private things. If any of my children spoke like that, I would beat him to teach correctness.'

Nathan curled his lip towards Ezekiel. Then, confronting the man's steady stare, uncurled it again, not quite knowing why. He picked at the grass, forming the cuttings into mounds. 'OK, OK,' he said.

'All this green!' exclaimed Ezekiel. 'All this green!' He lay on his stomach and put his face to the short-cropped grass. 'I wish I could show them this.' He gestured to the Pavilion. 'This.' And his prone gesture took in the whole of Brighton. 'All!'

'Who?'

'My family, my pupils, everyone! You, Nathan, are with somebody who is looking at everything for the first time. Brighton is by the sea, isn't it?'

'Yes.'

'I have never seen the sea, you know. I've seen pictures, of course. I have a large collection of pictures of the sea. I have a pen-friend in Maine, USA, and she sent me many pictures of the sea. But I have never seen it.'

'Never?'

'No. Niger is a landlocked country. And I have not travelled outside before this. On the plane coming to Britain I kept looking out of the window.' Ezekiel blinkered his eyes, made them big. 'Look, look, look, all of the time. I would not leave my window even for a minute. I wanted to use the bathroom, but I wanted to catch sight of the sea much more. But there were clouds. Clouds were wonderful, too, of course. I sat in my seat, saying, "Ah!" all the way over. The people next to me thought I was very simple, I think. But I did not care. I wanted to see the sea.'

'Sea's sea,' said Nathan.

'How weary you sound, Nathan! If I could beat amazement into you, I would!'

'Sounds to me like you do a lot of beating in . . . where was it?'

'Niger. Not very often. But we do not have many Nathans there.'

Nathan could not understand why he was so supine before this man. Normally no-one tangled with Nathan Pales and got away with it. It was lucky that none of his friends were around. Had they been, he would have been forced to stand up to this guy who kept putting him down. But as they were not he did not feel inclined to.

'Will you show me the sea?' Ezekiel asked.

'Maybe,' Nathan replied, thinking of his schoolmates. Then he forgot them. 'Sure, I will,' he said.

It was during lunch that the gloom descended upon the Arab contingent. Arthur, deep in discussion with Rachel, was approached by a Saudi who showed him the contents of his sandwich and asked, 'Please, what is this?'

Arthur surveyed the pink overlaid with a yellow smear

157

and said, 'Ham,' before returning to telling Rachel about his worst fears. The Arab returned to his masticating compatriots.

A few seconds later, mastication had turned to expectoration and thence to vituperation.

'What's the problem over there?' Rachel asked, wiping her eyes, then looking over at Omar, who had half his hand down his throat.

'Good God! Ham!' said Arthur. 'The silly buggers have put ham in the sandwiches. Surely the three Sues must have told them about that!'

Rachel and Arthur got up and tried to reassure the disgusted students. But there was nothing either of them could say. The Arabs looked at their infidel teachers, half in misery, half in anger.

'This is a very bad thing, missis,' said Ismaeel.

'We're terribly sorry. The kitchen people know that they mustn't use ham, or pork of any sort,' said Rachel.

'There must have been a mix-up between your sandwiches and the Open University's,' tried Arthur, though no-one was listening.

The Arabs, with Eisa tagging on for form's sake, made off for the gents'. Rachel, agitated, went around warning students to keep tight hold of their valuables. When the Arabs returned, she aimed bridge-building smiles at them but all the Arabs except Eisa, who smiled back, looked through her – out to a scene that would live forever in infamy wherever pork was abjured. They aimed hating stares at the Pavilion with its insulting minarets; at the lap-dogs, led by pork-gobbling infidels, that cocked their legs, squatted, barked, tripped up humans with their long leads.

Eisa tried to console them. 'You are not to blame. It was an accident. You have no culpability,' he said, legalistically in Arabic.

'I have never eaten pork before,' said Omar. 'I think I will never be well again. If my father knew . . .'

'At the Judgement, the people responsible will pay dearly,' added Ismaeel. 'Think of that, brothers, and be calm.'

Ezekiel and Nathan sat cross-legged, facing one another like Indians at a pow-wow. Opening the plastic receptacle of his lunch, seeing the little packets, the round juice container that turned into a glass when you peeled off the foil, the plastic knife, the sealed sandwiches and biscuits and fruit-cake, the tiny sachet of mayonnaise, the encondomed Cheddar, Ezekiel had turned into an observer, watching his children opening this novel meal. He ate his sandwiches, but could not bring himself to unwrap the cheese or cake. He put everything unused into his plastic bag to take home with him. These would join the airline packets of sugar, salt, pepper and milk as part of his growing booty. He asked Nathan, in the act of scrunching up his lunch-box, for anything that he had not used. These items he picked out and pocketed. Then he winked at him, stood up and went round the group of students, offering to dispose of their lunch litter. When the Arabs returned they were unwilling even to touch their lunches, and Ezekiel bagged many almost-perfect lunches for his collection.

While he did this he was aware of Nathan's eyes upon him. He knew that Nathan knew but, just as in the dusty area around his school he went round picking up stones in order to give a good example so, here and now, he wanted to open Nathan's eyes and keep them open. His secret was out. He had bared his poverty before the child. And, once having done this, for sound educational and practical purposes, he no longer felt in the least embarrassed.

'What are you going to do with all that?' Nathan asked.

'Take it back to my country. For the children. It will amaze them.'

Nathan looked hard at Ezekiel as Ezekiel saw assembly under the Doud tree. He would tell the children about his lunch in Brighton by the magical building which a rich prince had built for himself on a green carpet by the sea, a building that looked part product of the imagination, part mosque, part nonsense.

'Take me to the sea, Nathan.'

159

'OK. I'll tell Mum.'

'You've got a new friend,' Rachel said, reaching up to his face to clear up crumbs from his lips and chin. He squirmed away.

'Zek, you mean?'

'Is that what you call him?' Rachel asked, thinking of the stern formal man who had made her keep her head against the chalk-face during the lessons, had written everything down, discouraged levity.

'Yeah,' said Nathan. 'He doesn't know I call him that, though.'

'No. Are you coming with us?'

'I'm taking Zek to the sea. He's never seen it.'

'Hasn't he? Goodness! Anyway, Arthur and I are off for a bit of a shop, after we've been to the beach. If you and Zek wander off, don't forget to be back at the bus at five-thirty. Have you got enough money?'

He jiggled on the spot. 'I'm not sure.'

Rachel reached into her wallet and gave Nathan twenty pounds. 'Buy yourself something nice,' she said.

He looked at her. He wondered what the matter was. 'Thanks,' he said.

Rachel made to kiss him but he was running back to Ezekiel, pocketing the money. She saw him buying Tipp-Ex; saw him stealing away to a park bench to rub himself out with it. She shook the thought from her head and shouted to the disconsolate Arabs, 'Come on, you lot! No use crying over spilt milk! Sea-time!'

Eric and Moira Trotter had volunteered to stay around the environs of Heathcliff College to be on hand in case of telephone calls or emergencies. They had spent the morning happily enough in the deserted common room reading all the papers.

'I can't remember a summer school like this one,' Dr Trotter said.

'What do you mean by that? It seems the usual fiasco to

me.' Moira spoke brusquely from behind her *Telegraph*.

'You're not in the thick of it,' said Dr Trotter.

'So what's the news from the front?'

'Nothing really. It's just different. Maybe Keith not showing up has something to do with it. And Harry, of course.'

'It was bound to happen,' said Moira philosophically. 'I could tell last year that Harry wouldn't be back. You could see it on his face.'

'Arthur's still the same, though.'

Moira laid aside her paper. 'Do you think so? I don't. Seems to me like he's putting on an act. Can't put my finger on it. He goes through all the motions, but I'm not sure his heart's in it.'

'He may have it, too.'

Moira turned a page.

'I said . . . ,' began Eric.

'I heard what you said. I'm trying to read the paper.'

'Do you think I ought to retire?'

Moira laid her newspaper aside and stared at Eric over her half-moon glasses. 'It's a bit late now, isn't it?'

'What sort of answer is that?'

'What sort of question is that? I told you you ought to retire twenty years ago. Tell you the truth, I'm amazed anyone still employs you.'

'Thank God there are some races on the planet that have a bit of respect for age,' said Eric, thinking of Japan, Hong Kong, Saudi Arabia and Mongolia.

'More than I have. They should try living with it.'

'So you don't think I should retire, then?'

'Suit yourself,' said Moira, returning to her paper.

They read in silence for half an hour.

'Moira?'

'What?'

'I was talking to this German chappie.'

'Not the Faith Healer?'

'Yes, him. Do you know what he said?'

Moira flicked her paper. 'Not a clue.'

'He said that my dicky pancreas is psychosomatic.'

161

'Did he indeed? And you believed him?'

'Well, I though about it. I've only ever had attacks when I've been in a really miserable situation. He also said that shellfish would bring on an attack. Much more likely than alcohol, he said.'

'Did he?'

'And, when I thought about it, it began to make sense. I've only had trouble near the sea. Hong Kong, Bombay, Dhahran. I was as fit as a fart everywhere else.'

'Eric, how many doctors have told you that it's booze that does it to you? Tell me, how many?'

'A few.'

'*Quite* a few. And you think they've got an axe to grind, do you? Just a load of killjoys? You'd prefer to believe this German nutter, would you?'

'I don't know; but it's interesting, you have to admit it.'

'So drink youself into the grave, if that's what you want to do. See if I care.'

The telephone rang. 'I'll go,' said Moira. She strode out of the room.

'Who was it?' Eric asked when she returned.

'Someone for Lynn Weaver.'

'Not Keith?'

'You know, I think it might have been,' said Moira. 'Shocking line. I asked him his name but he rang off . . . Anyway, the line went dead.'

'Rum do.'

'I think she'd be better off without him myself.'

'Why do you say that?'

'Experience. Also, while you are in the thick of the summer schools I have time on the sidelines to keep my eyes open and observe. You don't know the half, what with trying to get people to help you spend your bloody cedis and drinking when you fancy my back's turned. There's a lot going on that you never even dream of.'

'Is there indeed? Like what, for instance?'

Moira Trotter ignored her husband. 'You finished with that *Independent* yet?' she asked.

162

He handed over the paper. 'Like what?' he repeated.

'You wouldn't believe me if I told you,' Moira said.

Eisa arrived at the carpark at six, only to find that the Demolish Babel bus had gone without him.

When Rachel and Arthur led the way to the seaside, Eisa had tagged along with Ezekiel and Nathan, though they spoke too quickly for him. He had a lot of nodding to do in the face of incomprehensible sentences.

Now Eisa walked back towards the centre of Brighton, looking for the railway-station. He smiled, remembering how Ezekiel had stopped dead when the shining carpet of sea came into view, passed his right hand quickly across his hair from front to back, shaken his head from side to side, then walked away from them, the walk changing to a trot, to a mad dash. Down the stone steps he had gone, disappearing from sight for a while.

Nathan ran after. 'He's never seen the sea before,' he told Eisa. 'Come on! This should be brilliant!'

Ezekiel was now halfway across the beach, making for the water. He must be making noise, Eisa thought. People were pointing. He saw Nathan running behind Ezekiel. Eisa, though he did not like to run, began running, too.

'What he do?' Eisa asked Nathan when he reached him, puffed, standing on the sea's edge.

Nathan looked up at Eisa happily. 'It's obvious, isn't it?'

Ezekiel was swimming a version of the crawl that took his small head through 180 degrees with each stroke.

'But his clotheses; he is wear his clotheses!' said Eisa.

'He took off his shoes and socks,' said Nathan delightedly. They sat akimbo on the shore, next to a dead crab, the socks two brown balls on the sand.

'But what he do after?' asked Eisa.

Nathan shrugged and watched Ezekiel, along with half the beach.

Ezekiel was now lying on his back in the water, blowing

sea out of his mouth, hooting and kicking the water to whiteness with his feet.

When at last he tired, he walked towards them, smiling happily. 'The sea!' he said to them, watching the water leaving him, sucking his clothes against his body.

'What you do now?' asked Eisa.

Ezekiel pointed upwards to the sun. 'The sun will dry me,' he said.

Eisa looked at the sun doubtfully. It was such a pale cousin to the Egyptian sun. 'I don't think. It very tepid,' said Eisa.

But Ezekiel was not listening. He had turned and was looking out, past the pier, to the horizon. His arms hung by his sides, their fingers pianoing his soaked cotton trousers. He was thinking of familiar small hands in his, watching and wondering, too. 'I shall tell them that it is salty; that it is like a blue desert.'

A ship was making its way towards the Western Approaches, heading for the horizon at an oblique angle. Ezekiel watched it, wondering what it would do when it hit the line between sea and sky. He sat down on the sand, pushed his socks into his shoes, rearranged them neatly beside him, and decided to watch the ship so that he would be able to convey exactly what happened. Eisa and Nathan, catching the silence of their baptized companion, sat down next to him. Eisa made to cover Ezekiel with his cardigan, but the man shrugged it off.

Yes, any moment now the ship would disappear. He was having to squint in order to see it at all. Over the edge of the world it would go, falling off. Of course he knew well enough that that did not happen but he now understood why those wives in his pictures of the sea, those wives on cold clifftops, wrapped in shawls, watched the disappearance of their men's ships with such sad expressions. Those men had gone off to unknown places, did not know what would happen when they reached the thin line between earth and sky. Perhaps they would drop off the edge into a hell that swallowed the arrogant who dared wander far from home.

The ship, he saw with a shock, seemed to have lowered itself in the water. Down, down, it went, until only the funnel was visible. Then it, too, was gone. He thought of his geography books. Yes, now it was over the horizon and facing one more. Just as the ship had disappeared from his eyes, so, from the ship's perspective, the land had fallen away, gone into memory. Now new horizons. New horizons! Now he understood. *New Horizons in Educational Psychology*. He'd read that for his teachers' examination. New horizons.

Nathan said, 'You're shivering, Zek.'

Ezekiel looked at Nathan. Zek? Is that me? Nobody has ever called me 'Zek'. Still, he did not turn his headmasterly disapproval on Nathan. A new name after my baptism. It makes good sense. 'OK,' he said. 'You can call me Zek. Zek is a good name.'

Eisa had seen him shivering, too, and offered him his cardigan. This time it was accepted. The people on the beach had lost interest in the strange foreigner swimming with his clothes on.

'Maybe we walk. You dry quick,' Eisa said.

Nathan picked up Ezekiel's shoes and the plastic bag containing the debris of the lunch, Zek's trophies. They walked back across the sand to the promenade. Nathan found an empty bench and they sat down. He watched Ezekiel looking out at the sea, panting, his eyes glittering. His body was shaking with cold. Some punks passed and looked at them. Nathan looked through them in his practised manner. He touched Ezekiel's cold shoulder, felt himself leaning towards him. 'You're cold, Zek,' he said. 'I know what.'

The ladies in the Oxfam shop had been having a quiet day. Apart from Mrs Stone dropping off a consignment of knitted tea-cosies fresh off the needles, not a soul had entered the shop. In fact, Angela had just been remarking to Harriet that the world was going to go hungry today if their branch was any indication. Harriet, ever the optimist, had replied that something would turn up.

It was an answer to prayer when a small wet black man

entered the shop in company with a large brown man and a beautiful brown child holding a twenty-pound note. Harriet automatically pushed her collection-box towards the front of her counter.

'Good afternoon, gentlemen. Lovely day!' said Angela brightly.

Ezekiel smiled broadly at the two women. 'You see how wet I am!' he told them.

'Yes, you are! Very wet! What happened?'

'He went for a swim in the sea. You see, he'd never seen sea before,' said Nathan.

Harriet nodded understandingly. The customer's wet shirt showed his black rib-cage. The sight, echoing the posters all around, made her go weepy. She tidied a stack of tea-towels from Madras to distract herself.

'We need some clothes,' said Nathan.

'That's what we're here for,' said Harriet.

She stepped out from behind the desk, carefully avoiding a display of basketwork from the Philippines. Then she led the group up the aisle to rows of old clothes on coathangers. 'Shirts. Trousers. Jackets.'

'Shirts and trousers, I think,' said Nathan. He started rooting through the display.

Ezekiel wanted to tell Nathan that he could not afford new clothes. As he was about to do this, Harriet said, 'Are you a visitor?'

'Yes, madam. I am from Niger.'

'Niger!' whispered Harriet, half in wonder, half in confusion about where in the starved world it was.

'I am a headmaster in a small school.'

'Welcome to Brighton!' said Harriet.

Nathan had selected a number of shirts and trousers. 'Do you like any of these?' he asked.

Ezekiel nodded. 'But . . . ,' he said.

'Try those on.'

'We've got a changing-room over there. It's a bit cramped, I'm afraid,' said Harriet.

'We've had to store old books in it,' added Angela. 'Still, you can have a little read while you choose. You won't get that service in C & A.' She excused herself, grazed past Ezekiel, showing him the way.

Eisa stood by the door looking at the craftwork. 'Where are you from?' Harriet asked him.

'Egypt,' he said.

'That's nice,' she said.

'Are you Brighton?' he asked, trying to practise.

'Yes,' she said. 'I am from Brighton.'

'Are you have husband?'

'No. He passed away. I am a widow.'

'Sorry?' he said.

'Never mind,' she said. 'It happens, doesn't it?'

Eisa, not sure, nodded. Harriet nodded back. 'This is very beautiful shop,' he told her, thinking it hers.

'Thank you,' she said. 'We try to make it cheerful. To tell you the truth, it's been a bit slack today. Everyone's enjoying the weather.'

Eisa, stuck for something else to say, picked up a small pottery piece. It showed a brightly painted open-backed van. The van carried an open coffin and mourners sorrowing beside it. 'What this?'

'It's wonderful, isn't it? It's made by a peasant co-operative in Colombia. Look how detailed it is!'

Eisa, nodding, followed Harriet's finger to take in the red-painted lips of one of the mourners. 'The man is die,' he said to her.

'Yes, the man is dead,' she said.

Ezekiel came out of the changing-room in his new clothes.

'They suit you. Bright colours go well with your complexion,' said Angela.

'They are very bright,' said Ezekiel, surveying the crimson trousers and the Hawaiian shirt, liking them, seeing himself at home in them, surprising the elders who did not expect flippancy from their headmaster. They would say England had done it to him, had turned him childish. No, he thought. The sea has done it. I have seen the sea. I will tell them about the sea. I will tell them my new name.

Nathan was paying Harriet. Harriet let him have everything for a pound less. Ezekiel looked over and saw what was happening, saw his wet clothes pushed into an Oxfam plastic bag. He had sensed that it would happen, was happy to be dry, wondered if he should feel humiliated. Decided not to.

He went over to Nathan, beaming. Harriet wanted to cry. The sight of anyone of African origin always made her want to cry. She supposed that it was overdosing on famine posters that did it, though it might be something else. She could not tell. 'Thank you,' she said, though she would have preferred to place a kiss on the black man's lips, sneaking a crafty feel of his hair while doing so. 'Come again,' she added.

'Alas, we are in Brighton only for the day,' said Ezekiel.

'So we won't see you again?' asked Angela.

'I think not. I think we will meet in heaven,' said Ezekiel quite matter-of-factly.

She looked at him and saw that he was serious. 'Do you think so?' she asked. 'I don't know. Oh, I do hope so!'

'See you, then,' said Nathan, corralling his friends confidently. They waved their way from the shop.

Harriet and Angela looked at one another. Then they made themselves a cup of Tanzanian coffee. They did not speak of Ezekiel. They did not speak at all.

Nathan, Ezekiel and Eisa looked in the shop-windows for a while. It must have happened then. Eisa lingered too long, gawking at Ratner's. When he came to himself there was no sign of his companions. He looked up and down the street for half an hour, then found himself distracted by W. H. Smith and, in the presence of stationery and magazines and books and CDs and pens and maps, doilies and paper plates, forgot about the time.

On the train, as the light was ebbing away, Eisa had fallen asleep, only to be awoken by the shouting. A youth wearing dirty jeans was arguing with a girl in the seat two away from his. The girl was crying. Eisa looked around.

Three other passengers had their heads buried in newspapers. Then the youth hit the girl. Eisa stood up and shouted in Arabic for him to stop.

The youth cursed him, came up to Eisa and pushed him. Eisa pushed back. The youth made to head-butt Eisa, and Eisa pulled back and then put all his strength into a push.

And later, in the police station, hearing 'is dead' again and again – thinking of the Oxfam import, the day just gone, Ezekiel safely back at Heathcliff – Eisa had remembered the way his push had sent the youth flying across the carriage to the waiting faulty door, and how the body had seemed so light. Hollow.

The screaming of the train as it lurched to a halt. The silence. Guards coming along the train: 'What's happening? What's going on?'

Eisa, sitting alone, not understanding, nodded and shook his head.

'I'm sure Arthur was only doing what he thought was right, Astrid,' said Molly.

'He called me "Mother" and bruised my arm,' replied Astrid. 'He insulted me in front of his . . . his . . . comrades.'

Molly sighed. 'But Arthur said that—'

'Oh, yes! Believe him. You will stick together. I know that. I am speaking the truth. It is he who should feel shame.'

The word made Molly jump. 'Shame? What do you mean? What for?'

'I know him,' said Astrid.

Molly gripped the banister of the staircase leading towards her room. 'Why don't you forget your little disagreement and make friends?'

'Never!' said Astrid vehemently. 'Not if he comes to me on his knees.'

'He won't do that,' said Molly. She sought around for a change of subject. 'Why didn't you tell us you'd been here before? Agnes told me. Usually I pride myself on remembering students. I must be losing my touch.'

'No,' said Astrid. 'I have changed. I am not the same as before.'

'None of us are. I'm sure I'd have remembered you if you were . . .' She tried to retrieve the situation. 'I enjoyed my dinner.'

'You were my son's teacher.'

'Was I? What was his name?'

'João.'

Molly thought. 'I remember João. Oh, yes. I remember him.' She stepped back, appraising Astrid. 'You're João's mother! Yes, I can see it now. How could I have forgotten? João had really lovely blond hair. And . . . er . . . so did you.'

Astrid shrugged and looked away.

Molly had spent the afternoon with Astrid, ferrying her round Kew Gardens, hoping that the peaceful place would balm Astrid's unhappiness. But nothing she showed her, nothing she said, seemed to help. Now, after dinner, she felt tired and stiff. Her back was playing her up. She wanted to be alone for a while. Perhaps have an early night.

'How's João doing? What's he up to?'

'I told Arthur,' Astrid said.

'Told Arthur? What did you tell him?'

'Ask him. Ask his *comrades*!'

'Astrid, I really think—'

But Astrid interrupted. 'And Arthur's friend – the one with the grey hair – where is he?'

'You mean Harry, don't you?' Molly replied, alarmed at Astrid's cold eyes. 'Didn't Arthur tell you? He passed away.'

'Passed away?'

'He died. He was at last year's summer school. But he wasn't well even then.'

'Of what did he die?' Astrid asked.

Molly looked away from those eyes. She'll turn me to stone, she thought. 'Er . . . I don't think it's my place to tell you. Can't you ask Arthur?'

170

'Of what did he die?' Astrid caught hold of Molly's thin upper arm.

'I don't . . . ow!'She pulled away from Astrid's grip. 'He died of AIDS, Astrid, but don't tell . . . I mean, he lived in Egypt. It might have been a dirty needle. He lived in Egypt.'

Astrid was smiling. Then she nodded and let go of Molly. 'My João died of this. Two years ago. He was twenty-five. His studies were finished. He was starting his life as a doctor.'

Molly stared at Astrid, but she was seeing João in her class. He had been too good for that class really, but he'd been content with the lower level and had helped the others. Once – yes, it was coming back now – he had stood in front of the class and told jokes. They had gone to Greenwich. Some nasty kids had tried to charge them for standing on the spot where west becomes east. João had frightened them away. 'Astrid, I'm so sorry. I don't know what to say.'

Astrid nodded. 'Do you remember how friendly Harry and Arthur were to João? Very friendly. Do you remember that?' she asked.

Molly shook her head.

'So friendly! So friendly!'

Molly saw what Astrid was thinking. She shook her head fast both to deny the idea and to forget it.

But Astrid just kept on nodding. Molly could see the woman she had been and the woman she was advancing and retreating, twisting out of focus and into perfect clarity. Finally she managed, 'You mustn't say that.'

Still nodding, Astrid turned on her heel and walked away.

Having knocked several times without getting an answer, Molly was jittering outside Astrid's room when Jordan Bostock nearly collided with her.

'Molly! Thank God!' he said. 'Can you do something for me? I've got to go to Bexley. Eisa, the big Egyptian, has been taken in for something. I just happened to be

171

passing the public phone when he rang. A good job, because his English is a pig's arse.'

'What can I do?' asked Molly.

'Ring Dennis and tell him I'm going to Bexley police station. Then get somebody to see to the disco people. They'll be arriving any minute. They need to be paid afterwards. Here's the money. Yes, and get the students to help clear the tables and chairs in the dining-room out of the way.'

'What's Eisa done? Do you know?'

'He pushed somebody out of a train, by all accounts.'

'He didn't!'

'Can't stop!' said Jordan, and he continued on down the corridor.

Molly made off in the opposite direction, trying to remember what she had to do. What, for instance, was this envelope doing in her hands?

A long-haired man was bent over the main door, trying to lift the bottom catch on the side of the door that never opened. He heard her clatter on the stairs and looked up. He was lined, much older than his hair had led her to expect. ''Scuse me. Can you help me with this?'

The band. She remembered what was inside the envelope. 'Yes, I don't know if that door *will* open. I've never seen it open.'

The man stood up straight. He wore a sequined jacket and black trousers. 'Don't say that, love. It's gotta open. No open. No show. Look at the stuff!'

Molly looked. Then she got down on her hands and knees, trying to move the stuck latch. She pulled with all her might but only managed to tear a nail on her index finger. This she hid in her hankie, offering up the pain for João and newly encrisised Eisa. 'I can't seem to do it,' she said. 'I'll see if I can find someone at the office.'

She made off up Kidderpore Avenue towards the administration office. It being Saturday, it was unlikely that that helpful chap Dominic would be about. Still, there would be someone. As she trotted up the road, she thought of the other errands she had to remember.

172

'Can you send someone to open the other section of the door into the summer school?' she asked the man behind the desk.

He sucked in air and shook his head. 'It's Saturday.'

'But there are musicians with huge things to get inside for the disco.'

'It happens every year,' said the man.

'So what did you do last year?'

'Don't remember. Tell you what, I'll send Security.'

'Right,' said Molly.

She returned to Heathcliff College by a different route in order to contact Rachel, who, she reasoned, would know Dennis's number. But there was no answer when she knocked.

Lynn was coming along the corridor, making for the kitchen.

'Lynn, you haven't seen Rachel, have you?'

'She went home, Molly. What's the matter, love? You look agitated.'

Molly told her. 'You don't know Dennis's home number, do you?'

'No, but I'll go and see if Agnes is about, if you like.'

'Would you? And, Lynn, could you get the students to help clear the dining-room for the disco?'

'Yes. What's happened to you, Molly?' There were drops of blood on the carpet and on the front of Molly's cotton dress.

'I hurt the nail on the door. Look, I'd better get on. I'm dying for the lav . . .'

'Leave it to me,' Lynn said.

When Molly came out of the toilet she felt she was missing something, but could not for the life of her think what it could be. She walked down the corridor, wondering, was distracted by the sight of her welcoming room, took the stairs two at a time, arriving at the main door just as the man from Security had released the catch, while his companion questioned the band, asking for a letter to prove their right of entry.

'This way, ladies and gentlemen,' Molly called to them.

173

'It's all right, then?' asked the security man, eyeing the long-haired musicians.

'Perfectly. They're the disco.'

The band struggled past her. One winked. 'Pocket Hitlers,' he said.

Molly nodded. 'They can't be too careful.' Then she saw Astrid, sitting on her bench outside the church.

She took a pace towards her, but remembered that she didn't know whether Lynn had contacted Dennis Harlow. She went into the crowded common room where Lynn was trying to make herself heard above the din.

'The disco can't begin until we have cleared the dining-room,' she was saying, but no-one took any notice.

Molly spotted Agnes Fogherty drinking a Guinness with Moira Trotter. She threaded her way over to her and told her what had happened. Agnes got up, sorting through her big bunch of keys to find the one for Reception. She passed by Lynn, who was still trying to gain the attention of the student body. 'I'll see to it. It's a knack.' She aimed her face at the ceiling and boomed out: 'CHAIRS! TABLES! MOVE!' The room went quiet and looked at her. She corralled a third of the students and gestured them to follow Lynn. Then she continued on to Reception. Molly followed.

Agnes dialled Dennis's number. It was answered by Lady Porn-Chai. Agnes asked for Dennis.

'They're in the middle of dinner,' she whispered to Molly.

Molly nodded, then remembered. She had left the envelope with the payment for the band on the cistern in the toilet.

'Agnes . . . ,' she said.

'Shh . . . ,' said Agnes. 'Hello, Dennis? There's a bit of a crisis. I'll put Molly on.'

'Hello, Sir Dennis, I'm sorry to interrupt your dinner-party but . . .' She told him everything she knew.

Molly looked at Agnes. 'Dennis is going to the police station himself. He only lives a few miles away.'

'That's something. Have you any idea how it happened?

I think Eisa's the one with the plug problem,' observed Agnes, as if everything suddenly fitted.

'There must be some mistake,' said Molly, thinking kind thoughts about the big man. Then she remembered.

'Agnes, I've got to go to the lav. I've left something on the cistern.'

'You do that, Molly,' said Agnes. 'It isn't that Brazilian woman, is it? If it is, I'd leave her there. Better yet, a quick push followed by a fast flush.'

'Shame on you,' said Molly. 'No, it's the money for the band. Jordan gave it to me.'

She left Reception and ran up the stairs.

'Thank God!' Molly exclaimed, when she found the envelope on the cistern next to her room-key. 'I'd forgotten all about the room-key.'

She jittered in the corridor, wondering what she should do next. She tried to think. No, that's everything. I'm free. I just need to pay the band. Then I can go to bed and have a little worry.

Agnes had shut up Reception and was nowhere to be seen. She went downstairs to see that everything was being cleared away for the band. All was in hand. The band was tuning up to an accompaniment of shuddering cutlery and crockery and a babel of foreign voices.

Molly went up to the man who had had trouble with the door. 'I'll pay you now,' she said. 'That'll give us one less thing to worry about.'

'Appreciate it,' said the man, taking the envelope.

A cereal-plate fell off a table being manhandled into a corner by Teresa and Assumption. Teresa screamed. The plate bounced loudly three times, but did not break. Lynn approached them, looking to Molly at the end of her tether. She thought of Keith. Then she thought of Astrid. Then she went to help Satoko and Mitsuko, who were vainly trying to move a table.

'You two take that end and I'll take this end.'

A drop of blood fell on a fork. Molly took a napkin from the dispenser and wiped the blood away, then folded the napkin round her finger. She lifted the table, carried it

175

with the two girls towards the corner. She felt her back go and dropped the table, leaning over it, one hand supporting her, while the other held the small of her back.

'What is the matter?' asked Satoko.

'Can you get me a chair, dear?' Molly asked. She felt a chair against the back of her legs and sat down, barely managing to stifle a cry.

Lynn came over. 'What's the matter, Molly?'

'It's my back. It's happened before. I should lie flat,' she said, angry with herself for forgetting what the fundamentalist doctor had told her about lifting.

'On the floor?' asked Lynn.

'Maybe. What a thing to happen!'

They helped her down to the floor. Molly cried out in pain as they moved her. Then, flat on the cool wood, the pain ebbed. She saw Satoko and Mitsuko looking down at her. Then the man from the band. He was holding the envelope over her.

'It's empty!' he said. 'Bloody empty!'

Molly shut her eyes.

After getting through to Jordan Bostock, Eisa had felt better. A friend who would explain was on the way.

A policeman in Bexley Police Station had brought him a cup of tea while another tried to ask him questions. They were very polite, and Eisa was starting to think that they knew he was not a bad man. The trouble was that he could not answer any of the policemen's questions. The shock of what happend had driven everything he had so tortuously acquired in English out of his brain. When he opened his mouth to speak and saw the reactions of the police to his multiply fractured utterances, it was clear that they did not understand anything. 'Wait for! Wait for!' he kept saying, sweating letters.

The other people in the carriage had been brought to the station, too, though not in the same police car. After the train had come to a halt, there had been a long silence in the carriage. The girl who had been hit by the youth had not moved from her seat, just sat there, her eyes wildly wandering between the open door and Eisa. He sat down heavily on one of the seats, wiped the palms of his hands down his face, looked at them and then used them to hide his eyes from the reality of the situation.

But that hadn't worked. Other realities impinged. Men he knew in coffee-houses pulled on their hubble-bubble pipes as he passed, their faces impassive. He turned and saw the gossip start. He made for home, past the chanting children. Leila was nodding at him ominously at the painted threshold, all her worst imaginings confirmed. How many times she had warned Eisa that leaving Zagazig would bring him to grief? Why could he not be content merely to attend Mr Fathi's English Academy? His prices were reasonable, his morals impeccable. Why venture at such expense across the ocean? Only moral laxity prevailed on those far stripped-off shores.

The trouble was that Eisa had not thought he was learning anything important from Mr Fathi. Mr Fathi taught his large class from a single copy of *English for Gentlemen*, wrote on the blackboard a lot, talked in Arabic like a politician lecturing fellahin, had not managed to teach Eisa much that would be useful to him.

When Eisa had announced his intention of travelling to Britain to learn English at Demolish Babel, his wife had pulled her veil about her face and sulked. She had consulted the muezzin at the mosque, who had collared Eisa after Friday prayers, warning him of the corruption he would be exposing himself to in London.

Eisa had not listened. Now, sitting in the police station, he longed for Egypt, wished he could put the clock back. But, then, it had seemed such a good idea. With the English he learned he would be able to approach tourists and seduce them into accompanying him to visit his perfume factory, located amidst the labyrinth of the old town. But what tourist would accompany a man who had pushed a fellow human being off a train?

177

A policeman entered the office and whispered in his interrogator's ear. The policeman looked relieved, nodded and stood up. He left the room, returning a moment later with Jordan Bostock.

Eisa made to kiss Jordan's hand.

'What happened, Eisa?' Jordan asked, pulling back.

Eisa told him everything.

'It sounds like an unfortunate accident,' said Jordan to the policeman. 'He tried to stop a man intimidating a woman. The man pushed him. Eisa pushed back and the man crashed back into the door. The door opened and the man fell out.'

'That seems to agree with what the woman said. And the other passengers,' said the policeman.

'What about the man who fell out of the train. Did . . . ?'

'Yes. He fell into some trees. Shocking mess.'

'I see. Does he know?'

'I don't know. I think so.'

Jordan translated. Eisa moaned and hid his face in his hands. From that position, he said to Jordan, 'I only wanted to help the girl. The man was very bad to her. What is going to happen?'

'Don't worry, Eisa. It was an accident. The other passengers have told the police what happened and they agree with your story.'

'I am very sad, sir,' said Eisa.

'God will give you the strength,' said Jordan. He turned to the policeman. 'What do you think will happen?'

'Well, it sounds to me like the chap got what was coming to him. If there's another culprit, I suppose it's British Rail. Just hang on, and then I'll talk with my colleagues. We'll probably be able to release Mr Eisa into your care. He's a tourist, is he?'

'Sort of. He's studying English at a summer school.'

'You haven't done much for him, have you? He can't say a word.'

Jordan shrugged. He turned to Eisa and spoke to him, reassuring him that everything would be all right.

'You can wait by the station desk, if you like,' said the

policeman. 'The station sergeant will make you a cup of tea.'

Eisa and Jordan stepped outside and sat on a long wooden seat. Jordan tried to engage Eisa in conversation but did not get anywhere. He collected the two teas, sat down and wondered how things were progressing at the summer school in his absence.

Then Dennis Harlow was led into the station between two policemen, who took him up to the desk.

'Failed the breathalyser. A hundred miles per hour along the M2.'

'Name?' asked the desk sergeant.

Before Dennis could answer, Jordan Bostock called out, 'Sir Dennis! Over here!'

'Name?' repeated the policeman.

'Sir Dennis Harlow. Actually, I was on my way to see you chaps.'

'Well, you're seeing us.'

Jordan stood up and went over to the desk.

'Jordan,' said Sir Dennis. 'How are things? Is that student all right?'

'Yes, Dennis. It seems to be going all right.'

'I came as soon as I heard. Got into a spot of bother on the way. Failed the damned breathalyser. I know I shouldn't have driven but I got so agitated.'

'You know this gentleman?' The policeman was addressing Jordan.

'Yes, he's the owner of the school I work at. He came here to see about Eisa.'

'If you'll just follow that officer, sir. We need a sample,' said the policeman.

'I think you'd better phone my lawyer, Jordan. Kill two birds with one stone. God, I feel such a fool. The summer school's always been a bother. But nothing like this. What's happening?'

'They should never have left him behind,' said Jordan.

'Who left him? Molly O'Connor?'

'No. I believe it was Rachel and Arthur.'

179

Dennis shook his head. 'It's the bloody last straw,' he said. He turned to Jordan. 'And you can quote me on that. Quote it back to me if you like. Next time I get sentimental.'

Jordan nodded.

The policeman gestured Dennis towards a door. He walked past Eisa. 'Don't worry, young man,' he said. 'You'll be out of here before me.'

Eisa, not understanding, looked up into Dennis's eyes. Then he looked down into his mug of tea and his tears were falling into it.

'Poor sod!' said Sir Dennis. Then he looked down at his own elbow, which the desk sergeant was gently but firmly using as a lever to push him towards the half-closed door.

'Well, if you want to know what I think,' said Agnes Fogherty, 'I think they should pay us to listen rather than the other way round.'

Molly O'Connor nodded. She was lying flat on the floor of her bedroom, a double whisky at her elbow. Agnes had got a group of students to lift her off the dining-hall floor and carry her up to her room in Churchill. All the time Molly moaned as the dicky vertebrae in her back, surrounded by trapped, deeply offended nerves, were further insulted. Once placed on the floor, the incessant beat from the unpaid disco band sound-boxed through the building and further irritated her back.

'Are you going to be able to pay them?' she asked.

'I'll have to rifle the emergency fund,' replied Agnes.

'It's all my fault.'

'No, it isn't. Not at all. You were landed with much too much to look after. It's what the fund's for, after all.'

'Of course, I should never have used the mattress,' said Molly. 'At St Cedric's I sleep on the floor. I was an accident just waiting to happen.'

'It's been one of those days,' said Agnes.

'I haven't seen anything of the three Sues today. To tell you the truth, Agnes, I could have done with them tonight.'

'Well, give them their due. They were here this morning to get the trips off. They looked like something the cat brought in. You probably didn't recognize them, Molly.' Molly grimaced. 'You don't think I ought to get the doctor for you?'

'No. I've got my anti-spasmodics. The fundamentalist doctor gave me them when I was laid up at St Cedric's.'

'So they're not all bad, then.'

'No, nobody's *all* bad, Agnes.'

'No, of course not,' said Agnes, not believing herself for a second.

'We had a sort of peace conference for them last Easter. I was helping to lift a wild pig on to the spit when my back went,' said Molly, back in her other world.

'I wonder how Jordan Bostock's getting on,' said Agnes.

'Don't!' replied Molly. 'I can't bear to think about it.'

'That Eisa was lucky to have a plug at all, even if it was too small. I haven't got a plug.'

'Yes, I'm sure you're right, Agnes.'

'Of course I'm right.' She looked at her watch. 'I'd better go and grub up the money for the er . . . musicians. Back soon.'

Back in Reception, she raided her hidden cashboxes for enough money to pay off the band. The theft – and theft it must have been – had hardly impinged on her until she found herself clasping a handful of notes and realized that what she held in her hand represented what had been stolen from the envelope in the toilet. Of course, it was pointless calling the police or making an issue of it.

I'm not going to think about it, she thought. She stuffed the notes into another envelope, sealed it, picked up her bag and left the office.

As she was locking up, Lynn was passing.

'Still at it?' Lynn asked.

'It never rains,' said Agnes. She started walking towards the din downstairs.

'You're not going to the disco, are you? I was looking for someone to have a snifter with.'

'You just stay where you are. I'll be back in a jiff,' said Agnes and she darted down the stairs into the midst of strobing lights and chaos, where the band were banging out what Agnes regarded as a cynical version of 'Yesterday'. It ought not to be allowed, she thought. She waited, leaning against the banisters, finding herself rendered quite giddy by a light set up on a tripod that nodded about at high speed, changing colour. The sight it illuminated of the students dancing wildly, united by a common language at last, did nothing to cheer her up. She paced over to the lead singer. 'I think you'll find your er . . . fee is all present and correct. Sorry about the problem before.'

The man, sweating, took the envelope, opened it and counted the money. The thought occurred to Agnes that he could have pocketed the contents of the envelope the first time. No, he couldn't have been so brazen, could he? Still, if he were brazen enough to push such noxious noises on an uncertain world, was there nothing he would not stoop to? He replaced the money in the envelope. 'Thanks,' he said.

She noticed Satoko and Mitsuko looking up at the singer adoringly, perched on the edge of the makeshift stage. Then she saw the singer wink at them.

'They're well brought up girls,' said Agnes to the singer, killing two birds with one sideswipe.

'Yeah,' said the singer. He struck up the next number, sending Agnes Fogherty scurrying back upstairs.

'I know I say it every year, but this is definitely the last time,' she told Lynn.

Lynn picked up Agnes's remark and ran with it towards her precipice of preference. 'You know, I think that, too,' she said.

'How do you mean?'

'I don't think I'll be coming here again.'

'I was joking, Lynn.'

182

'I wasn't.'

'Buy me a drink, why don't you?' said Agnes.

Half an hour later Lynn knocked at Molly's door, and it was opened almost at once by Astrid.

Lynn was taken aback. 'Is Molly all right?'

'And your name is?' asked Astrid.

'I'm Lynn, a friend of Molly's. Er . . . I'm a teacher on the summer school.'

'Ah, yes,' said Astrid. 'I have seen you but we have not introduced ourselves.'

'No.'

'I am Astrid from Brazil.'

'Pleased to meet you, Astrid. Of course I've seen you, too.'

'Good evening, Lynn,' said Astrid.

Lynn stood there, feeling foolish. 'How *is* Molly?' she asked.

'A moment. I will enquire.' And Astrid shut Molly's door.

She's shut the door on me! thought Lynn. That's a bit thick. She put her fist out, readying herself to knock.

The door opened, and Astrid was facing Lynn's fist. 'My teacher will see you,' she said and opened the door to let Lynn pass through.

Molly was lying on the floor, a pillow under her head, the covers neatly tucked in under her. Astrid had moved the coffee table to a position within easy reach of her patient, placing the desk-lamp on top of it. Molly's whisky was sitting on a folded napkin atop the table.

'Hello, Lynn,' said Molly. 'You've met Astrid, I think.'

'Er . . . yes,' said Lynn. 'You don't look very comfortable, Molly. Won't the floor make it worse?'

'Oh, no! It's firm, you see. Firm's what I need.'

Lynn sat down on the bed. 'This mattress is a bit rum,' she said.

'Coffee stains,' said Molly.

183

'Maybe coffee,' said Astrid.

'Talking of coffee, I could murder a cup of tea,' said Molly.

Astrid stood up straight. 'I will prepare it.'

'And what about you, Lynn? Do you fancy a coffee?'

'That'd be lovely.' She smiled at Astrid. 'Thank you.'

'You will be all right?' Astrid asked Molly.

'Oh, yes. Perfectly. You're an angel.'

Astrid nodded, and left the room.

'You're being well taken care of,' said Lynn, not without irony.

Molly, either unaware or unwilling to pick up the tone, replied: 'Yes, she's only been here five minutes. She's really sorted me out.'

'And you're sure this is the only treatment? We could always phone the doctor, you know.'

'I'm just where I ought to be,' said Molly. 'On the floor. It really is the best place for me.'

'Anyway, tomorrow's Sunday,' said Lynn.

'Today's Sunday. Lord, I hope I'll be able to get to mass. I've only made it the once this week. This is what I get for it.'

'Do you really believe that?' Lynn asked.

'Yes.'

'Moira Trotter thinks she spoke to Keith today.'

'That's great news!' said Molly. 'But how do you mean "thinks"?'

'It was a very bad line. It's only a slim chance, I know. Will you say a prayer for it to be true, Molly?'

'Of course. I'll offer this up for that intention.' She slipped her watch off, replacing it on her wrist upside down to remind her. 'No news from Jordan about Eisa, I suppose? I am worried about him. Such a nice chap. Not that I've spoken to him, but he has something about him. You can just tell he's decent straight off. At least, that's how I felt.'

'Arthur and Rachel should never have left Eisa behind,' said Lynn.

'Where is Arthur, do you know?'

'I think he may have gone off to the pub. He likes to get away.'

'I hope he's behaving himself.'

'I doubt it,' said Lynn.

Astrid returned with two cups. 'I forgot to ask if you take sugar. I do not think you do,' she said to Lynn.

'That's right. Thank you, Astrid.'

'Don't mention it,' said Astrid.

'Haven't you got yourself one?' said Molly.

'No. It is very late for me.'

'Yes, it is late. I was just looking at my watch.' She looked at it again, saw it upside down and remembered. 'Why don't you go to bed, Astrid? You must be really tired.' She turned to Lynn. 'Astrid and I went to Kew today.'

'Did you have a good time?'

Molly looked at Astrid, expecting a 'No'. But Astrid surprised her. 'We had a wonderful time, didn't we?'

'We did,' said Molly. 'Yes, we did!'

'I will see you in the morning,' said Astrid. She left, giving Lynn a smile.

'She seems more cheerful than I've seen her,' said Lynn.

'Yes, I don't know what's come over her.'

Lynn thought for a moment. 'I was wondering, Molly.'

'What?'

'Do you think it would be a good idea if I phoned my friends in Kano? I've been thinking about it all week but I worry about what I might hear.'

'I don't understand,' said Molly. The pain in her back seemed to be getting worse. She shifted position.

'It's just that if my friend there hears what's happened to Keith she may tell me something I'd rather not know. She's very honest, you see. An American.'

'Yes, they can be a bit that way,' said Molly. 'What would you do if Keith didn't turn up?'

'Don't, Molly, please.'

Molly persisted. 'It has to be faced, Lynn. Could you manage?'

'No, I couldn't. I've got nothing.'

185

'Well, think about this, Lynn. If push comes to shove, you could come and work at St Cedric's. We need a good teacher. I know it probably isn't what you want. You've done Borneo, haven't you? Still, it might give you a breathing-space. Perhaps more than that.'

The well-worn programme in Lynn's brain started up. She saw herself by a river in the middle of dripping jungle. Towering rainforest above her and beautiful brown children learning at her knee. Then she thought of Friday.

'I couldn't,' she said.

'You could if you want,' Molly said in a throwaway way.

'Thank you, Molly. I'll take your cup back to the kitchen.'

'Thanks. Could you switch off the light on your way out? The desk-lamp is enough.'

'What about the loo?' Lynn asked.

'Astrid saw to that most efficiently just before you came. I think I'll be all right,' Molly replied.

'Nathan?'

'What?'

'Not "what?" Say "pardon?" or "Yes?"'

'Yes?'

'That's better. Have you got anything that needs washing? If so, could you bring it downstairs now, please? I'm about to do a load.'

'OK.'

It was Sunday morning, and Rachel had been up since seven. She had slipped out of the house, walking a hundred yards to pick up the Sunday papers. She returned home by way of the shop on the ground floor, where she took some items from stock for breakfast: vegetarian sausages and hamburgers, a loaf of wholemeal bread, milk. Back in the kitchen she had put the sausages and hamburgers in the oven, brewed herself a pot of coffee and sat down with the papers.

At eight she gave Nathan his first call. Fifteen minutes

later breakfast was on the table but there was still no sign of him. That was nothing unusual, and she went upstairs and pounced on him in bed, hugging him, then pulling away the clothes.

'Mum!' he said, bad-tempered, turning over, burying his head in the pillow.

'Breakfast's on the table, young man!' she told him, feeling as ideal as a TV advert, enjoying it. 'Up you get. Five minutes.'

After breakfast Nathan returned to his room. She could hear his computer shooting soldiers as she cleared away the papers, putting them in the recycling bag, and set about her Sunday-morning jobs.

'Is that all you have for me?' she asked, when Nathan appeared with a small bundle of socks, underpants and shirts.

'Yes, that's it, Mum,' he said.

'What about your shellsuit? That could do with a good wash.'

'No, it's OK,' he said.

'Look, I've got some room. May as well wash it. Up you go and bring it down like a good boy.'

He stood there, looking sulky. She took his cheeks between her fingers and squeezed, making his lips pucker, and he bothered her away. 'Don't give me a hard time. I've got to get on!' she told him.

Nathan just stood there, looking at the floor, his trainers kicking the leg of a chair.

'What's the matter?'

'I don't have the shellsuit. I gave it away,' he said.

'Gave it away!' said Rachel. 'How do you mean, "gave it away"?'

'I gave it to Zek.' He looked at her for a reaction. 'I was tired of it anyway.'

'Why did you give it to Zek?'

'He wanted it,' he said.

'And he just came out and asked you for it?'

Nathan thought about that. 'No.' He looked at her. 'I was tired of it, Mum. Nobody wears dayglo colours any

187

more. I just told Zek I was tired of it and he said his son would like it. So I gave it to him.'

'When?' she asked. 'You were wearing it, weren't you?'

He kicked the chair-leg, watching the chair as it skittered across the cork floor an inch at a time. 'When we got back from Brighton I changed into the jeans and T-shirt in your room at school.'

'I didn't notice.'

'No,' he said.

'And what did Zek say when you gave it to him?'

'I put it outside his room. I haven't seen him since.'

Rachel sat down. 'He'll probably be angry when he finds it,' she said.

'No, he won't. He wasn't angry about the Oxfam clothes,' Nathan replied.

'Oh, yes! I'd forgotten. Look, I'll tell you what. Bring down the jeans. We'll wash those.'

'You aren't angry, are you, Mum?' he asked.

'No. Just a bit confused.'

'I don't know why. Zek doesn't have a bean to spend. He couldn't even go into the Brighton Pavilion. He said he didn't want to, but I knew. I saw him looking at the prices. And he collected all the little things out of the lunch-boxes. He wants to take them home for the children in his school.'

Rachel nodded. Nathan brought her the jeans. She stuffed them into the washing machine, and he went back upstairs to his computer.

Having switched on the washer, Rachel set about washing up. She reached for the radio in time to hear the conclusion of 'The Week's Good Cause'. It was for WaterAid. *How far are you prepared to go to turn on a tap?* the celebrity was asking.

Rachel turned off the hot water, thinking.

The telephone rang.

'Hello?' she said, drying her hands and her eyes. 'Jordan. What can I do for you? Is everything all right?'

Jordan told her everything that had happened.

'And where's Eisa now? God, I feel so guilty. We should

have waited. We could have waited longer but—'

Jordan told her that Eisa was back at Heathcliff, that he would have to report to the police station when required. There would be an inquest. Then he told her about Dennis.

'I'll be up there in half an hour,' Rachel said. 'There's nothing else, is there?' She listened. 'Poor Molly! Look, I'll be there shortly!'

Rachel put the receiver down, regarded the clothes going round in the washer. She did not like to leave it on. Still, there was no alternative today. 'Nathan! Let's go!' she called.

'Where?'

'Got to go to work!'

'But it's Sunday!'

'Five minutes, young man!'

Ten minutes later Nathan was sitting beside her in the car pulling at his seatbelt, snapping it across his mouth like a gag.

'You'll regret that if we have a crash,' said Rachel. 'You'll lose all your pretty teeth.'

'Yeah, yeah,' he said, looking out of the car window at the Holloway Road.

Then Rachel, as she often did, lost herself in logistics. By the time they were turning into Kidderpore Avenue she had worried about Eisa and Molly, bitten her lip about Arthur, but had not considered the thought that had crossed her mind on getting into the car with Nathan: *What are you doing with that stuffed-full sports-bag? You look like you're going away for a week!*

And once inside Heathcliff College – having given her room-key to Nathan, telling him to study – she had other things on her mind.

Book Four

Upper Intermediate

Ezekiel was studying a difficult chapter in Rachel Pales's advanced grammar when Nathan knocked at the door of his room.

'Entrez!' he called, thinking it might be Sebastian Palumbo, who had said he would be coming to see him about an urgent problem.

'It's me,' said Nathan.

'Ah, my benefactor! Come in, come in!'

Nathan, stepping inside, saw immediately his shell-suit on the desk, wrapped in a clear plastic bag. Next to it, also in a bag, the bits and pieces collected from the packed lunches. He grinned at them, remembering. 'Are you working?' he asked. 'I'm supposed to be working.'

'That is good,' said Ezekiel, smiling. He turned to the neat package on the desk. 'Did you leave this for me?'

Nathan nodded, embarrassed. 'I should have got it washed first. Sorry,' he said.

'Not necessary. Sit down, Nathan. Perhaps you can help me more.'

'Er . . . I've brought a few other things for you – for your children'. He held out the sports-bag. 'I need the sports-bag back,' he added, though he didn't really need it, but sensed that the limitation placed on the giving would prick the bubble of embarrassment around the transaction. Then he watched as Ezekiel unzipped the bag and started sorting through the clothes inside. He looked hungry. Nathan turned away.

'Football shorts, trainers, vests – so many vests – in so many colours. And what's this? A watch? My son does not have a watch.'

'No,' replied Nathan. 'It's a compass. You wear it like a watch. I never use it. I thought I would, but I don't.' He filed away *watch*, and remembered last year's forgotten *Swatch*.

Ezekiel nodded. He folded everything carefully, placed the trainers and compass on top of the pile, and handed Nathan his now-empty bag. Then he just sat, looking at the boy.

'Thank you,' he said.

Nathan looked back hard at Ezekiel, waiting for something to happen, wanting to know what kept him thinking of Ezekiel all the time.

Ezekiel continued looking back, unblinking. Then he released Nathan, let him off the hook with a smile. 'How's your grammar?' he asked.

'So, so.'

'Come and sit down here and teach me. I have a great trouble with these verbs that have two words. See: "John looked up the street." Now, the object of the sentence is "the street". But you can't say "John looked the street up" or "John looked it up", can you?'

'Nathan worked his lips, puzzled.

'But see this: "John looked up the word." And you can put the object in a different place. See: "John looked the word up" and "John looked it up". Now, why is this so? It has always been a difficulty for me.'

'I think you can say "John looked the street up."'

'Yes, I know. But it has a different meaning from "John looked up the street." Say he looked up the street to see if the bus was coming. Now, that's different from "John looked up the street" – on a town plan – isn't it? I cannot see the difference between "up" in those two sentences.'

'Isn't "up" a preposition?' asked Nathan. 'My mum—'

'But your mum isn't here, is she? Can't you help me?'

'Let's see,' said Nathan, pulling the book over. 'It says here that you can replace the object where the second word of the verb is a particle.' Nathan pocketed his upper lip. 'But I don't know what a particle is.'

'These are the things I must know,' said Ezekiel. 'I have many clever children in my classes. They will ask me for rules.'

'My mum says there are more exceptions than rules.'

Ezekiel sat back in his chair. 'Yes, I have heard her say that. But the exceptions must have rules, too, mustn't they? By the way, did you tell her you have given me these clothes?'

'Yes,' said Nathan.

'Did you?' He was caught in Nathan's gaze, so like the

look he got from teachers at school. What differed was his reaction.

'She knows about the shellsuit. She found out this morning.'

'And was she angry?'

'No.'

'What about the other things?'

'She doesn't know about that yet. I'll tell her, though. She won't mind.'

'Your mother is a very clever woman.'

'I suppose so.'

'Aren't you sure?'

'There are lots of things she doesn't know. She thinks she knows everything, but she doesn't.'

'What, for example?'

Nathan thought about that. 'She never has any time,' he said.

'For what?'

Nathan shrugged, looking sulky. He replied, but Ezekiel could not hear. 'Pardon?' he asked.

'Having a good time; just hanging out . . . with me,' he said.

'That's because she must work hard to make you comfortable.'

Nathan hung his head.

'How old are you, child?'

He thought about 'child'. 'Thirteen.'

Ezekiel nodded. 'Almost a man.'

'Remember that big guy who was in the shop with us?'

'Eisa? The man from Egypt? Yes, I remember him. He missed the bus.'

'He got into a fight on the train. He killed someone.' Then seeing Ezekiel's face, Nathan added, 'It was an accident.'

'Very terrible . . .'

'Mum shouldn't have left him behind. He hardly spoke any English at all. It wasn't fair.'

Ezekiel could remember the argument on the bus between Rachel, Arthur and the bus-driver, the repeated head-counts, the anxiety, time passing, the driver's impatience. He said, 'My son at thirteen is doing all kinds of things. He helps in the garden, grows vegetables, herds the cattle.'

He doesn't want to talk about it, Nathan thought. 'What's his name, your son?'

'Tanja.'

'Do you have a picture of him?'

'Yes, I think I do. It's an old picture. He's with his mother. My wife.'

'Can I see it?'

Ezekiel reached into his desk drawer and produced a zebra-skin wallet. Out of this he took a black-and-white photo, smiling at it as he passed it across to Nathan.

Nathan stared into the snap of the tall young man standing to attention beside the African woman, Zek's wife. He was wearing a pair of shorts and a short-sleeved shirt. He looked very like her, the resemblance far stronger than to his father. His feet were bare.

'You see his feet are bare. His shoes are in a plastic bag,' said Ezekiel.

Nathan looked at Ezekiel questioningly, wondering why he had said that. Ezekiel looked back, knowing why.

'I want to go home,' said Eisa to Arthur.

'We've only just got here, lovey!' Arthur replied, taking in the sight of the Sunday-morning Heath.

'No. *Home*. Egypt.'

Arthur switched to Arabic to make Eisa feel at home. 'I can understand that. Of course I can. If I were you, I'd want to go home, too. The trouble is, though, you can't until the police say it's all right.'

'I shall die, Arthur,' said Eisa.

Arthur didn't say anything. He just looked at Eisa, folding his fleshy face into question-mark wrinkles.

'What?' asked Eisa.

'Don't be so bloody daft,' he told Eisa in English.

'Sobloodaft?'

'Crazy, mad, loco, silly,' said Arthur. 'You're a hero, Eisa.' Back to Arabic. 'A hero. You did something which most people would not have done. You saw a bully and you did not just sit back and let it happen. Did anyone else in the carriage stand up to help you out?'

'No. They sat. They read newspapers.'

'There you are, then. But they *knew* what was going on. They knew, Eisa! I can picture the scene. The man you stopped could have done far worse and they would have sat on.' He sighed, looking towards the ponds. 'It happens all the time.'

'Why?'

'Fear, lovey. Fear pure and simple. Now, don't you dare talk to me about dying. People like you can't die. There's too much bullying going on. We need people like you.'

Eisa thought about that.

'I'm sorry, Eisa,' said Arthur.

'Sorry? Why sorry?'

'I shouldn't have left you behind.'

'Sorry?'

'In Brighton. I should have made the bus wait. You see, Rachel was having an—'

But Eisa interrupted. 'No. I understood. You said five-thirty. Five-thirty means five-thirty. I was late. It was my fault.'

'But . . .'

'There's the swimming-place you brought us to, Arthur.'

'Let's go this way.'

They walked between the ponds, stopping to watch some radio-controlled boats zoom around and around. Then a flock of Canada geese flew low overhead, startling them with their tolling, toiling wings, then landing on the lowest of the three ponds.

They walked around the pond, taking a route towards the lowest pond, following the flight of the birds.

A woman was sitting behind a table on the edge of the path. She smiled at them as they passed. She pointed to the notice tacked to the table, *Save Our Geese!*

197

'Gentlemen!' she called. 'Gentlemen, will you sign a petition?'

'What does she want, Arthur?' asked Eisa.

'Let's go and find out.' He guided Eisa over. He whispered in his ear, 'Ask her what she is doing.'

'What are you doing?'

'I am trying to get people to sign a petition,' she said, smiling at Eisa. 'The council want to cull the geese. They say there are too many of them. I think this is a very bad thing.'

Eisa looked at Arthur. 'Tell her you don't understand.'

'I don't understand.'

'Ah,' said the woman.

'He is a student of English,' said Arthur.

'Yes, he is, isn't he?' She turned towards Eisa, frowning. 'They want to cull – to kill – the geese. Can you see the geese? Over there?' She pointed.

'Those?' asked Eisa, pointing towards a group of about fifty large geese, grazing on the grass.

'Yes. They want to kill them.'

'For eat?' asked Eisa.

'No, they say there are too many.' She looked at the flock of geese happily. 'But the more the merrier, I say. There's plenty of room.'

'Not for eat?' asked Eisa, thinking what a lot of meat there would be on one.

'Where are you from?' asked the woman.

'My name is Eisa.'

'Don't let me down, lovey. *Where are you from?*'

'Ah, understand,' said Eisa. 'I am from Egypt.'

'Are you enjoying your stay in England?'

'No, madam. I am very sad.'

'Why?'

'Yesterday I kill a man.'

The woman gnawed her lip and looked to Arthur for clarification.

'He didn't really,' he said.

'I kill a man!' repeated Eisa, louder.

'Now, Eisa, lovey . . .'

198

Eisa looked away from them, towards the flock of geese. Tears were flowing down his big cheeks.

'I say, are you . . . all right?' asked the woman. She had only slept fitfully the night before, thinking of all the possible embarrassments her petition might cause her. But none of her nightmares had stretched to the situation now confronting her.

'No, I am very bad man,' said Eisa.

'No, you're not,' said Arthur. He turned to the woman. 'He isn't,' he told her. 'It was an accident, pure and simple. The man got what was coming to him.'

'So your friend *did* kill a man?' the woman asked. She snapped her Bic in half.

'Sorry,' said Eisa, who had heard the crack and looked down to see the two pieces, like twin pieces of a severed finger joined by a tendon.

'Don't worry. I've got another one,' she said mechanically. She turned to Arthur. 'How did it happen?'

'Eisa was on a train coming back from Brighton, weren't you, lovey? The bus – I – had left him behind.' He looked to Eisa for both confirmation and permission to tell her his story. Eisa, for his part, though he did not understand everything, understood what was happening. He wanted to know what the woman would think. If she started to shout at him and bay for his blood and tear her garments in disgust and encourage the geese she loved to peck out his eyes, the dogs running free to savage him and tear him to pieces, he could . . . He looked around at the sensuous curve of the green hill behind, with kites flying like the slides and ribbons in his daughters' hair . . . He could run away from her, from them all. He turned back to look at them. He nodded.

'He was sitting by himself and fell asleep . . .' Arthur told the whole story, while the woman looked steadily, seriously, back at Arthur, once or twice letting her gaze stray to Eisa.

When Arthur had finished, the woman turned to Eisa solemnly. Then she smiled at him. 'Jolly good!' she said.

'That's just what I told him,' said Arthur.

'Jolly good!' she repeated. Then she put out her hand, stained in Bic ink, to Eisa. He hesitated, then seized the woman's hand and shook it hard. 'Of course, it's sad about the man. I know how you are feeling. Who knows what might have happened to him if he had lived? But none of it was your fault. The door should have been properly shut. I hope the woman you helped thanked you.'

Arthur translated.

'No,' said Eisa.

'Well, she should have,' said the woman. 'You're a hero, young man! Will you sign my petition? I would consider it an honour to have my petition signed by a hero like you.' She held out another Bic.

'Go on, Eisa. In English.'

Eisa bent low over the table and wrote.

'A beautiful hand,' said the woman. 'Eisa Al Kishka. What a nice name!'

'Eisa is Jesus,' said Eisa.

'Is he? Jolly good!' said the woman. 'I'm Joan. Joan Lunt.'

'Please to meet you, lovey,' said Eisa.

Arthur signed the petition.

'Arthur Arthur. That's unusual.'

'I had an unusual mum,' said Arthur.

'Are you . . . er . . . Eisa's teacher?'

'Yes, I am. But his English is usually better than this.'

'I sometimes have overseas students staying with me. I live over there.' She pointed to Highgate.

'Lovely,' said Arthur.

'It's a bit big for me now.'

Arthur looked at the people passing. 'I think we're stopping you getting that petition filled up.'

'You are, a bit. Will you be passing this way again? I'll be here all week,' Joan said.

'Are you coming here again?' Arthur asked Eisa.

Eisa nodded. Then he took Joan's hand and shook it hard once again. 'Thank you, madam,' he said.

She looked into his eyes. 'You're a hero!' she said. 'And don't you forget it!'

200

They walked up the hill towards the kites. Eisa turned back to wave at Joan, but she was deep in conversation with prospective customers.

'Do you feel better now?'

'English. Speak English,' said Eisa.

'I thought you'd never ask. You're OK now?'

'Yes,' said Eisa.

'That's good. Let's walk back through Hampstead. I fancy a beer. You can have some juice.'

'Thank you,' said Eisa. They were passing the edge of the Heath. 'What is that big building?'

'It's the Royal Free Hospital,' said Arthur. 'I'm going there tomorrow.'

'Why? You sick?'

'I hope not, lovey. I hope not. Just going for a little check-up.'

'What is a "check-up"?'

Arthur thought of Eric Trotter. *Have you heard this one? Doctor asks woman, 'You had a check-up recently?' 'No,' replies the woman. 'A couple of Yugoslavs.'* The throw-away line suddenly made him want to cry. 'A check-up is an examination from a doctor. Some tests. Some *checks*. A check-up.'

'A check-up,' said Eisa. 'This afternoon I want go to the mosque. There is mosque near. I see on bus.'

'Yes, there is a mosque, Eisa lovey. I'll come with you. I've nothing to do this afternoon.' Eisa seemed to understand. 'You can say a prayer for me while you're there.'

'You are good friend me,' said Eisa. 'I love you.'

'Do you, lovey?' Arthur felt that in a few swift Arabic sentences he could make Eisa think twice about that. 'Now, in English we have two words, *like* and *love*. I think you mean *like*. You like me.'

'No, I am know that lesson. I love you,' said Eisa.

Arthur could not let it pass. He looked at the hospital, thinking of the Arabic words he would need for his confession. No, he thought. I can't use Arabic. I can talk about prices in Arabic but not the price of freedom nor the price you pay for it. He set off in English.

'I think I'm going to die, Eisa. I think I may have caused the death of my friend, Harry. If I'm positive for the virus, it will mean that I passed it on to Harry. There's no other way he could have got it. Harry never played about. He strongly disapproved of me, but I couldn't resist all the beauties. Astrid thinks João caught the virus from Harry. That didn't happen. But the way she looks at me I feel as if she's the one mother representing all the other mothers who've lost – or will lose – their sons to my lust. I knew. Harry told me. He passed the articles over to me with a look, left them open on the right page. But when the door knocked I answered it. If I'm positive, I'm to blame. I don't think you can love me, Eisa. No, I don't think so.'

Eisa looked at Arthur steadily.

'Have you understood the lesson, Eisa?'

'Sorry?'

'Did you understand?'

'Some,' replied Eisa doubtfully.

'If you'd come out of the dark with "I love you" a few months ago, you wouldn't have been safe. You might have been signing your death warrant, my friend. Count yourself lucky you caught me after chucking-out time.'

'Arthur, you are sad,' Eisa said. His teacher had successfully lost him linguistically, but Arthur's body language was international.

'You didn't understand anything I said, did you?' Arthur asked anxiously.

'You and me. Same same boat,' said Eisa.

'The same boat?'

'Yes. I remember lesson. " We're in same boat." Ten on ten?'

'If you say so, Eisa,' Arthur replied. He felt suddenly very tired.

Eisa took his teacher by the arm. 'Allah Karim,' he said. 'I love you, teacher.' And Eisa guided Arthur back towards Heathcliff College.

*   *   *

'I think you should go. It would make it all so much more *convenient*,' said Sue. 'Anyway, you know how *attached* to Dennis you are.'

Sue looked grumpy. 'You call Sidcup *convenient*?' she said. 'Have you ever tried getting to Sidcup?'

'I don't know why he doesn't just get the train in,' said Sue.

'He's above public transport. Anyway, he and Lady Porn-Chai like to go out of an evening. They've got a season ticket at the National,' said Sue. 'You'd be useful to him day and night.'

'That's what I'm worried about,' said Sue.

'It's never worried you before,' said Sue, looking over at Sue.

Sue laughed. 'Anyway, you'd earn some Brownie points.'

'I don't want no Brownie points,' said Sue. 'I want to stay here. There's lots of interesting things happening. Before you know it, it'll all be over. I think you should go, Sue.'

'Not me,' said Sue emphatically. 'I'd be missed.'

'And we all know by who!' said Sue.

'And I bet you're still not taking precautions,' said Sue.

'You're your own worst enemy,' said Sue.

'He's scrupulous,' said Sue defensively.

'That's what they all say,' said Sue.

'Well, one of you's got to go,' said Agnes, unwrapping the last packet of Molly's Sweet Aftons. 'I don't know where they've gone,' she said to herself.

'Down Red Lane,' said Sue.

'I think you should toss for it,' said Agnes.

'All right. If it lands on its side, I'll go,' said Sue.

'I don't know why he doesn't just hire a driver. It's not as if he's strapped for cash.'

'Why should he when he's got the three Sues?' said Agnes. 'You don't hire dogs and then bark yourself.'

'Thank you very much for nothing in particular,' said Sue. She nodded to the other Sues, who aimed livid looks at Agnes.

'I didn't mean it in the way it sounded,' said Agnes.

'Yes, you did,' said Sue.

'Only a bit,' said Agnes. 'Look, Dennis is waiting. You know how he gets.'

'All right, I'll go,' said Sue. 'Only for a week, mind. Share and share alike.'

'That sounds reasonable,' said Agnes.

'That includes you, too, Agnes,' said Sue.

'It does, thump!' replied Agnes. 'I'm your superior.'

'Hark at her!' said Sue.

'So how am I supposed to get to Sidcup on a Sunday?' asked Sue.

'Here's a railway map of Greater London,' said Agnes, as if addressing students.

'I'm going by minicab. It's the least he can do,' said Sue.

'He'll moan,' said Sue.

'Well, he shouldn't have got his licence taken away in the first place,' said Sue. 'Silly bugger should have been more careful.'

'That's rich coming from you,' said Sue.

'Right you are. I'm glad that's decided,' said Agnes. 'Now, Sues, leave me alone. I've got to juggle the petty cash.'

'You're good at that,' said Sue.

'What's that supposed to mean? And where were you lot last night when we needed you?'

'Not a million miles from here, was you, Sue?'

'Give it a rest,' said Sue, who felt she needed one badly.

Agnes ordered the three Sues out of her office.

'Thank you very much!' said Sue.

'*My* office, is it?' said Sue.

'I'm going by minicab,' said Sue.

'Maybe you'll get Derek,' said Sue.

Jordan Bostock came into the office. 'The three Sues. Good,' he said.

'Ooh, Mr Bostock, you look dead beat,' said Sue.

'Yes, I am. I've got a favour to ask you,' said Jordan. 'I'm supposed to be taking a group of students to Speakers' Corner. I was wondering if one of you would take my place. I really am tired.'

'Sue will go, won't you, Sue?' said Agnes.

'Only if Sue comes with me,' said Sue to the spare Sue.

Sue, out on a limb, said, 'Oh, all right!'

'Thanks,' said Jordan. 'They'll be outside in a few minutes. About ten of them. Now I'm going back to bed. I'm *très fatigué*.'

Sue watched Jordan leave the room. 'He's wonderful at languages, isn't he? He's like the complete works of Linguaphone,' said Sue.

'I don't know why he does the summer school. He's as rich as they come. Have you seen his snaps?'

'I know. He doesn't need the money.'

'He's got a timeshare in Bermuda,' said Sue. 'He lent it to Dennis and Lady Porn-Chai. That's why he's so well in. Apart from the lolly, of course.'

'Must be a workaholic,' said Sue.

'And he's got the strength of the insurance companies round him. He gave me a long talk about TESSA the other night. He told me it's never too early for me to plan for me retirement,' said Sue.

'You're not going to have a retirement at the rate you're going,' said Sue.

'What about that vodka?' responded Sue.

'Shouldn't you be in Sidcup?' said Sue.

'I won't tell you again,' said Agnes.

The three Sues shambled out.

Muchtar came in. 'I am going to Speaker's Corner,' he said.

'That's nice. You need to wait outside,' said Agnes.

'It is raining,' said Muchtar.

'That's nice. We need it.'

Muchtar left the office, feeling aggrieved.

He stood in the tunnel under Molly O'Connor's room, watching the rain falling and some old ladies leaving the church opposite waving to the vicar. He felt dissatisfied. Everyone he spoke to spoke English worse than he did.

Talking to all these foreigners was beginning to make him lose his certainty about what was correct. So often did he hear incorrect utterances that they slowly but surely entered his repertoire. The Germans whom he had latched on to massacred the Present Perfect until he was coming out with it instead of the Past Simple. Yes, the past was simple. Home was simple. The present less than perfect. What was he doing here, after all? What did the teachers have to teach him except confusion? If he heard Rachel say *That depends* once more, he'd . . . To pay good money in order to learn only confusion!

'Are you go Speaker Corner?' asked Mahmoud.

Muchtar frowned. 'Yes, I am go-*ing* to Speakers' Corner. Are you?'

'I think,' said Mahmoud, 'my friend no is present.'

'He will be late.'

'I don't hope so,' said Mahmoud.

Muchtar nodded. Then he moved away from grammatical error, knowing that it would follow him like a carcinogenic cloud of unknowing.

'We are just like the animals. No better and quite often a great deal worse,' said the Animal Rights speaker.

'That's complete nonsense!' shouted Muchtar.

'That's right. You tell 'im! Stupid berk,' said Sue.

'I wouldn't buy the ice-creams round Speakers' Corner, Ito. They'll cost you an arm and a leg,' said Sue.

'But I am very hot,' said Ito.

'Have an Everton mint,' said Sue, offering her bag to Ito. Ito took one, looked at it, then put it in his pocket when Sue turned away to watch the speaker.

'And another thing,' continued the harassed man on the soapbox, 'when you arrive at the Last Judgement all the animals you have enslaved will be there to accuse you.'

'Rubbish!' shouted Muchtar. 'Animals are for man the use of . . .'

'They will show Him their wounds, their cut-off beaks,

their sores from concrete floors and He will shake His Great Head and say: "Be gone from me, ye cursed. You could not love my creation, my innocent ones, you cannot live here."'

'Fairy-stories!' shouted Muchtar.

'I will not rise to the bait, ladies and gentlemen. You see how aggressive the eating of dead flesh has made him!'

Muchtar gave the man a dismissive gesture and walked on, taking most of the summer school students, bemused by his performance, with him.

'You can go to the toilet in the subway, dear. But I'd hold it in if I were you,' said Sue to Lourdes.

'And watch your handbag if you do go, though I agree with Sue. Best to hold it in if you can,' added Sue.

'Watch it anyway,' said Sue.

'And, having lost most of the rainforests on earth, the life-support of the planet has been severely compromised.'

'And why did the rainforests get cut down? I'll tell you why: to satisfy the demands of the insatiable Western world, that's why!' said Muchtar.

'I agree with you, sir,' said the man.

'You English agree with everyone, that's your trouble,' said Muchtar.

'I'd have to think about that. It's an interesting point. I'm not sure.'

'Ah, not sure! Not sure! Well, *get* sure and then you'll have something to discuss. What's the use of Speakers' Corner if you don't *know* anything? How are your children ever going to make sense of life if they're not sure? Go on, answer that!'

Muchtar looked round him for support. He found some, too, most of the crowd being made up of foreign tourists.

'Yes, answer that!' said a bespectacled African.

'The world is too complicated for easy certainties,' said the speaker. He swept his arm across his audience. 'There must be several conflicting creeds among you. We only get on by compromising and tolerating and seeing the other chap's point of view.'

'There speaks the country that dominated the world!

207

See what dented Tin Gods they are!' said Muchtar.

'I might say that we taught others to be Tin Gods and have moved on,' countered the speaker.

'Moved on to what, may I ask? Everywhere there are people begging, families breaking up, a country of lost souls! I was brought up to believe that the British has the key to everything. Now I know that you lose it . . . have lost it, that you never even had had it . . . had it . . . You never unlocked any doors. Just slammed them in the world's face! *You* are truly wretched because of your *that depends* and *but on the other hand* and . . . and . . .' Muchtar was shouting himself out of steam. He slumped.

'You all right, Mr Muchtar?' asked Sue. 'You really gave him what for.'

'Buy him a Mr Softie,' said Sue.

'At that price?' asked Sue.

'It doesn't have to be a Ninety-Nine, does it? Get him an ordinary one to moisten his tubes,' said Sue.

Muchtar allowed himself to be led away. 'You see,' he said to the two Sues, 'I am a disillusioned man. You are not what I expected at all.'

'There, there,' said Sue. 'I know exactly what you mean and I agree with you wholeheartedly. Sue's gone off to buy you a Mr Softie.'

'I don't want a Mr Softie,' said Muchtar sulkily. 'I want to go home. I want to be granted a little respect.'

'But you've only just come! Anyway, I respect you!' said Sue.

'Do you?' asked Muchtar. 'I do not think so. I think it is all a window-dress.'

'That's not true,' said Sue. She appraised Muchtar, admiring his black moustache, wondering. 'I've respected you ever since you came.'

Sue returned with a Mr Softie cone. 'Guess how much?' she asked Sue, holding it out for Muchtar.

'I dread to think,' said Sue.

'Pound bloody fifty,' said Sue.

'Typical! I wonder what they want for a Ninety-Nine,' said Sue.

'More than I'd give, I'll be bound.'

Sue gave Sue a look and Sue shunted her.

Muchtar licked his Mr Softie disconsolately. 'I think you said some very interesting things,' said Sue. 'My dad says we've lost our sense of mission.'

'He's right,' said Muchtar. 'You don't even know how to teach any more.'

'It's terrible,' agreed Sue. 'My sister's eldest, Shaun, is nine and he can't even read the big words on the back of a Rice Krispies packet. I know because I tried to get him to.'

'Well, "crackle" is a bit of a mouthful, but he should be able to manage "snap" and "pop" by now,' said Sue.

'All my children were reading Enid Blyton by the time they were seven. And they could read in Bahasa Malay and Arabic also!' said Muchtar proudly.

'You don't say!' said Sue.

'I blame the teachers,' said Sue. She saw the students wandering off. 'Don't wander off!' she called.

'I do not see wisdom anywhere! And I cannot understand!' said Muchtar. 'My teacher never says, "Make the students memorize! Make them learn! Have them study for three hours every night!" And everyone laughs at me when I suggest it. But how else can you learn? How else?'

'Search me,' said Sue.

'It's all projects these days,' added Sue.

'What a bloody skive they were!' said Sue.

Muchtar munched on his cone, pushing it into his mouth. Then he rubbed his hands together gleefully, as if an idea had come. He chewed his ice-cream quickly.

'I couldn't do that. I've got sensitive teeth,' said Sue.

'You ought to soak them in *Sterident*,' said Sue.

'What do you mean, *soak*? Silly cow!'

Muchtar ignored the two Sues. 'I am going to speak!' he said. 'I am going to tell the English what I think of them!'

'Do you think you ought?' asked Sue.

'Don't you want to see Buckingham Palace?' added Sue.

'No. This is where I should be. I have a mission. I see it now,' said Muchtar.

'But you haven't got a soapbox.'

209

'I don't need a soapbox.' And Muchtar strode away from the two Sues to an empty space between the anti-vivisectionist and the Catholic Evidence Guild. The Sues followed, looking at one another.

'Ladies and gentlemen!' began Muchtar. 'I have some-thing important to tell you . . .'

The group of students from Demolish Babel wandered across to Muchtar, wondering what was afoot. They were soon joined by others, along with two policemen.

At home that night, Rachel put down the phone angrily. She looked up at her books to console her, grabbed for one at random, sat down and started to leaf through it.

Volume 2 of *English for Your World*, first published seven years before, was, if her friend at Tongue to Tongue Publishing was right, not going to console her for much longer. Her friend Joanna had just come out of a meeting of the editorial board of the publishers. Professor Salt had dropped his bombshell. Time for a return to Square One.

Rachel leafed through the textbook. True, it had dated. Mrs Thatcher frowned out at her from the opening page of unit 3. She looked combative yet callow. Almost young . . . Next to her *The Belgrano* was sinking. When Rachel had written the text, just after the Falklands War, her head had been full of Argentinian students from her time in Buenos Aires. She had been angry and had forged the unit around Mrs Thatcher's wartime speeches. But what had seemed then like being relevant, on the ball, to the point, now had the sepia quality of a period piece.

She turned over page after page. Michael Jackson looked black, Sid Vicious alive, Docklands only half-finished. Rachel closed the book and put it back in its place. She made herself a cup of coffee.

The trouble was that Tongue to Tongue Publishing did not seem to be in any hurry for an update of the course, an update she could see was in order. No, if Joanna was to be believed – and usually she was – Professor Salt had persuaded the publishers to embark on a new set of textbooks. And it did not look as if they would have her name on the covers. Rather, the name that Joanna had heard mentioned was Jordan Bostock.

She thought of Professor Salt's speech at the Welcome Dinner. At the time she had thought the booze was to blame for what he had been saying. It was absurd to go back to the discredited methodologies of decades ago, wasn't it? They hadn't worked then. Or, if they had worked, they had bored students rigid. Why should they suddenly work now? Still, it was clear that the knives were out for her eclectic approach. The pulping machine had started to make mincemeat of her professional life; the presses to churn out a success-story for someone else.

'Nathan!' she called. Her cry up the stairs, designed to penetrate his Walkman headset, came out as a screech of need. 'Nathan, come down here a minute, please!'

Strangely, Nathan was at her side before she had thought to repeat her call. 'Yes, Mum?' he asked.

'You look tidy,' she said.

He shrugged, then smiled at her. She clasped his hair with her fingers, kissed him, and he did not pull away. She hugged him in the old way. 'I've had some news,' she said. 'I want us to go and stay up at Heathcliff College. Of course, you don't have to come if you'd rather not. I could make arrangements with Dot if you'd rather.'

'I like it up there,' said Nathan.

'Do you?'

'Yes.'

'OK. Let's pack a bag. Don't worry about forgetting things. We can come back. You may have to sleep with me tonight, but I expect we'll find you a room after that. Bring your study-books, though.'

He went off upstairs, taking them two at a time.

The telephone rang. Rachel answered it and listened to Dennis.

'Yes, I'm on my way to the school anyway,' she told him. 'Yes, Dennis, I'll be staying there from now on. Don't worry.'

211

She listened to his woes in her practised manner. At last he let her go.

Of course, she knew why Dennis was in such a state. He was realizing the implications of losing his licence. It was not as if the summer school was any different from previous years. It was always a ship with a loose command-structure. There were enough people who were prepared to stop things from degenerating. This year there had been an unfortunate combination of circumstance. Nothing could have stopped that, could it?

She thought of Eisa; of her argument with Arthur and the driver. But she had needed to be back in London. Anyway, they had left students behind before. It had been a baptism by fire visited upon at least one unfortunate. Usually the victim managed to get back, like a Scout from a night hike, to be congratulated and given a drink.

But perhaps that would have to stop. If Ezekiel had been left behind, for instance, would he have had the money to get back to London? People concealed their poverty with great guile most of the time, hid it behind a token of wealth. That is what Ezekiel's son would do with Nathan's cast-off shellsuit. It would become an icon . . . *My dad went to England and brought me this.* Like so many of the designer items that poor people wore – the trainers, sweatshirts, cheap watches dressed up to look like Rolex – they were just a talisman to ward off cries of *Poor boy!*, to instil some self-respect, skin-deep, but it was the skin that was important, that blushed, burned and bruised.

Rachel wrote in her organizer, *Stipends for scholarship students*, then added, *See how Eisa is,* zipped closed her bag and called up to Nathan.

'What, Mum?'

He was standing beside her, two large grips packed to bursting. She had not heard him come downstairs. 'You're taking a lot, young man,' she said.

Normally she would have expected him to moan, as had been his custom. But he did no such thing.

212

'Let's get going,' he said.

It was worrying really.

'Of course, I'm hoping against hope that I'm not. I could have got away with it, I suppose,' Arthur said.

'The drill is that we'll draw some blood and test it. We should have the results by five this evening.'

'I'll be here,' said Arthur.

'That's fine. Ask for me at Reception.'

The counsellor then ushered Arthur outside to wait his turn.

As he turned the pages of his newspaper in the waiting-area, Arthur saw Sebastian Palumbo coming through a door, in company with a nurse who was doing his best to make himself understood. Instead of approaching to see if he could help, Arthur lifted the newspaper higher, blotting the sight, and the implications, out.

It was not until an hour later, when Arthur arrived for the second hour of his class, a plaster on his arm, that he was able to stop going over the ramifications of the test he had just taken, both for himself and for the people of his village. In a few hours the results would be known, sentence be passed. He set about marking the work he had left for his students. A tear came to his eye which he did not wipe away fast enough.

'What's matter, Teacher?' Amy from Finland asked him as he pored over her paper.

Her beauty made him feel faint. 'The, you forgot the, lovey,' he told her. 'What's the matter? There's nothing the matter.'

'So why you are crying?'

'Almost. "So why are you crying?"'

'So why are you crying?'

As she repeated the question Amy's eyes widened, twin lakes of pure blue. Her flawless skin, her golden hair, pricked his tear-ducts again. What did she know? What need had she to dread? Back home in all-day Finland, doubtless with young-looking parents, a couple of Volvos, skis piled up against an outside wall, lakes and friends and marriage after university, crèches and saunas in the winter dark. As warm as toast, insulated from the freezing cold by thick wood walls.

'I wasn't crying. I've got something in my eye,' he said.

'No, Arthur. You are sad.'

'I'm homesick for Egypt,' he said. And he commenced marking her paper, circling mistakes, cutting huge flamboyant red ticks, cancelling large crosses, like graves, down the page of her work.

He taught them on automatic pilot, thinking of Abdul-Kadir, who was engaged and would shortly be marrying. He had to take back a gift for him. But Abdul-Kadir had been his regular for about six months, until Samir the boatman had happened along. And he, Arthur, holding back for a while, had then fallen for Shukry, the policeman, who had handed him on to friends . . .

I didn't know . . ., he kept repeating to himself.

Yes, I did. I knew. But the passion was stronger than the knowledge. My lust longer than my attention-span.

'I'm going to tell you a story. It's a very simple story. Pay careful attention.' He drew a donkey on the board, a smiling donkey. He drew it in a few seconds, making it appear as simple to do as a Chinese character must be to a Chinese. Then two men beside the donkey. Some villagers. A few lines showed the outline of an Arab village behind.

'This is Abdul and this is Abdul's father, Ali. And this is . . .' He pointed to Pablo.

'A donkey.'

'Yes, but whose donkey is it, Pablo?'

'Their donkey.'

'Correct. Abdul and Ali were going to market with their donkey.' He pointed to Amy. 'Who is going to market?'

Amy answered him. He did not hear her. Those blue eyes caught him again. He pulled away, staring at the village on the board.

214

'I think we'll continue this tomorrow,' he told them. 'Can you get on with your worksheets?'

They looked at him. Then those who had understood searched for the worksheets and those who had not understood watched and imitated.

Arthur rubbed the village off the board. Slapping the dust from his hands, he wandered round the class. *Please, let me have got away with it! Please! It could have been a dirty needle! Harry had some injections at the clinic. Please!*

Eisa looked up from his work. Arthur went over to help him.

'Ezekiel,' Rachel called to her student as he was leaving the classroom in company with Muchtar. 'Can I talk to you for a moment?'

'Certainly.' He watched her watching the door to see off the other students. Then she turned to him. He waited for her to ask for Nathan's belongings back. His room was full of them. He was already worried about the flight home.

'I didn't want to talk to you in front of the others,' she said. 'The thing is that I've got a couple of spare seats for the theatre tonight and I was wondering whether you'd like one. It's a play at the National Theatre. *Worlds Away*. It's quite good, I believe.'

She saw him look unsure and realized. 'They're complimentary. Free. We have bought a dozen and get two free. Could you use one of them? I'm giving the other ticket to Eisa.'

He smiled at her. 'I've not ever been to the theatre,' he said.

'Well, you might enjoy this one. It's had very good reviews. Don't worry about making your own way there. A coach will take us. Nathan's coming, too.'

'That's very good. We are friends.'

'I know that,' she said. 'What's your secret?'

'My secret?'

'Yes, Nathan's been in such a good mood since he met you. I don't know what you did, but I wish you'd give me the recipe.'

Ezekiel shrugged. 'I like him,' he said. 'He is a kind boy. A good heart.'

'Thank you,' said Rachel, choosing to take the compliment to include herself. 'And how are things going generally? Are you enjoying the course?'

'Oh, yes. Thank you. I am learning many new things. Of course, some of the techniques I cannot put into practice with my students. The procedures with overhead projectors, videos and et cetera. We do not have electricity at the school. Not yet. Still, I will remember what you taught and keep it all in my head for the day when these things come. The simpler things I will act upon. The flannel boards and flashcards, I am looking forward to trying. Also, the Oral Reconstruction.'

Rachel did not know what else to say. 'We'll have an early dinner. Just wait outside the main entrance at six-thirty. You'll see Nathan there, I expect.'

Ezekiel hesitated. Then he said, 'I hope you are not feeling very bad.'

She looked at him. 'How do you mean?'

'About Eisa. I am a teacher, too. I know how you must feel. He was your responsibility. You must feel that you let him down. I can understand that. It is a very heavy burden.'

Rachel bothered her fringe back. 'Yes . . . well . . . I'd better get on.'

'Thank you,' he said.

'Thank you?'

'For the chance to see a theatre.' And he aimed a smile in her direction that made her step back a pace.

'It's nothing,' she said.

'No,' he replied. 'It is far, far away from being nothing.'

*   *   *

216

'This evening's performance of *Worlds Away* will commence in the Olivier theatre in five minutes,' said the Tannoy.

'God,' said Rachel. 'Where're Ezekiel and Nathan? I was a fool to let them wander off.'

'They went to see the view from the top balcony,' said Lynn, rounding up stray students, zooming into Rachel's orbit, then flying out of it again.

'But that was ages ago!' She turned abruptly in the queue and found herself hard against Eisa. 'Well, at least you're staying close,' she said.

Eisa smiled but did not say anything. He stood next to a subdued Arthur. Rachel tried to melt the ice with Eisa by telling him that if they were late they'd miss the first half. They wouldn't be allowed in until a suitable break in the performance.

Eisa nodded. Then he looked at Arthur. But Arthur hardly responded. Rachel noticed, but the queue was moving fast and she readied the clump of tickets to be checked. 'It's too late now,' she told a group of students in front of her. 'I've got their tickets,' she told the usher, who had his hand out but had been given nothing.

'Mum!'

'Where have you been? You almost missed it.'

Ezekiel replied for Nathan. 'We saw the view. The river, St Paul, everything,' he said.

'Right, come on. Don't get lost again.' She looked around. 'Where's Lynn?'

'I'm here,' said Lynn. She was standing next to Arthur, pushing her hand under his arm.

'Right, everyone. Follow me!' said Rachel. 'We're row B.'

There was another log-jam as the group of Demolish Babel students passed through the corridor and got their first sight of the huge theatre, already almost full. Rachel had to direct them to their seats. She stood at the end of the row and told them to move right through to the end. She excused herself past three patient inhabitants of the first seats, settling down into her seat, like a cork sealing a bottle.

The stage was bare, its surface covered in what looked like gravel raked into lines of latitude and longitude. It seemed an odd acting-surface. She could already imagine each step of the actors scrunching the gravel, distracting her from following. She looked along the row. Arthur was looking at his hands while Lynn whispered to him across Eisa. She had never seen Arthur so subdued. She would ask Lynn at the interval. Farther along the row she could see Ezekiel staring at the stage. He nodded once or twice, responding to whatever Nathan was saying to him.

The lights went down. The hum of the audience abated. Ezekiel did not think he had ever been in such dark. He tried to stare through it to see what was happening on the stage. A scream from every loudspeaker made him jump. 'Oh my God!' he exclaimed.

'Shh!' said Nathan, delighted.

A single beam of light from the stage caught the audience. It swung back and forth, taking in the whole theatre, stalls and circle, slowly, section by section. Then it was extinguished, the stage lit up by a bright light that made him blink, seemed like the desert at home at midday. But the stage was different. In the time between the dimming of the lights and now – how long? thirty seconds? – a small bungalow had been erected. He could see into the main room where a middle-aged woman was sitting at her desk. A fan rotated above her. Beside the house there was a tree, but only that.

There was a knock on the door of the room. An elderly man came in, wearing the robes of a priest. The pair talked. Ezekiel worried because he could not take in what they were saying, so concerned was he with watching a group of blacks treading stealthily around the bungalow, machetes and pistols in their hands. He wanted to tell the couple inside the bungalow to watch out. Something terrible was going to happen.

Then the priest took the woman in his arms and they embraced. Did they know what was about to happen? He tried to concentrate. The blacks were getting closer. The man who seemed to be the leader, a cartridge-belt swung

218

diagonally across his sweating chest, was staring at the couple through the louvered window leading on to the veranda. Then he and his companions were still.

The couple were talking again. Should they go or should they stay? Ezekiel wanted to tell them that either way it was curtains for them. There did not seem to be any place to hide. The only thing they could do to save their lives was to offer the robbers everything they had. They might be spared. It was hard to tell. He closed his eyes for a moment when the woman made to open the door to the veranda. But the dark only made the suspense worse. When he opened his eyes again the woman was holding the door half-open and the leader of the robbers had his machete raised in the air, preparing to strike.

'Missis! Don't!' Ezekiel called out.

From all around came a chorus of shushes and comments. Rachel looked along the row. Nathan smiled happily. Ezekiel pushed himself down in his seat to watch between the heads of the people in front what would take place.

The woman opened wide the door on to the veranda, looked out over the audience and said. *This is my home! I do not want to be anywhere else!* Her face was exultant. She stepped outside into the blinding sun. Then the sun went out and strobe lights caught the carnage. As in a silent film, the priest moved behind the woman and machetes from the other stealthy men came together and fell and rose and fell and rose, sending streaks of ghastly light around the theatre.

Then the Africans disappeared and the couple, caught by a single beam from the back of the theatre, covered in wounds and in dripping blood, fell together, but slowly, slowly, swooning to death in one another's arms. The light went out.

'No!' gasped Ezekiel.

'Shh!'

'Oh, very terrible!'

But the darkness clung only for a moment. The stage lit up in a trice to show the same African who had wielded

219

the machete dressed in a suit behind a large glass-topped desk. He was speaking on a white telephone. There were many telephones on the desk. Ezekiel knew such men. He sat patiently and humbly outside the offices of such men, waiting to be admitted to plead for chalk, for desks, for unpaid salary. But this man sat at his desk set upon the raked gravel. He did not have a house. Where had it gone? And how had he managed to get into that suit? He did not seem to be sweating at all now. And what about the bungalow and the bodies? Where was the blood?

A white man came in and started talking to the African. Two white missionaries had been murdered at their mission station some years before. The Pope, the man said, wanted to make the priest a saint. What did the minister think of that?

The minister replied that he had other things on his mind. The desert was encroaching. There was a civil war to fight. His people were dying in the famine. But, as long as the investigators from the Vatican were not intrusive, permission to investigate the priest's life would be given. The two men parted amicably enough, arranging to meet one another for a round of golf at the Club.

Ezekiel nodded happily, for the scene had contained much that he knew but had never talked about. The ex-patriot minister who had fought for independence by fair means and foul who then, when power was offered, sipped, quaffed, forgot the people he had been fighting for, became a stranger insulated by Mercedes' windscreens and sharp shiny suits; who lowered automatic windows to beat with an ivory-tipped cane the poor who came to sell him simple things from a tray.

Black again. Ezekiel waited for the next miracle. Lights up on an English drawing-room set up on the gravel. Lights shone only on the room. A woman entered the room whom Ezekiel thought he knew. Yes, it was the woman who had been done to death in the bungalow. So what had happened? Had she really only been wounded? There did not seem to be any scars.

'But she's dead!' Ezekiel told Nathan.

'We've gone back in time,' Nathan whispered back.

Of course.

The woman seemed very upset because her father was dying. The doctor left shaking his head. An older woman entered whom the dead woman called 'Mother', though she did not look old enough to be mother to this girl. She said that her father had passed away. The woman looked sad. The two women talked for a long time about what the man had meant to them both but, when alone, the daughter did not look sad at all. She looked straight out at the audience, exultant, as though life were about to begin for her. Ezekiel fancied she was looking at him and returned to her a look of reproach.

'Why isn't she sad?' Ezekiel asked Nathan as darkness returned.

'Search me,' said Nathan.

'Ungrateful daughter!'

The stage was bare, and the priest came on. He was young, too, and he gave a sermon about serving the missions and converting the benighted heathen. The young woman who had just lost her father came up to the priest after the sermon was over. She wanted to devote her riches to the performance of good acts. She wanted to be a missionary.

The priest asked the woman what she felt she had to contribute. The woman did not answer. She and the priest froze on the stage, and Ezekiel sighed audibly. He had wanted to hear how the woman would answer.

The frozen couple went into the dark. He thought he could see their ghosts walking towards the wings. Then another priest was interrogating an old woman. She had been the housekeeper at the mission. She had loved Father and Sister. Yes, there had been miracles. A man of the village, blind since birth, had miraculously received sight; a woman wasting away had been restored to health . . .

The action shifted to the other side of the stage. The priest kissed the men Ezekiel recognized as his murderers, now dressed in rags and holding crutches. The priest touched the men. They threw away their crutches and began to dance. Again and again the priest embraced the maimed and deformed. Ezekiel drew in a sharp intake of breath when the priest kissed a man whose face was covered in sores. The man swooned into his rug, emerging in a second, his face bright and smooth.

'Miracles!' shouted Ezekiel.

The stage was aglow with light and the sound of the restored men dancing on the gravel. The light grew in intensity and seemed to concentrate upon the priest in the centre of the stage with the people dancing their joy around him. He lifted his arms up and out to the audience. The light around him became unbearable. Ezekiel made to stand with the exaltation he felt at the sound and light and glory of it. Nathan tried unsuccessfully to pull him back to earth. Then all went black and he collapsed back into his seat.

There was a silence and then a whoosh of applause. The lights went on.

'It isn't finished?' asked Ezekiel.

'No, it's the interval. Let's ask Mum for an ice-cream,' Nathan said.

They filed out into the foyer. Ezekiel found himself being looked at by the people who had been behind him. They smiled and nodded at him, and he smiled and nodded back.

'What's the matter, Arthur?' Eisa asked, seeing Arthur rubbing at his tears. Eisa had not understood what was going on but had, like Ezekiel, loved the effects.

'Nothing, lovey. It's good, isn't it?'

'Yes, Arthur,' Eisa said.

'Don't you think it's a bit predictable?' Rachel said to Lynn.

'Well, if it is, I don't know what to predict,' said Lynn quietly.

'Well, it's obvious, isn't it? The minister's going to stop the priest from being canonized by exposing his affair with the woman.'

'Is he? How does he know?'

'Because he saw them at it before he murdered them.'

'You mean the minister was one of the murderers?'

' 'Course! How could you have missed that?'

Lynn thought about that. 'Well, I must admit that it crossed my mind but I just couldn't believe he'd changed so fast.'

'They use Velcro,' said Rachel. 'You notice he didn't turn his back to the audience. Probably that suit was just something over his front tied with Velcro.'

'But what would be the point of him stopping the canonization?'

'I'm not sure really. Perhaps it would strike a blow against neo-colonialism. Something like that.'

'Maybe,' said Lynn. 'I like the effects.'

'So does Ezekiel. I thought he was going to get us chucked out once or twice.'

'It's nice to see somebody carried away by it all. We've been spoiled by CinemaScope,' said Lynn.

Rachel looked at Lynn. They wandered around the bookshop. As Lynn showed her a postcard of Peter O'Toole, Rachel asked, 'What's the matter with Arthur?'

'Arthur?'

'Yes. He looks like a wet weekend. What's the matter?'

'Doesn't Peter O'Toole look young?'

'Lynn . . .'

'I'm not supposed to tell anyone, Rachel.'

'It can only be one thing.'

'You know, then.'

'He's got it, hasn't he?'

'I didn't tell you,' Lynn said.

The bell rang. Rachel and Lynn circled the Demolish Babel students like sheepdogs, aiming them back towards the classroom of miracles.

'You have gone out hungry for sensation into the starved world and let them feed you. They thought that your colour and cultural credentials would ensure that you bestowed a blessing on them, that you would lift them

223

up to your exalted level. Poor fools! They – child-like – allowed you to keep your delusions, to stay childish, to live within your pampered flesh as they never could, as you never deserved. For what did you give them, after all?'

'Yes! That's the speech! How did you remember it?' Lynn asked Arthur.

'I've got that sort of brain. Some things stick. Only some, mind. I know when I am hearing certain things that I'll remember them. It never fails.'

They were sitting in the almost-empty common room. The bar had closed half an hour before, but Arthur and Lynn had got themselves a stock in, a stock they had almost exhausted.

'It's funny. That was the speech that hit home with me, too,' she said. 'The play had begun to lose me in the second half. I suppose I believed that Rachel had got it right. And there weren't so many dazzling effects after the interval, were there?'

'The gunshots had that African chap going wild,' said Arthur, remembering the way his seat had jolted as Ezekiel had jumped up in alarm.

'Ezekiel really had a good time. You didn't seem to, though.'

'Good-*ish*, as Molly would say. But I had other things on my mind.'

'Of course. Do you feel better now?' Lynn asked, concerned again.

'*Ish*,' he said. 'The trouble is that, even though I'd been expecting it, it still came as a shock. I'd thought that if I thought I had it hard enough it would mean I didn't.'

'Well, you've just got to keep yourself fit.'

'I shouldn't be doing this,' Arthur said, gesturing to the line of pints.

'Me neither. I'm getting much too fond of it for my own good. Maybe we should both quit tomorrow.'

Arthur looked at his watch. 'It already is.'

'So that's it, then. Cheers!'

'Do you know what really hurts?' Arthur asked. He did not look to her for a response. He had to say it, if only once.

224

And he might as well say it to Lynn before he made his general confession. 'I feel like a murderer.' Lynn started to speak, but he held up his hand. 'I knew about this disease in 1982. I can remember reading an article in *Time*. Of course, I was fascinated and appalled all at the same time. I combed the papers for information. As the years passed I heard of friends who had died. But I never put my knowledge into practice. God, I should have been going around the village putting up posters, but I didn't. I had built up quite a little fan-club. Never in all those years did I think to apply my knowledge to the situation in our backwater. I fucked about as if everything was as per normal. But I knew, I *knew*.'

'It's no good blaming yourself. There's lots we know that we don't act upon,' said Lynn.

'You're right. It's no good at all. Do you know how many people I could have infected?' He looked over at Lynn. She took a sip from her drink to avoid his eyes but when she had finished he was still looking at her. She shook her head.

'Neither do I. Lots. Harry for starters. I keep thinking of collapsing sets of dominoes. One after another they fall.'

'It's the booze talking. You've had a shocking day. Things will look better in the morning.'

'No, they won't, Lynn. I've been living with this knowledge for a year or more. Until today it was possible to think that maybe – hope against hope – I wouldn't have been to blame. But not now. Not ever again.'

Lynn fought for something to say. A phrase came. She knew it was lame as she said it. 'Don't be too hard on yourself.'

He looked at her. Then, still looking, he reached for his pint, raised it to his lips and drained the glass. He stood up. 'I'm going for a walk,' he said.

'Do you think you ought to? It's very late.'

'Yes, it is rather.' And he walked away from her, stepping over a carpet of ruined newspapers.

Lynn sat back in her seat, holding her glass on her collar-bone. No, she hardly had a problem at all, compared with Arthur. If Keith did not show up, it would not be the end of the world. She could go off with Molly, could go back to Leominster to lick her wounds. Of course, her garden in Kano would wither, Friday be let down. But she had let things wither before, forgotten about people she had never thought she would forget, shaken continents of dust from her feet. In a minute she had even forgotten about Arthur. God, I'm shallow! she thought. Shallow enough to bash your brains out.

She was about to gather her courage together to get up and return to her room when Eric Trotter walked into the common room.

'What are you doing, Lynn, there on your own?'

'I was just going,' she said.

'Don't go. Look what I've got.' Dr Trotter reached into his jacket pocket, bringing out a half-bottle of gin. 'I hate drinking alone.'

'You shouldn't be drinking at all.'

He thought about that. 'Don't you start. No, I shouldn't. Still, you know what expats are like. We drink to forget.' He held out the bottle over her glass.

'Go on, then,' she said. He poured her an inch and sat down. 'Why do expats drink to forget, do you think?' she asked.

He thought about that, sipping on his gin, poured into an empty used glass on the table. 'We've seen too much, Lynn. Too many friends made and lost, too many houses assembled and disassembled. But in my own case I think it's disappointment. I was always looking for another country, one that I could throw myself into heart and soul. I never found it, of course. I don't suppose it exists. We know something that the stand-stills don't. We understand our strangeness on the earth. We've proved to our own dissatisfaction how the world turns perfectly well without our presence. Blowing in and blowing out, we cause hardly a ripple. I think that's why I drink. Of course, It might be something else.'

'Like what?'

'Like loving to be blotto.' He poured himself some more.

'Where were you this evening? It was very quiet here.'

'We went to the theatre.'

'I've got my dose still to come. It's Stratford next Saturday. If I can get shut of the trouble and strife, I might get reacquainted with Flowers Bitter. I'm very partial to it. Was the play good?'

'It made me think,' said Lynn.

'I wouldn't think too much if I were you. Where's Arthur?'

'He's gone out for a walk.'

'More fool him. He's missing a nice spot of hooch.'

'He'd already had enough.'

'Is Molly better?'

'She wasn't this morning,' said Lynn, remembering that she hadn't thought to pop in. 'Pop in,' she said out loud.

'Sorry?' asked Dr Trotter.

'Nothing, I was just thinking,' said Lynn.

Arthur sat on the bench on the West Heath which Astrid had come to with Satoko and Mitsuko two weeks before. The world was going round. He sat up straight and breathed deeply. It did little good, and he lay down on the bench, looking up at the few stars to escape the influence of the city's lights. The sight of their denuded light made him think of the dense stars of Egypt, and he longed to be sitting in his cane chair outside his house there, waiting to see what would come out of the night.

Then that pleasant thought turned to wormwood, made him nauseous, and he sat to attention again, willing the sickness away. He thought about his future. There were going to be a lot of such feelings to fight.

A dry stick cracked behind him, but he didn't look round. He could imagine what had caused it. Behind the trees a quiet urgent form of life was proceeding as it had always proceeded. He knew because he had been there. Only last year he had left a lethargic Harry on several occasions to walk into the exciting dark of the

West Heath. Had he been careful? He could not remember. It took alcohol to give him the courage to venture out, so, if he could not remember, it probably meant that he hadn't been.

It comforted him strangely to know that he was not the only fool who courted death for himself and others. No, he was not the only fool. The only difference between the invisible shadows and himself was that now he *knew*. But had he not always known? No, I didn't; not really, he told himself.

Then he thought of a Thai student from a past summer school, a woman called Nee. For some reason, though she was not in his class, she had tagged on to Harry and Arthur, gone around with them. She had worked at a refuge for women in Bangkok and had told them what brought women to knock on her door. After the summer school had finished, Nee had sent them bookmarks and little postcard-sized embroideries made by the women.

Nee had told them of two sisters who had escaped from a brothel by jumping from a second-floor window. One had sustained severe back injuries in the fall. The other was already blind from some unnamed venereal disease. They had found their way to the refuge and told their story to Nee. Both had been sent to Bangkok by their parents, hill-tribe people who thought they would get jobs as domestic servants. But that had not happened, and the girls had soon found themselves enslaved in a brothel.

Later Nee wrote that the girls had died of AIDS, communicated to them by the foreign tourists who came to Thailand for the free-wheeling flesh, for whom worries stopped at the frenzied airport. The Thai government had kept quiet about the disease, for fear of frightening away the tourists. And the two girls, not yet seventeen, had died.

Somehow he and Harry had lost touch with Nee. This happened after every summer school.

Thinking of Nee, imagining her angry beside him, Arthur stood up. He felt dizzy but ignored it. Then he walked back into the undergrowth.

He reached a clearing. Shadowy forms of men, some with cigarettes, the red glow illuminating faces for a moment as they pulled on them. Arthur walked to the centre of the clearing and stood there, swaying. Then he started shouting in his teacher's voice:

'Stop it! Just stop it! Don't you see what you are doing? You're risking your own lives and the lives of the people you fuck about with! Hardly any of you are sober! Stop it! Learn from someone who knows, who has learned the hard way!'

He looked around and he was alone in the clearing, the unaccustomed noise having frightened the nervy residents. He moved on, towards Jack Straw's Castle, stopping every few yards to shout into the invisible undergrowth. 'I've got the virus! I didn't think it would happen to me but it has! Now stop what you're doing and go home. Sober up and find yourself a friend! I know why you're here! I *understand*! But you have to put life first! You have to put your brothers first! Stop killing one another! Stop it!'

A voice from the distant undergrowth told him to fuck off. He pursued the voice, marching towards it in the same way as he had marched down the aisle between desks in classrooms to chastise a cheeky student. He elbowed the branches of trees apart. The undergrowth seemed so thick that it would stop him passing through. He saw himself caught in it, his eye put out, his clothes ripped, surrendering to its secrets, lying down to sleep. But with a mighty effort he was through.

He was alone, the noise having put the nervous men to flight. He was sad that they had gone. He wanted them around. He wanted his prodigal brothers to understand how he felt. An owl hooted. The siren of a police-car on the West Heath Road. He leaned against a tree trunk and then slid down it and sat, listening to the retreating siren, the advancing silence which soon, apart from the pulsing of blood in his ears, became the only sound.

Arthur looked out through the black branches of trees. And a thought came to him, as clear and sad as the hoot of the owl. *When the time comes, the burden*

229

too great, when I see pity in friends' faces, when I weave and stumble, I shall come to a place like this. A pine forest. A palm plantation. I shall seek out the thickest, most wooded part. The densest part of the forest. There I shall settle myself down with a bottle and some pills. He thought of Abdul-Karim, the liberal pharmacist; he thought of Adnan, the Copt who made strong liquor. Yes, it would be easy. *And nobody will know.*

Arthur Arthur passed out. After some minutes a stick broke under a foot, a branch was parted and sprang back. The life of the West Heath slowly got back to normal as if he had never been there.

'Guess what?' said Sue, twiddling the car-keys of Dennis's car.

'What?' asked Sue.

'Yes, what?' added Sue.

'This may well be the last summer school,' said Sue. 'Dennis said he's tired of all the hassles.'

'Come off it!' said Sue. 'He just *said* that.'

'No,' said Sue. 'He didn't just say it. He means it.'

'Pull the other one,' said Sue.

Sue ignored Sue. 'So how did you come upon this information, Sue?' she asked.

'Dennis was talking on his car phone.'

'That's typical Dennis, isn't it?' said Sue.

'How do you mean?'

'Car phone. It's typical. You'd think he could wait. They cost a bomb.'

'He puts it down against tax,' said Sue.

'Yes, but it's so typical,' said Sue.

'He was talking to his chum at the British Council. He sounded really pissed off with all the things that have been going wrong. The drink-driving was the last straw.'

'That hundred and fifty pounds Molly lost can't have helped.'

'No. He went through everything that had gone wrong. Then he said it.'

'What?' asked Sue.

'Time to call it a day,' said Sue, mimicking Dennis.

Eisa came into the office. 'Hello, misses,' he said.

' "Miss," ' corrected Sue.

' "Ms" would be better,' said Sue.

'But you are three,' said Eisa.

'How may we be of assistance?' said Sue.

'Sorry?'

'He doesn't understand,' said Sue, wondering if she had time to seek out Sebastian Palumbo. Maybe she could call him out of class. It would be a bit brazen, but she was suddenly feeling a bit brazen.

'What do you want, Eisa?' said Sue. 'Why aren't you in class?' asked Sue.

Eisa clapped his hand. 'That is! No teacher. Where Mr Arthur?'

'Isn't he with you?'

'No. I am come for this. No Mr Arthur. Class is very sad.'

Sue got up. 'I'll come with you. We'll check his room. What's the number, Sue?'

'Two five nine Churchill,' said Sue.

'Come with me, Eisa.'

'He is fine?' asked Eisa.

'He's probably overslept,' said Sue. 'How are you, Eisa?'

They were walking along the corridor of Churchill. From an open door a cleaner was singing. 'I doubt even Arthur could sleep through that.'

'I am fine,' said Eisa.

'This is Arthur's room.' She tried it. 'It's locked. Arthur! Arthur!' she called. There was no answer. 'No, it doesn't look as if he's there. Let's try Molly's.'

Sue knocked on Molly's door. She went in, to be greeted by the sight of eleven students ranged around Molly's bed on the floor. Astrid was holding up a large sheet of paper while Molly talked about incorrect usage of apostrophes.

'Sorry to interrupt, Molly,' said Sue. 'Have you seen Arthur?'

231

'No, I haven't. Not for a couple of days. Not since I've been here, in fact. When you find him you can tell him I'd like a visit. You've tried his room, have you?'

'Yes, I have.'

Molly beamed when she saw Eisa. 'And how's my favourite?' she asked him.

'I am worry, miss. No teacher.'

'I don't know where he could be,' said Molly.

Sue ushered Eisa out of the room, thanking Molly. She walked with him to the classroom in the Finchley Road. There, all of Arthur's students sat chatting.

'I'll ask Lynn,' she told Eisa, leaving him in class.

Lynn was relieved to hear Sue's knock. She had been getting into deep water with Ursula over the use of 'one' in place of 'you'. Lynn had been saying that she thought it outmoded and pretentious; that she never used it. Ursula responded that she had heard it on the radio. 'Ah, Sue,' said Lynn.

'Sorry to disturb you. Have you seen Arthur? He isn't in class.'

'I thought something was the matter. It's been so quiet.'

She told the class to study their books and went outside with Sue. 'I was with him last night. He was a bit down, to tell you the truth. Not like Arthur at all. He left me at about midnight to go for a walk. I haven't seen him since.'

'God. More trouble,' said Sue. 'I don't know what Dennis will say. He's terminally fed up with the summer school as it is.'

'There's no need to tell him just yet, is there? He may turn up before the morning's out.'

'But what about his class?'

'I'll go up and give them some work to do. That's no problem. Nothing for me?' she asked without hope.

'No. Sorry.'

'I don't know why I ask.'

'Don't give up,' said Sue.

'No.' She shook herself. 'I'd better see about Arthur's class.'

She went up the stairs, wondering what she could give

232

the class to keep them amused. She opened the door without knocking.

'Arthur! You've turned up!' she said.

He had turned in the act of drawing on the board. A perfect village. God, he was good at drawing! She had forgotten. 'Yes, Lynn lovey. Back. Better late than never.' He looked towards the class.

'Better late than never!' they repeated.

'Sue was worried about you,' said Lynn. 'Where were you?'

'Later, lovey. Later.'

Lynn left him and went back to her class. She hoped that Ursula had forgotten her query, but as soon as she had installed herself behind the teacher's table Ursula said, 'We were talking about "one" . . .'

'Yes. As I say, it is a form that I don't use either orally or in writing. Still, I will concede that it *is* used. If you do use it, just make sure you use it consistently. For example, don't say: "One enjoys the theatre, don't you?" You should say, "One enjoys the theatre, doesn't one?"' She winced as she said it.

'But the sentence sounds correct. "One enjoys the theatre, don't you?"'

'Er . . . yes, I suppose it can be correct in a certain context. Er . . .' She heard banging from Arthur's class, followed by laughter. Playing for time, she wrote the two sentences on the board while Ursula watched her. As she wrote she desperately tried to think how the sentences worked. How am I going to get out of this?

'Er . . .,' she began, looking at Ursula. She explained the difference, looking at the young German girl who seemed to have the world on a string. She'd probably already started a pension plan, had a neat box with stocks and shares, a pretty little runabout, a fiancé in computers, everything in order. What, if she knew, would Ursula make of the chaos of Lynn's life? What would she think?

'Your explanation does not satisfy me,' said Ursula.

'Well, let's try another way,' said Lynn. No, she can see how I am through my teaching. It's as messy as the rest

233

of me. She knows! I am transparent to her. Before this blue-eyed success-story I'm a diseased body in a scanner. She can see right through me. 'Do you mind if we discuss this later, Ursula? I need to prepare. The problem with "one" is not the main point of the lesson, and I think I'm ignoring the rest of the class. I'll prepare you a more cogent explanation by tomorrow.'

Ursula nodded and looked down at her desk.

'Open your books at page seventy-nine,' Lynn said. 'Masood, read.'

I can't do it any more, she thought. I can't teach anything to anyone. I can no longer make them believe my bluff.

'Stop there, Masood,' she said. 'Try to give a falling intonation in that question. Listen. "What, then, is the answer to the conundrum? Where does the international community go from here?"'

She made the class practise.

'Good. Continue, er . . . Maria.'

Ursula was looking at her. Lynn looked back at her, then dropped her eyes, stared out.

Astrid was humming a tune as she tidied Molly's bedroom. She smiled when she caught sight of Molly frowning in her direction and paused to ask her if she'd like another coffee.

'No, I wouldn't, thank you very much,' Molly said bad-temperedly from her mattress on the floor.

'Nor something with milk? For strength?' pursued Astrid, bending delightedly, as though in the act of discovering a rare flower, to pick up a crumpled handkerchief by the washbasin.

'No,' Molly replied ungraciously. 'I've had it up to here with drinks.'

'I understand,' said Astrid serenely. 'I think I will take some of your clothes to the wash.'

She set about gathering together Molly's dirty clothes. She folded each item neatly to form a pile on the coffee table, still humming a tune.

Molly watched her for a while from the floor. 'I don't know why you fold them, Astrid,' she said sharply. 'They're going to get all messed up again when you put them in the wash. I don't see the point.'

'It is my custom,' said Astrid pacifically.

Molly frowned, scouting about for *something*, for the source of her irritation. She found a symptom, mistook it for the disease itself for a moment, seeing it reveal itself as only a sympton as it came out of her and made her ashamed at her pettiness. 'That tune you keep humming. It's really getting on my nerves, to tell you the truth.'

'I am sorry,' replied Astrid. 'You should tell me before.'

'Right . . . well . . .' said Molly. '"You should have told me before," would be better.' She returned to watching Astrid folding, and felt her irritation bubbling away. She could not think how to turn off the gas that fuelled it, could not understand why she was feeling it in the first place. 'What I don't understand is . . . ,' she began.

'Yes?'

'I just don't understand how you've changed in the last few days! It's almost as if my problem had given you a new lease of life!'

'I'm sorry. What is "lease of life"?'

Molly tried to think of a way of explaining. Then she thought, I'm a sick woman. Why should I have to explain these things? Don't I do enough of that in class? 'Ask me in class, Astrid. But why aren't you depressed any more?'

'You prefer me depressed?' Astrid asked. 'I think you thought I was a silly old woman. You should be happy that now I am happy.'

Molly thought about that. A spring inside her was fighting to uncoil as it had always uncoiled, to power the smile and the *That's great. You're better, thank the Lord!*

But something was stopping it. Astrid's sudden happiness irritated her beyond endurance. It was worse than the nagging deep pain in the small of her back. Why is that? Molly wondered. It's Original Sin, that's what it is, or something very much like it. Original Sin always turns up when I think I'm on top of things.

'Tell me some more about Borneo. It is so nice for me to listen. Speak to me about Tankiti,' said Astrid.

'I thought you were going to do my washing.'

'I have time for both.'

'I'm tired,' Molly said, seeing herself as she spoke, like an irritable child. 'I want to sleep.'

Astrid nodded understandingly. 'I am very sorry, Molly. How very inconsiderate I am. It's just that everything you tell me about your life interests me greatly.'

'Yes . . . well . . .,' said Molly.

'I will go now! Sleep well!' And Astrid left the room. Molly rubbed the place where her heart was or, anyway, the pain. It was as if a dagger had been twisted there by a strong efficient arm attached to a sweetly smiling assailant.

God! Make me better! I can't stand being cooped up like this! Do you hear me? prayed Molly, aiming a look at the grey ceiling of the room of an intensity sufficient to strip paint.

'So that's where the Brooke Street Bureau is!' said Sue, looking at Dennis through her driving-mirror.

'What's that got to do with anything?' asked Dennis.

'I think I might go temp again,' said Sue, stopping at a zebra, though she might have been able to make it across had she felt so inclined.

'Get a move on, Sue! I'm late.'

'He had his foot on the crossing, Sir Dennis. The law states—'

'Since when did you obey the Highway Code? You really can be infuriating, Sue,' said Dennis.

'It's my nerves,' said Sue. 'What I need is a change of routine.'

'You're just saying that,' said Dennis. 'You wouldn't leave DB. You've got it too cushy.'

'You call this cushy, do you? Driving you and Lady Muck round and round? *I* don't call it cushy even if you do.'

'Don't talk about Porn-Chai like that!'

'Why not? I know what she thinks of me. You've told me often enough. She thinks I'm a slag, which is rich coming from her,' said Sue, revving the car on to Hyde Park Corner in a manner which Dennis judged to be reckless.

'What brought all this on?' asked Dennis.

'Lots of things,' said Sue. 'Closing the summer school, for instance.'

'How did you know about that?'

'I've got ears, you know.'

'You haven't told anyone else, have you?'

'Not yet, but don't you think I won't,' lied Sue.

'It's not fixed, you know. There's nothing decided. I just think it's more trouble than it's worth.'

'Trouble for who, I'd like to know?'

'Turn left here,' said Dennis.

'Who's coming to the meeting?'

'Just a few of the shareholders. Look, will you wait for me? I'll have some time afterwards. Maybe we could go to the flat for an hour. Porn-Chai's having a hen night.'

'Is that what she calls them?' asked Sue. 'Well, I might be here when you finish. Then, again, I might not. Just don't drag it out.'

'No.' Dennis got out of the car and slammed the door. He watched as Sue drove off, then he went into the hotel.

'Sir Dennis, we're over here,' said Jordan Bostock.

'Ah, Jordan . . .,' said Dennis, aware that people in the reception area were looking at him and seeing him as a man entitled to respect. The novelty of it still slapped him on the back.

Rachel Pales was seated next to Harry English, a major shareholder in Demolish Babel. Dennis kissed Rachel and shook hands with Harry. 'Let's go straight in to dinner. I'm a bit pressed for time,' he said.

When they were seated, Dennis opened the discussion. 'I've been very unhappy with the conduct of this

237

year's summer school. It's been one thing after another.' He stopped, looking at Rachel. He lost the thread, but seeing Harry English nodding encouragingly he continued, 'Now, I have long thought the summer school a bit of a distraction from the normal work of Demolish Babel. We are known throughout the world as the company of preference for all major business corporations. Our business is business English – Business English in its broadest sense – and we do it damned well. We're second to none. What I'm saying is that I really don't think that the summer school fits the new image of Demolish Babel. It's always been a loose tramp-steamer of an event, but this year it is really beginning to break up. Time to call enough, I say.'

Dennis looked around the table. He could not gauge what the rest of the quorum thought. 'Right. I've said my piece. Do any of you have an opinion on the matter?'

'I do,' said Jordan. 'I can understand completely what you're saying. I agree with most of it. Where I part company with you is in thinking that the whole notion of a summer school is a dead duck. On the contrary, I think it could be a money-maker, a prestigious event, a flagship instead of a tramp-steamer, but in order for it to be that you would have to get rid of most of the present staff, change the caterers, perhaps the venue. You need to attract the top end of the market.'

'But that's what we do for the rest of the year!' said Rachel. 'I don't think you're being fair, Jordan.' She turned to face Dennis. 'Dennis, it was you who established the ground rules of the summer school. It was to be, first and foremost, a place where people from all over the world could get together and learn. Remember that?'

Dennis did remember. He nodded.

Rachel continued, 'It was also to be a school to which the same teachers would return year in and year out. And that's happened, and it does not happen a lot in this business. Also, the very fact that it is different from what goes on in the Oxford Street school for the rest of the year is a reason for keeping it going. When you started DB the classes were full of waiters and au pairs and refugees. That's all gone, but the original intentions continue to flourish at the summer school. It's a nod – and only a nod – towards your original intentions. You wanted to demolish Babel, to bring about better understanding between peoples. The summer school does that. It's not earth-shattering. It isn't as much as we could or should be doing. But it's something. A bit like a poor man's Rhodes Scholarships.'

'But this year . . .?' said Dennis.

'This year has been exceptional. We've had bad luck.' Rachel stopped. Then she added, 'Bad luck that can be partly laid at my door. And I'm sorry about that. Truly sorry. But we're muddling through. I'm afraid I don't agree with Jordan. I know he disapproves strongly of several of the teachers, but they keep the students happy. They work hard. They come back. I think that says a lot.'

'If I may have a word,' said Harry English.

'Go ahead, Harry,' said Dennis.

'It's a matter of profit and loss. The summer school has never made a profit. Most years we've come out even, but this year there's going to be quite a hefty loss.'

'Why is that, Harry?' asked Dennis.

'You've been doling out scholarships too freely, Dennis.'

'I can't say no,' said Dennis.

'Of course, it's admirable, but would not scholarships be better invested in the mainstream business courses? It seems to me that it's the businessmen of the Third World we should be helping out. Then we might get a return on the investment.'

Rachel saw Jordan nodding his agreement. The aura of sweet reason poured like a sauce over the unattractive pudding that she now saw Dennis to be was making her feel very queasy indeed. Looking hard at him, she said, 'I think the summer school in its present form is very much worth preserving. It makes the rest of the year just about bearable.'

'How do you mean?' asked Dennis.

'I just get terribly tired of pedalling a thin gruel of language to fat cats.'

'I thought you loved your job!'

'It's OK,' said Rachel. 'But I *love* the summer school.' Did I say that, she thought. Me?

'Well, I'm sorry but my mind's made up,' said Dennis. 'This summer school will be the last.'

Jordan and Rachel exchanged glances of ice. Harry English sat back in his chair, nodding. 'I think that's a wise decision, Sir Dennis,' he said.

Rachel looked around the table. 'So that's it, is it? We stop the summer school just like that? You can't do that! What about the other shareholders?'

'Sorry, Rachel,' said Dennis. 'We've already sounded them out.'

'You're the only one who is objecting. You could say that this little supper is just for you,' said Harry English amiably.

Rachel did not reply. She was thinking about Lynn and Arthur and Molly. Then she thought of Nathan and Ezekiel. She looked at the three men in front of her and hated them.

Without a word she stood up and left the table.

Only when she was sitting in the back of a taxi did she think: That's exactly what they wanted me to do. I've been set up.

Book Five

Advanced

Molly was dodging a blow from a panga wielded by Tankiti. She heard it crash next to her ear. Her eyes wide open, she found herself gazing at the luminous face of the alarm-clock. The panga fell again.

'Molly, are you awake?'

She sighed with relief. 'Arthur? Is that you?'

'Can I come in?'

'Sure you can!' she said, reaching for the switch of the desk-lamp.

Seeing her lying flat on the floor in a pool of light, Arthur thought of Harry. 'I'm sorry, Molly. I didn't think.' He made an unconvincing move to leave.

'No, don't go. Come on in and stop jittering at the door. I'm glad you woke me up. I was in the middle of a nightmare. It was terrible.'

He sat himself down on the edge of the armchair. 'Are you all right now?'

Molly smoothed down the counterpane. 'Yes, fine now, thank you.' She smiled up at him. 'I haven't seen you in ages, Arthur.'

'No, I'm sorry, Molly. It's just I've been rushed.'

'So it's my fault, then.'

'How do you mean?'

'Well, if I hadn't hurt my back I'd have been able to help you and you'd have been less rushed and had time to visit.'

Arthur thought about that. 'Molly . . .'

'You went to see *Worlds Away*. I was sorry to miss that. We get videos at St Cedric's, but a good play – they're gold. A production of *The Browning Version* visited us once from Kuching but that was years ago. Was it good?'

'It made you think.'

'Oh, one of those plays.'

'Yes. Molly . . .'

She stopped him. 'I know what you're going to say, Arthur.'

'Do you?'

'Astrid told me what you said to her.'

'So you know it all, then?'

'Yes.'

'I'm sure Harry and João never did anything. It wouldn't have been in character,' said Arthur.

'And what about you?'

'I might have had a go. I was quite capable of it, but I didn't. Not that time.'

'I think Astrid came back convinced that João caught the virus here. She told me that João didn't have friends *like that* in Brazil.'

'How would she know, Molly? How many mothers know? Mine is still convinced I'll settle down. We probably stood out in Astrid's mind because we made no secret of who we were. João latched on to us for fellowship. As far as I remember, he talked of having a pretty full life back home.'

'Arthur, I . . .'

'She didn't react when I told her I had the virus.'

'What did you say?' Molly asked.

'"I've got the virus." I told Astrid that.'

'Oh, Arthur! I didn't know that!'

'You mean she didn't . . .?'

'No. Arthur, I didn't know that. I don't know what to say.'

'There's nothing *to* say, Molly.'

Molly thought about that. 'No, Arthur. There is something to say. You can't go back to Egypt alone. Who's going to look after you, to make sure you eat right? You need people around. I'll tell you what, you must tell Rachel. When she finds out what's happened, she'll offer you a job with Demolish Babel in London.'

'Have you been talking to Rachel?' Arthur asked.

'A while ago, yes. She's been worried about you, Arthur. We've all been worried.' She saw him flinch. 'You can understand that, can't you?'

'Everyone will know soon enough, I suppose.'

'Only friends. You need your friends now, Arthur. More than ever. Look, if you don't want to stay in London you must come back with me to Borneo. St Cedric's needs good teachers. I'd love to have you there.'

'Molly . . . it's kind of you – more than kind – but I've got to go back to Egypt. I have debts to pay, friends there who need to know. Aaron would call it *damage limitation*. It's got to be done.'

'No, Arthur, you can't go back there. You said yourself that going back hastened Harry's death. At St Cedric's you'd be near medical attention. Say what you like about those fundamentalists, they're good doctors. And the climate's healthy. It suits me, anyway.'

Arthur did not feel he could tell Molly any more. To tell her what he proposed to do back in his village would terrify her. Even to think it himself made him break out in a sweat. 'OK,' he said. 'I'll think about what you've said. Thanks for asking, Molly.'

'Why do you think Astrid is so damned cheerful all of a sudden?' Molly asked. 'Agnes thinks it's because she's got someone to take care of. My back going gave her a task.'

Arthur shook his head. 'It's obvious, isn't it? She thinks justice has been done. It's lifted a weight off her. Lucky Astrid . . .'

Molly thought about that. 'But it hasn't, has it?'

'Yes and no. If she thinks Harry and I are responsible, then let her continue to think it if it makes her happy. It's good practice for me.'

'Arthur . . .'

'Highgate Ponds was shut,' he said, 'but Egypt's open still.'

'Arthur . . .'

'Try to sleep, Molly lovey. I'm sorry I woke you up,' Arthur said and he tip-toed from the room before Molly could think of another thing to say.

Rachel stood with Agnes at the door of Reception, watching Lynn talking on the payphone. 'I wonder how that story's going to end?' Rachel observed.

'It doesn't look as if we're going to find out, does it?' Agnes replied.

'How do you mean?'

'Come off it, Rachel. Don't forget I work with the three Sues.'

'You know, then?'

'Of course, I know. I think it's a crying shame. It's made me think of taking early retirement.'

'I'm resigning,' said Rachel. She ignored Agnes's reaction. 'I'd always been prepared to give Dennis the benefit of the doubt, before last night. But when I saw him being led by the nose by the shareholders I knew it was time to get out. We're like any other business now. The English language castrated, stunned, dismembered and extruded into sound-bites. English for Specific Purposes! God, I hate it! We produce the dynamite but withhold the peace prizes.'

'I don't get you,' Agnes said.

'In the old days those robber barons gave something back. Carnegie libraries, Ford foundations. Not any more. Now, I know we're small beer, but the summer school does give something back. Not enough, but it's something. Now we're just going to be smoothers of palms. Don't quite know when it happened. Dennis's first student-procurement trip to the Middle East, I expect. We sell our language in any form the punter likes. It's all we have left to sell. Most nations love their language, hate to sell it short. Not us. Not the pragmatic, supply-side, take-the-money-and-run Brits.'

'This isn't like you, Rachel.'

'No, it isn't, is it? Well, perhaps I'm just arriving at the stage that Lynn got to when she put her foot down and said, "Keith, I want to stay put and cultivate a garden." I've taken my time, I know. Perhaps the summer school was an interlude each year when I could remember why I took up teaching in the first place. Rich, really. I dread it at the same time. All those faces coming back a bit older, a bit rustier, a lot untidier. Still, they do show me some light – the teachers and the students – and now the light is being turned out.' Rachel gestured to the office. 'Well, time to move on.'

'But do you think you'd be happy in the shop? I can't see you weighing out lentils.'

Rachel smiled. 'I can't see you taking early retirement.'

'Just watch me,' said Agnes. 'I might spend it visiting teachers and students around the world. I've got a few addresses.' She looked at Rachel. 'You may not think it, but I have.'

'I'm sure you have,' said Rachel.

'I know people see me as a carping Tartar, but someone has to be.'

'Yes, I suppose so. But the whole messy event *worked* – at least, until this year. And even this year . . .'

'Rachel, if you feel so strongly about the summer school, I don't know why you don't set up your own.'

'The very idea,' Rachel said.

It was a surprise for Lynn when Jordan Bostock approached her the following day as she was standing in front of the notice-board, worrying. She had just passed Nathan Pales in the corridor of Churchill. The boy had been carrying a great pile of books. When she said hello, he had looked at her as if he had never seen her before. Then when she, determined to get a response, had said it was nice to see him making himself useful, helping his mum, he had turned his back on her and walked away. She had watched him go, thinking that a turned back, a blank look, was going to be her lot in life.

'Ah, Lynn. Just the person I wanted!' said Jordan Bostock.

'Who, me?' Lynn replied, the sight of him reminding her of another thing to worry about. 'I'm very worried about the rumours,' she said.

'You mean the summer school?'

She nodded.

'It's true, I'm afraid. Dennis seems determined.'

'But what will you do, Jordan?'

247

He shrugged – no doubt thinking of off-shore accounts, Lynn thought. 'I'll be all right. It's probably about time I had a change of routine. Also, I may have to get my head down and write a few textbooks.'

'That's nice,' said Lynn, trying to appear pleased. But she was not pleased. To see him standing there, cushioned for the rest of his life by wise investments and a fat salary, writing gainfully and at ease, made her feel an envy she had not thought herself capable of. If only she and Keith had kept still. That job in Saudi Arabia had been a money-maker. If they'd stuck it out until now, they could have been in a position to retire.

Not that she had minded leaving Saudi Arabia. *Life's too short*, she had told Keith. But standing in front of Jordan, who, in Lynn's book, had sacrificed everything in life for a safe old age, she could only see him as the very personification of good sense and efficient management.

'There ought to be classes,' she said.

'How do you mean?'

'Well, I was just looking at you and envying you. It's been such a waste of time. My life, I mean. I'm looking back at all the places Keith and I have been. If we'd known then what we . . . what I know now . . . I . . . we . . .'

'You'd have managed things differently.'

'Yes. Very differently. It's one's –' she thought of Ursula – 'perception of time. So long looking towards the future, so short towards the past. There really ought to be classes.'

'But you must have known it would be like that.'

'Yes, I suppose I did. People keep telling you, don't they? I just couldn't take it in. I don't know why.'

'I can't believe that you envy me,' he said. He looked pleased. She didn't like that.

'It's probably just a bad mood. I've got enough reason to be in a bad mood.'

'Nothing from Keith?'

'Not a dicky-bird.'

'He probably couldn't stand the idea of doing another summer school. I can see his point.'

Was that Jordan Bostock's idea of a joke? she thought.

'There's nothing wrong with the summer school!' she said. 'It's always been the high point of my year.' She saw him smile. 'If you felt like that, why did you come back year in year out? You didn't need to, did you? And it's not as if you have any friends here.'

She saw him blanch.

'I mean, not close friends. You haven't, though, have you?'

'Yes, I have several very close friends. I thought you were one.'

Is he serious? Lynn thought. Does he really think I'm a close friend? Is that what friendship means to him? No, he's having me on.

'You're having me on,' she said.

'No, I'm not.'

'But you're always so distant!'

'I don't *feel* distant,' he said. 'It's true I don't like many of the things that go on here. But I have developed an attachment towards the staff.'

'Of course. I shouldn't have said that. We feel an attachment to you.'

'Yes, well . . . ,' he said.

They dithered, separated by continents.

She wanted to be elsewhere but did not feel she could just walk away. 'Do you know how Molly is?' she asked, not for a moment thinking that he would.

'Much the same, I think. I expect they'll be keeping the news from her.'

'About the summer school, you mean? I doubt Molly would worry too much.'

'No,' he replied. 'Not that. The news from Sarawak. I'm surprised you haven't seen it. It's in all the newspapers.'

'I don't read them. What's happened?'

'There's war between the Army and the Kass. The report in the *Guardian* even mentioned St Cedric's mission. That's where Molly is, isn't it?'

'What did it say about St Cedric's?'

'That it's been taken over by the Army. The authorities reckon that it was a centre for resistance to the loggers.

249

There was a pitched battle for control of it. A priest was killed.'

Lynn leaned heavily against the notice-board. Her brain dismantled the gleam of hope for her own future. Brown children ranged round her feet in a rainforest setting disappeared off the screen to be replaced by a fading dot. Only then did she think of Molly. 'No, she mustn't see that. She mustn't. She's been worried about St Cedric's. She mustn't see it.'

Dot was bagging beans when Rachel came into *Inner Cleanliness*. The wind-chimes placed strategically against the door clanged.

'Hello, Dot. You all right?'

Dot stared at Rachel, mouth open. 'Yes. I hadn't expected to see you again until after the summer school. Nathan said . . .'

'Yes, we are rather snowed under,' Rachel replied. She stopped, placing her other thoughts on hold. 'Have you spoken to him on the phone?'

'Not on the phone. No. He comes in every day. It's looked like he's moving up to the school for good. He leaves loaded down with stuff. He took his computer this morning. And more books. I told him it was nice to see how studious he was getting.'

'What time was this?'

' 'Bout eleven.'

'That's odd.'

Dot banged down a kilo of pinto beans and taped the bag shut. 'You're going to have one hell of a job getting all that stuff back into the flat. I wouldn't like to be in your shoes.'

'No. See you later, Dot. I've got some things to do.'

Rachel went upstairs, unlocked the front door and stepped into the flat. She looked about her. Apart from the empty aura the flat always had when Nathan was out, everything seemed to be just as she had left it. An unwashed glass, left by Nathan, stood on the kitchen table. Rachel looked around further, walking up and down the kitchen-diner area. She passed her fingers along the spines of *English for Your World*.

Funny . . ., she thought.

She looked at the row of her books closely, discovering with a start that complete sets of volumes 1, 2 and 3 were missing. This discovery set Rachel into motion, and she turned and made for the stairs, taking them two at a time to Nathan's attic bedroom.

The room was tidier than she remembered. It took her a walk around the bed and half a minute sitting on top of it eyeball to eyeball with a Prince poster to make her realize why. Most of the things in the room had disappeared. The desktop was bare of computer, tape-recorder, tapes, CD-player. She opened the cupboard and found it completely bare except for some underwear and woollens.

Rachel had returned home for an hour or two for a bit of peace, to lick her wounds and, perhaps, draft out a livid resignation-letter full of all the things she had stored in some negative corner of her brain since joining Demolish Babel. But that was all forgotten. Now she could only sit and wonder what Nathan had been up to. He could not possibly need all those things at Heathcliff, could he? They would not fit on the desk of the single room he occupied. She thought of drugs. She thought of Ezekiel. But Ezekiel would never be able to take those things home! So why?

Dot had changed to bagging Lexia raisins when Rachel stormed through the shop.

'They're a bugger, these raisins,' she said. 'I found a dead beetle in this bag. Quality control needs a good shake-up in Lexia. You off, then?'

'Yes,' said Rachel. She stopped, helped herself to a raisin. 'Everything all right with you, Dot?' she asked.

'You've asked me that once.'

'And what did you say?'

'I said, "Yes". I might not have meant it, but that's what I said.'

'Well, that's the main thing.'

'What's the matter with you, Rachel? Is anything wrong?'

Rachel sat down in the old-customer chair across the counter from Dot. 'You'd be better asking me if anything was right, Dot.'

'Would I?' Dot asked. She prepared herself to listen, as she often had to. She thought of her own problems for a moment, then pushed them out of her mind to concentrate on Rachel.

'Have another raisin and tell me all about it,' she said.

They had been throwing a ball against the blank brick wall of the library They had kept it up for eighty-seven throws between them and neither had fluffed a catch. Nathan was seeing himself participating in the new event of throwing at the Olympics. He was representing Britain, Ezekiel Niger. Thus far it was evenly matched. It would take only one slip by either for the match to be decided. Whoever dropped the ball first would stand on the lower step and take only silver.

Nathan made to catch the ball, felt it in his hand, then dropped it.

The crowd roared for little Niger.

'I am tired,' Ezekiel said.

They sat down on the grass. The cars passing in the Finchley Road could be made out between the houses, but the noise of it hardly reached them.

'Zek,' Nathan said.

'Yes, little brother?'

'Is your school a good one?'

'Of course it is good. I am the headmaster!'

'I was thinking . . . ,' he said.

'What was it that you were thinking?'

'I was thinking that . . .' He rushed into it. 'You could take me home with you and I could go to your school.' He stopped then, looked down at the grass, picked handfuls, which he teased into heaps.

'But what about your mum?'

'Oh, I'd ask her, of course. But I think she'd go along with it. After all, I am part African and she would trust you. I know she likes you a lot. She thinks you're great.'

'But where would you live?'

'I could live with you and your family.'

'I don't—'

But Nathan was ready. 'I know it must sound weird but it's no weirder than English kids going to Europe or America, is it? You said yourself that I should see Africa. England isn't my home. Not really. Also,' he added, hoping that this might be the clinching argument, 'if I went home with you we could carry more stuff back.'

'It is not possible,' Ezekiel said. 'Your mother needs you. You can't leave her. There is no man to protect her.'

'She'd manage OK. In fact, I think everything would be easier for her without me. She's got her work and her writing. Say yes, Zek. Go on! Say yes, then I'll ask Mum.'

Ezekiel thought for a moment; then, confident that Rachel would say no, replied, 'OK. I'll think about it.'

'Great!' Nathan said.

Ezekiel looked at his watch. 'I must go to the language laboratory now.'

'OK. See you later.'

After banging the Coke machine, hoping for another miracle, Nathan bought himself a can. Then he wandered back towards his room. He passed through the common room, picked up the *Sun* to have a look at page 3. He threw the paper down after a minute and was leaving the room when he saw three students standing looking into a large box on the table in the corner. They were choosing items from the box. Three piles of books, tapes and items of clothing sat on the table. The students were arguing over who should have a Walkman.

Nathan took a step towards them, then changed his mind, sat down, opened another tabloid, flicked over the pages and watched the possessions he had given to Zek a few days before being redistributed. Hey, he thought to himself. Hey . . .

253

*   *   *

'Molly knows,' Arthur said, placing his lunch-tray on the table beside her.

'How can she?' Lynn asked.

'Astrid steals a paper for her every morning and takes it in on her breakfast-tray.' Arthur saw Lynn's agitation. 'She's taking it in her stride. She told me it makes her feel part and parcel of everything.'

'What does that mean?'

Arthur shrugged. If Lynn didn't know by now . . .

'I must go and see her. You know she offered me a job at St Cedric's?'

'Me, too. I said no, though. Can you imagine me on a mission station?'

'You've heard about the summer school?'

Arthur nodded. 'It figures.'

'Jordan Bostock said some odd things to me yesterday.'

Sue passed with a tray. ' 'Scuse I,' she said. 'What's your maiden name, Lynn?'

'Why?'

'There's a letter for a Ms Lynn Cupper. That's not you, is it?'

'Cupper was my maiden name. You're joking, aren't you?'

Sue did not feel like a discussion as her salad was slipping down the tray. 'It's in the office. Sue's still there. Anyway, she was five minutes ago.'

Lynn looked at Arthur. 'What do you think it could be?'

'Search me, lovey. Go and find out.'

'Save my place,' she told Arthur.

She returned in a couple of minutes, holding the envelope.

'What does it say?' Arthur asked.

'I haven't opened it, but it's in Keith's handwriting.'

'Where was it posted?'

She showed him the envelope.

254

'Chile,' said Arthur. 'Fancy putting a blind sheep on a stamp.'

She did not hear him, just sat down, placing the envelope on the table.

'Go on, open it!' he told her.

She sat regarding the envelope on the table between them. 'I can't. It isn't for me. I'm Lynn Weaver.'

'Yes, but—'

'The shit! The nasty little shit! You know what he's saying, don't you? He's saying that we're finished. And look how he does it! The shit!'

'I'll open it for you,' said Arthur.

She nodded, seething, watched as Arthur removed a piece of paper. 'What does he say?'

'It's a cheque for . . . Lynn, I think you'd better see it.'

She grabbed it from him and was looking at a bankers' draft for £17,000 made out to Ms Lynn Cupper. 'Is there a letter?'

He searched the envelope, opening it wide, pushing his fingers along it. Then he showed the empty interior to her.

'Nothing? Is that it?'

'It looks like it,' he said.

'The bugger's in Chile.'

'Yes.'

Lynn picked up the envelope. She held it close to her eyes and regarded it closely. Like a drunk, Arthur thought. Obsessed. Shaky. 'We never got to Chile. We meant to. Had it all arranged. But Allende was killed a week before, and we couldn't go. Well, we could have but it didn't seem right.'

'Do you think he's found himself a job there?'

Lynn started to laugh.

'Lynn . . .'

'*Ms* . . . *Ms* . . . I never liked *Ms*. I liked the idea of it but I never liked the word. Well, I suppose I'd better start trying to get used to it.'

'Get that cheque cashed,' said Arthur.

Lynn took the cheque and looked at it on the table

next to her pudding. She scrunched the envelope up and placed it on her empty dinner-plate. 'Seventeen thousand pounds. We were together for seventeen years, you know. Where did he get seventeen thousand pounds? Something else I never knew.'

'Maybe he's had a breakdown. It happens, you know.'

She took the cheque, folded it and put it in her bag. 'It's possible, I suppose.' She stood up. She felt her eye-patch, then she ripped it off and stared at Arthur, presenting him with the sight of two clear eyes. 'I don't need that any more.'

'Lynn, your eye looks fine,' Arthur said.

'It was always fine. The patch was just a sort of defence mechanism. I thought it might make the students . . . feel sorry for me or something. Pathetic, isn't it?'

'Where are you going?' he asked. 'Don't forget to get that cheque cashed.'

'No, I won't. Just as soon as I've seen Molly,' she said.

'Excuse me, ladies,' said the policeman. 'What are you doing here?'

Satoko and Mitsuko were standing before a pair of high iron gates, gazing through the whorls of wrought iron at a large house.

'We wait for Grid Reference,' said Satoko.

'He's moved,' said the policeman.

Mitsuko, who had tired of the fruitless search for pop stars, nudged Satoko.

'Where?' asked Satoko.

'Search me,' said the policeman.

'Where that?'

'They all move on, the pop stars.'

'Who own the house now?' Mitsuko asked.

'Oh, I don't know that, ladies. Some foreigner, I expect.'

In the light of the setting sun, Satoko studied her pop persons' map. The policeman saluted them and walked away, adjusting the strap of his helmet.

'I am tired of searching,' said Mitsuko. 'They have all gone away. We should have accompanied the disco band when he asked us to the pop festival.'

Satoko was still studying her star-map. 'No, they were second rate. Have you heard of John Keats?' she asked.

'No. Why?'

'Sandra Sayarama says you can go into his house and feel him everywhere.'

'Sandra is so bold!' said Mitsuko. 'How far away is it?'

'It is almost on our way back. Look!'

'Yes. Let's go. We must find somebody. I cannot go home if we do not find a pop star.'

'We can use the pictures we took at Madame Tussaud's, if we have no success.'

The two girls, following their map, walked back across the Heath towards John Keats's house. They snapped one another under the trees. They passed Highgate Ponds. Some policemen were cordoning the area while a number of bystanders stood around Joan Lunt, who was carrying her placard, waving her petition, shouting and weeping.

'What is happening?' Satoko asked.

Some geese took off from the pond and flew low over their heads, flapping and calling.

'Beautiful!' said Mitsuko, shooting them with her compact camera.

Satoko and Mitsuko wandered hopefully into the spectacular sunset, on their way to John Keats's house, which had closed for the day four hours before.

Eisa stayed close to Eric Trotter as he led a group of male students around a crowded Stratford the following Saturday. This time nothing would go wrong. Nothing bad would happen. This time he would go back to London on the bus after seeing the play. He stayed so close to Dr Trotter that the old man felt like telling him to give him some breathing-space. He kept treading on Eisa's foot.

Moira Trotter had been reluctant to let her husband out

of her sight, but Eric had said that she should take the women on her candlewick hunt around the shops.

'Just give me tickets for the theatre. You'll see, we'll all be sitting there like good boys when you arrive,' he had told her.

'Well, you just make sure you are. It starts at half-one. What time?'

'Half-one.'

'Right. And half-one means half-one. It doesn't mean twenty to two.'

'No.'

'What's wrong with you?'

'What do you mean, what's wrong with me? There's nothing wrong with me, Moira.'

Moira looked at her husband suspiciously. 'You haven't got some trick up your sleeve, have you?' she asked.

'What do you take me for, Moira?'

'What I've been taking you for for sixty years, Eric. I know you, and don't you think I don't.'

'I'm hurt, Moira. Anyway, what could I get up to with all these students around? Not a chance.'

'Knowing you, you might try to lead them astray.'

'I'm still hurt, Moira. You're questioning my professional integrity.'

'Not as hurt as you'll be if anything goes wrong. I'm giving you eight tickets.' She counted them out. 'One for you and seven for the human beings. I'm going to count you all out and heaven help you if I can't count you all back.'

Dr Trotter saluted his wife. 'All pleasant and correct, ma'am.'

Moira Trotter looked out of the window of the coach. 'Silly old fool,' she said.

'But you do love me, don't you?'

'I'd love you better with sense. It's been like being married to a kid, Eric.'

'You don't mean that.'

'See them houses?' asked Moira. 'They're Cotswold cottages. We should have been happy residents of one of those for the last two decades. You'd have been pottering about in the garden. I'd have been a pillar of the Mothers' Union.'

Dr Trotter looked at the houses with some distaste. 'I bought you a jigsaw of one like that,' he said.

'A jigsaw isn't quite the same, though, is it?'

'It'll have to do you, Moira. It'd have done me in.'

'I know that, Eric,' said Moira. She patted Eric's hand and turned to watch the passing scenery, an activity that had been the *magnum opus* of her life.

'You having a good time, Eisa?'

'Very good. Beautiful city,' said Eisa, looking admiringly at Stratford.

Eric Trotter nodded but didn't say anything. Eisa, not because he wanted to know, but for something to say that he could say, pointed to a church tower. 'What is this, Teacher?'

'That? It's a church tower, Eisa.'

'What it for?'

'A good question, Eisa. A profound question. What *is* it for? Well, let me see. They have bells inside. Shall we go and see?'

Eric rounded up the other students. 'We're going in here,' he called.

'Is this Anne Hathaway's cottage?' Muchtar asked.

'No, young man. It's a church.'

Inside the empty church they looked around. Then, back in the porch, Eric gathered the students together. He counted them to make sure. Yes, all present. 'We've just enough,' he said.

'Sorry?' Eisa asked.

'You see these ropes, lads? These are bell-ropes. The bells are in the tower, and by pulling the ropes you can make them chime.'

The students looked at him.

'I'll show you.' He reached out and pulled the nearest rope. High above them a treble bell chimed. 'Right, all of you take a rope.' He guided the students to stand

259

beneath each of the bell-ropes, leaving one spare. 'Now, you grip the rope in the right hand. You see the bit like a carpet? That's the sally.' He reached up for the red soft part of the rope. 'Now, you keep the rope in this hand and you pull down on the sally.' The bell chimed. 'But don't let the rope go slack or you'll be in trouble. Like this.' The bell tolled repeatedly, mournfully, over summer Stratford. 'Right, now you try.'

A cacophony of chiming bells rang above them. 'Go on, you'll soon get the hang of it.'

'But why?' asked Eisa.

'It's like your Muslim call to prayer, Eisa. Not that it works.'

'It is very noisy,' said Muchtar.

'Very English. Let's try again, shall we?'

The group tolled the bells for five minutes. 'It's not as easy as it looks, is it, lads?'

'What's going on here?'

They turned to see a man in a grey suit and a clerical collar, standing at the door.

'Ah, Vicar. I was showing my students how to ring the bells.'

'It isn't allowed.'

'Isn't it?' asked Eric, all innocence. 'You see, we're strangers here. I'm from New Zealand. In New Zealand you can have a go on the bells. The vicar in our parish reckoned it helped get rid of youthful excess of energy. Bell-ringing stopped the young men worrying the sheep.'

The vicar was looking around at the strange assortment of nationalities and colours standing under his belfry. He suddenly saw things in a new light. People from the whole world coming to his church to summon the faithless faithful to worship. It was, if not the answer to prayer, at least to his Sunday sermon. Yes, he could see it now. He would tell the Miss Gentrys and Mrs Yeoman and the smattering of tourists who came to service that the day before he had been at the end of his tether . . . no, his rope . . . Close to despair for the nation and the church that was supposed to help the nation, but was failing. Yes, he had been in despair and then . . . and then . . . he had heard the bells ringing as he was preparing his modest lunch. The bells on a Saturday morning! Yes, he would say. Uncharitable thoughts filled my head. I imagined marrauding punks swinging drunk from the ropes. Most terrible blasphemies, I imagined. But what did I see when I opened the door of the church? I saw seven men. Seven. From all the races of the earth. There were Muslims and Buddhists and Hindus and perhaps a don't-know or two and they were there with their teacher – an elderly New Zealander – pulling on the ropes and making the bells sing! In truth the song was strange and some might say untuneful. But the chaos of all life was in their song. The outside world was calling us – calling us to remember what we have forgotten! And my despair melted away in front of this little sign. It just melted away.

'Welcome! Welcome, all!' the vicar cried. He went around the group of bell-ringers shaking hands, beaming, chatting. 'The bell you are ringing', he said to Ito, 'would have been heard by William Shakespeare. Isn't that wonderful? Toll it!'

Ito did so, and the vicar beamed. Perhaps a series of sermons, he thought, elated for the first time in a long time. 'All of you! Chime those bells! Let us drown out the traffic and the Mr Whippy vans and the children asking their parents for things they cannot afford! Chime!'

Eric Trotter, at first relieved that the vicar had been tolerant of their taking liberties, was now worried that he would detain the group so long that they – or, rather, Eric – would be deprived of the longed-for couple of pints of Flowers bitter before the play began. He looked at his watch. 'I say, Vicar . . .' he began. But his words were drowned out by the tolling of the bells.

'That's it! God, that's it! Toll those bells!' exclaimed the vicar.

The students did their best to oblige. All were getting the hang of it, each tuned in to the tolling of his own bell but unable to achieve any kind of sequence. This, however, did not faze the vicar. He smiled seraphically

261

at his blow-in bell-tollers who had so lifted the day.

No, it was not mere chance! The very idea that it was a random occurrence was a blasphemy! These people were messengers sent to his church by the Almighty to tell him things he had been in danger of forgetting. 'Oh, you make me so happy!' he shouted above the clashing of the bells. 'You make me feel alive again after such a long period of spiritual moribundity! Thank you! Thank you!'

Christ, thought Eric. Trust me to find a nutter.

The vicar then insisted on taking all the students up the bell-tower in shifts. Eric Trotter was left below, murmuring to himself, thinking of the pub.

'Right, lads, we'll have to get a move on. I want to go to the pub. How about you?'

'I want to see more of Stratford,' said Muchtar.

'Right. How many of you want to go off and how many want to come with me?'

Nobody spoke. 'Come on! I haven't got all day!'

'I come with you,' said Eisa.

The others, their ears ringing, wanted to follow Muchtar.

'Here are your tickets. There's the theatre. Be there by twenty past one at the latest, do you hear? Don't be late! You'll catch it from the missis!'

Eric turned to Eisa. 'Looks like it's just you and me.'

'The man was a very good man,' said Eisa.

'Which man?'

'The man in the tower.'

'If you say so, Eisa,' said Dr Trotter.

'He has my address and I have his address,' said Eisa.

'You swapped addresses, did you? Very nice. I haven't bothered with addresses for years. Ah, there's the pub. Still there!'

Dr Trotter said it was his treat. 'What's your poison, Eisa?'

'Juice,' said Eisa.

'Come on! That's no drink. Have a beer. You're on your hols.'

Eisa nodded. They sat down behind their pints in the

crowded pub, watching the pleasure-barges going up and down the canal.

'That's a nice drop of piss,' said Eric as Eisa eyed his own pint doubtfully. Eric looked at his watch. 'I think I've time for another.'

As Eric rose, reaching out for his glass, he sat back down heavily. Eisa saw him look at him hard. He wondered if he had not understood something, had caused offence.

'Sorry?' he asked.

Eric Trotter did not say anything. He continued looking at Eisa, wide-eyed. His body jerked, then the head slouched sideways on to Eisa's shoulder, continuing down to rest on his lap. His right arm fell forward, the hand banging the table and knocking his glass to the floor. Then the arm slithered off the table and seemed to wave as it slumped around the head of the dead man.

Eisa looked down, then out at the crowded bar. The drinkers stared at the strange *pietà* in the corner, their pints and glasses of wine frozen, as in a photograph of a wedding toast.

'Where's Dr Trotter?' Moira asked. She counted the students. 'And there's another one gone AWOL.'

'Don't worry, madam,' said Muchtar. 'Dr Trotter and Eisa are coming. We separated after we rang the church bells.'

'It was you, was it?' asked Moira, who had scowled at the church tower while negotiating the High Street and, still hearing the bells even in Marks & Spencer, had told the assistant that it ought not to be allowed.

'It's very unusual,' the assistant told Moira. 'I'm sorry we don't have any candlewick. I'm very fond of it myself.'

'You're a woman of taste and discernment.'

'Thank you. I shouldn't say this, but have you tried Peacock's, down the High Street? It's next to the bank.'

'Thank you. I'll have a go.'

'A pack of blessings light upon thy back,' said the assistant.

That was a funny way of putting it, Moira thought. Still, a nice turn of phrase. Better than what you usually got. 'It's becoming more and more difficult.'

'I know what you mean. There's nothing like candlewick. It's wonderful next to the skin. Shall I tell you something?'

'Tell away,' said Moira.

The assistant came close to Moira. 'I like to kick off the rest of the bedclothes and just feel the candlewick bedspread next to the skin. It's ever so sensual.' She pulled away, nodding conspiratorially.

'I have nighties made of candlewick for that very reason. Now, a shop-bought candlewick nightdress is impossible to find. I've been cutting up bedspreads for years. But even they're disappearing. I don't know what the world is coming to.'

'I know,' said the assistant.

'Me and the husband live abroad. Hot old places in the main. But it's amazing how cold it can get at night. And if it isn't cold, then the damned ceiling fan is giving you a chill; that or the AC. If it's not one thing, it's another. And you know what?'

'What?'

'No mosquito I know has ever been able to poke through candlewick. They can get through Eric's jim-jams – Eric's the husband – but through my candlewick, never. It's typical of the world to drop candlewick. Much too versatile. Works far too well.'

'A double blessing is a double grace,' said the assistant. 'I've been telling that to the powers-that-be here.'

'I bet they don't listen.'

She looked to right and left. 'You're right.'

'There's none so blind as them that will not see,' said Moira, trying to show the assistant that she, too, had a few quotes up her sleeve.

'He that is strucken blind cannot forget the precious treasure of his eyesight lost.'

264

They exchanged a nod of understanding, a protest against the chaotic world whirling around them, out of control and candlewick. The assistant looked into the chaos. 'I'd better get on. "Labour, wide as the earth, has its summit in heaven." Leastways, that's what I tell myself. Nice talking to you.'

'Very nice,' said Moira.

It had been, too. It did not happen very often that she was able to have a chat off the cuff like that. Usually unknown languages cut communication to sound-bites of baby-talk and gesture.

At one twenty-five everyone sat down in the Royal Shakespeare Theatre. Two seats were empty, Moira scowled at them, but then she decided that she wasn't going to let her fool of a husband interfere with her enjoyment of the play. She settled back and opened a box of Maltesers.

At the interval she looked around the foyer for signs of Eric and Eisa. Muchtar came over. 'They are missing the play,' he said.

'It isn't the first time. What's your name?'

'Muchtar.'

'It isn't the first time, Mr Muchtar. I can tell you that.' She looked towards the entrance, surprised to find herself coming out of a dark theatre into daylight. She thought of the Regal in Victoria. 'How do you rate the play?'

'I don't understand . . .,' said Muchtar.

'The play. Do you like it?'

'It is very strange.'

'You can say that again. You know how it ends, don't you?'

Muchtar said he didn't.

'Well, I better hadn't spoil it for you. Anyway, Edward gets what's coming to him, I can tell you that. Enough to make your hair curl. Just stick around, Mr Muchtar. When that husband of mine turns up he's going to get worse than that. Stick around.'

But when Moira came out of the play she saw Eisa, haloed by the sunshine light outside, and flanked by a policeman and the theatre manager. Eisa pointed to her, and the policeman stepped forward.

But, before he was able to say anything, Moira said to him, 'So he's finally shuffled off, has he?'

The policeman, who had been waiting half an hour in dread at the task assigned to him, felt relieved. The manager led Moira to his office. Moira told the mystified students, 'Mr Muchtar, you're in charge. Take them to the bus and tell the driver to wait.'

'How did it happen?' she asked the policeman.

'He keeled over in the Bard. That big chap was with him. He was already dead by the time the publican got to him. It must have been instantaneous.'

Moira nodded. '"We, though our flower the same, think we are rooted in earth." Right, I'd better get back to the kids. We've got a bus to catch.'

'Er . . . madam. There are some formalities . . .'

'You want me to identify the body, do you?'

'Yes, and there are some forms . . .'

'There are always bloody forms. How long will it take?'

'Not long.'

'Right,' said Moira Trotter, picking up her handbag and the parcel containing a candlewick bedspread from Peacock's, 'I'll show you where the bus is. We'll follow you.'

The policeman nodded; then, as Moira made for the door, aimed a look at the theatre manager.

Moira sat alone in the front of the bus. The students behind were silent, the news having filtered through despite language barriers. Lourdes sat weeping at the back. Eisa, also alone, looked out of the window and saw flesh fall at the sight of him.

'I'm sorry about this,' said Moira to the driver. 'I hope it won't delay you too much.'

'Don't worry about it, dear,' said the driver. 'I'm really sorry about—'

'He had a good innings,' said Moira. 'Lived longer than he had a right to expect.'

The bus-driver didn't say anything. He turned into the hospital service-road and followed the police car to the mortuary.

'Yes, that's Eric all right,' said Moira Trotter to the concerned mortuary-attendant. 'Can I have a mo alone with him, please?'

'Certainly.'

Moira looked down at the body of the man she had followed around the world for almost sixty years. 'So long, mate,' she said and went outside to do the paperwork.

Nathan lay face-down on his bed, his head buried in the pillow. Rachel could not tell whether he was crying or not. She knew this gesture from early childhood. Whenever Nathan was pressed beyond endurance his reaction was the same. He would take to the pillow on his bed or, if bullied in the school playground, find a wall, preferably the corner of a wall or the place where a buttress made a suitable mourning-space, and there hide his head, turn his body away from the world, blot it out with his hands.

'That's no good! That doesn't solve anything!' Rachel said. 'I'm staying here until you tell me why. You've given everything away. Everything!'

A sound came from the pillow, but she couldn't hear. Her hands itched to grab Nathan by the shoulders and pull him round. But that had not worked in the past and there was no reason to think it would work now. Such actions only served to send Nathan farther and farther away, to regions she could not reach, had never reached. She shook herself and contented her ire by saying, 'I haven't got all day! Why?'

He turned ever so slightly, and said, 'He needed them for his family.' Then returned face-down back to the pillow.

She had tackled Ezekiel about it earlier in the day. When he had let her into his room she could see some of Nathan's things in a neat pile by the desk. But not everything.

'I've come about Nathan,' she said.

'Yes.' He smiled. 'I knew you would come. I have been thinking about it. If you consent, I think it would be good for him.'

'I'm sorry . . .,' she began, not understanding, feeling she was being cleverly deflected from the matter in hand.

'He is a good child. His instincts are right. You can see from the gifts he has given. He has been like a river to me. So much that I have had to pass certain things on to others.'

Rachel had not been able to help herself. 'You mean, you've given away the things he gave you?' she asked.

'Most of it, I fear. How can I take everything home with me? The baggage allowance is very little, and I cannot pay for extra things. I thought of posting things, but the service is unreliable and—'

'But you had no right.'

'Right?'

'To give away his gifts. They were meant for you!'

'Rachel,' replied Ezekiel serenely, 'English is not my language, although I am trying to make it mine. But in my language a gift is given out of love or duty, and possession is freely surrendered. If I choose to pass it on, then I am exercising my right as owner.'

'But . . .'

'You must know that there are many students here at the summer school whose countries are much worse off than mine; who cannot afford to buy anything to take home to loved ones. I have spoken to many at length in the dining-room and elsewhere. They are my friends.'

'But he had no right to . . .' Rachel could see that Ezekiel was in his teaching mode. She had seen it many times in class. She had been able to imagine him in front of classes back in Africa, teaching his certainties from a little wooden soapbox.

'Imagine this. I am a farmer living by a river. The river bestows its water upon me freely and my field is green, green, green.' He stretched his arm, his face animated by the sight he was conjuring up. 'All green. My family will smile at harvest. Their stomachs will be full. But there are

268

other farmers less fortunate. Their fields are away from the river, and the irrigation channel goes through mine. Do I block the channel and say, "There is too much water from the river, but I do not want to give you any. It is mine!" That would not be human, would it? That would diminish me and my enjoyment of my own good fortune.'

Rachel did not appreciate Ezekiel's lecture. 'Nathan should never have given you so much. He didn't ask me, you know!'

'Ah.'

'He just took everything without a by-your-leave. It will all have to be replaced.'

'Ah.'

'I haven't had an easy life, you know. It's been a struggle for me.'

Ezekiel nodded. 'I thought you approved of what Nathan was doing.'

'At first, yes. But he's gone too far!'

'You have decided that your poor neighbours have had enough, and have dammed the irrigation channel,' he said.

'How dare you! How dare you!' Rachel exclaimed. 'How would you feel if your son gave things away that you had worked hard to provide for him?'

Ezekiel thought about that. 'I would be proud. I might be upset for a while. But mostly I would be proud.'

She had not known what to say. She had left him then – turned away livid – without another word.

'Now, Nathan, I'll tell you what you're going to have to do,' Rachel said. 'You're going to collect together everything you gave to Ezekiel. I want to see it all back in your room by the end of the summer school. Is that clear?'

Nathan moved on the bed, turned his head. She could see his small ear, the ear she had loved to pull and play with when he would let her. She approached it. 'Is that clear?'

Quite suddenly he was sitting on the side of the bed, looking at her, a stranger. 'No!'

'I'll pretend I didn't hear you,' she said.

'No!' he shouted. 'No way! No fucking way!'

'You . . .!' She struck him hard across the cheek. He blanched but in a trice was back, staring steadily at her. She hit him again but she might have been chastising a rock.

They regarded one another icily. Then Nathan said, his voice strange, for the first time adult, broken, 'I want to go back to Africa with Zek.'

Eisa sat down next to Moira Trotter on the bus back to London. She smiled when she saw him there but did not say anything. As they turned on to the M40, he had tried to express his condolences. But, hearing his stuttered sentences, she had patted his hand, shaken her head.

'I know, dear. I know. Let's not say anything, OK?' Then she had turned back to the window, watching the scenery passing in reverse.

A cottage reminded her of what she had been saying to Eric on the outward journey; a war memorial of the thoughts she had been thinking when last she saw it. *Ulan Bator! Who goes to Ulan Bator? Who goes to Ulan Bator at our age?*

Well, Ulan Bator was out. Eric had been looking forward to it; might have gone down well there – as he had gone down well wherever they had travelled. The older he got the better he'd gone down. The odder he became the more foreigners took to him. Silly old humbug!

'You all right, love? We won't be long now,' said the driver, as they passed signs to High Wycombe.

'Fine, thank you,' said Moira.

Her words could be heard right through the silent mourning bus.

At Heathcliff they held back for Moira to get off first. Eisa made to help her down the steps of the bus, but she did not take his hand. Once on the pavement, she walked steadily towards the entrance and disappeared up the stairs of Churchill, carrying her Peacock's bag in her left hand, thinking of a place in her suitcase where it would go just right.

The students watched her go. Then, nodding to the driver, they trundled off the bus and disappeared to their rooms.

Eisa was left with the driver.

'I've got to tell someone,' said the driver, holding up a sheaf of papers.

'Sorry?' asked Eisa.

They went to the locked door of Reception. Eisa found Arthur sitting in the common room. 'Mr Arthur! Come!' he said.

'Are you in charge?' asked the driver.

He explained what had happened. 'The deceased's missis doesn't seem interested. The police are going to arrange a post-mortem. Then arrangements will have to be made. But I'm not sure you're going to get any sense out of his widow. Shock, I suppose.'

Arthur looked at the papers. 'This is everything, is it?' he said.

'Think so. They've written a number for you to ring,' replied the driver. 'Well, I'd better be off.'

'Thank you.'

'It's the least I could do.'

'It can't have been easy.'

The driver nodded. 'One thing – well, two really. It was quick, apparently. He just keeled over in a pub. And he had a good innings.'

'Yes, he did,' replied Arthur. 'Was anyone with him when it happened?'

The driver pointed to Eisa. 'You're the one I left behind in Brighton.' He shook Eisa's hand. 'I'm sorry,' he said. Then he waved and left, happy not to have bumped into Rachel.

'You're having all the luck, aren't you, Eisa?'

'Sorry?' Eisa asked.

Arthur repeated his sentence in Arabic. 'What happened?'

271

'I went for a drink with him. He began to drink it and died. He fell over on to me,' said Eisa.

Arthur reached over and hugged Eisa, thinking that when his turn came he would like this good man nearby. 'I'd better try to find Agnes,' he said.

He went into the common room, scouting about. Seeing Muchtar sitting alone, he approached him. 'Were you at Stratford?' he asked.

'Yes,' said Muchtar.

'Will you stay with Eisa? I think he needs someone with him.'

'Of course,' replied Muchtar, happy to have duties.

Arthur went off to find Agnes. He got no reply from her room and was about to return to the common room when he heard laughter coming from the kitchen. There, Agnes was sitting with Lynn and Sue, an empty wine-bottle on the table in front of them.

'Bad news,' said Arthur. He told them what had happened.

'Where's Moira?' asked Agnes, watching as Lynn broke down again.

'I think she's gone to her room.' Agnes stood up. 'Agnes, she'll need careful handling.'

Agnes at once strode down the corridor to Moira's room and knocked quietly.

'Come in!'

A suitcase lay open on the bed. Moira Trotter had already packed most of her clothes. A pile of shirts, shoes and trousers lay higgledy-piggledy on the floor. 'I know why you've come,' she said. 'I don't want to talk about it.'

'Moira . . .'

'I don't want to talk about it,' she repeated. 'I'll say it once and I won't say it again. I warned him. You heard me warn him. I sometimes think I spent the whole of my married life warning him. Well, he didn't listen. It's a big relief for me, tell you the truth.'

'You're in shock,' said Agnes. 'You should take it carefully.'

'You can tell everyone I'm in shock if you like,' replied

272

Moira, settling her new candlewick bedspread down into the hole in the suitcase. 'It won't be true, but if you want to tell them that . . . well, go ahead.'

'Aren't there people who should be told? What about the funeral?' asked Agnes, trying to put practical obstacles in the way.

'There probably are. I can't think of them offhand, but there probably are. Don't worry about it, I'll do it. As to the funeral, let the dead bury their dead, I say.'

Agnes changed tack. 'Would you like a cup of tea?' she asked.

'Never say no,' replied Moira Trotter. 'Two sugars.' She did not look up from her packing.

'Right.' Agnes left the room and closed the door behind her. Then she stood in the corridor, thinking about tactics. Nathan, loaded with bags, had to excuse himself twice to get past her on his way to Ezekiel's room.

'Going on your holidays, dear?' she asked.

He looked at her and smiled.

She clanked the kettle into position under the tap, filled it and placed it on the gas. Then she sought around for tea-bags, smelled the milk in the fridge before pouring some into one of the stained mugs. *A good dollop of Ajax wouldn't come amiss!* Then she thought of Eric Trotter and shed a tear.

'Here you are, Moira,' she said.

Moira Trotter was sitting in her easy-chair. The suitcase, now closed, sat at her side, next to her handbag.

'You look ready for the off,' Agnes said.

'Always ready for the off,' said Moira. 'Thanks for the tea.'

Agnes tried her strict tone. 'You're not going anywhere, Moira. I can't allow it,' she said.

'It's a free country,' Moira replied.

'But where do you think you're going?'

Moira looked at her. 'Away. Any objections?'

'But where?'

Moira thought for a moment, warming her hands around the mug of tea. 'Ghana.'

Agnes gasped. 'Ghana? Do you still know people in Ghana?'

'Not that I know of.'

'So why Ghana?'

'I liked Ghana. Always did. It was Eric who insisted on leaving.'

'All right, Moira. You can go to Ghana. But wait a while. What about the funeral?'

'Put him in the bin,' said Moira Trotter.

'Moira, you can't mean that. You're in shock!'

'I do mean it,' said Moira. 'The old fool was always asking me what I'd do if he went first. I said that I'd put him in the bin and head off for Ghana. Now it's happened, maybe I owe it to the daft bugger.'

'But what about your kids in New Zealand?'

'What about them?'

'Don't you want to be near them?'

'Not in the least. No, I'll be better off in Ghana.'

Moira Trotter drained her tea. 'I know what you're thinking,' she said.

'What's that?' asked Agnes, wishing she knew herself.

'You're worried about the undertakers' bill. That sort of thing.'

'The thought hadn't crossed my mind.'

'Well, be that as it may, you can take Eric's summer school cheque. Anything over, give it to charity. I'm rather partial to the Donkey Sanctuary, but I'll leave you to take your pick. I know you think I'm being daft.'

'You're in shock.'

'Agnes, will you stop *saying* that? I'm not in shock. The shock's been seeing him turning up in the early hours all these years blowing his booze fumes over me and making excuses when by rights he should have been dead. The shock's been seeing him taken on by one more college or university that should have known better. The shock's been trundling myself to yet one more beginning. This isn't a shock. This is a relief.' She looked up, past the cracked ceiling to the sky. 'For this relief – though it took its time coming – much thanks.'

'You sound like you didn't love him.'

'Oh, I loved him – after a fashion. And it's probably because I loved him that I don't want my last contact with him to be a bloody funeral. We've said our goodbyes.' Moira Trotter stood up. 'I'm off!'

Agnes could see her point. 'But will you be able to manage?'

'Agnes, I may have been daft in many ways but I wasn't *completely* daft. I held the purse strings.'

'Well, that's something.'

'Say goodbye to the gang for me.'

Agnes nodded. 'I'll help you with the suitcase.'

'Not necessary. I carried it up. I'll carry it down.' She looked at Eric's suitcase and clothes on the floor. 'See if you can find a home for those, would you, Agnes? There must be someone at the summer school who can use them.'

And Moira Trotter handed her room-key to Agnes. She picked up her belongings and led the way out of the room. 'I'll leave you to lock up,' she said and disappeared round the corner by the kitchen.

Agnes locked up and followed after. She did not see Nathan, his packed bags on the floor beside him, his head on the kitchen table, weeping.

'Where's the other Sue?' Agnes asked, the following Friday.

Sue looked at Sue. 'Search me,' she said.

Agnes looked from one Sue to the other. 'No, I don't think I will. I'd be afraid what I'd find,' she said. 'I'll hear soon enough, I expect.'

'Not from us you won't, will she, Sue?'

'No fear,' said Sue. 'We're sworn to secrecy.'

Sue frowned at Sue. 'That is, if we had anything to be secretive about. Which we don't,' said Sue.

Agnes made a stab in the light. 'Sue's gone off to Chile, hasn't she?'

275

The two Sues looked at Agnes.

'How did you know?' Sue asked.

'Who sorts out the mail round here because you two are too busy sleeping it off?' she said. 'Who collects the faxes?'

'Well, we didn't tell you, did we?'

'No, you didn't. And don't you dare say anything to Lynn.'

'You can rely on us,' said Sue.

Agnes lit a Sweet Afton. 'I think you should change the flowers for Eric,' she said, gesturing towards a large plastic bottle inside a sealed plastic bag on the filing cabinet, in front of which drooped a dozen carnations in a jam-jar. 'And make sure they give you something fresh this time. Give them a good shake before you part with the petty cash.'

Sue looked at Eric Trotter's ashes, nodded and took a five-pound note from Agnes. 'What'll we do with him?' she asked.

'I can't make up my mind,' said Agnes.

'It doesn't seem right,' said Sue.

'There's a lot that's not right round here,' said Agnes. 'I'll have a think about what to do with the ashes. Who knows, maybe Moira will come back.'

'She won't. I feel it in my bones,' said Sue.

'"Let the dead bury their dead." They was the last words she said to me. On the Churchill stairs,' said Sue portentously. 'We've seen the last of Moira, if you want my opinion.'

'Go and get those flowers, Sue,' said Agnes. She turned to Sue. 'And you can photocopy the panto script. One copy each for every class and one each for the teachers.'

'There's no more toner,' said Sue.

'Well, make do. I'm not going to order any more at this stage.'

'All right,' said Sue. 'But they won't be up to our usual high standard.' She set about her task.

'When did you find out that Sue was going off to join Keith Weaver?' Agnes asked.

276

'It's been on the cards for ages. I don't know what she saw in him myself,' said Sue.

'Yes, but when did she tell you she was going?'

'Ages ago,' said Sue. 'These copies are really faint, Agnes.'

'By "ages ago", do you mean prior to the summer school?'

'Oh, yes. Long before that.'

'What I'd like to know, Sue,' said Agnes, 'is how Sue could have kept quiet about it when she knew how unhappy Lynn's been. You, too, for that matter. Didn't you ever feel you were being really cruel? You see how she's been.'

'I didn't like to,' said Sue.

'What's that supposed to mean?'

'These copies are really bad. They'll never be able to read them,' said Sue. 'I think I'd better go and see if the Open University have any toner.' Sue made to leave.

'No, don't go,' said Agnes. 'I asked you a question, Sue.'

'What about you? You're not so pure and don't you think you are!'

'What's that supposed to mean?'

'Well, you knew about Keith carrying on with Sue at the summer schools. Why didn't you tell Lynn then? If you had, it might not have come to this.'

Agnes was silent for a moment. Then she said, 'I thought she knew.'

'You did, thump, think that she knew! You did, thump! It was bloody obvious that she didn't know.'

'I didn't think it was my place to interfere.'

Sue turned to Agnes. 'There you are, then. Neither did I. Now I'm going to get that toner.'

Sue left the room hurriedly. Agnes lit another cigarette.

The door of Reception opened, seemingly of its own accord. Agnes was looking at the empty corridor, the dingy concrete, the stain below the coffee machine. Then Eisa stepped into her vision, smiling broadly. He gestured with his right hand, patting downwards. Then he disappeared.

277

'What now?' Agnes wondered. She sat, waiting.

Then Eisa was standing at the door with Molly O'Connor on his arm. Seen next to the large man, Molly looked smaller than ever.

'Agnes!' said Molly. 'I'm better!'

'I can see that, Molly! But are you sure . . .?'

Molly was looking up at Eisa, who was looking down at Molly. 'I owe it to Eisa here! Of course, I was sceptical, but it's worked.'

'What's worked, Molly?'

'Eisa's massage. I don't know what he did. But the pain's gone and I'm my old self again! Isn't that wonderful?'

'Yes, it is. Well done, Eisa!' said Agnes.

Molly walked into the office. Eisa made to help her, but she squeezed his arm to tell him it wasn't necessary.

'Gosh, that's good!' said Agnes. 'I should set him to work on me.'

'You should, Agnes. Mind you, it hurt. He's no light-weight. Then I felt a click and I knew straight off I was better. Astrid's going to be tickled pink when she finds out.'

'Where is Astrid?'

'She went off to get her hair done.'

'Miss, I go now,' said Eisa.

'Must you, Eisa?'

'Must,' said Eisa.

'Well, thank you very much for your help.'

Eisa smiled and left the room.

'It's funny, Agnes, but I wouldn't let him do it to me at first. I was embarrassed.'

'Well, I'm glad you got over that, Molly. I wonder if Eisa could work some more miracles. We have need of a few,' said Agnes.

'I know,' said Molly. 'Lord, it's wonderful to be well again, Agnes. As long as you've got your health, you've got everything.'

'I must write that down,' said Agnes. 'It's lovely to see you again, Molly. I needed something nice to happen.'

'I've been hearing a lot of bad news,' said Molly. 'A lot

278

of it I haven't been able to take in. Any sign of Moira?'

'None. There's Eric over there.'

'How do you mean, Agnes?'

Agnes pointed to the plastic bottle.

'Do you mean . . .?'

'Yes. Moira must have told the authorities to cremate Eric and send his ashes to us. But the only address we have for her is Hong Kong, their last posting, and Ulan Bator, their next. Neither applies in the circumstances.'

'Oh, that's terrible, Agnes. What are you going to do?'

'Search me.'

'Moira didn't say goodbye,' said Molly.

'No. But she didn't say goodbye to anybody. Just upped and left.'

'And Lynn is in a state,' observed Molly.

'I know,' said Agnes. 'Perhaps we should be thankful that this is the last summer school. What are you going to do, Molly?'

'I haven't the foggiest, Agnes. The missionary house have told me not to go back just yet. I'm to go to Runcorn to see them after the school's finished. They might offer me another posting, but to tell you the truth, Agnes, I don't want to go anywhere else except St Cedric's. There's nowhere like it. I can't bear the idea of never seeing the Falls of Sense again. The future's uncertain-*ish* at the moment. Still, we're all in the same boat. It takes something like this to make you realize . . .'

Lourdes and Ursula beat Lynn as she kneeled on the floor in front of them. They attacked her with her own blackboard duster. 'Right, then,' they said, as chalk rose in a halo around Lynn's head while the rest served to turn her hair white. They said she was old and ugly; that she would be laughed at if she ever went out in public. No, it was far better for her to stay and be treated abominably by them.

Lynn wept, hiding her face in her hands; then, when Lourdes and Ursula lost interest in her and stomped out,

Satoko and Mitsuko hopped up to her, nuzzled her face and told her not to be so sad. But Lynn was inconsolable. She looked out towards the light and exclaimed, 'Oh, what an unlucky person I am!'

'Don't worry, Cinderella!' Mitsuko squeaked. 'Something will turn up!'

'Oh, I don't think so! I really don't.' Then she turned her wet eyes to the audience. She wanted to shush a small group by the bar who had not yet stopped chattering. In a voice louder than the acoustics of the common room required, she asked, 'Do you really think something will turn up?'

'Yes,' shouted the strategically situated two Sues, Agnes and, using the microphone, Arthur.

'I don't think so. Do you *really* think so?'

'Yes!' shouted the majority of the summer-school audience, getting the idea.

She turned back to the mice. 'Do you think so? Do you *really* think so?' she asked them, stroking their tin-foil ears.

'Yes, of course, Cinderella,' replied Satoko. 'But don't go on and on; it's really boring.'

A loud knock from stage right. 'Postman!' cried Mr Wehrli, who had borrowed a cap from Security. 'I have a letter for the beautiful girls of this house. It is from the Prince. It is inviting pretty girls to a great ball which is to take place on Saturday next from eight until late. To get to the palace you take the Jubilee Line southbound to Green Park. Alight there and mind the gap. Follow the signs to the Victoria Line southbound and take the Victoria Line to Victoria. Anyone there will be able to tell you how you do you go to the palace. Just ask: *Excuse me. How can I get to the ball from here?* That'll do nicely. It's as easy as pie!'

Satoko grabbed the letter from the postman with her teeth and gave it to Cinderella. 'It isn't for me,' she said. 'I never get any nice letters. It must be for my sisters.'

'But they're so ugly!' remarked the postman. 'It can't be for them! It must be for you, Cinderella. If you would just clean yourself up a bit, you'd be really beautiful. I could quite fancy you myself!'

'Do you really think so?' asked Cinderella.

'I know so,' said the postman. He looked at his watch. 'Still, I must be off now. I have yodelling practice at eleven.'

Cinderella was about to open the invitation when the ugly sisters entered. 'What's that? A letter?' Ursula asked. 'One so likes to receive letters! Give it to one at once, Cinderella!'

'But it's for me!' exclaimed Cinderella.

'How could it be?' said Lourdes. 'You can't even read!' She grabbed the letter from Cinderella. She read the envelope. 'Thought as much! It's addressed to *The Pretty Girls of This House*. That's us, isn't it, Sister?'

'One would say so, yes. Definitely,' said Ursula.

Lourdes opened the envelope and jumped up and down. 'We've been invited to a ball at the palace!'

'A ball! We must see to our outfits.' The ugly sisters left the stage. From the wings Ursula shouted back her exit line to Cinderella. 'I'm not surprised you didn't get an invitation, Cinderella! You're so ugly and pathetic! Not like us!'

Cinderella stood up. The mice tried to console her, but she did not even notice them as she boo-hooed off the stage.

The lights went up, and Arthur's voice was heard. 'Next group to their places. Quick!'

There was some delay in restarting the pantomime because the second Cinderella – Teresa – was trying to get in a round at the bar.

When, finally, the lights went up, Jordan Bostock was on stage. He addressed the audience. 'It just isn't fair. Cinderella never goes anywhere. I don't know what the world is coming to, I really don't. Although I am only a humble butler, I would marry Cinderella straight away if I were asked. Of course, I would never dream of telling her of my love.'

Teresa entered, putting her pint of Lowenbrau on the

stage apron and gesturing to Assumption to guard it with her life. She started weeping as she approached Jordan.

'Poor Cinderella!' said Jordan. 'What's the matter?'

'My ugly sisters they go to the ball and I no. I didn't go out since I see the quarter final of the synchronized swimming at the Olympics in 1992!'

'Oh, I'm sorry,' said Buttons. 'I know how difficult it must be for you. Have a cigarette.'

'I don't,' said Cinderella.

Ezekiel and Sebastian entered, dressed in bin bags and a couple of blond wigs, borrowed from Rachel.

'Don't we look lovely?' shouted Ezekiel raucously. 'We shall be very admired at the ball, sha'n't we, Sister?'

'Oh, yes!' said Sebastian.

'Of course,' continued Ezekiel. 'I shall be much more the admired of we two!'

'Oh, no!' said Sebastian. 'I shall be much more admired from you!'

They approached Cinderella and recommenced cuffing and kicking her.

'I have never seen such an ugly girl in my life!' exclaimed Ezekiel.

'A mirror! I must see my beauty in a mirror. Buttons, bring me mirror.'

Buttons exited, returning a moment later with Sue, a plank tied to her front, over which had been laid tin-foil. The ugly sisters admired themselves in Sue's front while cameras flashed and a world of students saw themselves opening wallets of new photographs worlds away to show what had been happening worlds away.

'Ah, beauty!' sighed Ezekiel at his own reflection. 'Surely the handsome prince shall be mine!'

'How we shall go to the ball?' asked Sebastian.

'We shall take public transportation. It is ecologically sympathetic,' Ezekiel replied.

'Good! I shall have time to read *The Times* in order to show everyone how very educate and upper-classed I am!' said Sebastian.

Two chairs were brought on by Aaron. 'Sit down here,

ladies!' he said. 'It isn't often I have two such beautiful girls on my bus! If you'll give me a kiss, I'll let you ride for free.'

Sebastian puckered his lips, readying to be kissed. Aaron leaned down towards him. But Ezekiel placed *The Times* between the approaching lips. 'Shame on you! We shall pay our fares, Sister. We have to be careful from now on. After I am married to the prince this bus conductor might sell his story to a tabloid. It is from the gutter. It is not a broadsheet. It would be our undoing.'

'After I'm married to the prince, you mean!' countered Sebastian.

'You'll never marry the prince. He's mine!'

'No, he isn't!'

'Yes, he is!'

Aaron came between them. 'No trouble on my bus, please, ladies!'

But the ugly sisters just kept on rowing.

'Ding!' announced the bus conductor. 'Palace next stop! Everybody off for the ball!'

The lights went down, and Arthur shouted for the next group to take their places.

Astrid, a blonde again after her trip to the hairdresser, kneeled at the centre of the stage. The lights went up. Someone wolf-whistled. 'I am so lonely and sad. There is no consolation for me,' she said.

Paula appeared, wearing her own white dress, her hair garlanded with roses from a garden in Kidderpore Avenue. She carried a stick of Toblerone with a star on the top. 'You shall go to the ball, Cinderella. You shall be the star of the ball and shall marry the charming prince. You shall have many babies and will breast-feed them all without benefit of Nestlé products!'

'But I can't go like this!' said Astrid, surveying her ragged clothes.

'No, you certainly can't! Also, you will need appropriate transportation. Come, mice!'

Satoko and Mitsuko reappeared, pulling Fatos, plumped out with the orange curtains from his bedroom and most of that day's newspapers, as the pumpkin.

'Ibrikidibri!' called out the fairy godmother.

'But . . .,' said Astrid.

Students came on-stage whirling bed-sheets to hide the scene. Someone threw sparkle into the air and over the audience, and the lights dimmed for a moment.

Arthur appeared in a ball-gown, surrounded by students with plumes on their heads and tin cans on their feet. The students whinnied. Arthur looked out over the cheering audience. 'Now I can go to the ball!' he said.

'But,' said the fairy godmother. 'There has been an error. I have turned Cinderella into Cinderfella!'

'That'll do nicely,' said Cinderfella. He got aboard his carriage and was lifted away to the ball by the horses.

'Be careful, Cinderfella, if you know what we mean! There's a chemist's on the way! And be back by midnight! The magic ends at midnight!'

'Don't worry! I will!' shouted back Cinderfella. 'I can't believe I'm going to the ball!' He tripped on the stairs and collided with Astrid. 'I'm sorry,' he said.

'I am sorry, too,' Astrid replied.

After the interval, light went up on the ballroom. There, the ugly sisters were desperately trying to attract the attention of the prince, played by Paolo. The prince was rejecting the ugly sisters, now played by Ito and Mr Eng.

'I want to dance with a beautiful girl!' said the prince. 'You two are not beautiful at all!'

Assumption came on shyly, dressed in a sheet. 'Where is my prince?' she said.

'Will you dance with me?' the prince asked.

'I'd be glad to.'

They danced, but then Eisa appeared stage right as Big Ben. He positioned his arms at five to midnight. In his minute-hand he held a wooden spoon. On his head he wore a Prestige pressure cooker missing its handle. As the dance neared its close his hand crept up to midnight and he banged the side of the pan with the spoon.

'How time fly!' Cinderella exclaimed, and she rushed

from the room, leaving a shoe on the dance-floor.

'Ah, she's gone!' exclaimed the prince. He caught sight of the shoe and held it up. 'Whoever this little slipper fits shall be my wife!'

Back in the kitchen Molly and Florence were swanking to Cinderella and Buttons about their night at the palace.

'The prince liked me much more than he liked you, Sister!' said Molly.

'That isn't so. That isn't so at all!' replied Florence. 'It is true he danced with you first, but once he saw me he couldn't keep away! He was a fly to a honey-pot!'

'Oh, no, he wasn't!' shouted Molly.

'Oh, yes, he was!' replied Florence and the audience.

A knock at the door. 'It's only me,' said Agnes. 'Your nosy neighbour from across the road.'

Nobody seemed to remember her.

'Don't you know me? I keep your keys for you. I mount the Neighbourhood Watch single-handed! I'm a pillar of the community! Surely, you remember me, don't you?'

But they didn't.

'Anyway, I have news. The prince is going from house to house looking for the owner of a slipper. He says that whoever lost the slipper will be his wife!'

The ugly sisters sent two single sensible shoes flying off their feet into the audience. Teresa's tappas-bar boyfriend, annoyed at having Florence's shoe-heel land in his beer, threw it back. It was neatly caught by Mr Molina, playing Buttons. He dropped it over the apron.

'I've lost my slipper! I wonder where it is!' exclaimed Molly.

'That's odd! I've lost mine, too!' added Florence. She looked around the stage, where everyone was holding their nose. 'The prince must have found my shoe. He must be on his way to the house now!'

'No! He must have found my shoe!'

'No! Mine!'

Molly and Florence started to slug it out.

'Fanfare for the Common Man' bugled from Rachel's

classroom tape-recorder, operated by Nathan.

'The prince is coming!' exclaimed Molly. 'And look at the state of this room! Cinderella!'

Cinderella resignedly started brushing the floor.

'Faster! Brush faster!' the ugly sisters told her, cuffing and kicking and screaming.

'Franco is dead!' said Cinderella, to much applause.

There came an insistent knock and in came Muchtar, followed by a United Nations of courtiers. Yaohan, wrapped around with a splendid batik, carried a high-heeled shoe on a Heathcliff pillow.

'Your highnessness!' exclaimed Molly.

'Your ineffableness and correctnesses!' added Florence. 'You are welcome to our humble house.'

'I have been seeking my beloved,' said the prince. 'I have been seeking her but nowhere I can find her. One says "Go there", another "Try there". But wherever I go I do not find she whom I seek. I am sad.'

'Sit down, Prince,' said Assumption.

They looked briefly into one another's eyes.

'Will all the women in this house try on this shoe? Whoever it fits shall be my wife!'

'Me, me, me, me, me,' shouted the ugly sisters, making for the shoe on the pillow.

Florence sat down on the floor and tried to get it on. When it was half-on, she stood up and exclaimed: 'It fits! It fits!' .

'Oh, no, it doesn't!' shouted the audience.

Molly tried the shoe on, with the same result.

'Is there no-one else who can try on the shoe? Don't tell me I will have to continue my search! I am tired! So tired!'

'There is no-one else,' said Molly dogmatically. 'Only us.'

Ito approached mouse-like and whispered in the prince's ear.

'Cinderella? Where is she?'

'She's over there.'

'Bring her to me!'

Assumption approached, humble and hangdog. The shoe fitted perfectly.

The prince kneeled at Cinderella's feet. 'Will you marry me?' he asked.

Cinderella opened her mouth to reply. The cast froze.

Rachel entered, dressed as the fairy-godmother. She sprinkled great quantities of fairy-dust – supplied by Agnes – over the frozen actors and audience. They rubbed their eyes. They coughed. She waved her wand. She spoke:

'And now our story nears its close . . .
The question's popped, the answer's . . . well, who
　　knows?
Will Cinderella take the prince for groom
Or soldier on with brush and blackboard . . . with
　　bucket, chalk and broom?'

'Yes, I marry you,' said Cinderella.

Applause and more fairy-dust thrown over the audience to quieten the babel.

'Autumn golds approach; our time its day has had,
A Heathrow star of vapour trails us sad
From all the pretty people gathered here away.
Remember, DB! Come back another day!'

'Does this mean the summer school can continue?' asked an ugly sister.

'Yes, of course!' Rachel replied. 'If it helps to make a happy ending.' She threw more fairy-dust around.

Agnes smiled at seeing Eric Trotter so appropriately disposed of, his ashes mixed with sparkle.

'And you who watch this scene all shall
By bus and train, BA and JAL,
Zoom off, away from this smoke-filled room . . .
We wish you luck, long life, be strangers one and all
　　to gloom.'

The audience clapped. The cast took a bow, filling the stage with its Cinderellas and ugly sisters, cats and mice, many an undone Buttons and one Big Ben. Arthur disengaged himself from Astrid to help Nathan on to the stage to receive applause for his sound-effects. Rachel made him a place between her and Lynn. He looked at his mother, smiled at her, but went and stood next to Ezekiel. The world applauded itself until its hands hurt. Then, from the basement, came the thump of the disco, announcing the last act of this year's stab at demolishing Babel.

THE END